Trails of Grief, Hope, and Triumph

and Triumph

Familial Terrorism and Other Stories

T. W. GABRIEL

NEWMAN SPRINGS PUBLISHING
320 Broad Street
Red Bank, NJ 07701

First originally published by Newman
Springs Publishing 2022

ISBN 978-1-63881-326-2 (Paperback)
ISBN 978-1-63881-327-9 (Digital)

Printed in the United States of America

To my sons Aman and Adam

Author's Note

On Christmas Day 2009, a young Nigerian, aged twenty-three, by the name of Umar Farouk Abdulmutallab boarded Northwest Airlines in Amsterdam on a flight to Detroit, Michigan. His plan was not to visit the motor city but to detonate an explosive with all passengers to be blown to smithereens.

This young man was born into wealth and privilege. His father, a banker, had great ambition for his son and sent him to an elite school in England. But he had other plans. He was infected with religious extremist ideas. He diverted his travel initially to Yemen and met people with the same misguided ideology.

When I read the news, I started to ask, "How is it that a person of his background chooses to be a terrorist?" Certainly, it was not religion. If it were, we would have a billion terrorists. Nonetheless, it became the inception for my story, "The Honor Killing: Familial Terrorism."

My other story, "Wailing Voices," is a story of people displaced through deportation, friendships suddenly broken, and livelihood disrupted. The cruelty of deportation has been written about for a long time. However, it continues unabated, creating misery for people.

The third story, "Goatherd in Exile," shows how people with limited exposure to modernity can adapt to new experiences in a foreign land. A young man, following rebels on flight, crosses the border into Sudan where his vision and life is completely changed.

Introduction

The event started in Northeast Africa where conflicts had been prevalent for over a century. The causes of the conflicts had been mostly for usurpation of power of one group or another. War and fear of persecution was the cause for the exile of the families whose stories we are to follow.

Honor Killing: Familial Terrorism

The season was spring, right after the end of the big rainy season. The mountains and hills were adorned with wildflowers offering their comely color as hurrah to the new season. The ubiquitous yellow daisies were spread on the sloppy hills. The few trees, left from the relentless axes of the loggers in the destruction of the thick forest of a century ago, were green with leaves. The fields were carrying a bounty of harvest to come—cornstalks, sweet corn enveloped with the sheath protecting it from the greedy eyes of birds that contributed nothing to the hard labor of the farmers, and the humble sorghum stalks with the bowing seed bunches, ready to be harvested. The farmers, after working hard for months, ploughed with the oxen-driven tools as their long-gone ancestors looked with hope that their family would pass the year without hunger and desperation. Birds seasonally appeared after migrating to other areas during the rainy season. The weather was comfortable with crisp, cool air blowing from the east, crossing the valleys between the mountain ranges. The whole environment exuded hope.

On the political scene, however, there was a growing disaffection. It was reaching a breaking point. Young people were calling for rebellion against the regime. In reaction, the regime had become more repressive. The prison population had grown with many prisons filled beyond capacity. People were imprisoned for any and all kinds of reasons.

It was at this moment that the month of fast and prayer was observed by adherents to Islam. In the month of Ramadan, every Moslem, unless sick, devoted body and soul to the Creator. For about a month from sunrise to sunset, you were not to eat any food or imbibe any fluid, including your saliva, and pray five times a day. A hungry stomach and dry mouth would certainly remind you of your need to glorify and pray to your creator but also remind you of the need to help the poor and hungry around you. It was a humbling experience. At the end of almost a month of fasting, the Eid al-Fitr holiday was celebrated.

In the family house of Mr. Mohamed Nur and his wife, Fowzia, Ramadan was celebrated with friends and family gathering. It had become a tradition for the family to invite several people and feast together. A sumptuous variety of food and beverages, albeit nonalcoholic, was ready. With all the food, the air was so aromatic it tingled the senses, and the nostrils quivered. The friends were from all walks of life and faith. Mr. Nur was a very spiritual person without any prejudice against the others' faith.

The family was blessed with four children—two boys and two girls. The children were healthy and happy. Their rosy personalities were welcome additions to the pleasant atmosphere of the home. The house was located in an affluent neighborhood of the town. It was festooned with bougainvillea covering the surface to the east and vine tree to the west. The vine tree had stretched itself leisurely to the canopy that was built to the end perimeter of the property. It was in that area where the feast was organized and guests gathered, besotted by flowers and other tasteful ornaments. During the celebration, the political turmoil in the country weighed heavily on the celebrants.

The growing resentment among the youth in the economic hardship was turning into crisis that challenged the ruling authorities. The students were in the forefront, articulating and leading the populace into resistance. A call for active resistance and overthrow of the regime was made daily. Manifestos, flyers, and posters clandestinely were distributed at strategic locations of the towns and cities of the country. Soon, underground movements started to emerge with less than ten people in each group. Each member of the group recruited more people to expand the resistance movement without compromising too much the security of members. The underground movement exploded in membership and activities. Every social stratum of the community was affected. At times, whole families unbeknown to each other belonged to different cells. Politics was unavoidable. The state was in panic. The security apparatus was greatly expanded. An intensified surveillance of individuals and organizations was initiated. Individuals were brought to security offices and interrogated. Physical and psychological torture was applied. The arrest of people was announced over the media to create fear on the population. However, it never helped as resistance continued to intensify.

Early morning on April 17, the air was oppressive. It was unusually warm. The birds started to chirp, and one could hear the roosters crooning their salutary crowing for a new day. The muezzin, in earnest, called on the believers for their early prayers, and church bells could be heard from afar. The familiar sounds belied the tense atmosphere of discontent and fear.

Suddenly, there was a knock at the door of Mr. Nur. The footsteps of several people could be heard. *Knock! Knock!* It was a knock of an unwelcome visit.

"Open the door!" somebody shouted.

The family was startled by the loud knock, and footsteps could be heard going out of the bedroom.

Mr. Nur ordered all to stay put as he advanced toward the door. He asked, "Who is there?"

Someone replied forcefully, "Open the door before we knock it down."

Mr. Nur opened the door. To his amazement, there were seven officers outside his door. One with a pistol drawn pointing at the door was in the middle. Everybody was armed with handguns, some drawn out and a few placed in their holsters.

The leadman was known to Mr. Nur, a major in the special forces unit of the army. The major advanced and commanded Mr. Nur to follow him to the army garrison at the edge of the city for a brief inquiry.

Mr. Nur, still in confusion, said, "Any problem, Officer? Why am I called to the army headquarters? Are you sure you are looking for me?" To make sure that there was no mistaken identity, he started to recite his name and occupation.

The major, with abrupt voice, responded, "Do you think we are stupid? It is you that we want. Follow us or we will have to drag you."

Mr. Nur, clad in his pajamas and sandals, followed the officers. He could hear his children crying in the background. An army van was parked a block away on the corner, and everybody mounted, including Mr. Nur. In the van, they shackled him with a metal frame. He pleaded that was unnecessary, for he did not commit any crime.

Few people were out in the streets. No one spoke in the van; the soldiers had kept their guns drawn, looking on all sides of the streets. Soon, the van arrived at the garrison. At the gate, the van stopped for inspection by heavily armed guards, and after inspection, they were allowed to pass through the gate.

The garrison was an enclosed area with walls high enough to block any vision from outside. There were homes within all the perimeter where the officers lived. In the middle was an open area the size of a football field. There were tanks, trucks, and other mechanized vehicles parked. On west end of the ground were a few structures with military police as guards. The van pulled close to the door, and the soldiers started to jump off.

Mr. Nur was taken into one of the rooms, still handcuffed. The room was dimly lit. A uniformed officer with a stack of paper on his desk was seated in the corner of the room. Mr. Nur was pushed to the left of the desk and ordered to sit. Momentarily, he was relieved when they started to take the handcuffs off his hands. However, they firmly shackled him to a metal with chain protruding out of the wall. The seated officer ignored his presence, except for a short glance as he was brought in.

He could hear a faint cry of pain from somewhere in the building. The cry seemed to be from someone who was in deep pain but weakened, maybe someone who was tortured immensely and left to die. His emotion was heightened. All the people who were important to him—his children, wife, friends, brothers, and sisters—passed through his memories in procession. He was bewildered. *Why am I brought here? What are they going to do to me?* He asked himself. The anguish was palpable. The silence in the room with the cry in the room next to him wrought havoc to his emotions. Though he was only about an hour there, he felt that he was in that miserable room with a chunk of his life. Suddenly, he released a cry of anguish. It was loud.

The officer was startled. He stood to his feet and started walking to where Mr. Nur was shackled. The anger in his eyes was visible. Standing close to the prisoner, he started to spout insults. "If you do that again, I will break every bone in your body," he threatened.

Mr. Nur regained his composure, and his natural dignified self was visible.

The officer seemed to be ashamed by his reaction and moved from where he stood backward. "Listen," he muttered in a conciliatory tone, "I have a job to do. You are accused of a serious crime against the state. I have a file here that shows you have been supporting the outlaws in their terrorist activities. I am looking into the evidence. Soon, we will get your side of the story. In the meantime, be seated and stay calm."

Jaded by what he heard, Nur closed his eyes and made a brief prayer. The accusation was mortally serious. In a country where being a suspect was enough to send individuals to their death, his situation was dangerous. Justice was arbitrary in the country. Formally, one could hire an attorney for defense. However, all the lawyers had been cowered by the state that they had effectively become an extension of the prosecutorial arm.

The family of Mr. Nur was stunned by his arrest. His wife, recognizing the urgency and dangerousness of his situation, started calling on his friends and relatives to alert them and beseech them to find ways to get him out of his predicament. Soon, the whole town started to speak about the incident. People were worried as he was the pillar of the community.

Friends scrambled to reach the powers that be to help with his release. The military governor had a far-reaching power as the country was under martial law. However, there were friends who did not agree with this proposal, their argument being once the governor denied a release, it would be almost impossible to undo it. They agreed to get his release by corrupting officers to help free him from prison.

The likeliest person was an army major. He was known as a person who lived beyond his means. He had been divorced by his wife a few years ago. He liked the company of beautiful young ladies. He was regularly seen in some of the best clubs and restaurants in town, it was rumored, for a price he could deliver. The challenge was to find a way to negotiate the price. The best way everybody agreed was to approach one of his lady friends. They all went to find who to approach, where they lived, what vocation they had, and who their families and friends were. It was agreed that they would meet early morning and decide.

In the military cells, Mr. Nur was taken into the interrogation room, a dark cell with a small vent. The place was musty. On the wall, splattered dried bloodstains were visible. There was a big metal worktable—the kind you find in restaurant kitchens—with metal rods, whips, and batons lying on the top of it. There were only three chairs. Work light on stands were placed on two sides. The lights were off. The time was early evening, around six o'clock, as the church bells could be heard from afar. The atmosphere was eerie. Men on boots could be heard marching on the corridors. Maybe three or four officers were walking by.

Suddenly, the door opened, and a ray of light was visible in the corner. Nur could not see the people as there was a black curtain blocking his sight. The officers talked in inaudible, hush-hush words, except for someone saying, "Maybe not tonight." After about fifteen minutes, the two officers left. And soon, the major followed them, closing the door forcefully.

No one talked to the prisoner. He was left in suspense. As the hours dragged, the prisoner was exhausted. He could not sleep as there was no mattress or cover to give him warmth from the cold concrete floor. He was still shackled by the wall. Soon though, he started to doze off while still seated on the stool. Torturous nightmare disturbed his sleep. He saw his youngest daughter cry uncontrollably on the floor. He tried to reach her, but as he stretched his arm, a muscular man hit him with an iron rod. He cried loud, and that made the guard posted outside to open the door and direct flashlight on him. His whole body was sweating. He thanked his God it was only in his dream. He resolved to remain strong for the sake of his family.

Daylight started breaking. A light, through a vent, showed a glorious sunny day outside. He hoped that the day would bear good news for him. Instead, he was transferred to the main prison.

*****

As appointed, the friends met at the prescribed place and time. Most of them were gloomy, except for Zerai. Zerai was a government employee and the closest friend of Nur. Their friendship dated back to their youth. They were inseparable growing up some had called them "radio" and "antenna" on the account of the differences in height and in compliment of their characters.

Zerai was haggard from lack of sleep. But his head was kept high, and his eyes sparked, effusing hope and confidence. As soon as everybody was seated, he said, "My friends, with God's will, we may get our friend out in a short time." Anxiously, everybody waited for his word. But he said, "I could not tell the details of it, but rest assured, someone is working to get his release soon. Mind you, nobody should speak to anyone about our conversation. I could not even tell my dear wife. You know how she feels about Nur. She is on the brink of nervous breakdown. However, I could not tell her. I repeat—do not tell anyone until the situation is resolved." Thus, everybody went their way, hoping for the nightmare to come to an end. They promised to keep in touch with one another.

Zerai did take off from his work and walked to the central part of the town. On the way, he met an old friend, Aregawi, who at one time was a business partner of Nur. Surprised that he did not see him to help with Nur's situation, he commenced to tell him about Nur's tribulation. To his surprise, the friend showed no emotion. What bothered Zerai most was how nonchalantly he commented that Nur should have not involved himself in illegal political activities. Zerai was in a rush to go meet the intermediary and left Aregawi. On the way, he was bothered by the comment. *What does he mean? Why didn't he show some sympathy on the arrest of his friend?* He even suspected maybe he had something to do with the arrest.

He rushed to the appointed place. The place was a conspicuous open market area where people from all walks of life would come to do shopping. Mothers with their children, young people in groups, and gentlemen after work were assembled. People were involved in their own business without minding others.

Zerai sat on a corner café with a bottled water on hand. He was eyeing all corners of the store. After almost half an hour, a young lady, clad in an ordinary garb, stood about fifteen feet away. She walked slowly. He stood and followed her. Once they reached the most crowded section of the market, he handed her an envelope and parted without talk. He prayed that she would succeed in her mission.

In the prison, Nur had spent two days in a confined cold room. He was not interrogated; it was both a relief and bewilderment to him. Usually, the interrogators would be harsh and would take no time to lay their hands on the victim. The sadistic brutality of the officers was well-documented. Their notoriety had broken the will of many courageous men and women. It was a matter of surprise and talk when Nur was transferred to the central prison without being molested by the officers. Some thought it was because of his influence and affluence. Others were even suspicious. It was a charade on the part of the regime to procure some information from some prisoners. In prison, Nur was despondent, talking to nobody and most of the time staying in the corner, looking upward to the sky. He was oblivious to the people around him and the filth in the cell.

Each cell housed great human suffering. The prison was a big structure built with heavily fortified walls with watchtowers on all four corners. It was heavily populated, far beyond its capacity. There was no segregation of age and type of crime. Political prisoners, murderers, and petty criminals were all kept together. In each cell, you would find hardened criminals and first-time prisoners. Some juveniles who were caught distributing the opposition flyers could be found among them. The living condition was abysmal. No sanitary facilities were available, except for a few plastic drums placed at different corners, and those were where the prisoners would relieve themselves. The prison was not equipped with medical service. Sick prisoners were left to die. The scene was most horrific it drove sane people to lose their sanity. Meal was provided twice a day, mostly of stale bread and bean stew. The taste was revolting. New prisoners would have to starve before they ate it. It was permitted to get food from outside, but it would be difficult to eat your own when hundreds were looking and cavorting for your plate. The family of Nur made sure to send food that could feed several people. Most of the prisoners were provided with some goodies of the goodwill of Nur's family and friends.

The amazing thing to observe in the prison was the spirit of the prisoners. The political prisoners took their punishment with stoicism as a price to pay to regain their rights. They had a purpose, a mission if you will, to free their people from the fetters of dictatorial rule. They labored to politicize and organize the prisoners. Their success was evident in the manner by which the prisoners carry themselves with their heads up. Notwithstanding the squalid living conditions, the camaraderie among prisoners was amazing. That helped Nur to open up slowly and create friendship, in particular with the young prisoners. He was captivated by their youthful idealism and energy. He was patient to listen to them. Every now and then, he expressed his opinions and added wisdom to them. They loved him. Some called him "Pops," and others called him teasingly "Old Warrior." Most of all, they admired his modesty.

*****

Ms. X met her friend, the major, for lunch at a place they both frequented and enjoyed. She was charming and elegant; the major had great fondness for her. He ordered a succulent lamb dish with potatoes and salad. She was careful with her diet and ordered salad. The day was bright, breezy, but crisp, a delightful day. She suggested they should spend the rest of the day together.

The major did not respond immediately. He looked like he was thinking of something. A moment later, he said, "Why not! I enjoy being with you."

She feigned delight and said, "I love you."

Lunch was over. He grabbed an imported bottle of wine from the store, and they headed to his place of residence.

At his home, he shed off his uniform and wore only his underwear. He started to undress her, button by button, each time caressing her velvety, soft body. She was seated in a love seat with legs folded underneath her. He stood behind her, lovingly looking down, with his hands busy unbuttoning and touching the breasts that had not lost their youthful protrusion. She was endowed with a well-sculpted body. In her bare, she looked like God had spent the best of his talents in making her. Her smile, with those well-chiseled teeth, was captivating, as if to add garnish to her beauty, she had dimples that would melt anyone as she smiled. The major was enthralled. He moved as if he was on a trance. In her presence, neither could he think right or act right. They both lay on a set of pillows on the carpeted floor. He started stroking her hair, at the same time enveloping her with kisses all over her body—the eyes, ears, nose, lips, neck, and nipples—with his lips and tongue voraciously. He kept caressing her all over her body. Ms. X was not only cavorting all these in delight of the sensation it created in her body but also on the powers she had on the man. Her ability to make strong men squirm in front of her had become a legend.

With her mind fixated on getting things her way, she was unflinching and cunning. On this night, she had set the stage for drama. The ambience was set to induce love, with candles burning in the two corners of the room. An aromatic essence, the kind that soothed the body, was effusing scents all over the room. "Ahh!" She stretched her legs with self-satisfaction. In such romantic atmosphere, she was at her best, both good and bad. She could evoke the most pleasure to her partner or design the most cunning plan and trap the victim at his most vulnerable moment. Such was the situation tonight. All the activities of the night were rehearsals to the entrapment of the major. She played the game to the hilt, gave herself to his amorous desires, kissed, hugged, caressed, and made love.

Ms. X brought the subject at his tender moment. All the while stroking his back, she asked, as if curious to know if he knew about the arrest of Nur.

Unsuspectingly, he said, "Yes, we are holding him on suspicion of facilitating the activities of the opposition in the city."

"But he is a prominent businessman and highly respected in the community," she added.

"I know that," he rejoined without any display of anger or suspicion.

She kept quiet momentarily to impress that she was not manipulating him. She gave him her most seductive look with head tilted, eyes partially closed, and a smile. He was smitten by this goddess of beauty and caressed her. At this moment, noticing the prey was snared, she made her move. "You know, my love," she said, "Mr. Nur is a father figure to me. He had always been supportive. It pains me to see him in prison." And she started to cry with tears rolling on her cheeks. "How come a man so gentle, wise, and generous be treated like a common criminal?" she queried.

The major, taken aback by her emotional outburst and distress, started pleading with her. "Dear," he said, "wise people make unwise decisions and are accountable for their actions. Mr. Nur made a serious mistake, and now he finds himself in jail."

To this, she angrily reacted, "What did he do? Didn't you say that he is only under suspicion? Isn't it possible to keep him with his family? He is no flight risk. You know it. Why is that the government have to humiliate our elderly? How do you expect to get the support of the population by continually showing disrespect to the most respected members of the community?"

The major was stunned by her forceful statement. The passion and anger in her every word disarmed him. He knew deep in his heart everything she said was right. But as an officer of the state, he had to defend the policies. "Hmm," he said, contemplating on how to respond. After some thought, he said, "Dear, you don't understand the situation. This is a revolutionary government under siege by different enemies who do not want change. I admit the government does make mistakes. Sometimes innocent people are hurt. But in view of the goals and achievements for the improvement of the life of ordinary working people, it is a small price to pay. Yes, Mr. Nur is prominent in the community. His generosity is legendary from the information we gather. However, there is compelling evidence that he was generous in supporting the opposition too. The government has no choice but to keep him confined in prison. Honey, can we lay off this topic and enjoy the evening?"

But she was persistent. "What evidence do you have?" she sneered. "Isn't it customary for the state to jail individuals on information provided by people who are untrustworthy to score against personal enemies or curry favor from the government? I dare say, my love, Mr. Nur is put in jail because someone had snitched on him—and I may add—falsely, either out of jealousy or enmity."

The major admitted that they had their informants, and the evidence against the accused was provided by one who knew him closely. That said, both were quiet. The quietness in the room was depressive they needed diversion. The bottle of wine the major brought was on the corner table. He uncorked it and offered a glass to her and poured on his glass too. They kept sipping on the wine without much talk. He refilled his glass, but she declined another.

As he drank more wine, he started to become more voluble. His speech slurred by alcohol, he started to recite his life history. He talked about the bitter feelings he had on his previous wife, who was currently married to a high-ranking government official with whom she had an affair during his marriage. The haunting nightmare he experienced from the cry of the tortured prisoners. He admitted that he did neither love his job nor did he have conviction on the goals of the revolution. To the amazement of Ms. X, he started harshly to condemn the leadership. He confessed the revolution did not have aim; the barbarity meted on individuals was for the sake of creating fear on the population. Fear was the guarantor for their stay in power, thus survival.

"To survive, they torture, rape, and kill," he lamented. "And, my dear, I have been a willing partner on this charade—actually, crime. I have condemned individuals to their death on flimsy evidence—most often, evidence that have been fabricated. I rationalized for my despicable action initially as revolutionary necessity. Later, I started to lie to myself by saying that the action is not acted by me but an office that I represent. I try to separate myself from the career I had chosen. But this also is becoming difficult. My conscience, at least what is left of it, is not letting me rest at peace. God knows how long I can do it. At times, I would want to end it by committing suicide. I argue it is a cowardly cop-out. Coward I am," he mused.

Foreboding an alarm, she intervened by caressing him and planting kisses on his face and lips. She told him, "You and thousands like you are victims. You joined the revolution with idealism, only to be entrapped by its vicious turnaround."

It was amazing what the caress of a beautiful woman could do to a man. His nerves were calmed. He was erotically aroused and moved to embrace his willing partner. They made love, and both were orgasmically satisfied. In that state of elation, he promised to atone himself of the wrongs he had done to many people. He gave her his word that he would find a way to release Mr. Nur. She thanked him profusely and lunged the tenderest kisses on his lips. Thus, relaxed they went to sleep.

Early morning, they woke up. They both had to go to work. Work started at eight for her, and she had to go home and change clothes. Curfew was not lifted before six. Anyone who was found outside prior to six was subject to detention, unless one carried a special pass. Army officers were exempt from such restrictions.

The major had to drive her to her place. His mood was relaxed. "It is going to be a wonderful day," he greeted her as he dropped her by her home. They exchanged kisses and promised to call each other during the day.

The officer headed toward a cafeteria where he frequented for his breakfast. He grabbed the daily paper and sat in a corner. He had the vantage of looking at all those who came in and out of the cafeteria. Every now and then, people would stop by his table to greet him. After finishing reading the paper and eating his breakfast, he headed to his office.

Most of the time, he did not go to work that early. However, today he felt he had to go early and accomplish the mission. The conversation of the night before was still fresh in his memory; he had made a promise and had to keep it. Most importantly, he had resolved to atone himself from the injustices he had committed on others in the service of an unjust government. He remembered Emerson's adage that he read long time ago: "Nothing is at least sacred but the integrity of your own mind." He had to amend his ways to live with himself. Thus, a new chapter of the life of the major had started, the consequences of which he might not know for some time.

Nur was released the same afternoon. As no one was informed of the imminent freedom of Nur, nobody was waiting for him outside the prison compound. He stopped a taxi and went home. Only his wife was at home. The children were not back from their school. His wife was so shocked she froze. He grabbed her before she fell to the ground and kissed her to snap her from the shock. She started sobbing uncontrollably. This time though, it was tears of happiness. She could not believe that he was at home. She studied his face by grabbing both his cheeks and thanked God. She ululated so loudly a few neighbors were startled, thinking their neighbor had gone crazy. Some rushed to the house, only to be extremely excited to see Nur as he was a beloved friend and neighbor. Nur graciously acknowledged the presence of the friends; however, he was concerned as he was advised to stay low until things settled down.

The major had taken him to his office and counseled him to find safer haven for himself and his family. "I am not to name names," he told him. "But you have an enemy closer to you. Be careful! Stay away from the limelight," he concluded.

But he had to inform his friend Zerai as he would surely go to prison for his daily visit. *He would be worried to death if he did not find me there*, he mused. He called over the phone and broke the news to his ears.

Zerai could not believe his ears. He called Ms. X "the miracle worker." He never thought that his beloved friend would be home in such a short time. As soon as he was out of work, he rushed to meet his friend face-to-face. The meeting between the two friends was highly emotional. Both had a feeling they might never see each other alive, knowing the serious accusation and the brutality of the regime. The friends stepped onto the verandah and huddled together, speaking so low so no one could hear.

Nur had to inform Zerai the counsel the major had given him, which was a clear suggestion to leave the country. Both understood that once you were put under the radar of the regime, every move would be fraught with danger. It could also be dangerous to friends and extended family. There was no alternative but to find a safe haven outside the country. It had to be arranged the soonest and with utmost secrecy. It was not possible for them to travel through formal ports of exit that would require an exit visa and entry visa to another country. The only way was to travel clandestinely through the forests and valleys and cross the border to a neighboring country. They studied the logistics required to travel six members of family. First, a guide that knew the route and any possible traps set by border security should be found. Second, the need to organize food, water, and clothing to sustain them for the duration of the travel. Third, to identify a contact on the other side of the border that might give them shelter and guidance once they arrived in the country. Last, to exchange money into hard currency, preferably American dollars.

The plan had been set, and immediately, they embarked on their way to find the guide—a reliable guide who could be trusted to lead them all the way to the neighboring country safely. The resourceful Zerai left no stone unturned to come up with somebody who could be entrusted with his dearest friend's family.

By next day, some information was gathered on who could lead the way and how to contact the individual. The candidate was a contraband trader who crossed the border frequently on cross-border trade. He had an intimate knowledge of the route and had many officers on the pay to help him in the event of being apprehended. He had transported hundreds of people for a fee.

After much thought and consultation with Nur, Zerai decided to approach the gentleman himself. He went to the area and neighborhood hangout which the gentleman patronized. Shortly, the gentleman arrived and sat by the counter. And thus, Zerai went to join him by the bar counter. He took a chair next to him and ordered a beverage.

The man saw Zerai and recognized him. After greeting him with due respect, he could not contain his surprise to see him in a bar frequented by contraband traders and other hustlers. He said, "I did not know you are a bar hopper," without sounding rude.

Zerai, as he was known for his directness, responded by saying, "No. Actually, I seldom go to a bar. I had reason to come here. That is to meet you."

"Why do you want to meet me?"

After a short surveillance of his surroundings, he said, "I am here to request a big favor of you, for which I would be willing to recompense you generously."

The greedy eyes of the gentleman widened. Money was the demon that drove him. Zerai, without hesitation, told him that he wanted to hire him as a guide for some friends to go abroad. Like a dog in his own turf, the gentleman said it would be of little inconvenience and that he was ready to give his service anytime. Thus, they agreed and parted ways after setting time to meet the next morning.

Zerai immediately went to his friend's home to apprise him of the arrangement. To his surprise, he found a group of friends, the children of Nur's, and his own family in a festive mood assembled at the patio of the house. *This is not good*, he thought. *It is thumbing at the noses of the angels.* He led his friend to a corner and gave him the information. It might be time to end the festivities and prepare for the inevitable departure in a couple of days.

On the eve of their departure, Nur remembered a part of the lyric from his favorite Egyptian crooner, Mohamed Abdel Wahab: "Let us apart without kisses so I live in hope of seeing you again."

Now that the date of departure had been decided, they scrambled to get everything ready. The children would have to be told before bedtime. Money had already been collected by exchanging local currency into American dollars at the black market. Food supplies—mostly biscuits, dried fruits, and dry powdered milk—were packed. Clothing was kept at bare minimum as the weather was pleasant during the season. Carrying heavy clothing was unnecessary. It was decided that they would act and behave as usual so as not to arouse any suspicion. The time was ticking.

It was at ten o'clock in the evening, the hour when the children would go to bed. They had arranged their books and homework papers to get ready for school the next morning when the parents called them to come to the kitchen table. It was very unusual for the father to gather them at the kitchen table. Fleeting feeling of uneasiness passed through their mind. Everybody assembled at the room. Their mother was facing against the wall, looking at the closed cabinet.

"Hey, Mom! Why are you there? Come over and sit at your chair," the youngest child asked.

When she moved her head to see her children, her eyes were swelling with tears. Obviously, she had been crying for a long time. Nur, without hesitation, explained to the children about their trip to a foreign country the next morning. Everybody was stunned. To depart from their home country, friends, and relatives was too much to digest. It took them awhile to react. They agreed their father was in danger and he had to leave, but was it necessary for all of them to go? In their youthful mind, the departure of their father would only be for a short time, until the situation improved in the country.

"We will wait for you here, Dad," said the oldest son.

Nur said, "I had thought of that, my children, but things will take a long time to change. Besides, this government has a policy of punishing members of a family for a crime committed by another member of a family. I can't leave my family in danger. We will be okay. We have people on the other side of the border."

After reaching consensus, the manner in which each would depart was discussed. The children would go to their school as normal. During break time, someone would pick them up, and they would meet at a place just outside the city.

The morning started with an unusual drizzle wetting the earth. A few people were outside on the streets, helping the escape less exposed. Everybody left on time without raising a suspicion from their neighbors. Their package had been loaded in a car owned by the guide, parked some distance from the home.

Nur, accompanied by his wife, drove their car to their warehouse, which was five kilometers away. They left their car key with a longtime employee, instructing him to take it for an oil change. The husband and wife walked a block away to be picked up by the guide. As appointed, the car, identified by the model and plate number, was parked on the corner, away from any eyesight of doors or windows. It was shaded by a big tree. Nur and his wife, after observing in all directions, jumped into the car. The driver, who was already seated in the car, started driving at legal speed to the northwest direction of the city. Twenty-five minutes later, they were at their destination. Their children arrived ten minutes later without their schoolbags. The bags were left on their desks at school. Each had told their separate homeroom teacher they had medical appointment. That way, no one had any suspicion why they did not attend the second half of their school day.

Now everyone was on spot. The long trek to the unknown land started. On their faces, uneasiness could be observed. The journey through forests, valleys, and desert was fraught with the dangerous attack by bandits and venomous snakes, and the risk of being apprehended by the military could send them to certain death.

The responsibility had weighed heavily on Nur. He had to act both as a determined chaperone and cheerleader. So the journey started. A journey to the unknown from the life of comfort, family, and friends to a life of exile. To eke out the life of refugees in a land alien to their culture. Nur was very optimist by nature and a very hardworking entrepreneur. Deep in his heart, he was confident in making it. He surely believed that his children would be successful in their education. He was determined to give them the best education, come what may. He had another advantage, the mastery of several languages. He was fluent in French, Italian, Arabic, and his native language. *Language opens many doors and opportunities*, he thought to himself. That gave him much comfort.

The guide, as said earlier, was a man of much talent. As a contrabandist, he had to be able to operate under very difficult situations. He should be flexible and adaptive to conditions. He had cultivated contact with several well-positioned individuals along the route, and they had saved him many times. He was generous with them. On this mission, he had felt special responsibility. The family to whom he was responsible for safe passage was very important to him. He had always had great respect to Nur and his friend Zerai. They were men of great stature and deservedly well respected in the community. The comfort and safe passage became of utmost priority, and he decided to charge them not a penny more than his cost. Along the way, he had arranged safe houses, inconspicuous places where they could eat and rest.

On the first day, they drove ninety-five kilometers and decided to spend the night at a place owned by a friend of the guide in proximity to a major street. It was conveniently located near a major artery and sparsely built houses.

After dinner, the guide warned them that they had to depart before daybreak to avoid any likelihood of being identified by people. From there, they had to walk or ride a camel a distance of a hundred seventy kilometers. It might take them as long as a week to traverse the distance. They would sleep under trees, caves, and farmlands. There wouldn't be a fire or light burning at night. Cigarette smoking would be done camouflaged. "Speak very softly at all times. Most importantly, all of you will wear the traditional folk garb of the local people. In the event we are caught by border patrol, most likely, they do not understand the local language. Let me do the talking. I will tell them that we are local people on a pilgrimage to a shrine some distance along the way. Now let us rest for few hours," he instructed.

They woke up at three o'clock in the morning after a few hours of sleep. The guide said, "Splash some cold water on your faces." One by one, they did. A sweetened hot tea with flatbread was eaten for breakfast.

"The trek that we follow is the most arduous," said the guide. "Elevation changes drastically, and so does the clime. In the highlands, the weather is pleasant with moderate temperature between seventy to eighty Fahrenheit most of the year. Whereas, the lowlands' temperature could rise to one hundred Fahrenheit or more. Vegetation is sparse, except for the thorny bushes that survive the most horrible of weathers. Walking in that kind of environment saps the energy of the most energetic person. For an older person with some pounds to carry, it could be downright miserable."

But there was no turning back now. Everybody was ready to take on the challenge. They prayed together, and the voyage started slowly but steadily.

They dismounted the rocky hills with the guide leading in front, pointing to the steady rocks, walking like a marching band in a single file. They reached the sandy plain, exhausted and thirsty. They rested under an acacia tree, which gave a little shade, and looked yonder at the horizon the endless flatland with a mirage of distant body of water and the long trek that they had yet to cover. The course that they followed was not straight, avoiding the expanse of the flatland. They walked for a long time, but they did not seem to have covered a long distance as the hills were angling every few yards, elongating the distance to cover. At the end of the day, they might have traveled fifteen to eighteen kilometers. Tired and hungry, they rested under a big rock to pass the night. Their resourceful guide asked them to help him move good-sized boulders to build a fence around them, both as a shield from the cold desert wind and unwanted nocturnal visitors. The night passed uneventful, except for the ache they felt sleeping on a hard surface.

In the morning, the guide congratulated them for the day before. "You really are resilient. At the start of the journey, I was apprehensive, but I am confident we will reach our destination in time. Today's trip is a lot easier, and if we are lucky, we might hire camels and mules to cross us for most of the distance. We are going to follow a dry riverbed until we reach a small village of mostly nomadic tribes. I have built friendship among residents and arrange for camels and mules."

They started their journey with much hope and better spirit. Owing to its depth, the dry, sandy riverbed was a good camouflage and a shade from the sun. Its soft surface was easier on the feet and joints. They walked for about four hours, when the sound of life started to be heard. The camels and mules were braying with dogs barking in the background. Their guide told them to wait for him. It took almost an hour before he came back with an elderly gentleman, turbaned and slightly stooped with age.

After a cordial exchange of greetings, the old man started to speak. He expressed his sorrow to see so many people, young and old, flee their country, crossing by there to go into exile. Mothers were left childless, and sometimes whole families were uprooted. "Allah, save us," he prayed. With that, he negotiated with the guide on how he could provide them camels and a guide to return the animals once they reached the border. At this point, they parted with their guide who brought them all the way there from their home. Before he left, he gave Nur a note and an address to his friend across the border.

Ensconced on a camel, holding the hump for stability, they continued their journey. The ride on a camel was not as scary as they thought once they were settled. Actually, the young ladies were so tickled by the experience they could not stop giggling. The camel rider was whistling melodic tune of the tribe. The dexterity with which he handled his camel showed his experience. The camels were obedient to his command. The communication by gesture, words, and sound gave the impression that the camels and the man were in uncommon understanding. Camels were highly intelligent animals. Folkloric stories told of the camels' unfettered loyalty to their master and terrible temperament when crossed.

"Be good to the camels," the guide forewarned. To make a point, he told them that once a man struck a camel with a cane while eating shrubs. That must have upset the camel. Few minutes later, the man walked in front of the camel. It caught him by the neck, choking him to death. Message well understood, everybody was in their best behavior.

Riding a camel was like riding a slow-moving swing, only that the camel continuously moved forward. It was amazing. This rather-clumsy-looking animal could traverse distances intersecting valleys, flatlands, and hills with ease and speed. The advantage of a camel was that it wouldn't need water or food for a long time.

On this day, they crossed almost fifty kilometers before they decided to rest for the night. The camel rider-guide took them to a village close to an oasis and planted posts to set a tent by unfolding a tarpaulin. The guide went to the village were some of his extended families lived to fetch water and possibly milk. Few minutes later, he came back with two jugs made of goatskin filled with water and milk. Since they had a powdered milk, they mixed it with water and drank it. They offered him the milk, but he declined it, preferring the camel milk, to which they didn't have a palate for. Again, the night passed uneventful. Rested, they were ready for another day of journey.

The clock hit 4:00 a.m. when their guide gave his command for the camels to move. They did not have a map or compass; however, direction was never a problem as their guide had traveled this route many times. He seemed to identify every hill, tree, nook, and crook. As they came closer and closer to the border, they were told to be extra careful as they might encounter military scouts on surveillance mission on cross-border hostile activities. They were still dressed in the tribal garb. With their unkempt look, they had blended quite splendidly. Unless one observed very closely and carefully, they were unidentifiable as people from an urban area.

After they traveled for about three hours, there was an alarm on the voice of their guide. "Stop! Stop!

Dismount from the camels." He commanded the camels to kneel down under a tree. The cause of his alarm was a dust blowing on a trail some three to four kilometers away. He said that was an army truck, and they would have to check on what direction it was going before they moved. Few minutes later, the dust settled, and soon, none was visible. Their guide was not satisfied. He said he was not sure if they had stopped and camped in front of them or they had changed direction. He decided to go alone on his camel to survey the area. He nimbly jumped on his camel, and off he went to the direction where the dust was blowing. It took almost an hour before he came back. He assured them that they were safe, but it was necessary to move westward to go farther from the direction of the movement of the army truck.

The part of the country that they were moving on was rugged with a chain of mountains. The mountains were denuded of plant life. The midday sun was so intense everyone was sweating profusely. Actually, they were afraid of sunstroke. Thanks to their guide, they kept hydrating themselves frequently. As they moved farther northwest, the steep hills to the east shielded them from direct sun, and the ground and air cooled noticeably. Owing to the change of weather, the camels were sprinting, covering a long distance in a shorter time. Long after sunset, it was decided that they ended their journey for the day. This time, their camp was spread in a sandy valley with mosquitoes humming around them. The mosquitoes were vicious. They penetrated the covers which were laid on top of them and bit them incessantly. None of them could sleep the night. By the morning, their bodies had swelled all over from the onslaught of mosquitoes. The itch was miserable. There was nothing to do but withstand the pain with stoicism. Their guide was apologetic for resting them on a shallow place where mosquitoes breed. He promised to get them a cure for the itching and swelling from plants a short distance away on their route. He concocted a mixture of some leaves and juice of aloe plants and smeared the exposed part of their bodies. The effect was miraculous as it relieved them from the itching, and the swelling subsided. Each one of them admired the wisdom and knowledge of the humble nomadic people. The understanding and respect of their environment was the lesson that they repeatedly learned from their trip. Every creature had a purpose, according to the tribal people, and they treated all with some sort of sanctity, to be relished and used appropriately. Their creed was that treating all of God's creature with sanctity was the highest respect to the Creator.

Beyond a small hill lay the border. The guide gave them information with a sigh of relief. "Shortly, you will be crossing the border to the Sudan."

Their life as aliens in foreign land was to start in a matter of few hours. Their guide would depart from them to join his family and clan in his village. He might travel day and night before he would reach the safety of his home. He was a wonderful guide—gentle, patient, wise, and courageous. They would miss him dearly. In the last three days and nights, they had built a kinship with this tribal man. Alas, they might never see him again. He took them almost to the border before he bid them farewell. He prayed for their safety, and off he went to the land of his ancestors. They, on the other hand, were forced to flee the land they loved and cherished, the land of their forebears.

On the border, there were no distinctive markers, no posts planted, and no line drawn. Except for the line drawn on a map in reference to latitude and longitude on the ground, no one could identify where one country ended and another started. They crossed anyway, with their paltry earthly possession. Their guide had informed them that a military outpost of the host country was located not far from the border. They had two choices—either to go and surrender to them or to pass the outpost clandestinely. The danger was that they might turn them back if they surrendered to them.

Some fifteen kilometers after crossing, a small town was located. It was a bustling trading town where a sizable number of their countrymen had settled over many decades. Among them were several successful business people. They went into town without raising any curious look from the citizens.

Soon, they were at the door of a huge warehouse. The sign read Kassem Warehouse Store in Arabic. The note that their first guide gave them was addressed to the owner of the store, Omar Kassem. On the side of the warehouse was a small office with windows open. A balding man was seated on a desk with his head down. There were two other young men lazily standing on the side. The young men saw them and reported to the gentleman their presence.

The man raised his head and smiled a little as if he had recognized them. Nur asked him if he was Omar Kassem. He responded affirmatively, and Nur handed him the note. He read the note carefully. And in excitement, he said, "You are Mohamed Nur." Before he had a chance to respond, he jumped and hugged him with the reverence and love that one would exhibit to a long-lost uncle. Indeed, the man had reason to be so enthused by the presence of a man so reputed and who was a benefactor to his brother. He introduced himself as the brother of Shariff Kassem.

Nur was so surprised at the turn of events; of all places, his first stop would be to the place of Shariff's brother. Shariff was a young entrepreneur in his country until he was framed up by a business competitor to be thrown in jail. A stockpile of small arms was planted in his warehouse, and police discovered it on a tip from an informant. For weeks, the government-controlled media had feasted on the crimes of Shariff. They were calling for blood. Shariff denied that he had any knowledge of the arms brought as an exhibit. He suspected his enemies had framed him. His case was so hot and so dangerous nobody dared to defend him. All erstwhile friends deserted him. The courageous Nur was the only one to come in defense of the accused. He gave an alibi and acted as a character witness. It was a dangerous thing to do.

The stature of Nur at the time was so high the government rationalized the release would give it mileage on rehabilitating its damaged reputation at least among the business class of the population. Shariff's release was conditional that he would refrain from political involvement.

Shariff sought asylum and chose to live in exile on his first opportunity of visit abroad. In exile, Shariff became a successful businessman. He had spoken to all who could hear that he owed his life to Nur. That was why his brother Omar was so elated to have the family of Nur as guests at his home.

"I know my brother will instantly come here to visit you," he told Nur. Omar was single with a big house and a maid to take care of it. He opened his home and heart to them.

Encouraged by the words and support that Omar provided them, they thanked God. They prayed and went to rest their tired bodies in the accommodation set up for each of them. It did not take them long to be in deep sleep. They slept for almost ten hours.

In the morning, they all sat at a table and ate a sumptuous breakfast. Omar had left early to attend to business. He left a message that he would return during the day. He advised them to wait for him at home. Waiting, they thanked God for their good fortune.

The wife could not stop her blessing. "He is an angel to open his home so generously," she blessed. She would tell her husband that what he did was a call of the conscience to save the life of an innocent man and that what he was doing was a charity of the heart. Each in its way was a celebration of God's will. Fowzia was a woman of few words but a grand heart. She had an uncanny ability of soothing the bereaved, the sick, and the hard of luck and also the ability to bring the arrogant and powerful to common sense and decency. Between the husband and wife, it was a marriage made in heaven as all their friends would attest.

Few hours later, Omar came back to the house. One could read a sense of triumph and joy on his face. "I talked to my brother over the telephone," he said. "And he is coming to visit you soon, in a few days. He had beseeched me to keep you here until his arrival. Jokingly, he even told me that he will recompense for my expenses. I am sorry to say you are stuck with me for a while. Appeal is denied," he concluded in good humor.

On their third day in town, Nur, accompanied by his sons, ventured outside to explore the town. Omar gave them directions and places of interest to visit. The bus number and where to fetch taxi he carefully jotted on paper and gave them some local currency folded in the paper.

Nur was well conversant in the local language. They visited the central part of the city with its bustling business quarter. He was amazed at the vibrant economic activities in the stores, cafés, and sidewalks. As a business person, he imagined all the possibilities and opportunities. He even imagined himself setting up a distribution center of commodities and consumables like he had in his country. Of course, reality set in. He teased himself. *I am just dreaming. My struggle is survival of my family at this point*, he mused.

After a long walk, they decided to sit in a café with local people lounging. They ordered tea and bottled waters and sat at an empty table. The mood in the café was friendly, the customers laughing and relaxing to an outsider; it looked like some kind of a family gathering. After few minutes, the people seated next to them asked them if they were new to the place.

Nur said, "This is our first time to visit here." And he added, "We are new to the country."

Immediately, the people asked them if they did not mind to join them at their table. In no time, they became part of a great family. Food and beverages were brought to the table, and everybody started to feast with gusto. The hospitality was genuine; they made them feel welcome. The legend of the Sudanese generosity and conviviality was known throughout the African Horn region. Names were exchanged before they returned to Omar's place.

By the time they reached Omar's home, it was early evening. Fowzia and the girls were worried. As soon as he saw his wife, he apologized for being late and told her about their visit to town and their newly acquired friends. He even prophesied that the country would be a welcome place for them to stay.

Shariff arrived the morning after. He was expensively attired and grown a tad plump. The moment he saw Nur and his family, with a broadened smile and stretched arm, he hugged his savior. They were all excited, for they did not expect him to come in such a short notice. After exchanging pleasantries and gifts to everyone, he seated himself beside Nur to listen to the story of their exile.

Nur revisited the horror of his incarceration and flight to exile, concluding by saying, "Allah has been good to us. We arrived safely here and landed at the hands of the most generous person, your brother. We are treated royally. *Alhamdulillah!* Allah has a way of taking care of his good children."

Shariff said, "I am happy for what my brother did, but it is little sacrifice. He did not put himself in harm's way to help you. I know, sir, that you had put yourself in grave danger to help me. That is a greater sacrifice and a courageous act. My family—that includes my brother—is forever grateful to you. We are honored to have you in our midst."

Shariff had come only for few days, but he wanted to make sure that the transition to the new life of the Nur family was as smooth as possible. After consulting with his brother as to what should be done, they decided to help Nur establish a business. They agreed that since he was a successful businessman in his country, it would be easier for him to succeed. As agreed, Omar took the responsibility of arranging for the family to get proper documentation and permits from the host government. With his extensive contacts among government officials, he promised it would be done in a short time. The idea was brought upon to Nur.

Nur could not contain his joy. "My dear friends, benefactors, I do not know how I can repay you for your kindness. When I left my home, my life had darkened. Honestly, I was scared for the future of my family. I trusted in Allah. Allah guided me through the maze of flight to safely arrive here and brought me here to you. Am I not the luckiest person? I thank you. Thank you!" he blessed.

Few weeks later, the documents were filed with the appropriate offices. Omar made his rounds to lobby on behalf of the family. All officials were sympathetic. However, the wheels of bureaucracy turned very slowly. It took almost six months for them to get the necessary documents and permits to start a business. In those six months, the family busily acclimated themselves with the town. The different neighborhoods, schools, and mosques they discovered.

Every society had its business culture. Transparency and codified business were entrenched in the West. In the developing world, business was done mostly in a haphazard, constantly negotiating terms and conditions. Those who did not understand these subtilities of mode of doing business were doomed to fail.

Nur, as a seasoned business person, was observing and studying the manner in which business was done in his new home. He took time to look into the different nuances of wheeling and dealing. He was well prepared before he started the business.

Shariff was willing to contribute the initial capital. He told Nur, "You would pay me back when you are in a position to pay." He was sure that Nur would not accept a handout from anyone.

Thus, a new venture was born, the importation of consumables and selling on wholesale. Before they invested though, they made a thorough study of the market and competition. Nur had the experience and connection with manufacturers and distributors. The warehouse was set in an industrial zone of the city with easy access. From the start, business was brisk. With a comfortable income, they planned their future. Education of the children was given priority.

The children were enrolled at a private school famous for its academic rigor and discipline. Secular schools, Nur reasoned, would give his children an outlook less indoctrinated. Tolerance to other religions, ideologies, and racial and ethnic affiliation was a hallmark of his life. Certainly, he wanted his children to understand and respect their religion, Islam. He had encouraged them to study the holy Quran. Only time would tell how his children would turn out to be.

Friday was the day when stores were closed in the city. Some of the businesses, especially those who dealt on a wholesale distribution, would close on Saturday too. Nur's wholesale distribution company was closed both days. It gave the family time to go out together and recreate.

Of late, Amin, the older son, avoided the family outings. He simply said he would rather go to the mosque and the Islamic center, even though the family pleaded with him to join them. He adamantly refused.

The three children, with their parents, customarily went to places that gave some quiet and relaxation away from the drab and crowded city. They brought food and beverages and some camping gears to throw a tent and enjoy.

It was on a return home from one of those picnics that they saw a huge demonstration of people chanting, "Death to the infidel, death to the bitch!" The people were carrying placards, sticks, and some daggers. It was a battle-ready crowd. But what was going on? Was there a change of government, a revolution, or a riot? Sure, it was a riot. A single woman had allegedly made a disrespectful mention of the name of the Prophet. She had called one of her male cats Mohamed. For this, the crowd wanted blood. They were heading to the woman's residence which was by then cordoned off by phalanges of riot police and paramilitary unit. The riot police were in full gear.

As Nur drove carefully and very slowly in the opposite direction of the crowd, his daughter, Amina, the youngest, saw her brother Amin sweating and chanting with the rioters. He saw her. His blood-shot eyes were red, his veins swollen with anger and emotional chanting. She waved at her brother and called him by his name. The rest of the family saw him too. Each one of them was stunned; they could not believe their eyes. He did not respond to the call nor did he seem to slow down. He continued on his march to the war front against a single European woman. Nur calmed the family and reassured them he was coming home, and he promised them that he would do everything in his power to bring sanity to his son. It was agreed that he was the only one to talk to him on the matter.

The rioters, before they reached the concrete walls of the house were the woman resided, were stopped by a wall of well-armed security forces.

The police chief, standing on armored vehicle and surrounded by sharpshooters, called for the attention of the crowd. He used a high-decibel megaphone to address them. It took a few minutes to get their attention. As soon as they were calmed, he skillfully and respectfully addressed them. As a good Moslem himself, he was angered when the Prophet—peace be upon him—and Islam were insulted, and he was always ready to lay his life for the honor of Islam as they all were. "Now," he added, "go home as the woman is under the custody of the security forces. She will meet appropriate punishment under our hands, and we will teach her and others who disrespect our beloved prophet—peace be upon him—a lesson."

There was a great murmur among the crowd. Those who were in front started to walk away. Thus, a major riot was averted and the mob justice that was to be rendered avoided.

Nur was totally shaken from witnessing his son's participation in the riot. He tried to find an answer to what influences had pushed him to be such a zealot and why. How was a son born and raised in a liberal, albeit religious, family became so fanatic as to be part of a potential murderous crowd? The challenge was how to start a dialogue and delve into the inner sanctum of his thinking and be able to bring him to his senses. For few days, that was the question that dominated his mind.

Two days later, Amin came home. He was quiet, unwilling to speak with his siblings other than grunts and short answers. As instructed, the family did not raise the riot.

The mother only expressed her worries of him not coming home for two days. "I had two sleepless nights, my son," she told him.

"Ema!" he said. "I am a grown-up man. I can take care of myself." Dismissively, he said, "Do not worry about me." He moved to his room and closed the door until late in the evening when he came out to eat his meal. He gave a short greeting to his father and went to the kitchen. With food on a plate, he went to his room where he stayed the next two days.

Nur decided to challenge his son on a religious basis, scripture by scripture, and maybe win him back into mainstream Islam without hate and extremism. He understood that was not going to be easy but would establish that the Quran expressed the universal themes of human experiences and spiritual fulfillment.

Few days later, Nur decided it was the day to start a dialogue with his son. He had prepared himself to be patient and let the son express what drove him to extremism.

By evening when the day's hectic activities had subsided, the hot sun had given into cool breeze of crispier air. That was when he asked his son to escort him over a walk. Nur had a habit of talking to his children individually while doing his daily evening walk.

Amin knew what was coming. He wanted to do it too. He had always felt his father's liberalism was at fault because his sisters and brother were irreligious. He was particularly angry at his youngest sister. She befriended and socialized with people so easily, young men and women of all races and religions. Her personality was so gregarious people liked to be around her. For Amin, this was sacrilegious, lack of humility, and considered it an affront to Islamic values. Every time he tried to lecture her on proper "Islamic decorum," she had dismissed him by saying, "Sheik Amin, keep your advice to your future children." She had grown so weary of his constant harangue that, for the most part, she avoided his company.

Nur wanted to deal with the issue of his son's understanding of how women, particularly his sisters, should lead their lives. The route Nur took on his daily walk was predictable. It was constant that the neighborhood owners of small stores and cafés and office workers gauged their time by his crossing the sidewalks. He greeted them cordially, and they responded wishing him peace and good health.

On this day, he was so preoccupied with his son he did not notice the neighborhood nor the people. The discussion started rather uncomfortably when Amin accused his father of neglecting the most important duty of a father, the inculcation of religious duties to his children.

Amin said, "Eba, you are a good provider. We have more clothes than we need, more food than we can eat, larger house in the neighborhood that betrays modesty, drive a car that is both stylish and new. But we lack religious guidance. Look, Eba, the way Amina dresses, the friends she has, men and women. And my brother, had you ever seen him go to mosque or pray with regularity as demanded by the holy Quran? He spends more time dribbling a ball or going to cinemas that are corrupt and sinful. When I ask him to join me for salat, he ridicules me. He said that I will hold the key to the gate of heaven, and I would help him entry to it. This blasphemy and insult to Islam makes me suspect that he is no more a Moslem. Maybe he has converted to Christianity to be among his friends. Is that what you want, Eba? When are you going to be an Islamic father guiding the family in a pious Islamic way?"

The indictment was severe, and Nur understood that it would take more than a single walk to resolve the schism created among the siblings and possible total breakup of relations. From the earnest and serious tone of his son's discourse and accusation posited against his role as a father, he understood it might lead to grave consequences upon the family.

He was worried that his son might cause harm to his youngest sister Amina. He was more condemnatory of her and her lifestyle. Without spouting the words, he intimated that she had brought dishonor to the family and Islam.

It was time for Nur to peel the layers of condemnatory statements from his son. Like a good prosecutor, he wanted to crack them layer by layer until the root of the ideas was exposed. He started to ask him the simplest and most obvious questions. He wanted to take him back to his native country where he had fond relations and friendship with people of all faith, region, and ethnicity. "Do you remember when you were much younger back home? On weekends, you used to spend time at my friend Zerai's home."

Amin seemed to be taken aback. For a minute, he did not know how to respond. Nur could observe, for a while on that hesitation to respond, a nostalgia for the old ways—when things were uncomplicated and when young people were young and the old were to be ignored. This short show of emotion, though subdued, gave a flicker of hope to the father. *All is not lost*, he thought.

After a short interlude before getting response, Nur continued, "You know I have been in contact with my friend Zerai. He had lost his job for suspicion that he may have played a role in my release from prison. He is in dire financial condition. As a matter of fact, I have asked him to send his two children here to be with us and continue their education. It was your mother's suggestion, and I agreed. Your friend will join you soon. You were inseparable as children. That was a long time ago."

Amin attempted to change the direction of discussion. "Eba, I am glad you are helping your friend. Islam teaches zakat, helping the needy. But that is not what we set to discuss. My concern is about my family here. The ones that violate every Islamic tenet."

The father was slightly irritated by his son's irascible behavior and his holier-than-thou attitude. After a short contemplation, Nur wanted to explore the issue of women and how they should maintain themselves. The issue of women under Islam had always been controversial. There were those who were conservative and maintained that some Islamic injunction should remain forever valid without taking into consideration the changing social dynamic of societies. "For me and many modernist Moslems, Islam is not such static with rigid unchangeable laws but a religion that adapts to changes in social conditions. But the changes should not violate the fundamental Islamic values and basic principle."

Amin was impatient, listening to his father's lecture. He quoted a scripture of the Quran in support of his displeasure with his sisters' lifestyle, "And stay in your homes and do not go about displaying yourselves like the display of the days of ignorance" (Quran 33:33). He further quoted, "O prophet, say to your wives and your daughters and the women of the believers that they let down over them their Jilbab. This will be more proper than they may be known, and thus they will not be molested" (Quran 33:53).

"The Quran is clear on how women, young and old, should cover themselves and directs husbands and fathers to make sure they do so. The Quran further admonishes women who display their body parts by saying, 'Say to the believing women that they cast down their looks and guard their private parts. That is purer for them. Surely, Allah is aware of what they do. And say to the believing women that they cast down their looks and guard the private parts and not display their ornaments except what appears thereof, and let them wear their head coverings over their bosoms and not display their ornaments except to their husbands'" (Quran 24:30–31). "You see, Eba, the Quranic instructions are clear, the way my sisters, especially Amina, violate every Quranic teaching in total abandon. If one does not know her, they may think she is non-Moslem. Even non-Moslems in this country, for the sake of modesty, cover their hair with scarf. My sister, on the contrary, she unfurls her hair and walks the city streets as if she is on a fashion show with all public attending. This is anathema to our religion and tradition, and you as a father should have stopped it."

With patience and a measured tone, Nur started to respond. "Listen, son," he said, "your sisters and brother are good children. They are pious in their own way. As a father, I am proud of each and every one of my children. Allah has blessed us with children who are kind, moral, and hardworking. The verses that you quoted are not strange to me. I have read them and reread them several times over the years.

58

Let me tell you how I differ in interpretation from you. Interpretation has to be viewed with context. Otherwise, you will make them irrelevant. At the time of the Prophet—peace be upon him—in pre-Islamic Arabia, morality was loose. Women had multiple amorous relationships. Conflicts and civil strife was rife. The Prophet—peace be upon him—wanted to bring order and form the new Islamic community. Peace, order, and the establishment of strong families was essential to the new community, and women had a central role in it.

"Back to the verses, if you look at the verses taken literally, it orders that women should not go out of their house. Is that what you want to happen to your sisters and all women? I don't think so. As far as covering of woman's body parts, it was mainly meant to protect women from molestation. This again have to be seen within the context of the Arab situation, where chaos and warring tribal groups raided and captured women and molested them. In our situation, I do not foresee any of my daughters being molested by a marauding group. I hope at least that such situation may not arise. This is not to say that young women should not show humility. Of course not. The greatest disservice to Islam is the extreme, narrow view that you have taken on the issue of women's rights. You cannot enslave women and expect to form a harmonious family and, hence, society. Our view should progress with the development of society and make essential readjustments demanded of a new society."

Amin was dumbfounded by his father's out-look which was no different than the nonbelievers. With much earnest, he wanted to argue his case on the broader Islamic mission both as a spiritual and worldly guide to humanity. "The misunderstand-ing of Islam as religion who treats women is unfair and erroneous. There are voluminous historical and current events that show women in Islam are treated as equal and with respect. The problem is there is a confusion on the traditional treatment of women with Islam. Right from the time of the Prophet—peace be upon him—women, like the Prophet's wife, Aisha, played a significant role in the Ashura. The Quran succinctly and without equivocation asserted the equality of women and the complementariness of the relation between man and woman. In the Quran, it is written, 'They are apparel for you and you are an apparel for them'" (Quran 2:188). "What this verse tells us is the obvious natural differences of man and woman, nonetheless that each had an important role no less equal one from the other to make life full. That is where the ignorance lies. The Quran had made it plain and clear in other verses the equality of women. 'They have rights similar to those against them, in just a manner'" (Quran 2:228). "The Prophet, in many occasions, had reminded his followers that women should be treated with respect and dignity as their male counterparts. The context you have men-tioned is well-considered in the Quran as the rights of women spring from biological, sexual, and social realities that are immutable in time. But Islam has more compelling and important calling. The Quran assures every Moslem, 'You have become the best community ever raised up for mankind, enjoining the right and forbidding the wrong and having faith in God'" (Quran 3:110).

Amin continued his pitch for his faith and its broader calling. He said, "Islam is the first religion that has called for humanity to unite in brotherhood, irrespective of region, race, and gender."

Nur, surprised by the audacity of his son, stopped him by remarking, "You are preaching to a convert. The issue is not the teachings of Islam. There is no dispute on that. What I am against is the way some people are trying to impose their beliefs on others through intimidation and violence. Utterly un-Islamic way. By using violence with teachings of Islam, they make it look as if both are inevitably linked. Teach about Islam and its basic tenets, its faith in one God, generosity, commitment, sacrifice, and renewal. Those who commit violence in the name of Islam are truly damaging to the true calling of the faith of human brotherhood."

It was getting late, so they decided to go home. The issues were hanging, both not totally satisfied with the outlook they held on the role of Moslems in both practicing and teaching their religion. Nur felt he had at least made his son pause and think about the way he related to his siblings. The future would tell. It might be parental wishful thinking. Like a desert mirage, it could be deceptive. Nur was watching every gesture and word of his son, in particular toward his younger sister.

As they entered home, Amina came and hugged her father without acknowledging the presence of her brother. The dye was cast. There was no love lost between the two of them.

Nur had a restless night. He had a nightmare whose image he couldn't recall in the morning. However, it left him anxious and tired in the morning. Since his imprisonment in his country, he did not recall a nightmare episode. He wanted to put it aside and start his day with a fitting disposition, the perennial optimist unflinching by setbacks. Even his wife Fowzia noticed something on his face and asked him if he was falling sick. "No, dear, I am perfectly all right. I just did not have enough sleep."

She was concerned the evening before that her husband was somber and her son went into his room and never came out to eat. Since her husband had instructed the family to leave the issue to him, she did not ask him anything. But under the circumstances, she had no choice. The suspense was driving her insane. Prudently and gently, she asked her husband how the evening went by with their son.

Nur, knowing his wife's sensitivity and love for her family, felt it unfair to keep her in the dark. He gave her a summary of their discussion by concluding that the young man was exploring both the spiritual and worldly life. "No need for alarm," he comforted her. "He will be all right sooner than you think and join his siblings in guiding his life." Thus said, he left to work.

As for Amin, as soon as his father left, he snuck out of the house. It was only about midday that his mother knocked by his door to ask him to come out and eat his meal. Nobody was answering. After a few more knocks and calls, she opened the door to find that he had already left. To her surprise, the bed was set well as if no one slept on it. All his clothing was neatly hung on the closet rack. Shoes were dusted off and cleanly layered by the shoe shelves. All books were symmetrically stacked on the bookshelf. Initially, she thought that her son had grown up and taken responsibility, but there was a nagging feeling. There was something unusual about it for a young man of his age. It was too good to be real, she surmised. *Why would he leave without eating and bidding me good day?* She asked herself. In spite of the nagging feeling that something was amiss, she intended to praise her son for the upkeep of his room.

Evening came and everyone came back home as usual, except for Amin. Amin's lateness was not of concern because his arrival was irregular. Time kept ticking late by nine thirty in the evening. Everyone was concerned and started to ask where Amin was.

At ten o'clock in the evening, Fowzia advised her husband to check into Amin's bedroom if he could find any clue. The neatly organized room surprised the father. He expected to see socks on the floor, item of clothing strewn everywhere, and the bed with bedsheets and blankets partly on the floor.

This time, everything was meticulously organized. The clothes were neatly folded and in the proper place, and the floor was clear and clean. He looked into the shelved books; most of them were religious books. He picked up a few of them and started to leaf through them. There was nothing unusual about the books. Here and there, there were questions written and comments and highlights on some verses. Amin did not come home for the night.

Early morning, Nur decided to go places where he thought most likely his son might hang around. He crisscrossed the streets on the car and walked the neighborhood's narrow streets. After almost three hours, most of the businesses were open, and the sidewalks were teemed with people going to work. He did not know what to do or who to ask, for Amin had kept his contacts secret. He decided to sit in a corner tearoom where he could observe people walking on all directions. Amin was not to be seen. Understanding the futility of his effort, he went back to his home where he found his wife huddled in a corner with her face furrowed out of her concern for her son.

As soon as her husband entered the house, she leapt to her feet and started to ask him a barrage of questions. "Did you find him? Did you meet someone who knows his whereabouts?"

Nur, deeply saddened by his wife's agony, tried to comfort her. "Do not worry. He will be back. He is only going through self-discovery." Deep in his heart though, he knew the schism between his son and the family had deepened. Maybe it had reached a point of no return. The group that so captivated him with their ideology had, by far, deeper and firmer grip on his imagination. *Where it will lead him, Allah only knows. I pray it will not take him to the extent where he could cause pain and tragedy to other human beings. But where could he be right now?*

He decided to use his children's help to look for their brother. His son, Tarek, had many friends. Maybe they had seen Amin somewhere or with somebody. Tarek set to trek every information he could get about his brother, who was estranged from him for some time now. He set out to start from Amin's room. There could be hints, lists of names, or addresses that could be used in his search.

He entered his brother's room. It struck him that he had not been to the room since they separated their sleeping room. The other thing that amazed him was how it was neatly and orderly set up. He knew Amin as a disorganized slob. *What changed him so?* he wondered. In looking, he found that most of his reading was on Islam. There were few political and historical books that dealt with issues on the Middle East conflict. Books on Pakistan and India are the two on his bedside desk. It was clear from this observation that Amin was much interested in Islam and histories that involved "Islamic" people. Tarek remembered the last discourse he had with his brother. It was on how the West—according to him, "the Christian world"—had humiliated Islam and the Islamic people. The Israeli-Palestinian conflict was a constant reminder of how the West had attacked Islam and the Islamic people. In his mind, the West was the mortal enemy of all Islamic people, and all Moslems had a duty to avenge it. The extremist historic understanding of his brother amazed him. At dinner when all the family sat at the dinner table, Tarek raised the issue.

The father who loved good discussion and reasoned argument encouraged the discussion. He offered Amin to make his statement first.

Amin, as expected, made a catalog of accusations against the Christian world led by the US from imposing retrograde regimes on Islamic people, the exploitation of Islamic resources, the military attack on Islamic nations, and the onslaught on their religion and way of life which had corrupted Islamic youth all over. The passion with which he made his indictment had taken everybody by surprise, but the sincerity of his conviction was transparent.

The father asked the youngest daughter Amina if she had anything to say. She simply asked her brother if he personally had felt corrupted, exploited, or oppressed by anybody. "I never felt anyone doing those things to me," she asserted.

Amin made a snide remark, which was censured by the father.

It was Tarek's turn to give his opinion, and he started by recalling the talk with Amin the night before which, of course, had initiated the discussion tonight. Tarek said, "The issues are complex for me to have an answer. However, I have friends with diverse experiences to give a little better perspective than my brother's few sectarian friends. Let us talk about the Israeli-Palestinian conflict which, for many, is the constant irritant of the West's biased support for Israel. Every time a conflict arises with Israel, in the Moslem world from Indonesia, Iran, and Arab nations, a riot-like protest is organized. It is always looked as an attack on Islam. What is forgotten is that it is essentially a nationalist struggle with Palestinian's demand to form a Palestinian state. Among the Palestinians, there are Christian nationalists, maybe minority, nonetheless with the same demand as their Moslem contemporaries. It is my opinion that the Islamization of the Palestinian struggle had not helped the struggle of the Palestinian people. On the contrary, it caused a backlash of sympathy for Israel as a nation under siege by nearly a billion Moslems. Why would a Persian, Pakistani, Indonesian Moslem be so worked up when the issue of Israel is raised? Israel does not border these countries and never had any conflicts with them. Palestinians would have world sympathy if the issue had remained as a nationalist struggle for land to call their home. Islam is misunderstood, I grant you, among many in the West. This could be because of poor scholarship, biased presentation of Islam in popular culture, and the misguided and destructive that has been done in the name of Islam. It is up to true and good Moslems to teach Islam and its message for universal brotherhood." Tarek concluded by advising his brother to come out of his cocoon and face the world with all its diversities. "Teach your religion. That is fine. But without showing any rancor or hostility against those who hold different religious beliefs. Condemn those who commit violence in the name of Islam."

The mother and older sister remained silent.

The father, after listening to each of the children's views and concerns, gave his opinion, careful not to antagonize the religious sensibility of Amin but at the same time remain true to his lifelong philosophy of tolerance. "The idea of religion is to give guidance in our life to create the best human relationship and to prepare us spiritually for the afterlife. Intrinsically, all religions have these essential elements. There are ritual differences which are the external manifestation of the religion. Rituals are the symbolic acts of the individual's expression of devotion. Because religion is both a social and individual practiced activity, some of it are incorporated from the practices of the society before the religion is established. Some of the rules on etiquette, culinary rules, and styles of clothing and grooming are adapted from the social norms of the society wherein the religion started. For Islam, it was from the pre-Islamic Arab culture. That is why in Islam you find variations on different localities. Moslems in India and Afghanistan have been influenced by their way of life, so are others in other areas. Even the sharia laws have been practiced in great variation from place to place. To insist that a person should abide by a certain way of dressing relating to others is to deny the reality of the different way Islamic people had lived, and it is also to condemn Islam to a static tradition, never adapting to a change in technology and way of life. The only things that remained consistent are the Quran and Hadith which are general systems of ethics and spiritual guidance. The holy Quran, in several verses, expresses the guide to life: 'Lo! He produceth creation, then reproduceth it that He may with justice recompense those who believe and do good works'" (Quran 10:4). "Good works, good deed is what leads to a blessed life, not by what they wear or with whom they socialize and befriend. We can go on and on, find verse and Hadith instructions to affirm this truth. My son, my word for you is to keep faith and good deeds. Be a guide by your deeds. Avoid condemnation of others. It is not for you to judge."

Amin kept quiet, but no one could tell if he was convinced. Such was the last talk on the dinner table with Amin's presence.

Since Amin left the house, the family started to describe situations before Amin left or after Amin left. Things had changed. The sudden and unexplained disappearance of a son and a brother within a close-knit family was hard. But life had to go on.

The three siblings succeeded in their education. Amina and Tarek were recipients of a coveted scholarship in the US to study in prestigious universities.

The older daughter, Zainab, was pursuing education to be a teacher. She was the closest to her mother, helping in the household activities. After graduation, Zainab became a teacher in the city close to her neighborhood. Soon, many suitors were trampling one another to betroth her. She was not in a rush to get married. However, she had a liking to a particular young man whose background was similar to hers. They were also from the same country and locality, with each family knowing each other for many generations. Both families encouraged the blooming relationship.

The educational progress of Amina and Tarek was phenomenal. She chose to go to a prestigious law school in the East, and Tarek was accepted in an Ivy League university to study engineering with a business minor. The father's business was booming. Because of the reputation, he had built great customers. His fame spread throughout the country soon, and that brought many accounts. He had amassed enough money to afford a visit to his children in the US. At least once a year, the husband and wife visited their children. They were very proud of their children. Amin was their heartache that could not be healed.

In one of their trips, Amina introduced them to one of her special friends, Derek. Derek was an African American young man who had graduated a year ago from the same university where Amina was attending. He was working in one of the most established law firms in the country. He was very courteous and carried himself with dignity. From what they could observe, he was very fond of Amina. Nur was not sure about his feelings on the whole thing. This rarely happened to him. As for the mother, she remained very quiet the whole time. They had a dinner together; it was formal with a limited conversation. Amina tried to enliven the party, but to no avail. It was the quietest dinner they had. After dinner, Fowzia and Nur were dropped at their hotel.

"You know, dear," Fowzia started as soon as she stepped into the hotel room, "since I became a mother, my wish had always been to see my children get married within their own people. I dreamed of having a good relationship with families of my sons-in-law and my daughters-in-law. But tonight, I was turned into a mute and deaf and looked so stupid because my daughter brought me, as a future husband, someone whose language and customs I do not understand. How in heavens is it possible to be a good mother-in-law if you can't converse with each other? How about my faith? Is he a Moslem?"

Nur was bothered by the issues. Since he was not sure of the length and depth and future plans of his daughter, he wanted to reserve his opinion.

Next day, Tarek was coming to meet his parents. He had few days' break. As appointed, he came to their hotel. After loving salutations, they went for a snack and coffee at the cafeteria located by the hotel lobby. While snacking and sipping coffee, Tarek brought the issue of Derek. Casually, he said, "So you met Derek."

The mother, astounded by the casualness of his comment on an issue as important as marriage, regarded, "So you knew about him. And for how long, and why did you keep it a secret from us?"

"Wow! Wow! Ema, take it easy. I was not trying to hide any secret from you. I thought it was Amina's business to talk about her relationship."

"Are they planning to get married?" the father asked.

"Well, most likely," Tarek responded. "Derek is a great guy, and Amina loves him," he continued. "He is responsible, intelligent, decent, and a great friend. They are good match," he concluded.

Nur snapped, "That is *finito*. How about the culture, language, religion? Don't you think that have some importance in marriage?"

"Yes, but love supersedes it," Tarek added. "The love they have for each other breaks ice and even rocks, so to speak. Language could be learned. Culture. What is culture? It is only a reflection of a way of life. As far as religion is concerned, the two are the most spiritual people I ever met."

At dinner, with Derek included, the five of them went to a place which Amina and Tarek suggested. Once they arrived at the place, they were seated in the best spot. It was obvious that Amina and Derek were very popular here.

The manager and staff came to their seating area and greeted them. The parents were introduced, and the manager said it was an honor to meet the parents of the lovable Amina. "Let the celebration start," he announced.

A sumptuous dinner was served. Tarek, with his usual voluble personality, kept the conversation lively. By translating what was being said to his parents, he made sure they participated in the conversation. The dinner party was more relaxed and cordial.

For the parents though, there were many concerns of a union of families whose experiences were so diverse. *What am I going to say when I meet them? The way we talk, eat, dress, and worship are so different.*

The next day, Amina and Tarek had planned to take their parents for shopping. It might also help the parents vent off their concerns with Amina. For tonight, the parents went to have some rest.

Nur hardly had sleep. The words of Amin came haunting him. *Did I make a mistake of being so liberal on raising my children? Should I have enforced strict "Islamic" way of life on my children, particularly my daughters? Would this kind of relationship be avoided?*

In the morning, they woke up early and were ready to get answers to some of their concerns. As appointed, Amina and Tarek came to the hotel where their parents were staying. After exchanging greetings and hugs, thcy headed to the part of town where the most elegant stores were located. Shopping was not in the minds of the parents. They wanted to have a good talk with their daughter. What were her plans, and what was the nature of her relationship with Derek? Nur remembered with nostalgia the days when he used to take his children to a walk when he had something to get off his chest. But now he had to do it in a corner, sitting in a café.

The café was sparsely seated at the time they entered it. They chose a corner seating to be more discreet. As the four of them were seated and ordered breakfast, the conversation turned into some left unsaid the evening before. Amina asked her parents what they thought of Derek.

"Hmm," said the father and returned the question by asking her what she thought of him.

Amina started giggling. One could see the glow in her face and sparkle in her eyes and unabashedly said she loved him and thought that he was the greatest person in the world.

"How long have you known him?" the father asked.

"Over two years, but really, we have been very close for about fifteen months."

"So the last time we visited, you had a relationship with him, and yet you did not introduce us to him. What changed now?"

"I know," she answered. "At the time, he was in Europe for business. I wanted you to meet him in person. That is why I kept it a secret. But Tarek met him many times, didn't you, brother?" she asked pleadingly, as if to say, "Come on, back me up."

Tarek said, "Many times."

Nur and Fowzia brought a parade of questions about religion, culture, language, and all the concerns they had in their mind.

Amina, with her lawyerly logic, answered all their concerns. At the same time, she admitted there would be some challenges, but love was the most important in any relations. Everything else was surmountable.

"Marriage is a union of two people," Nur said, "but that includes families and ancestors. At least that is how we understand it. The youthful love or romantic love, if you will, wear off as time goes by. And vicissitude of life brings small and big conflicts, and if you do not have a solid foundation buttressed by family relationships and cultural affinity, that union flounders. Did you know how many people end up in divorce in the US? Maybe more than half. That is what we are talking about. We are not judging Derek. He could be the most decent person in the world. It is the absence of all the things that help keep marriage pass through valleys that worries us. Do you know how many people are divorced among people you had known all your life—my friends, relatives, and neighbors? Only two. It is not because there are no conflicts within every marriage. Every marriage passes through problems. Whenever a marriage had a problem, families had a mechanism to resolve it. Intervention of relatives, censure by elders and religious leaders, societal approbation, and maintenance of reputation restrain people to go on divorce. I know your mother may have something to say."

Fowzia said, "Yes. You know, dear, let me tell you about your sister Zainab. She is getting married to Idriss in a few months. Idriss is the son of Ismael and Zemzem. We can go on telling you all their histories. We know each other from way back in our ancestral land. When both of them decided to be engaged, it was the happiest day for both sides of the family. Our families blend so well. Zemzem knows what I think before I open my mouth and vice versa. Your father and Ismael, when they meet, act like little children, laughing uproariously by remembering events that happened long time ago in their youth. A marriage built with such a relationship has the solidity that withstands the shocks and aftershocks that appear in life. This is the kind of marriage that I have dreamed for my children. If you get married to the young man, I will remain always alienated from his family and obviously not by choice. And I have to remind you the Quran forbids a Moslem woman getting married to a non-Moslem man. That is all I have to say. You are a good and smart kid. Think of all the advice we gave you."

Throughout, Tarek remained silent, in spite of the pleadings of Amina's eyes to come in support of her.

Amina did not want to argue her case. She preferred some adjournment. In her mind, she was planning to recruit her brother for rebuttal on her behalf. She simply said, "Do not worry, Ema and Eba, everything will be all right. And we will talk about it later. Besides, a wedding is not even planned at this stage. Let us go shopping."

All stood up and went to do shopping.

They browsed the stores, purchasing different items. Amina bought several gifts for her sister. After walking over the huge mall and the boutique stores on the main boulevard, they wanted to take a break. They dropped the parents at the hotel for a siesta.

The brother and sister decided to hang around the neighborhood café until the parents wake up for a meal.

Amina had her own plans; it was an opportune moment to plead with her brother to talk to the parents on her behalf. She had already planned her rebuttal. "What is the matter with you?" she scolded her brother as soon as they were seated. "Why didn't you intercede on my behalf? You know how much I care about Derek, and you are friends with him."

Tarek said, "It would have made matters worse. Besides, they did not say anything that deprecates Derek or his family or background. They were expressing concern any parent would have if their child is to be married outside of their religion or national group. On the contrary, I am glad they vented out their frustration, and in my opinion, they did it in a way that I had expected from my parents, the civil way—"

"Here is my plan now," she interrupted. "I have to give them answers to their concerns. First, I will ask, 'Do you believe in my right to choose my partner?' In that choice, there is an implied fact that I could choose wrong. If I choose wrong, I will have the right to correct that mistake through divorce. If I am forced to stay in the marriage to satiate the demands of family or society, it is no more a marriage but a bondage. I will also vigorously protect the integrity of Derek who is the most honorable person I have ever met. My relationship with Derek is not simply based on romantic love but a love based on mutual respect. Derek fulfills me in a way no other man did. He loves me. His intellectual acumen is first-rate. Honesty, hard work, and humility are the hallmark of his persona. Why won't I be attracted to such a man?"

"Take it easy, sister," Tarek advised. "Mark my word, our parents are not going to raise the issue again. They have made their point. Now they will just see your decision in the coming months. The burden had been lifted off them, and they rested it on you, so to speak. That is the way they have operated all the time. 'Hit and withdraw' is their tactic. I used to call it 'guerilla attack.' Because they understand quite clearly that if they persist and put us in a corner, rebellion is what they end up with. It has worked for the most part, except on Amin's case."

Lunch was simple fish and chips with spinach pies, which Fowzia loved. Shopping was limited to a few items they had not been bought the previous day. The rest of the afternoon, they decided to go on an excursion—the museum, a famous zoo, and the skyline of the city in the dark. By the time they came back to the hotel, it was late evening. Before parting to their places for the night, they had dinner at the hotel restaurant. Tarek was staying with his sister; they went to her apartment after they made sure the parents were in their hotel room.

On the way back, Tarek raised his brother's name. "How is it everybody is afraid to even discuss about him? It brings a lot of pain to the parents, so avoidance was the way they cope with it. But he is in the mind of all. Somebody has to raise it."

Amina intoned, "Not me."

Tarek suddenly looked somber and quiet. As he drove the car, he was gazing forward, avoiding his sister's face. Obviously, he was preoccupied with a thought.

After a few minutes, Amina asked, "Why suddenly are you quiet? Is there anything that I said that offended you?"

"No, sis. I do not know how to put this, except forthrightly. I heard a rumor that Amin is in the US. Mind you, it is only a rumor. I have been trying to get more information to verify it, but so far with no success. The person who gave me the information is credible, but he did not see Amin himself. But a former classmate of Amin's told him that he had seen him. The friend and I went to the area and browsed the whole neighborhood, the Islamic center, and mosques. He was not found. Neither could we find anyone to tell us if they had met him. We circulated a picture at the center, and they were kind enough to let us post the picture and contact information with my phone and name. So far, no one had contacted me. The next time I went to the center, the picture and contact information were taken down. By whom? Nobody knows. In fact, the front desk person was surprised. Without their permission, nobody would take down a posted information."

Amina was somehow uneasy to hear that the "sheik," as she used to call him, was in the US. In the last few years, their relationship was strained. By the end, they were hardly in speaking terms. Certainly, she was not enthused to hear a rumor that he might be close to where she lived now. "The guy has gone mad," she told her brother. "Should we tell our parents?" she queried.

"I do not know," Tarek responded. "How would they react to the rumor? Would Father forget about his business and insist that he would look for his son? Would Mother cry her heart out and long to see her son, forgetting that she had a wedding to organize in a few months? I am so sad, Amina, that they have to go through so much pain in the twilight of their life when they should look relaxed in their retirement and enjoy their life with satisfaction of doing the best they can to their children. Yes, Amin has gone bonkers, but he is driving us crazy. I can't believe he can be so cruel and can't even see it. What is the point of professing religion if you cause so much pain to people closest to you?"

They agreed not to tell their parents about the rumor until they had more evidence.

On Friday, Derek returned from a trip. In the afternoon, when the parents were taking a rest, Tarek and Amina went to the airport to pick him up. The flight was long and tiresome, but when he saw them at the terminal, he was all smiles. He gave a good loving kiss to Amina and a friendly hug to Tarek. On the way back to town, he told them all about Switzerland and shortly about the conference. He gave a bejeweled watch to his love and lovely gifts to Tarek. He had even brought gifts to Nur and Fowzia.

"Very considerate of you. I love you!" Amina said endearingly.

They dropped Derek at his place of residence to refresh himself and have some rest before they would meet for dinner. Amina and Tarek headed to the hotel to be with their parents. It was the last weekend before the parents fly back to their home. The betrothed daughter had been anxious being without her parents and siblings at these important weeks of her life before the wedding. She had made so many calls to her mother. Fowzia understood that her daughter was in love and excited. So was she with the impending union. The very thought of it warmed her heart.

Dinner was at a posh restaurant that opened only a few months ago to a rave review. It was located at one of the most fashionable part of town. The four of them arrived a few minutes before reservation time. They were seated a few minutes later. Sipping their beverage and nibbling on appetizers, they waited for Derek to come.

Derek came right on time, and after exchanging pleasantries, dinner was ordered. Derek talked a little about his trip and how the country was beautiful with a picture-perfect scenery.

Soon, the conversation turned a little personal. Nur wanted to know Derek better, and he felt he had only a day to do that. He rather deviously asked where Derek was born and raised.

Derek was born in the Washington, DC, area from two educator parents. That he had a brother and a sister. Sadly, his brother was killed in a car accident about seven years ago. His sister was a physician and married with two children. He was the youngest in the family. He added that Amina had met with his family, and they adored her.

Without commenting, Nur asked, "What is their religion?"

Derek did not know how to answer it. This very articulate young professional was kind of befuddled with the question. This was the first time in his life that anyone had asked him about his parents' faith. But he knew he had to answer it honestly to the best of his knowledge. To tell the truth, he asked himself, *When was the last time my parents talked about their faith?* He couldn't remember. He told Nur, "When they were young, they were members of the Baptist church—"

Before he even finished his sentence, Nur asked, "What is it? I have never heard of it." In fact, that was true. Nur knew only of Islam, Orthodox Christianity, Protestantism, Judaism, and Eastern religions. As worldly as he was, he had never heard of Baptist religion.

Tarek intervened and explained that the Baptist church was a denomination within the Protestant religion.

"Okay," he said, somewhat surprised to hear there were branches in the Protestant religion.

Derek continued, saying that his parents at this time were not part of any organized religion.

Nur tried to understand this part of the comment. "Do they have religion?" he asked.

Derek said, "Frankly, I do not think so."

Nur was clearly confused how people who were so educated and mature in age and had raised successful children could end up without religion. He left that issue and asked Derek what his religion was.

Derek obviously expected that question from the trajectory the discussion was going. He said he was exploring, and at this point, he did not belong to any religious group. But he added, in an attempt to assuage the disappointment of Nur, "I am very spiritual."

"What do you mean?" Nur asked.

"I mean I believe there is a higher being that created us and all heavens."

"When you said you are exploring, how do you explore religion and decide this is for me?"

"I should be honest." Derek stammered, "I...do not have any idea how one explores religion because, so far, I have lived fulfilling my worldly life, education, and profession."

Tarek, sensing that Derek was being put in a corner, asked his father with great respect to lay off the issue. Obviously, Nur was unhappy with the response. He knew when to stop. Importantly, he made his point to his daughter that her possible future husband was irreligious. That was sacrilege to him.

The mother and daughter had animated discussion about the impending wedding of Zainab in a few months. Amina was suggesting about that wedding should be organized, including decor and ambience of the hall. The mother wanted a small modest wedding that included family and closest friends, whereas Amina wanted the wedding to be a splashy one-of-a-kind wedding.

At the end of the dinner, Derek took out small packages and gave it to both parents, gifts brought for them from his trip. They graciously accepted. Soon, the conversation was joined by all. After dinner, Nur feigned tiredness and opted to go to his hotel, and Fowzia agreed with her husband. They were taken to their hotel for early retirement. The three headed to an ice cream parlor to have gourmet ice cream and coffee.

Derek brought up his conversation with Nur on the issue of religion. "I must have sounded atheistic to your father when I told him that my experience in religion is still on the stage of exploratory. It may have sounded an affront to his religious sensibilities."

Amina was sympathetic to her sweetheart and said, "My father does not rush to judge. You do not have to worry. I am sure he is going to think about it. At the end, he judges a person by his overall character. You have nothing to worry about. Trust me." She sweetly leaned close to his ears.

Derek had to finish a report on the conference he attended and decided to go and work on it. He left, promising to call the next day.

Amina and Tarek headed home, talking about the evening. Both had sensed that their father was prodding on the religion and lifestyle of Derek's parents to understand his background. It mattered little to him that the family held high educational and professional pedigree. Religion and their ethical standard was more important.

Saturday was the last full day that the parents were to be in the US. Amina wanted them to have lunch at her apartment to give them a full sense of her life. Tarek agreed. Early morning, they did some shopping at the closest Whole Foods store. Fish and vegetables and beverages were brought and stacked in the refrigerator. She set a table for five. Soon, she called her parents at their room and informed them that Tarek was on his way to pick them up. Time was set for 1:00 p.m. She prepared a real nice lunch of seasoned and baked fish as main course with several vegetables, soup, and salad. And the beverages were juices and coffee.

The parents arrived at 1:15 p.m. They were seated by the dining table. They were impressed with the setup. The choice of colors and arrangement of the small apartment was impeccable. It was a satisfying lunch, but the conversation was sparse. The father uncharacteristically was quiet. It must be the feeling of disappointment from the night before. They attempted to make him talk more, but he gave only short answers.

In desperation, Tarek brought the subject of Amin. He asked if they had heard about him.

The parents, with a clear sign of sadness, said they had not heard anything about him. The rumor was he was either in Pakistan or Afghanistan. "The group is so secretive that every attempt we made did not succeed. I do not blame Amin. I have come to realize, though belatedly, I have failed as a parent. It pains me to see that my mistake in not giving my children strong religious sense took them to extremes of both spectrums. One to become a fanatic and another to be an atheist."

Amina understood the indictment was partly on her. She attempted to explain by saying she was religious. But the evidence to the contrary was so pervasive she was unconvincing. She withdrew her mild protestation. She also understood the dynamics of her relation with her parents had changed, maybe forever. As she kept track of their lives, she knew this was going to have a serious implication on one another's life. Since the situation was new to all, they felt so odd and uneasy.

"Maybe it is better if we rest today for the long trip tomorrow," Nur suggested to his wife.

Fowzia was quiet the whole time, confused and saddened by the disappearance of her oldest son and her daughter's astray from her culture and religion, but she did not want to aggravate the situation. She loved her daughter as much as she loved her other children, and she knew Amina was smart and moral with a strong sense of purpose.

Tarek dropped his parents at the hotel. When he offered to pick them up for dinner, they said, "It is all right. We may not need to eat dinner."

With that, they parted, and Tarek went back to Amina's apartment. Amina was crying her heart out. When Tarek arrived, she dried her eyes and rinsed her face with cold water, but her bloodshot eyes betrayed her.

"Come on, sister, it is a temporary lapse of relations that could easily be amended once they know Derek better."

"You do not understand, Tarek. My father is faulting me like Amin. He said I am the other extreme of him, equally condemnable."

In the evening, Amina called the hotel. There was no response. She left a message at the front desk. Two hours later, there was no call back. "Better to go there and talk to them," she consulted with her brother.

He did not disagree. They drove to the hotel. No one was in the room. They sat in the waiting area, reading magazines. After almost an hour, the parents came back carrying small packages. They exchanged greetings cordially. The father looked a bit haggard. The liveliness and the easy smile was not present.

Amina felt so sad because she loved her father more than anything else in the world. Now she found herself in this classic emotional divide between the love for her father and the love for Derek. It was a situation she never expected to find herself in, and she did not know how to handle it.

Tarek took the packages from their parents and carried them to the room. Everybody was quiet. In the room, there were a few bottles of soft drinks and bottled water. They sat in front of the TV. Suddenly, Amina burst into this uncontrollable cry, her tears streaming downward. The mother tried to comfort her daughter, but she was so laden with emotion she joined her daughter in crying. Even the father had to wipe his tears. Tarek, with his jovial easygoing personality, tried to sooth all, but he himself was in an emotional distress.

Amina, in between her cries, kept saying, "Sorry, Eba. I love you so much I did not want to be the cause of your pain. I have much respect for you to defy you in any shape or form."

Nur could not see his daughter and the rest of his family in such distress. He went and hugged his daughter and started to stroke her hair and wipe her tears. "Do not cry, my daughter. It is the accumulated pain of Amin's disappearance that is coming to the surface. I am sorry for me to take it out on you kids. Let your mother cry. I know she had bottled her emotions for too long. I could tell that she had aged since her son left without any trace. I know she tries to hide it from me and Zainab, but as soon as we get out of the house, she lives with her pain alone. I am sorry, Fowzia, dear. I am so sorry," he repeated.

Soon, everybody was calm but enveloped with sorrow that only a family with a missing son could understand. Death had finality. There was a closure, but a missing child was a constant torture for the imagination to take you to places and images that were harrowing. From the time you would open your eyes to the time you would close them to sleep, you would think about what might have happened to your child. "Is he hungry, sick, tortured, dead, or shackled in a cave?" This was what would hover in your mind. The pain was real and all-pervasive.

Once they vented out their sorrow, they decided to spend the last evening in a more subdued and yet caring manner. Of course, there were issues that they had not dealt with, to anyone's satisfaction. Maybe for another time, God willing. It was agreed for Derek to spend the evening with them and bid them farewell.

The evening dinner was at a modest Middle Eastern restaurant, but the food was good. They ordered as much food in variety and quantity it looked like some kind of celebration was happening. Everybody was cordial. Nur actually was talking to Derek, and he extended his invitation for him to attend the wedding of Zainab. Partly, he was testing him on how committed he was to his daughter and her family. Derek was gracious. He thanked him for the honor and promised him he would try to be there and celebrate with the family. As the hour was getting late, they left to their respective domiciles and the parents to the hotel. Derek bid them farewell, wishing them a safe trip.

The departure of the parents was on a midday on Sunday. Since the airport was located some fifteen miles from where the hotel was, Amina and Tarek came early to pick them up. After breakfast, they drove to the airport.

Before departure, the parents advised the children to come earlier for their sister's wedding. "It will mean a lot for your sister and us."

Amina and Tarek promised them they would be there to help organize the wedding.

For Amina, there was something about this departure that made it so different. She was emotional and filled with some unexplained uneasiness, a premonition that she might never see one or both of her parents in the future. They were getting tired and, in her eyes, growing old fast. She gave a short prayer to make their flight safe. Until the airplane departed, they lounged in the airport terminal and then drove back to the city.

Tarek drove the way back to his home, which was a two hours' drive, and got ready to catch up with his studies. He was a semester away to earn his graduate degree in engineering and business.

Amina called Derek and told him the parents had just left. They made an arrangement for him to pick her up after work.

She was in the kitchen when the tragedy struck, preparing her favorite breakfast of cut fruits and yogurt. She was very careful with her diet. Some of her friends called her "diet fanatic." The apple was quartered and layered on her dish, and a little lime juice was squeezed on top to stop discoloration and give it a tart flavor. The berries were washed and dried by paper towel. When the door burst open, she had yet to put them on the plate. The yogurt, just out of the refrigerator, was as cold and addled as the intruder's eyes. He came hurtling into the kitchen near the breakfast table where her colorful breakfast was waiting to be devoured. Except for a slice of apple and a few berries, she did not eat. She had lightly eaten the night before and was ready to enjoy her breakfast. Breakfast was the meal that she enjoyed most. It set her mood for the day, she said, and she was looking for a great day with friends and her fiancé. In the morning, she was mortally wounded by a double-edged hunter's knife. She was only twenty-seven years old. Her death came agonizingly, about an hour after the attack. Her beautiful eyes were frozen with a look of terror and surprise even after death. The killer went to her linen pantry and covered her with the cleanest bedsheet for humility even in death. The door was left slightly ajar, maybe for someone to come and do the messy work that needed to be done on a homicide victim.

At the café, Derek was the first to arrive, and a young couple they had befriended arrived a short moment later. They were known to the staff of the café and well-liked. They were waiting for Amina before they ordered their meal. It was very unusual for her to be late without calling Derek. A half hour passed and Amina was a no-show and no call. Derek called her several times, and there was no response. It was unlike her; he was concerned.

Forty-five minutes later, he was agitated. "Something must be wrong," he intoned with a grave voice. "I have got to go to her apartment and check what is going on," he said while standing to walk to his car. The friends joined him and drove to her address.

In the corridors of her apartment, a couple on their way out saw drops of fresh blood. "Strange," they said. "Where is this blood from? Someone may have cut themselves." By the elevator, there was blood, visible and substantial, with clear bloodstained foot-marks. Alarmed, they decided to go back to their apartment and call security. They noticed Amina's apartment was cracked open. They liked her. As they came close to her door, a faint voice could be heard. A painful remote voice. They called the security and went inside.

Here lay a body covered with blood-soaked linen on the kitchen floor. Frantic, the security called 911. The police and ambulance arrived in a short time. The police cordoned off the area. One of the officers started to ask questions to the neighbors while the medical crew was trying to revive the victim. The neighbors did not have much information to provide, except for the blood on the darkish floor of the corridor and the more visible and more substantial blood on the elevator floor. The officer took note of the names and contact number of the neighbors. While giving them his address card, he asked them to call him if they ever hear or remember anything that could help the case.

By the time Derek and the friends arrived at the building, the area was swarmed by police cars and unmarked detective vehicles. The entry into the building was blocked, in the fear the culprit might still be in the building. The officers walked through the fire escape stairs all the way to the end of the building. The other officers searched the room where all the mechanicals were located and the parking area and all the public-accessible areas. They could not find anyone. Derek was distressed; his inability to see her face was agonizing.

That same day, the police started their investigative work. Forensic technicians took samples of bloodstains, footprints, and fingerprints. They went door to door to record any unusual observations by neighbors. They continued their collection of possible evidence from floor-level business employees and vendors. They recorded even mundane comments and observations.

The victim was a vivacious twenty-seven-year-old lawyer. Her name was Amina M. Nur. She graduated from an elite university. After graduation, she was hired by a prestigious law firm where she had been interning during her college days. As she was familiar with most of the partners and staff, she meshed quite easily into the team.

The investigation on the murder treaded slowly but methodically. It was started with her fiancé. Derek had a solid alibi on where he was, and his telephone records indicated that he was in touch with her before her death and called her number many times after. Even though he was in deep grief and pain, he cooperated with the officers. The officers eliminated Derek as a suspect.

Grief-stricken Tarek was brought for interview. He was so much in pain his grief was heart-wrenching. Even the battle-hardened investigators were so touched they decided to waive the questioning. The investigation's aim was not only to find out if one was involved in a crime but also to get any clues on who might be the culprit and what could be the motive. In other word, leads to an investigation were gathered through questions to members of families, neighbors, associates, and ex-lovers. The habits and routines of the victim were looked into. All these and more had been done for the case. But no tangible clue had been found. As far as the suspect was concerned, all those who were investigated so far had been discounted. As the investigation reached a dead end, the case was sided into cold case file. Investigators were moved to more current homicides and other heinous criminal activities.

Tragedy struck the family again. Five months after the murder of the beloved Amina and almost four years since the disappearance of Amin, Nur succumbed to a massive heart attack. His death was sudden. The weight of the pain of losing his daughter and the lingering feeling of guilt of failing to give a good paternal guidance to his children had burdened him massively. "Why could not I see this?" was the question he asked himself. His wife, battered by sadness, was in no condition to help him. The efforts by all his friends could not relieve him from the anguish.

The death of Nur, the pillar of the family and community, was a blow to many. The toll that would take on all was unimaginable.

The obituary on the major newspapers was almost a full page. In the front page with bold and big letters was written "The death of a tycoon and philanthropist." His biography was compelling. His generosity and integrity were recognized. The love for his family and many friends was fully described. Many of his friends gave testimonials; each had something great to say about the humble and very successful gentleman. They came from all over to pay their respect. On the following days, letters to the editor of the newspaper were coming on avalanche from humble people to the most powerful. The accolades were consistent and the condolences heartfelt. They were from people of all faiths; among them were prominent church leaders.

The news of Nur's demise was widely spread, even to the caves of Afghanistan, the hills and mountains of Yemen, and the border villages of Pakistan. Amin heard the news of the death of his father like everybody else. It was a shock he loved his father. Even in the years that he had departed to follow his calling, he looked at his father as the Rock of Gibraltar. Strong, wise, loving, and the most decent person he had known. Their differences were in the understanding of the role of religion and its interpretation in their daily life. Amin took the extreme interpretation and affiliated himself with like-minded people. Nur's understanding of the Quran was contextual. He looked at them as a spiritual guide to his life brought to mankind at a given historical epoch of the Arab world. He was very critical of the extreme and violent direction some had taken.

Amin recalled his childhood with his parents and siblings—the simple pleasures of walking, talking, and joking. The hilarity of having friends of the parents and their children. All the easy, uncomplicated friendships. The nurturing and patient advise the father gave to the children. Amin remembered how his father would listen patiently to some of the silliest cases they brought from school without interference. *He would let us express how we felt about them and why. He was patient. Only then he would give his advice lovingly and make us look at things, and if there are specific things he wants us to do, he does it tactfully, making us think that it came from our own volition.*

Amin was left in quandary; his sense of guilt was palpable. He could not even share his sorrow with his colleagues. They had already painted Nur as an apostate who deserved to die. Nur's liberal thinking and his criticism of their fanatical ways had angered them for a long time. His death was a punishment he deserved, they concluded. For Amin, his father's death was a jolt that hit so hard. For the first time in a long time, he started to think about his religion and the way he interpreted the book. Many questions that he had ready answers to in the past came haunting him, and no answer was readily available to him this time. He had many sleepless nights. His demeanor had changed. He became easily irritable and distracted.

The group leader had noticed a change and started to worry about Amin's continued commitment to the cause. Amin knew too much—all the strategy, structure, leadership, and financial sources of the organization. If he absconded from the group, he could cause a great damage. They were ready to sacrifice him, but a few of the leaders sought to be patient and follow his movements.

Amin knew the danger to his life. He was very cautious, but he was in a state of confusion. The certainty of his cause and mission with the organization betrayed him. His sense of guilt was getting deeper by the day. Outward, he was not showing it, but internally, he was planning to leave the organization and expose himself to the world. He was not afraid of death or imprisonment, but he did not want to die before he expressed his remorse and asked for mercy from his mother and two siblings. He wanted to fully account for his activities in the years he had disappeared. What had he been doing? Was he involved in any violent activities? Had somebody been hurt because of his actions? Maybe in due time, the world would know. There were forces that would want these truths to remain lidded forever. Mulling over the whole tragedy that had befallen the family and his role in it, Amin was remorseful. He was a harried man to meet his remaining family.

Tarek, in the meantime, had returned to be alongside his mother and sister and to manage his father's business. Amin had been in his mind since he heard the rumor that he might be in the US. *If the rumor was true, why didn't he contact us? How is it Amin could be so heartless not to care about the death of his sister and father?*

The organization had its own agenda in regard to Amin. A mission was set up to test his commitment and reliability. It was decided to send him to the US and assassinate an individual who was suspected as a double agent. He would travel from Pakistan to Europe with a minder escorting him. The duty of the minder was to kill Amin if, at any point, he attempted to defect. From Europe, he would transit to the US without spending any time. In the US, contacts would pick him up from the airport and take him to a safe house. Amin was not informed of the assignment awaiting him nor was he aware of the layers of individuals watching him. Any wrong move would lead to his death.

After a long travel, he arrived at the Detroit airport in Michigan. On arrival, he had to go through inspection of customs and immigration. At the immigration, because his point of embarkation demanded closer scrutiny, he was taken to a small room and was questioned why he was in Pakistan and Yemen. His response was simple: "I was studying religion and language." They kept him in the room for almost two hours until they gathered enough information. The Homeland Security officer suspected that he was a potential terrorist with a mission to accomplish. It was decided to let him go and follow his movement so as to apprehend all those with whom he had contact. The Federal Bureau of Investigation (FBI) assigned officers to surveil his movements. Amin was handed back his passport and form I-94. The officer wished him a good stay in the US.

At the terminal, he was met by two individuals. After a short introduction, they headed to where a vehicle was awaiting them. They traveled to a suburb of Detroit where he was going to stay. The FBI gathered the information on the vehicle registration and address of the place he was taken. The building was a two flat brick structure with six people calling it residence. All of them were young people of mainly Middle East heritage. There were two from North Africa. All the information of the individuals was gathered. In fact, the FBI had been aware of the young guys for some time.

For the next few hours, there was no movement from the house. Amin, after taking a bath, went to sleep. He was too tired to have any conversation with the group. The FBI had installed listening devices within different areas of the house. Most of the talk of the evening was mundane. It was only at one point that Amin was mentioned by someone who was assigning who would escort him the next day. Names were not mentioned, but someone authoritatively said, "You and you," obviously pointing fingers at the individuals assigned to the task. But there was no mention of the task.

Late in the evening, the vehicle that picked up Amin from the airport was driven by the two people who waited for him. An FBI unmarked car followed. They stopped at a U-Haul storage area located about two miles away from the residence. Fifteen minutes later, they came out with a box and drove back to the apartment. The box was unloaded and taken into the apartment. In the apartment, excitement could be heard. The man who earlier assigned the two young men told them to put the box at an area and asked for screwdrivers and pliers. The sound of the box cracking open could be heard. Soon, the click and clack sound of metal softly banging each other was coming over the listening device. Someone said, "Read the instruction carefully."

After almost an hour of some activities on metallic objects, they were silent. There was an Arabic news on the background. The FBI agent who spoke Arabic said, "It is news from Al Jazeera, a TV program transmitted from Qatar, a small Middle Eastern country." After the news, silence reigned, and all the lights were turned off.

Early morning, there was some activity in the house. The lights were turned on, and there was a talk in a hushed voice. It was hard to pick up from the listening device, except Amin's name was mentioned twice. Patiently, the agents waited until someone got out of the apartment. Surely, about ten o'clock in the morning, three people came out of the apartment and drove eastward. An agent followed them. They stopped at a parking space of a Target store. All three got into the store. They bought a baseball cap, neutral color khaki-like pants, and sneaker shoes. With the items packed, they drove back to their apartment.

There was a heightened activity in the apartment. Three voices could be heard.

The one with the authoritative sound was giving his instruction to Amin. Amin was to travel to Chicago with both of them. He called the other one, Rahul. "Here is the picture of the traitor. His name is Abdul, and he is Somali. He lives in the uptown area of Chicago. Most of the time, he hangs around the Edgewater neighborhood. There is no discernible precaution that he takes. Infrequently, he attends a mosque in the area. He has few friends but lives alone at an HUD-subsidized housing. He works at a store that is open up to midnight. On summer nights, he walks home, which is about two miles far. His route is invariably the same. He walks east on Foster Avenue and then turns left on Sheridan Road. It takes about twenty-five to thirty minutes to reach home. Sometimes he picks up a meal from the McDonald's on the corner of Foster and Sheridan. He does not show any concern for his safety. At night, you do not see many pedestrians, except for buses and some private cars. It is not crowded. Most of the mom-and-pop stores are closed early. Occasionally, police cruise the area on vehicle, but a site could be chosen where it is possible to observe the police movement."

Ahmed Gillani, the leader who spoke with authority, gave his final instructions to Amin. "You will be armed with a handgun which you have used in Pakistan. You are very familiar with the gun. That is why it has been chosen. It is fitted with a silencer. The two of us are armed too. If any need arises, we will use them. The gun will be provided at the point where the actions are to take place. We will trek Abdul from work to a chosen site. At the site, we will drop you a few feet behind him. You will get off the car, and as you reach him, call his name and extend your hand as if to shake it. Since you are left-handed, at that point, you blow his heart out. Make sure you hit on target, one single shot. Then you run to a corner and hop in the car and speed away from the area. There will be extra clothing which you will change into a few miles away, and dump your other clothes. With mission accomplished, we will travel back to Michigan."

All the conversation was heard and recorded by the FBI officers. The officers decided to let the group load their guns and travel a distance where they would be stopped for traffic violations and, with extra support officers, would be put under control. The rest of the group left at the residence would be picked up by other officers.

In a well-orchestrated action, the group were stopped about twenty miles outside the town on an interstate highway. A state patrol stopped them for speeding a few miles above the limit. As soon as the car was stopped, they were surrounded by unmarked and marked police cars with a sheriff and FBI officers. They were caught by surprise. One by one, they were dragged out of the car and ordered to crouch on the side holding, their hands above their head. The officers looked under the hood, and the guns were pulled out and loaded into the officers' cars. The automobile was towed to a police pound for exhibit and further investigation.

The most intriguing thing was what Amin said when they were encircled by the officers and were being pulled out of the car: "Allah Akbar! Allah Akbar! Thank you! Thank you!" He seemed to be relieved by being caught at this stage of the mission.

A search of the car exposed several munitions, handguns, submachine guns, and many rounds of bullets. It looked that the mission was more than killing an individual. Everyone was handcuffed and taken to detention. The three people left in the house were also detained by a squad of FBI and town police officers. The search of their home produced more ammunition and documents that would be analyzed by FBI forensic officers.

Local, national, and international media reported the apprehension of a terrorist group in the Midwest of the US on their way to kill an individual who had left the group and condemned the organization. They named the head of the group Ahmed Gillani of Pakistan and the others from Middle East and Northeast Africa. They named the Northeast African member as Amin Nur. They reported that Amin traveled from Pakistan to commit the assassination. The FBI and Homeland Security officers had suspected Amin upon arrival at the Detroit international airport. However, they allowed him entry into the country to follow his movement and expose the network of terrorist group working underground in the US. It was well planned and executed by the security agents which netted so far possible terrorist recruits and saved the life of a young unsuspecting individual in Chicago. Mr. Abdul, for his own safety, was given a new identification and moved to another place.

The news created shock waves in three continents. In the caves and mountains of Afghanistan, the frontier villages of Pakistan, it was a damning failure that would have repercussions. One of their key operatives was apprehended with information that would wreck their organization.

In Northeast Africa, in the family of Amin Nur, it was a tragedy that added to the tragedy that had befallen the family in the past year. They were so incensed and outraged by the actions of a son so misguided. It was beyond comprehension that a son so loved and raised by the most genteel and civilized parents could be involved in one outrage and another.

Tarek had the most difficult task. He had to maintain the sanity of his remaining family, his mother and sister. He had to nurse his deep sorrow of losing the father he dearly adored and respected and his beloved sister. She understood and loved him with all her living fiber. She did not deserve to die so brutally. All her life was filled with love and hope and goodwill to all. Tarek had some suspicion that Amin might have some role in her murder. He did not have any evidence, but the fact he had heard the rumor that Amin was seen in the US and in the town they lived and had not contacted them made the suspicion credible. Now that he had been caught in attempting to commit a heinous crime was a further confirmation that Amin was capable of doing anything in the name of religion. The latest scandal should not be told to the family, Tarek decided. He contacted all the people that could possibly pass the information and instructed them not to tell the family. For how long it could be kept a secret was an open question. The immediate dilemma for Tarek was whether he should share with authorities about his suspicion of his brother's complicity in the murder of their sister. After much thought and many sleepless nights, he decided to let the law enforcement investigate without his input.

The terrorist suspects were taken into prison, each kept at separate cells. The investigators prepared profiles on each prisoner.

Ahmed Gillani was the group leader who had organized the whole operation. He appeared to be a true believer in his cause and had remained very stoic with no apparent fear or show of perturbance at the time of his arrest.

Amin had surprised them by his remarks. What did he mean by "Allah Akbar! Thank you!"? Was he relieved by his arrest from committing the crime, or was he ready to be arrested and be a martyr? The question was "What induced him to shout the praise of Allah under the circumstances?"

The other collaborator was chosen as a trusted cadre. The three who were arrested at the home were suspected as accessories to criminal activities. The extent of their involvement was to be seen during the investigation.

The profile of the young group was of deep curiosity to all. Almost all of them came from a very privileged background, with families of upper-middle class. Most of them attended exclusive schools and had traveled extensively. They spoke multiple languages, hence exposed to multicultural experiences. They had lived among people of different religions and social and political systems. The question was "What drove them to be part of a group that would perpetrate terrorism?" They had asked this question before and were remained befuddled by it even at this point.

The investigators started their work in earnest. Since the media and the public were aware of the apprehension of the group, there was great interest both on the progress and outcome of the investigation. Investigators, cognizant of the sensitivity of the cases, were extra careful. On the other side, the suspects were well aware of the legal process in the USA. They must have been given orientation by someone who knew the US laws and, in particular, the rights of the accused—the presumption of innocence, the right to legal representation, and also to the right not to self-incriminate. From the start of the investigation, they were determined not to cooperate with law enforcement officers. The irony of it all was not lost on Amin as later found out. Amin came to violently disrupt and violate US laws and yet use it to maximize legal benefits out of it.

In prison, Amin had a nightmarish dream on the night he was detained. He was visited by his father in a remote area whose surroundings both did not know. The father would call his son by the same endearing name he used when he was a child. In the dream, the father was escorted by so many of his childhood friends and acquaintances, all taunting him and laughing at him. His closest friend, Zerai's son, Adam, seemed to have grown wings and sailed over him in protection. The father was speaking without stopping, each word coming out with much pain. Amin could not make any sense of what his father was saying. The closer he wanted to come to his father, the farther the father seemed to back away. As he woke up from his sleep, Amin was drenched with sweat. He tried to dispel the dream of his dead father's vision from his head. In his conscious state, he tried to understand the meaning of the nightmare. That turned out to be a wakeful nightmare. All the things that had gone in his life in the last few years came in a procession of painful exposure. *I am fiend,* he said to himself. *A sinner before God. I betrayed family and friends and destroyed what was dear to me, my family. Oh God, what would I do to redeem myself?* he asked with deep regret and sadness. He cried a painful cry. In prison where the cacophony of noises was coming from all corners, nobody would even hear him. He felt alone in the universe, isolated both physically by the four walls that surrounded him and mentally because the idea of rejecting the very ideology that bound him with a violent fundamentalist group had felt so alien to him at this point in time. The loneliness was crushing that even a strong sense of spirituality could not deliver him. He wished death. Death was the only deliverance to him. But before dying, he wanted to come clean. He did not want to carry the burden to the afterlife. The challenge was if he would be courageous enough to accept culpability.

Ahmed Gillani was difficult for the investigators. They had no clue who he was, how he came to the US, how long he had been here, and how many people he had recruited. Even his national origin was doubtful. He was unwilling to give any information, except for the name. Even with the name, no one was sure if it was genuine. The people around him did not have much information either. He had kept his movements and personal issues secret. He was very committed to his cause and religion. Most of his time was spent either praying or in Islamic centers recruiting potential candidates. Money never seemed to be a problem. He seemed to have substantial, but his lifestyle was austere. He was a vegetarian and drank water or freshly squeezed juices. Coffee and tea were no-nos to him. For the investigators, their work was cut for them. But they were resilient, and with enough resources, they would crack through the secrecy and bring sunshine to the individual's life history.

The three that were taken from their residence were lightweight members. They were recruited from the local Islamic center for no specific task. They were told that they could live free of charge and learn the Quran and pursue their educational goals. For the few months they had lived there, no one had told them to perform anything except live a good Islamic way. They had always thought it was a charitable act for young Moslems who were away from family. After a thorough investigation, the investigators decided that these individuals had not committed any crime or that there was no discernible anti-American feeling among them. The three were surprised by the activities that were going on around them without their knowledge. They were never aware of the munitions stored in Ahmed Gillani's room, which always remained locked, and they had no purpose to enter it. The recruiter instructed them that if they had any interest to pursue their education, with free housing and free meals, they were welcome to his place.

The investigation had dual purposes—first, to thoroughly investigate the plan to assassinate an individual who had a sanctuary in the USA and to find if there were other murders in the past and, second, to unravel the web of the terrorist organization. To identify leadership, members, origin of resources, and location. The investigation would use all resources of the government and all methods of investigation. The suspects were individuals highly disciplined, indoctrinated, and motivated. They were ready to die for what they believed. When they were recruited into the organization, it was not for personal gains. It was for sacrifice, hardship, and possibly martyrdom.

Tarek was following the development of the criminal and terrorist investigation of his brother and his group. The information he was getting was scant as the investigators were not releasing any further information. He decided it might be necessary for him to come to the US for a brief visit. He told his mother and sister and friends he had some unfinished business. He entrusted the protection of his family with his sister Zainab's fiancé. He contacted Derek and gave him his travel itinerary. Derek was going to pick him up from the airport and arrange his stay in his place.

The flight arrived on schedule, and Derek was waiting in the terminal. The meeting was very emotional, for both were still in deep mourning. Derek had changed a lot in the last year. He had grown a beard and added some weight. The easy smile on his face was nonexistent. He looked more contemplative. They drove to town with little talk. Both were afraid to mention Amina's name, for it might open the floodgates of tears that were held close to their eyes.

Derek had moved to another part of town. He wanted to change places. There were many reminders of his loss in his old neighborhood. The cafés, the streets they walked holding hands, and the parks where they lay on sunny days. Even with friends, in spite of their attempt to share his pain and give him solace, he had minimal contact, except for occasional telephone calls. He was engrossed in his job just to keep his time filled up and leave him with minimal moments of leisure. He volunteered for duties that needed travel more readily than before. In fact, he informed his boss his luggage was always kept ready.

In the morning, Derek dropped Tarek at the prison, and he went to work. He gave his extra keys to his apartment to Tarek.

At the prison office, Tarek identified himself as Amin's brother. There was an animated interest in knowing who he was, and the officer told him the conditions and schedule that he could visit his brother.

The officer said, "Mr. Nur, you should understand that your brother is a special prisoner, and visits are on prearranged dates. You may have to make an appointment by filling a form. In the form, name, address, telephone number, and relations with the prisoner are requested."

Tarek, without hesitation, complied with the requirements. With that, he left the prison yard to go around town until Derek was coming home.

Two hours after he left the prison office, he received a telephone call. It was from the FBI. The officer identified himself as Officer O'Malley and asked if it was possible to meet him for a few questions. Tarek told them there was no problem. They agreed on the time and place where they would meet. Officer O'Malley informed Tarek that he was coming with a partner, Officer Kern.

As appointed, the officers came a bit earlier. They were in civilian clothes, which surprised Tarek. After showing their IDs, they introduced themselves and briefly told Tarek they had a few questions to ask and if he had any information that he could share with them about Amin, his group, and activities. The first series of questions was about himself—name, address for the last five years, profession, and family. Without hesitation, Tarek gave all the answers.

Officer O'Malley asked, "Why did you go back to your country?"

"My father died suddenly after the brutal murder of my sister Amina," he answered before he started sobbing.

The officers were aware of Amina's murder and expressed their condolences for the death of his father and sister. They allowed Tarek to catch his breath before they started asking questions about Amin and his group. "How was it growing up with Amin?" he was asked.

Tarek, after a short pause, answered, "Amin was a great brother. Our family was a close-knit with a lot of love. Amin was a bit introvert unlike me, but he had a very happy childhood. At school, he was very studious. I was into play than doing my homework. Amin had many friends he had fun with. In family outings, my father and he were the ones who throw the tent and set the chairs and table while my mother and my older sister took the responsibility on food and beverages. My sister Amina and I were the happy consumers. He was very reliable and responsible until his senior year in high school. Around the time of his senior year, he started to change. He became more aloof and avoided family outings. Progressively, he was critical of our lifestyle, particularly of our younger sister's clothing and friends and our father's negligence of religious teachings. He blamed our father for his liberal upbringing of the family. Our father, with patience, tried to reason with him. Obviously, it did not help. Amin had answers for everything and anything he looked from the prism of a fundamentalist Islamic point of view. Our father tried to reason with him using Quran's teaching, but Amin's understanding of them was extreme. Our father thought it was a phase that he had to pass through. Patience he demanded from all of us.

"After a while, we started to ignore him. Amina ridiculed him every time he criticized her style. She started calling him 'the sheik.' Amin became secretive on who he meets and where he spends his time. My father tried very hard to find out where he spends his time and in what activities he is involved, to no avail. There were times when he did not come for days. He would worry my mother. But my sister and I did not care much. We were sick of his criticism. Almost three years ago though, he disappeared without any trace. He did not say goodbyes, nor did he leave a note. Our father, for months, tried to get information and went to all places possible. But there was no information. He changed the family mood. Mother was crying all the time, and our father became more pensive. He started to question about his fatherhood. It struck him as a personal failure. I tell you there was no better father in the whole universe, if you ask me. Amin's problem is being associated with the wrong people and indoctrinated to abandon all the good judgments under which he was brought up. That is the last time I heard of my brother for the last few years. There were always rumors that he was either in Afghanistan or Northern Pakistan with no substantiation.

"It saddens me to think that my father's premature death was brought by Amin's disappearance and the brutal death of his beloved daughter. When my father was visiting the US few months before Amina's death, there was a sense of foreboding in him. His optimistic disposition was gone. He was unsure how to deal with issues, in particular about the future of his children. And this is a guy who had protected his family from danger with confidence in the past. He was always able to face challenges unperturbed. The last I saw him alive, he was not that confident." The officers never interrupted while he was pouring out his heart. It was cathartic for Tarek. He wanted to know who the murderer of his sister was. At the same time, he did not want to accuse his brother as a potential suspect in the crime on the basis of rumor that he was in the US around the time.

Officer Kern asked if there was anything to tell them about the murder of his sister.

Tarek responded by saying the same things at the time of her murder—he did not have any clue who might have wanted her dead. "She did not have any enemies as far as I could tell."

Officer O'Malley added, "Do you think it was possible that she could have been murdered by some fundamentalist group for her lifestyle and getting engaged outside of her faith?"

Tarek admitted that had crossed his mind, but he did not have any evidence to back it up.

The two officers thanked him for his cooperation. They passed their cards to him, asking him to call them anytime he needed to talk about the case.

Tarek was intrigued by Officer O'Malley's last question and mulled it over his head. *Was there something that they know? Is the investigation of Amina's murder leading them toward Amin or his group? Do they have any information on the rumor that Amin's travel to the US was not the first time?*

On Tuesday morning, Tarek decided to go to jail to see Amin. After passing through the security checkup, he was allowed to go to the window where his brother's face was to face his. There was both anticipation and anger in his feeling. It was unbelievable that the brother he adored so much as a young man could be the source of much of his grief in adulthood. *What do you say to a person who is the cause of the destruction of your family?* he asked himself.

Amin showed up at the window with his feet dragging, obviously under shackles. He was changed. His overgrown beard was covering his handsome face, his eyes bloodred with an obvious lack of sleep. He looked much thinner and haggard. The head had been shaven. He would not have recognized him. After a minute of hesitation, they exchanged greetings. As much as Tarek was trying to look at his brother's face straight, Amin was avoiding him. He had difficulty to get words out. When words came out, they sounded more of a restrained cry than clearly stated words. Few minutes passed.

"Hmm. Huh?" Then suddenly Amin cried hysterically. "I am so sorry, my brother. I am so sorry for my father. I am so sorry for my sister." The words were coming so weak Tarek had to lean forward to listen. All of a sudden, Amin fell off the chair onto the floor. Prison guards, posted not too far, observed and rushed to help. They gave him mouth-to-mouth resuscitation until the medics arrived and took him on a gurney.

Tarek stood stunned. For a moment, he thought it was a bad dream.

One of the kindly-looking guard came and told him, "He will be okay. He is breathing on his own."

Fate was an inscrutable phenomenon. Who would have thought that what had befallen to the Nur family could happen in such successive occurrence, one tragedy after the other? Maybe the gods were envious of their charmed life.

Confused on what he should do next, Tarek left the prison premises. Since it was about midday, he went to the part of the city where people would promenade. By joining people leisurely walking on the sidewalk of the fashionable part of the city, he hoped he would be distracted from his agony. He made a few calls to Derek and friends.

Derek was anxiously waiting for him. He told him what happened. "Oh God!" he intoned. "Let us talk about it over dinner." They agreed and hung up the phones.

Walking up and down the street with a throng of people on all sides of him, he was so lonely, immersed in the thoughts of incidents that happened to him in the last few months. He remembered the first time he walked the street with his sister. She wanted to check every boutique it took them hours to walk the two sides of the street. It was a clear spring day with a perfect weather for a long walk. *Amina insisted that I buy a jacket and a shirt against my protest for it being expensive. We ended up buying it. She made me wear the jacket after the purchase by putting the one I already had in the new package. "Oh, my brother," she will joke, "be careful with the girls. You look great with that outfit." I had always enjoyed her company. She was full of life, energetic, good-natured, and generous. How I miss her*, he mourned.

Later in the afternoon, he called the prison office to check on his brother's condition. Amin had been transferred to the City General Hospital. He was admitted at the cardiology unit. Tarek talked to a nurse and got the information that he was stable after a heart attack. Since he was a prisoner, there were special protocols to follow for a visit. There were guards assigned to him twenty-four hours a day. A visitor would be vetted thoroughly. Only families would be allowed. They would not be allowed to bring anything—no food, beverage, and even flowers. All visits would be monitored, making sure there was no physical contact between patient and visitors.

The next day, Tarek went to the hospital not to visit his brother but to talk to his doctor. He was lucky to have met in the elevator a middle-aged, slightly graying physician with his name tag attached to his coat. It was indicated that he was a cardiologist. Tarek mustered courage and introduced himself as the brother of the terror suspect patient. It so happened Amin was a patient of Dr. Ducker.

The doctor told him there was nothing to worry about his health. All vital signs were normal. Since he was under tremendous stress, sometimes heart failure could be triggered. Some medication would be prescribed, and most likely, he would be released tomorrow. "We will just keep him for observation today." With that, the good doctor parted to fulfill his duties.

Tarek decided against visiting his brother in the hospital, afraid it might put pressure on him since he couldn't talk freely about what and where he was the last three years and why he decided to join an organization that committed terror—of course, if the allegations were true. He was afraid to ask questions about Amina's murder. He just did not want to face the truth of the suspicion he had. Truth in a situation like this was very difficult to grapple with a brother that you loved dearly killing a sister you adored with all your soul.

Officer O'Malley called again, asking Tarek if he could come to the office for some further exchange of opinion. "Exchange of opinion"—Tarek found it rather guileful, for the discussion was only one-sided.

However, he agreed to meet them in late afternoon. The officer agreed and gave his address and suite number again. He was not sure what this meeting was for. Now that Amin had the episode, most likely the interrogation of him might be postponed. How could they interrogate a man who was so vulnerable healthwise they might lose him before all the questions were answered?

With the arrest of Ahmed Gillani, the organization had lost one of its most important operatives. Gillani was an intellectual who could quote the classics and recite romantic poems as easily as he could recite from the Quran. He was well-built. With his daily regimen of exercise, he could pass for an athlete practicing for some competition. He had this charisma that had become a magnet for recruiting young people. No one knew about his personal backgrounds. He was not intimately involved with anyone. His recruits, young men, were selected for their youth, Islamic faith, and being born in the Middle East or Northeast Africa. Europeans did not make good recruits, he slipped one day after a prayer time, because they were not experienced in cultural shocks and alienation as people from the Middle East and Africa in the US.

With his strong commitment, Gillani was hard to puncture for the investigators. Keeping him in isolation for almost twenty-four hours a day did not seem to have any effect on him. On the contrary, as the days went by, he was more mysterious than the days he was taken to prison. The officers had several options to follow to nudge cooperation—among them sleep deprivation, isolation, maybe water-boarding. Each was controversial on its own, but in an attempt to preempt terrorist activity, they could be useful tools. Initially, a good police work on collecting every information to be assembled about the groups and individuals was followed. Their habits, telephone calls, credit card transactions, leases, travel information, friends, neighbors, everything and any-thing in their lives are peered to find clues that would tie them to terror activity. It was a multipronged investigation that involved many law enforcement officers.

Tarek met officers O'Malley and Kern at their office. It was a modest building. As you entered, you would see a wall of pictures of officers killed in the line of duty. It was very sobering it brought to reality that the law enforcement job was dangerous and that the officers that we would see in ordinary life as uniformed and menacing face danger and death every day. There were several officers in the reception area. A desk with a lady on duty was directing people to the right offices. Everybody went through body check after pockets were emptied and passed through a screening machine.

The office of O'Malley was roomy and modestly furnished. Both officers were in the room as Tarek entered it. They stood and gave him a warm handshake and invited him to sit on a chair already set for him. To relax the nerves, they talked about a few nothings, like weather, traffic, and sports. Soon, they started the reason why they had to meet.

Officer O'Malley said, "We had few gaps to fill in our exchange last time. Could you tell us what brought you to the US this time?"

Tarek answered, "I had few things left dangling at the time I left with my father's sudden death."

"Did it have anything to do with your brother's arrest?"

"That too, after I read that my brother had been arrested in an attempt to commit murder ordered by an organization. I wanted to find out for myself from my brother. Why, and where has he been the last three years? It is so unbelievable for me to see my brother involved in a situation that causes harm to another person. It is so incredible that nothing in our childhood could be traced to prepare him to it."

"Your sister was killed few months ago in her own apartment, and she was living in an exclusive building and affluent neighborhood, and yet there were no pictures in the cameras of a suspect and no traceable clue. What do you think may have happened?"

"I wish I knew. God, there is no day that passes without me thinking about my sister and who may have killed her. I have tried different scenarios where one or another may have done, but each fails the test of logic and motive. I have suspected a workmate for career envy, but she worked for a short time to create that deadly envy. Ex-friends. She had only been very close and intimate with Derek. Derek adored her, and she loved him dearly. They were planning to spend their life together. Besides, he had alibis to show that he was not even close to her apartment. He was waiting for her with friends to join them at their favorite café."

"Were there people who were unhappy with her relationship with Derek?"

"My parents were not that excited, nothing against Derek, except his being non-Moslem and not showing any care for religion. During his last visit, my father grilled him on that, but when he left, he had warmed up with him and invited him to my other sister's wedding."

"How about from some Islamic groups or relatives who may think that she is a traitor to her faith?"

"It is possible but far-fetched because she does not associate with them. I do not think she has been to any Islamic activities."

"Do you know a man named Kapoor Shah?"

"Yes. I know him in college. We took some courses together and became somehow friends. He is from Pakistan, a good student, and devout Moslem. He had never met my sister, and I never socialized with him outside the campus."

"Did you know that he is in detention for being a suspect in conspiracy to commit terror in the US?"

"Oh my god! I can't believe it. I did not know that. We lost contact after graduation. I believe he got a job in the West Coast with some technology company."

"Do you think he may have information about your sister from you and plotted to kill her for abandoning her faith?"

"I may have mentioned my sister as the only relative in the area. Shah had his entire clan in the US—parents, siblings, uncles, and cousins. To think that he may have been involved with my sister's death is far-fetched. From what I understand, terrorist groups have larger targets to destroy—public infrastructure, like train transportation, air transport, financial and military centers to create havoc in a given society."

"You do not think a high-profile person could be a target and marked for assassination? There are cases where individuals had been assassinated or fatwa had been declared against them—a Dutch artist, Author Salman Rushdie, a Somali member of the Dutch parliament."

"Well, yes, these are indeed high-profile people, who challenged the religion and the Prophet's teachings according to their accusers. I am not sure of the extent of the truth of their misdeeds. These individuals had wider reach, either through their writing or their politics. My sister did not have that kind of audience. She had not written about religion. Certainly, she had great legal mind, and I am sure if she had lived longer, she would have written maybe a legal book. I am not sure how she could be a target by any group."

"Did she ever tell you that she had nearly a dozen telephone calls from K. Shah? What reason did he have to call her? You never introduced your sister to Shah?"

"No, never. As far as I know, he had never met her. I do not understand. How did you find out he had called her?"

Officer O'Malley said, "From telephone records. Most of the calls lasted about a minute or two, which tells us they did not have much to talk about. It could be a threat, insult, or warning."

"Are you sure it was from Shah?" Tarek asked again.

"Certainly. The telephone is registered to his name."

"Oh my! Why would he do that? He knows her name, profession, and legal firm she was working for. I am sure I have told him that. But I had never thought of introducing him to her, and he never showed any interest to meet her. Like I told you, we were not that close as friends. I do not know what to say. I am shocked. Maybe my sister did not know who was calling her and dismissed it as a freak caller. She never mentioned any threat or curse. I do not know. Maybe she did not want to worry me. She felt very safe where she was living and working."

"Did Shah ever invite you to go to an Islamic center, mosque, or any kind of organized activities?"

"Not really. I do not remember when he invited me to any activities. We were casual friends who had spent some time having lunch after class. I remember he always ate food brought from home because it was 'halal.' I ate cafeteria meals. In terms of personality, we were so different. I have many friends, including a girlfriend. He is much reserved, very shy, especially with women, but never commented about my social life. Neither would have I allowed him."

"Did you ever meet his family?"

"Nope. From his description, they were clannish, deeply religious, and traditionalists to the extent of curbing their children's social life. I was not brought up that way. My parents, though religious, were very tolerant. In terms of our social life, as long as we remained moral and ethical, they never tried to control us. From the day I remember, we were friends with people of diverse cultures and backgrounds. So did my parents. Shah's family were not the type I was eager to meet."

"If you had to profile K. Shah, what would you say?"

"Studious, religious, shy, socially awkward, and nonadventurous. I think he could make a good engineer, not the innovative type but the one that runs operations."

"Do you think he is capable of committing murder and terrorist action?"

"I do not know. Hmm. If he joined a terror group or if a powerful person orders him, maybe. He does not seem to have a strong will, considering how he was brought up. I do not know, sir."

"Let us talk about your brother," said Officer O'Malley. "Does your brother use another name, an alias or nickname?"

"Not as far as I know."

"Were you aware that he had been in the US in the past?"

"If he had, he never contacted me."

"Is that a yes or no answer?"

"Neither, because I did not see my brother in about three years until two days ago at the prison."

"But you do not have to see him or hear from him to know that he was in the US."

"Officer, I have heard many rumors about my brother's locations in the past three years—Yemen, Pakistan, Afghanistan, and, yes, the US."

"Who told you that he was in the US?"

"It was someone who works at a store where I buy some baked stuff. He saw a person that had a physical resemblance to me and mentioned my name to him. And the person responded by saying, 'He is my younger brother.' When I heard that, I went to the Islamic center to see my brother or get some information. Nobody seemed to know of him, so I thought it was one of those rumors that can't be confirmed."

"Do you know the name of the person who gave you the information?"

"Yes, he is Bakri, a Pakistani. But he quit his job, and I did not have a chance to ask him more."

"So you do not know where he is now?"

"No."

"Well, he is in detention," Officer Kern stated.

Tarek seemed to get a little surprised by the news and remarked, "What is going on? Everybody that I have contacted seem to be involved in criminal activity. Please tell me Bakri is not suspected as a terrorist."

"Let us stop here. But if you think of any occurrence that may help us solve your sister's murder, contact us. Anything. Leads that may look trivial could help us."

After he left the officers, Tarek was confused. His world seemed to slip away from him. *Has the whole world gone crazy?* He tried to piece together the talk he had with the officers.

That weekend, he and Derek had planned to visit the burial ground of Amina. He had dreaded it, for it brought out all the pain and sadness of the last few months. The loss of his sister and then father had left an emptiness that nothing could fill in. Derek had been visiting the site quite regularly, in fact every weekend unless he was out of town on duty. For Tarek, it was the first time since the day she was interred into her lasting place. But that day was so vividly inscribed in his mind no amount of tears and therapy could erase it. The day she was buried, it was a cloudy, darkened day as to mark the sadness of the day. Friends, workmates, and Derek and his family had come for the burial. She had been eulogized by a friend from law school. Derek had read a poem.

Tarek was overwhelmed with the sudden and brutal loss of his sister he could not speak a word. He had a hard time carrying his body. The suddenness of her death and the brutal way she had been killed was too much for him to bear.

They started driving early. The cemetery was located about thirty minutes' drive away, but sometimes if traffic was congested, it could take longer. They arrived in time. Derek could walk to the burial spot blindfolded.

For Tarek, it would have been difficult. There was no landmark or marble mausoleum as could be seen in a Christian burial ground. Amina's burial ground was modest, level to the ground with only a well-trimmed grass covering. There was a small plaque with her name, birth date, and the date of her death inscribed on it. The day she was buried, there were no graves east and south of her burial place, but today she was surrounded by newly interred bodies. He wondered, *Did they die young like my sister or die at the ripe age after they had seen their children grow up and have their own children? Did they die of natural cause, or were they brutally murdered like my beautiful sister?* All the thoughts brought a ton of emotions and made him cry again.

Derek joined him in an anguished cry. Even people who came to visit the graves of their loved ones joined them in the orgy of crying. They cried their hearts out. They consoled one another. They prayed each in their way and talked to her.

Tarek told her how much he loved her and missed her. He told her of the death of their father and how heartbroken he was with her death. He also told her that, without both of them, the world was not the same and their family was not the same. *It is not the happy family anymore. Our mother is trudging through life, only to give courage to the two remaining children. I can see in her eyes she wants to join Eba and you. Amina dear, I want to survive until the day when who had murdered you is caught and brought to justice. I want to tell him how scum he is for killing the most beautiful, angelic person, my dearest sister.*

They cleared the area and picked up some weeds and bade farewell to Amina and drove back to town. On their way back, they were quiet. Without stop, they went to the apartment. They drank a glass of water each and decided to get into their respective bedrooms.

To Tarek's surprise, he went to sleep immediately. He took a nap for about two hours. Derek woke up earlier and was waiting to go out for dinner. After a shower, he joined Derek in the living room. He was ready, so they went to a restaurant not far from the apartment. He did not have much appetite to eat. He ordered a bowl of clam chowder soup, and Derek ate a salad with grilled chicken strips.

He told him about his encounter with the officers and the information they gave him about Shah, Bakri, and Amin. "Shah had been calling Amina many times, not long talk, about a minute or two long. The officers think it could have been a threat or a curse."

"But why?" Derek asked.

"Well, some people think that she was a traitor to her faith and culture, unworthy to live. There have been cases like that, Derek. They call it 'honor killing.' I have told them it is far-fetched. But I believe that there may be a nexus between Amin, Bakri, and Shah. I do not know."

Derek added, "But she never told me that there was any threat or curse against her."

"You know Amina. She would not worry you. Besides, she always felt safe in her apartment and neighborhood. It is something that we can't dismiss, especially that Amin had traveled to the US using aliases around the time Amina was killed. I have to think about it if there could be any connection."

On Monday, Tarek decided to visit his university and see his advisor and professors and a few friends who were doing doctoral work. He rented a car and drove there. He went to see his advisor, a long-tenured professor who was outstanding in the field but, more importantly, one of the most supportive. He was very happy to see him as he was too.

After he expressed his condolences, he asked Tarek if there was anything he could do for him. Tarek told him he just came to see him because he did not know how long he was going to be in the US. "I am glad you came," he said. "What have you been doing the last few months?" he asked.

Tarek gave him a synopsis of what had happened in the last few months. After twenty minutes, he had to leave, promising that he would come back to see him.

From there, he was walking to the Science and Technology Building when an engineering doctoral candidate, Aziz from Pakistan, saw him. Aziz called him and waved him to stop. They greeted each other.

Aziz expressed his condolences and asked him to have tea with him at the cafeteria. He accepted because he thought of Kapoor Shah, and he might give him some information about the person.

As soon as they sat, he brought the subject of Kapoor Shah.

"Have you heard about Shah?" he asked.

"Yes," Tarek answered, somehow muted.

"I heard he is in jail for suspicion of murders of three people."

Tarek said, "What are you talking about? Be serious. K. Shah can't involve himself with murders."

"So you did not know K. Shah is a suspect of three murders? And I am sorry to say one of them might be your sister."

"What do you mean my sister? He does not know her. How could he kill a person he does not have any contact with?"

He continued, "The rumor is that K. Shah and a few others were involved in assassinating prominent Moslems who had strayed from their religion and have brought dishonor to it."

"Do you know who else is involved?"

"I do not know them. But they are organized clandestinely, and they originate from different countries. Several of them are under custody. In few weeks most likely, we will know who the others are."

The whole time, Tarek's mind was accelerating, and his heart was beating faster and faster. What this could mean was that he was the one who gave the information to his sister's murderer. Somehow, he was complicit with her death. When he could no longer get any more information from Aziz, he rushed to go home and think thoroughly what the next step should be.

"Who was this Bakri?" was one of the questions that bothered Tarek for the whole evening. He had to get some more information, where else but the store where he used to work.

At the opening time of the store the next day, he went to the store and found the owner busy stacking the shelves with food items. Mr. Omar was in his sixties, very friendly, and an ebullient, proud father of two physician sons and a married daughter who was an accountant. He had been fond of Tarek since he met him. Mr. Omar said Tarek reminded him of his youth, full of energy with a quick smile. He had met Amina on several occasions. Every time Tarek came, he asked about her.

When Tarek came that morning and Mr. Omar saw him, he hugged him and cried for the loss of his sister and father. "I am so sorry, my son. I hope Allah burn the evil that did this to her in hell."

"Mr. Omar, thank you for your sympathy, but I need your help. I know Bakri, your former employee, is in jail. Do you know why?"

"Let me tell you what I told the investigators. Bakri had worked for me for two years. Initially, he was a good worker, trustworthy, so I used to let him open the store and manage it. He did a good job—always on time, proper cash handling, careful with inventory. I was very happy. As a reward, I used to give him extra money as a bonus every three months. After a year, he started to bring people around the store, always talking in a subdued voice as if they were conspiring to do something. Every time I came, they stop talking. They look at me sideways. I gave him many warnings that friends were not supposed to hang around the store. He did not seem to care about my warning. Soon, different characters started to hang around the store. I could not take it anymore, so I had to fire him. What surprised me, he did not seem to care about being fired from his job. Since then, I had seen him only once when he came to pick up some of his stuff left in the store. He drove a car on that day, a brown imported car which he told me he just bought. He can't afford a car on his pay. I wish I could give you any more information. That is the extent I know about Bakri."

"Thank you, Mr. Omar. Have a good day."

"Come back again, Tarek, and ask me for anything you need. God be with you."

"Thank you again," Tarek responded.

After leaving the store, Tarek was more suspicious of the Bakri, Shah, and Amin nexus. But how did they meet? Who acted as interlocutor to bring the three together and plot to kill Amina and others, according to Aziz?

Tarek went to the Islamic center to gather any leads that would help him in this increasingly puzzling mystery. At the center, there were a few people. After greeting the person at the front desk, a husky Jordanian with pleasant personality, he went to the

133

reading room. Sitting at the sofa, he read Arabic magazines that dealt with social issues, but he could not concentrate as his mind was wandering. He tried to look calm and not trifle, worried about anything that might create suspicion among the few readers. The center regulars had been edgy since the arrests and visits by investigators. The vast majority of the members were ordinary citizens who came to learn, socialize, and pray. They were hardworking, peaceful members of the community. The guidelines of the center, its main slogan, was "peace for humanity and friendship to all."

After flipping several magazines, he went to the front desk and started a conversation with the Jordanian gentleman. He introduced himself as Tarek Mohamed Nur, but the Jordanian had already recognized him from a previous encounter. Without fidgeting, Tarek started asking about Bakri, Shah, and other arrested individuals for suspicion of plotting to commit terrorist activities and allegedly committing murders.

The gentleman said sternly, "The center is totally and absolutely against violence of any sort. The individuals acted on their own. They were using the center like any member of the public. The allegation they used it to conspire, the center does not have any knowledge of it. The information we have about the individuals is no different than that of the general public. We got it from the media. I am sorry, my friend. I have nothing more to say about this issue." With that, the conversation was concluded.

As he walked out of the center, a young man followed him. Tarek was not concerned as there were comings and goings from the center. The man followed him about ten feet apart.

As he approached the car, the man said, "Hey!"

Tarek, surprised and a bit concerned, said, "Yes? Do I know you?"

"I do not know, but I have something to tell you."

"What is that?" Tarek responded.

"Let me tell you something. You have suffered enough with the loss of your sister. Do not go probe about the group. It is dangerous. This is a dangerous group whose tentacles nobody knows. To preserve their organization, they will do anything. If they think you may expose them, they would not hesitate to harm you. Let the professionals handle it. I have said enough. Goodbye." As fast as he approached Tarek, he left in a hurry. Tarek did not know what to make of it.

After much thought, Tarek decided to concentrate his probing from his brother. *If I confront him with what I know already, he might confess. I will use all the moral suasion and sympathy for the remaining family, especially our mother, for him to tell me all the things he knows.* Tarek convinced himself it might work. Once facts were established, he would beg him to come clean with the investigation. He would ask him to tell them what he knew. Sooner rather than later, they would find out anyway. He would also tell him of negotiating a plea bargain for his case for a reduced sentence. *We do not want to lose you in an electric chair.* He would plead with him. *We have lost enough. Have mercy on the family.*

Tarek made an appointment for a visit to prison. Unfortunately, he was informed the prisoners had been moved to another prison for security reasons, and it was located 120 miles south, and visitation was highly restricted. Another dead end, Tarek moaned.

In desperation, he came up with an idea of contacting the investigators and asking them to facilitate his visit to his brother and probe some information from him. He called Officer O'Malley and shared his opinion. Officer O'Malley thought it was interesting and promised that he would call him back with a response in the next few days. Tarek was a man on a rush. A few days was too long, but he did not have an alternative.

While waiting for Officer O'Malley's call, Tarek decided to do some business long distance, back home. He called his mother and sister and promised them that he was coming. He talked with his friend and his sister's fiancé. After an exchange of greetings, they started talking business. Tarek updated him what was going on in the US with his brother and other suspects. There was no clear suspect on who killed Amina, even though several people, including Amin, were suspects. Ibrahim, on his part, informed Tarek of the business conditions at the company his father established—that everything was well, the customer base was expanding, and the revenue and profit were also showing growth. They promised to exchange email message to each other. With that, they hung up the telephone.

Tarek always had an ambition to expand the product variety in the business. While in the US, he contacted some companies that produced consumer products and technological products to act as their manufacturer agent in the northeast region of Africa. Several of the companies were interested and requested him to send them business history, qualification, and business plan. He started to assemble all necessary documents to do just that. In the meantime, it kept him busy while waiting for Officer O'Malley's response. It was taking long.

Five days later, Officer O'Malley called Tarek and informed him that the clearance for him to visit the maximum security prison was cleared for Wednesday at 1:30 p.m. The officers were flying with him, and local officers would wait for them at the airport to drive them to the prison site. He further informed him that he was going to meet Kapoor Shah instead of Amin. Tarek was caught by surprise on why Shah. The officers thought that Shah was the weakest link that had joined them, mainly because of his weak personality rather than conviction. It was their assumption that, with a little prodding and bringing up of his wasted educational career, he might crack up. "We will have to discuss on how the discussion should follow, and we may have to wire you to listen from a distance and record what he says." Tarek reluctantly agreed.

On Wednesday, the three—Tarek and the two officers—flew, courtesy of the FBI, to the maximum security prison area. And a car was ready for them at the airport. In the flight, they talked on how the visit to Kapoor Shah should go. It was suggested that Tarek should tell Kapoor Shah that he had visited Amin and Amin was cooperating with the FBI after negotiating a plea bargain. That might create panic on Shah, which might induce him to open up and expose the workings of the group. "This should be done after you have established rapport by reminding him of college days. 'Why, K. Shah?' You should ask him he could have been the most successful engineer. 'Why spend so many years of rigorous college education if you are going to end up here? Tell me, Shah. I am trying to understand what drove you to be a member of an organization that advocates violence? You do not impress me as a violent person.' The idea is for Shah to open a little crack on the structure of the organization. Make him feel that you are on his side, except that you do not agree on their tactics."

At 1:30 p.m., Tarek was at a room divided by a thick glass and metal bars. On one side, he was seated safely. And on the other side, a prisoner in an orange jumpsuit, both hands and legs shackled, would be seated. The whole area, both in structure and dimension, was different than a regular jail. There were cameras peering from all directions. Every movement of the prisoner and visitor was monitored. A maximum security prison holds the nation's most dangerous criminals; the extra security measures were understandable. Even the guards escorting a prisoner were several, armed, and encircling the prisoner from all directions. To see Kapoor Shah with strong guards surrounding him made Tarek smile because he was skinny and not of strong built. One guard would have been more than adequate to tackle him and keep him under control.

Kapoor Shah was walking slowly, dragging his feet, maybe because of the discomfort of the shackles or the weight of the circumstances under which he was in. What would he think of a visit by a some-time friend from college? When he saw Tarek, he was bewildered. It was a total surprise. He said he thought finally some members of his family were here, which he resented as none of them had come to visit him. He was bitter and felt betrayed.

Tarek observed hesitation on the part of Shah to come to the window. His eyes were narrowed by suspicion on why the visit was allowed. To just break the ice, Tarek said, "I am sorry to visit you under the circumstances. I wish it was at the college cafeteria like we used to do."

Shah shrugged it and asked, "What brought you here?"

"Well," Tarek said, "I was visiting Amin, and when I heard from the guards that you are in the same jail, I came to greet you."

"And who is Amin?" he asked.

"You know Amin, my brother, who is in the same predicament as you are."

Shah responded, "I do not know him."

139

Tarek thought, *Maybe Amin is using an alias.* Tarek wanted to change the subject. "What happened, buddy? I never thought I would see you in this condition. I was expecting to see you work as an engineer at a prestigious company."

Shah quietly heard without any reaction; he was obviously very uncomfortable.

"Do you have an attorney to help you get out of the jam you are in?" Tarek inquired.

Shah said, "Allah is my attorney, and Quran is my law and the path to truth."

It was rather discomfiting to hear this kind of response from an educated person who must know the deep problem he was in. After several attempts to speak with Shah, Tarek felt spurned and gave up. He wished him well and signaled to the guards he was done. Shah left the way they brought him, shackled and encircled.

After the unsuccessful encounter with Kapoor Shah, Tarek and the officers had to redraw their strategies. They left the prison to have lunch at a local restaurant and discuss what just transpired. The restaurant was located close to the prison, maybe quarter a mile distance. At this time of heightened security, many people had a concern for public places to be in such proximity to a prison that housed dangerous characters. As they entered the restaurant, the officers looked into all directions, their keen sense of looking for potential trouble developed by training and experience. The place was fairly full, with most seats occupied.

In one corner, there were three guys seated that caught the attention of Officer O'Malley. At the time, he could not figure out why, but the way they were looking at their direction and, in particular, Tarek's gave him some concern. The young men's demeanor changed, and obviously, they were discussing the new entrants by the way that each had to check them simultaneously. Officer O'Malley alerted his friend Officer Kern and Tarek. "Check on those guys while I make a call for local police to help us check them."

The police were on their way when the guys stood to leave the restaurant. Two police squads arrived in a short time; however, the two guys had already left toward the parking lot with only one of them left in the restaurant to pay the bill. Officer O'Malley walked to the police officers and introduced himself and pointed to the two guys already seated in the car and the one coming out of the restaurant. Immediately, one of the officers blocked the car with his squad car. They were blocked from all directions with parked cars on all sides. The police ordered the guys to get out of the car with their hands above their head. They did come out as ordered. Each pulled out their wallets and handed over their IDs. Their heads remained bowed, and they avoided eye contact with the officers. An officer took the IDs and driver's licenses to check their authenticity. The first thing they did was run the license plate of the car, which was registered to a Toyota Camry 2003 whereas the car they were driving was a Taurus 2005. The IDs showed they were all forged with names, and the social security numbers did not match. Immediately, the guys were handcuffed and put under arrest. They were read of their Miranda rights and taken to the station. All the arrested spoke English well with no discernible accent. The first impression was that they were American born. Running the vehicle identification number of the car indicated it was owned by a man who lived in the Chicago suburb town of Oak Park. The gentleman had reported the car stolen about four months ago. Now the police had three young guys with forged documents and stolen car with a plate registered to another car.

Three guys—Who were they, and what were they up to?—became the focus of the police in the small town. The small-town police were never involved in cases that might have implication beyond their locality. There was excitement and commitment from all to work hard and expose the whole rubric of the case. Because of the nature of the case, the FBI was involved.

Tarek was dumbfounded. He was surprised how his life had become complex. He never had any inkling that he might be involved in a case that might change the course of his life forever. After the incident, lunch had a different flavor. Even the talk was different. "Who are these guys? What are they doing? They could not know of our visit to the prison. Was it coincidental that they were here at this time? Were they really dining at the restaurant or observing what goes on around the prison? The investigation will find out the facts soon hopefully."

The question of what to do next about the prisoners, Amin and his friends, was in Tarek's mind. He wanted to get some answers to the suspicions that dogged his mind for months. He wanted to get some finality on who the killer of his sister was and what role, if any, Amin played. He wanted to go home and be with his grieving mother and sister. He brought the question, "Why don't I talk to Amin now since the approach to K. Shah failed?"

Officer O'Malley had a pained look on his face. "Sorry, Tarek, that is not possible."

"Why?" Tarek asked.

"Well, Officer Kern took over. Your brother is in no condition to talk since he left the hospital. He had refused to eat his food. His condition is precarious They have started force-feeding him, so any discussion with him had to be delayed until the doctor approves it."

It was one more to the numbing, painful occurrences that were happening to Tarek. He did not have much to say, only to pray and ask when it was going to end.

Few days later, the preliminary investigation report of the three guys came. They were recent converts to Islam. Upon investigation, they were born and raised in Chicago. They did not know one another until they met at Cook County Jail. They were in jail for small-time drug use and distribution. Each had several run-ins with the law. Nothing big but getting in trouble all the same. In prison, a Moslem they befriended started teaching them about Islam.

They were attracted, for it was the first time that any-body had talked to them on religion and spirituality. Since it was almost at the end of his jail term, he gave them a telephone number to contact him upon their release. He promised them shelter out of jail. When they were released from jail, they each contacted the gentleman. As promised, he gave them a place to stay and food and continued to teach them the Quran. He introduced them to other Moslems and wel-comed them with open arms. It was a new experience for them. All their life, nobody had ever shown any regard for them. They converted to Islam and wanted to know everything about Islamic history and liturgy. They were regular attendees of the mosque, always ready to serve. They were true converts, and their life had been transformed positively—no more drinking, smoking, or drugging themselves. The more days that passed, the more they liked this new turn of their life. They assumed Middle Eastern names.

They made friends, among them a man, of about the same age like them, in his late twenties. He was always animated in his talks and teachings of the Quran. He was very interesting to them but also seemed to be an angry man. He accused the West of putting Islam under siege. He was convinced the "Christian West" wanted to destroy Islam. It was a new kind of politics to the new converts. A new kind of politics that they were not equipped to criti-cally analyze and discard the fantasy from the truth. The more they met with Othman, the angrier they became with the West. Othman was never a terrorist.

His intention was not to recruit for terrorist action. He just believed in what he was preaching. But there were others who were following the way the young men were responding to the fulminations and fantastic accusations of Othman. They observed that these young men were easy prey. They were the ones who recruited them to surveil for a possible attack on the maximum security prison and free Ahmed Gillani and his comrades. There was nothing to gain, no other motive other than to right the wrongs that had been done to Moslems as was told by their recruiters. The new recruits felt that they were in a great mission of jihad against those who had wronged the sacred. They were the most suitable recruits, with low self-esteem and low education. They were ready to do anything to gain acceptance and respectability from their new friends.

The investigation of the three young people from Illinois went rather easy. Their pictures were sent to Oak Park, Illinois, police department. The police took the picture to the owner of the stolen car. He immediately identified them as the guys who had moved to the neighborhood not long ago. He showed them the apartment where they lived. He had never spoken to them. With the information, they went to see the manager of the building, who gave them more information about the guys. They had lived in the building for only three months, whose lease was signed by Mr. F. Idriss. Rent was timely paid, and they were upright, with no trouble with neighbors. "Who is F. Idriss?" was the next question. The manager brought the lease contract where F. Idriss's personal information was included. Included were the address, occupation, and telephone number.

Two officers were dispatched to the address to collect whatever information could be available. When the officers arrived on site, the place was closed. It looked that it had been closed for a while, with strewn papers, empty cans, and bottles of beer all thrown on the gateway through the metal security bars. The telephone was not working. Further investigation showed the number was issued to a young African American lady. Upon contacting her, she knew no one as F. Idriss. How he had gotten her telephone number, she had no clue. The information was passed to the officer on the site of the apartment. The manager of the building could not give them any more information. According to him, he only saw the gentleman once. He paid the security deposit and first month's rent in cash. The second month's and third month's rent were also paid in cash, delivered by Ishmael, the name used by one of the tenants. The information on F. Idriss was a dead end.

In frustration, one of the officers remarked, "Maybe the city should pass an ordinance requiring all leaseholders' pictures to be kept on file with building management companies."

Othman was slender, excitable, and, from all appearances, a nice young man. He was very pious. Everyone at the mosque thought highly of him. He was always ready to serve and generous with charity contributions. He did think though that Islam was

146

under attack by some elements of the evangelical church in the West. The remarks of the likes of tel-evangelist Pat Robertson deriding Islam and Moslems and spewing anti-Islamic rhetoric through their tele-vised programs were the examples he quoted. The "merchants of religion," as he called them, were the most dangerous in driving individuals to extremes in defending their religion and culture. At the same time, he sincerely believed in his faith as the ultimate solution to human, moral, and spiritual problems. Islam would elevate human beings in the eyes of the Creator, he believed. One couldn't help but be impressed by the sincerity of his conviction. He had many friends of different religions, and all gave testi-monials on his behalf, saying that Othman, under no circumstances, would hurt any person. They admit-ted that he always tried to teach them about his reli-gion, and for that, they were appreciative. However, none had converted to Islam but had gained a better understanding of it.

When Othman was asked about the three young converts, he identified them as the three who were so confused in life and found the right path through Islam. "Islam will free them from their demons and will lead them to a righteous life. *Alhamdulillah*," he concluded.

Officer O'Malley informed Othman that they were in jail.

"They are in jail," Othman repeated with clear disappointment. "What happened? Did they go back to their petty criminal activities?"

None of the officers volunteered to answer the question. They asked Othman if he knew F. Idriss.

"F. Idriss! F. Idriss," he repeated, trying to bring to memory if he knew such a person.

"Do you know any person or persons that befriended the three guys?" was the next question.

Othman said, "Many people were interested in them. They were young Americans who converted to Islam, so a lot of people hoped they will be a bridge to a better understanding of Islam among young Americans in the area. During Friday prayers, everybody talked to them. As far as I could recall, no individual was particularly involved with them."

The officers had no reason to suspect that Othman was not forthright with them. They left their telephone cards and asked him, if he had any more information to share, to contact them at any time.

After the officers left, Othman was in deep thought. *Who could be F. Idriss? What has he got to do with the three guys? Is this F. Idriss recruiting for terrorist activity?* The more he thought about it, the more he got upset. *It is sacrilegious to hire potential terrorists from a mosque. And to involve young, unsuspecting, new converts for such heinous act is even more appalling.* He was determined to get to the bottom of it and help the police catch the bastard.

*****

For a moment, Tarek was untangled from the case. He pursued vigorously some potential business ventures. Many manufacturers were interested in hiring him as an agent to distribute their product in Northeast Africa and part of Middle East. He had presented impressive credentials and business plan to the companies which might decide to contract with him as their agent representative. He emailed a message to his friend and fiancé of his sister about the good news and advised him to look for a site to build a bigger and suitable warehouse. It was a welcome diversion from the tragic and intriguing situation that surrounded him. It was an antidote for the pain he suffered. He wanted to go home and help the family come to terms with the tragedies and normalize their life. Among the first things he wanted to do was to have the wedding for his sister. That was what his father and Amina would have wanted, he thought with much sadness.

Officer O'Malley was of the opinion there was a limited role for Tarek at this stage of the investigation. When Tarek asked what role was left for him to play, he told him, "Very little honestly. It is entirely police work that could untangle the maze henceforth. If you want to go back home, it is okay by us. When we have a conclusive resolution, we will email you, I promise."

Tarek expressed his appreciation for the hard work they were putting on the case, and he was confident they would get to the bottom of it. With that, they parted, wishing each other the best of luck.

Othman rang the telephone to Officer O'Malley.

Officer O'Malley answered the phone, the direct line, knowing it could be one of his contacts.

"Hello! I am Othman, the guy who you talked to about F. Idriss last week."

"Yes. How are you?" answered Officer O'Malley.

"I am fine, except I did not have enough sleep since I talked to you, gentlemen," said Othman. "The idea that someone is recruiting for violent acts from our mosque angers me. I am calling to volunteer my services in any way possible to catch Idriss or his comrades, if there are any, and bring them to justice."

O'Malley said, "Why do you want to do that?"

"Because I am opposed to terrorism, and most importantly, Islam is opposed to violence against individuals that had done nothing against the religion."

"Okay," O'Malley said. "You will be vetted for your background thoroughly if you had committed any crime or if there are suspicious activities."

"I am okay with that, Officer," Othman responded. "My life is an open book. I have no concern for anything," he said confidently.

"Okay then, Othman. You will hear from me soon. Have a good day."

"Thank you. Have a good day, Officer," Othman ended.

Officer O'Malley saw the opportunity of Othman, availing his service as a way to penetrate the inner workings of the mosque and the individuals that might be involved in hostile activities in the country. After consulting with senior officers in the FBI, it was decided to vet Othman and recruit him as a contact person. The vetting showed that Othman, except for occasional late payment of bills, had a sound financial situation. He had no criminal record of any sort. He had lived for almost twenty years in the same neighborhood and attended both high school and college in Chicago. After college, he had worked with other companies before he was hired at his current job. He had few friends, and each had been vetted without any blemishes on their backgrounds. It was decided to recruit Othman.

Othman had already started to gather information on who F. Idriss was. Nobody recognized the name until someone mentioned a name Idriss Abdelk Foukry. *Could it be the same person?* Othman asked himself. The best way was to look for Idriss Abdelk Foukry. Upon investigation, Othman found out that Foukry was a mystery man. No one knew what business he had, except that he had a small office close to the downtown area. He drove a new Nissan Altima, white color. He had been seen talking to the young men outside the mosque and, in fact, gave them a ride to where nobody knew.

The FBI wired Othman and officially hired him to do a job. They gave him two days' training on how to use both the listening and recording devices, how to identify suspects, and what to do in case he wanted to send alerts. Othman swore that he would surveil only those who most likely committed violent acts. He was not doing it for the love of FBI. He was doing it because he believed those who committed violence in the name of Islam were enemies of Islam. It was a personal crusade against those who gave his religion a bad name.

He apprised Officer O'Malley of the suspicion he had that F. Idriss might be Idriss Abdelk Foukry. He gave the address to where his job was located. Officer O'Malley took the information and promised Othman that he would run it through the bureau's database and perhaps the immigration.

Exposing the identification of Idriss Abdelk Foukry, alias F. Idriss, was the least difficult task for the bureau. His picture and all personal information were recorded in the Homeland Security database via US Citizenship and Immigration Services. He was born in Baghdad, Iraq, in 1956. He was hired and worked as an Iraqi government bureaucrat at different levels. He was a Shia Moslem. He migrated to the US in 1985 during the Iran-Iraq War and was granted political asylum. In the US, he was mainly working as a limousine driver in Chicago, according to his tax records. However, in the last five years, his income was very low, not enough for subsistence. He had lived rather lavish with comfortable apartment in a solid upper-middle-class neighborhood, drove a new car, and dressed fashionable attires. Where was he drawing extra income to support his lifestyle? After identifying who F. Idriss was, to corroborate, his picture was taken to the building manager where the three guys lived and also to the imprisoned three men. Both confirmed the picture was of F. Idriss.

In a follow-up to F. Idriss's activities and connections, Officer O'Malley and Officer Kern went to his workplace. The place was closed, and by looking at some of the letters and advertisement flyers, it must have been closed for some time. Contacts with the post office confirmed for three weeks a certified letter had been on hold since F. Idriss failed to claim it. Further investigation indicated that the content of the mail was certified cheques issued in London to Idriss Abdelk Foukry. The cheque was signed by Masood Abdel Azziz, a local activist and an Iraqi Shia. The information was immediately reported to Scotland Yard to look into the background of Masood Abdel Azziz and his connections.

F. Idriss was nowhere to be seen. He had already flown out of US into Pakistan via London. In Pakistan, he melted into the population and perhaps into the organization's strong base area of Northern Pakistan. The investigation would, however, continue to unravel any and all members of his organization. The news from Scotland Yard was no different. Masood Abdel Azziz had also taken the same flight with Foukry to Pakistan. Othman might be indispensable to unravelling the network that F. Idriss, also known as Idriss Abdelk Foukry, had. He was apprised of the investigation and the flight of Idriss to Pakistan. Othman promised he would do everything in his power to bring to justice all involved, even if it involved his brother or his best friend.

The three men were held in prison for almost three weeks. The US attorney was still to decide what

charges he would bring against them. He was awaiting the FBI report, upon hearing the whole story and
the role and the depth of their involvement, to make
a decision. They were hired by F. Idriss to survey the
activities around the prison hour by hour—when
the guards would change, how many at a time, visiting hours, and the volume of traffic. No action was
required on their part. After their case was looked
into, the US attorney decided to charge them with
felony of car theft and holding forged documents.

The attention of the officers was turned back
to the maximum security prison, Ahmed Gillani and
his group. The FBI had been trying to piece together
a bulk of information about the group, some trivial and some important with potential to break the
secret of the organization and its operations. The
most important information was the telephone
communications and the type of people he was contacting in many parts of the world. Three telephone
numbers, in particular, stood out—one telephone
number listed to Idriss Abdelk Foukry and two numbers listed to Masood Abdel Azziz. The two Azziz's
numbers were simultaneously used, which indicated
that one of the numbers was used by someone else.
The connection was made between Ahmed Gillani,
F. Idriss—also known as Idriis Abdelk Foukry—and
Azziz.

Othman had come up with two names who
had close contacts with F. Idriss—Bashir Nussredin,
the owner of the limousine service where Idriss had
worked intermittently, and a gentleman by the name

of Ishmaelov, whose origin was from Central Asia, a country that was formerly part of the Soviet Union. Bashir was the enabler of Idriss, a good financial supporter, and provider of legal shade by opening an office that really served nobody and nothing. Ishmaelov was an expert in high technology and educated in the US. He had become key in high-tech communication and database collection. The question for the investigators was to unwind the loop that connected all the characters.

After determining that Ishmaelov might be the person that could easily be extricated from the group, they decided to approach him. They wanted to add some drama to make it more menacing. They took two police officers to Ishmaelov's apartment early morning. He was still asleep when he heard a loud knock at his door. He folded the window shade to look who was waking him up at this ungodly hour. It was the police. Panic seized him. He wanted to make a call to Bashir before he opened the door. But the police ordered him to open the door right away.

Ishmaelov lived alone in a one-bedroom apartment that was tastefully decorated. This was a man whose life had been intertwined with an organization which had reached over several countries in different continents. His apartment, from the setup of few chairs and impeccably clean kitchen, did not indicate of any sign of human traffic crossing it. He had set an office in a corner of the room. A computer and well-stacked papers were on a desk. There were shelves on both sides of the desk with books on mainly information technology that were vertically placed.

Ishmaelov had calmed down. He invited the officers to have a seat and asked them of if it was okay for him to change his pajamas.

"We only have a few questions, Mr. Ishmaelov, and then we will let you go to your business."

Ishmaelov asked, "Do you have a search warrant?" And the officers produced the search warrant.

Officer Kern asked, "What is your full name?"

"My name is Mahmet Kedir Ishmaelov," the suspect answered.

"Where do you work?"

"Right now, I do not have regular work. I freelance as a software consultant to different people and businesses."

"Can you tell us the companies or individuals that you worked as a consultant for?"

Ishmaelov, afraid that he might trip on some of his answers, responded by saying, "I cannot give you the names because there is an issue of confidentiality."

When the officers persisted, he declined to answer any of their questions without legal representation. While Officer Kern was interviewing Ishmaelov, Officer O'Malley was looking into the stacked books and papers on the table. All the papers had to do with application of information technology, and there were few personal letters from family members.

The interview reached a stalemate. The officers huddled to make a decision on whether to take

Ishmaelov to the station as a suspect of terrorism support. Both agreed there was no other option as he might take a flight like F. Idriss. After reading his Miranda rights, they told him that he was under arrest. They allowed him to change his clothes before they took him to the police car waiting outside. At the station, he was allowed to make a telephone call, and his first call was to Bashir. But Bashir was unavailable because he was already booked in another police station. On the second attempt, he was able to contact an attorney that had represented Bashir on matters of business.

Bashir was gregarious, jocular, and mischievous as one of the officers called him "a lovable bandit." If anyone employed a recruiter and mobilizer for a dangerous mission, Bashir would best fit it. His personality would mask whatever design he was planning in his prodigious mind. He was quick-witted. He could quote the Bible and the Prophet's Hadith. Anyone who talked to him would leave impressed. If the allegations were proven correct, it would be sad, for Bashir would have made a great diplomat. As a diplomat, he could have bridged differences among people of differing political, national, and religious affiliations. Everybody in their heart wanted Bashir to be innocent of any involvement of terror plans. It would be seen what the evidence would bear.

All the suspects, on the advice of their lawyers, had used the constitutional right not to self-incriminate. The investigation had to prod without the cooperation of them. The officers had full confidence in time they would reach to the core of the organization's structure.

The offices of Bashir and Ishmaelov were located on the same street, separated by a wall. Bashir had leased them to run his limousine service business, but one office on the south side of the building was exclusively used by Ishmaelov. When the officers went there to collect any evidence, they were surprised by the serious oversight of the police when they arrested Bashir. They did not seal the place to maintain any possible evidence. This time, all the computers and documents were removed. Only books of no consequence to the investigation were left behind. Nobody knew who had removed the materials. It was a serious setback to the investigation. Both officers were furious. The arresting officers were not at fault. The order was only to arrest Bashir. Actually, at the time of his arrest, Bashir beguiled the officers with his charm and cooperation he distracted them on following procedures which should have been clear to veteran officers.

At the time Ishmaelov was interviewed by the officers, he gave them his email address and telephone. They were reported to FBI forensic analysis department for thorough analysis of where calls had been made and where email messages had been sent. A certain email contact in England caught the attention of the analysts. The content of the email was cryptic, coded messages whose meaning was a mystery. The FBI recruited the help of Scotland Yard to explore on their part on who the proprietor of the email address was and if there was any connection with terror groups. Exposing the email address was easy. The Scotland Yard found out it was a woman on the other end of the email. Not your ordinary woman who trudged through the daily grind of raising children and family, she was a highly considered professor at a prestigious university. She was a single woman with apparently active social life. Scotland Yard had to tread very carefully on the matter to avoid any besmirching of the name of the highly regarded scholar. To avoid any embarrassment, they hired a staff from the university to do some background check on the professor. The staff, in a matter of few days, brought an information that the lady had an unlikely male friend by the name of Mansour, who was considered as a bully within the Pakistani community in London. There were many allegations against Mansour, ranging from exacting funds from business and suspicion of murder. None of them was proven from the lack of cooperation from victims and witnesses. Scotland Yard had a few questions: "What is the nature of the relationship between the professor and Mansour—sexual, political, or both? How is it that socially incompatible people could have such a close relationship?"

The professor was at her office at the university when officers from Scotland Yard paid her a visit. She was working on her laptop, facing parallel to the door with the computer in front of her on a desk. Another larger desk was between her and the door, and two chairs were on two sides of the desk. The room was full of books shelved on all sides of the walls. The officers identified themselves by showing their IDs and sat on the chairs. The professor was quiet, unable to utter a word for a good couple of minutes. The officers gently waited until she regained her composure. The blood was sucked from her face. Her eyes were full of fear. With her left hand, she pulled some tissue papers from a box placed on the table where the laptop was situated. There was a small mirror underneath one of the shelves, and what was written on the laptop was partially readable. There was a name of Bashir and Ishmaelov and their being held in US prison. The officer could not read any further because the computer shut off in its energy-saving mode.

The first question to the professor was biographical—name, date of birth, address, and telephone number. And then what she taught at the university and for how long. She was an organization management expert and had been at the university for almost a decade and had worked as a consultant to some of the biggest corporations in the country. The second question was about her relationship with Mansour. When the name of Mansour was mentioned, she was demonstrably in a state of panic. "I am sorry I can't talk about him," she said, more out of fear rather than avoidance to give information.

"Why is that?" the officer asked.

"I am sorry. I just can't."

"Are you afraid of him? We know from his police record he is a rather-unsavory character, and we are a little surprised a person of your prestige will risk your reputation by having a relation with him." She was quiet. Maybe weighing her options. "Do you need any protection? It could be arranged," the officers suggested.

"I can't speak to you here," the professor said with some urgency in her voice. "There are too many snoops around. I will follow you to a safer place away from the university premises." She gave them an address about three miles farther east from her community and the university.

It was a café where mostly shopping housewives take a break from hectic shopping outing. They sat at a corner, watching who was coming and going.

The professor seemed much relieved to speak. She started by saying, "You are going to be either my saviors or executioners, but I am willing to take whatever befalls on me to unshackle myself from the clutches of Mansour and his criminal group. It is almost two years since I have become a hostage to Mansour."

She recalled how she had fallen as his prey. "Mansour is notorious in our community. He has been able to exact money from business people and services from professionals. There were rumors of murder, beatings, and blackmail committed by him. So far, the law has not caught up with him, and this has created an aura of untouchability and scares the hell out of people.

"Since I came to teach at the university, I had lived a rather-isolated life, for I did not know many people. My parents and siblings live in Canada. The community is very clannish, and if you do not know people, you are secluded from many social events. It was fine with me as I was able to concentrate on my career as a university lecturer. I kept writing on professional journals and traveled to different parts of Europe.

"On one occasion, the Independence Day of Pakistan, I was invited to a celebration organized by the community in collaboration with the embassy. The young man who invited me is a doctoral candidate at the university. He gave me the address and an invitation card. I had seen him before and had exchanged courtesies with him whenever we see each other in the campus. On the date and time of the celebration, I went to the site of the event. There were few hundred people already at the banquet hall. The celebration was opened with a speech by a 'community leader.' He gave a long-winded speech on the achievements of the nation since independence. For some odd reasons, he avoided the challenges and failures of successive governments, including the current, Musharraf's regime. A representative of the embassy also gave his speech. It was dull, boastful of the government that he represents. Kashmir and India figured prominent in the speech.

"I was already getting bored and ready to leave when the young man who invited me came with an individual who is tall and has a well-built frame dressed in the traditional attire of Pakistani men. 'Good evening, Professor,' he greeted me. 'Thank you for coming. I want to introduce you to an important person in our community. He really wanted to meet you because he respected your work of the university. This is Mansour...'he stammered without adding what he does and why he is important in the community. I gave my name, to which Mansour responded, 'Well, I know about you, and I am proud of your achievement at the university. People like you make all of us here very proud.' He flattered me. 'Thank you,' I said.

"I vaguely remembered his name, but for some unexplained reasons, he made me feel uncomfortable. Maybe it was his constant surveillance of the hall by gazing in all directions while talking. 'Mr. Mansour,' I interrupted him, 'it was nice meeting with you, but I have to leave now. I have an early morning commitment tomorrow.'

"'The celebration is only starting now, Professor. The banquet, music, and dance is about to open soon,' he said. 'I know,' I told him, 'but I have to go because I have to be at a meeting very early. I need enough sleep.'

"'Well, okay,' he conceded. And then he added, 'Maybe we will see each other soon.'

"'*Alhamdulillah*,' I said while walking toward the door. I left the hall with an unexplained but uneasy feeling. On the way home, so many questions came to my mind. Was the invitation a setup with Mansour and the young man? What is the reason Mansour wanted to meet me? And what does he do? Why didn't I ask him?

"Few days later, I had to go shopping to buy some spices and sweets from a small grocery store owned by a Pakistani man. I picked up the things I needed to purchase. At the counter, we exchanged greetings with the gentleman, and I asked him why I did not see him at the celebration. The gentleman said, 'Which celebration?' I gave the address. 'Oh! You went there,' he said with a voice that was clearly of a surprise. 'That is the one organized by Mansour. Professor, avoid that crowd. Mansour and his gangs are bad story,' he said. I told him I met Mansour. There was almost pity for me in his voice and gaze. 'Don't you know about the man?' he added. 'He is an unindicted murderer, a thief, and an outright criminal. Avoid him at any cost,' he advised me.

"After leaving the store, I was more gripped with apprehension as to why I was invited to the 'celebration.' What does Mansour and his group want from me? I was determined to avoid them and never to have any contact with them.

"Few uneventful days passed until the Friday after the celebration when I met the young doctoral candidate at the hallway to my office. I did not think it was by coincidence. 'Good afternoon, Professor!' he shouted. I thought of ignoring him, but there were several professors and students passing by it would create a scene. 'Good afternoon,' I responded. By then he had reached to where I was. Walking beside me, he said, 'Sorry you left early last week. It was more fun after the boring speeches. Mansour was very impressed with you. Since that day, he has been telling to all young women that they should follow your footsteps. You have become a role model.' Impatiently, I turned to the young man. 'I am busy. I do not have time for your nonsense, okay? Leave me alone.' Unperturbed, the young man responded, 'I am sorry. I did not want to make you angry. But before I leave, I want to tell you this message. Mansour wants to meet you for some consultation. Of course, he will pay.'

"'Tell Mr. Mansour I do not have time. I am way too overloaded for some time.'

"'Well,' said the young man, 'if I were you, I would not treat Mansour like that. Goodbye,' he said and left as fast as he had come. I was angry, worried, and afraid. What am I going to do? I asked myself. Report to the police? What is there to report? Or just ignore it. But how can one ignore a threat by a known outlaw?

"A couple of weeks later on a Monday morning while I was hurriedly walking into the campus office, four people emerged from a car parked on a side street. They were all dressed in a suit. The burly older man was dressed in a pink-striped suit and a tie. He waved at me and called, 'Good morning, Professor.' I immediately recognized the voice of Mansour. The three others dispersed themselves and stood at different corners as if standing on sentry. 'Good morning,' I responded rather timidly. 'What can I do for you, Mr. Mansour?' I asked, hoping to make the rendezvous as short as possible. Mansour had all figured it out. He was holding a folder on his hand, and he said, 'I have a business, and I need your expertise to make it more efficient and productive. I wish we could sit somewhere and show you the proposal. It will take only a minute. And I am ready to pay a fee for your professional work.' In hindsight, that was my biggest mistake—to allow him to make me look at the proposal. I should be honest I was intimidated by his show of force. I am a single woman who had few relatives and friends in London.

"Anyway, I allowed him to come into my office. What transpired in the office is something I was never prepared for. It scared the wit out of me. Mansour, as soon as he entered the office, closed the door and unbuttoned his coat. On his left side on a belt was a holster hanging with a handgun clearly visible. It was meant to be seen, to intimidate, maybe even to use against anyone who does not follow orders. He sat on a chair. I was behind my desk. Hesitantly, I asked him why he carries a gun. 'Oh, this,' he said in a pretentious jocular voice as he pulled the gun to show me. 'It is only for protection. London is a dangerous place,' he added. 'You should also carry, Professor, for your own protection. Maybe one day I will show you how to use it.' I immediately regretted asking him the question. 'Let us get to the business,' I asked him to end the meeting.

"'Professor,' he started, these are very sensitive documents. Once you have seen them, you have to promise me to keep them confidential—'

"'Mr. Mansour,' I interrupted, 'you are the one who came seeking my professional consultation. I did not solicit your business. Now it seems to me you are trying to put preconditions on how I conduct my business. I do not accept any preconditions from any, except those conditions that are delineated in my contract. I am sorry I am not willing to work for you. I am too busy already anyway.'

"'No! No!' he repeated. To my surprise, he emphatically said, 'The mere fact that we talked so far is an acceptance of the proposal, Madame Professor.' While standing, he pushed the folder toward me and said, 'Read the proposal. I will contact you in a few days. Remember what I said about confidentiality.' Before he left, he asked, 'Should I contact you at your home?'—and he recited my address and telephone number—'or here at the office?' I was so stunned I do not think I said anything. Just gazing and gasping like a deer pushed into a corner. He left the door slightly ajar. I was paralyzed by fear. The whole day, I could not function. I cancelled all my classes and meetings. For few days, I was even scared to touch the folder. It remained on my desk the way Mansour left it. I did not know what to do. Again, if I report it to law enforcement, I am as good as dead. The recital of my home address and the three bodyguards that escorted Mansour were clear message: 'I know where you live, and I have an army that will take care of you.' I seriously started thinking of moving back to Canada. But again, I was not sure what connections he had in Canada. I was concerned of putting my whole clan in jeopardy.

"After much fidgeting and hesitation, I opened the folder and started reading. There was nothing out of the ordinary, none of the things. I was expecting quotes from Quran or statements from Hadith. It was written by a person who had some knowledge of business organization, although rudimentary. It is seeking to find ways to expand the business by creating connectivity with people and business around the world. The use of modern technology to maximize productivity was what was sought in particular. In self-delusional moment, I thought I can give him a proposal or schematic plan so as to get him off my back. I started working on it. I drew charts, organizational structures, assets both human and technology, and the overall budget outlay it may require. Since I had worked on similar projects for other major products, it was not difficult. However, in the past, I knew the products and the profile of the consumers of the products. In Mansour's case, I had no clue of the products and consumers of the products. My work strictly was on the technical and managerial setting of the organization.

"Three weeks later, Mansour came to the office unannounced. This time, he was dressed casually, and there was no visible weapon of any sort. He had already made his point on the previous visit. He was polite. In fact, he was apologetic on how he behaved in our previous meeting, he said unconvincingly. 'How are you progressing with the project?' he asked. I answered, 'Mr. Mansour, I do not have all the information needed, like what products and where you want them distributed. I need to know them for me to give a fully developed plan.'

"'I understand, Professor. Let us go step by step. I want to know the nature of your preliminary proposal before I divulge the nature of my products and its consumers. That is why in our previous meeting, I insisted that everything should be kept confidential. I again reiterate how important that this transaction should remain secret.'

"'Okay,' I mumbled. I handed over the draft of the plan to Mansour. He read carefully, asking questions here and there. The man is smart. I give him that. He asked the right questions. At the end, he said he liked the draft. 'It may need some details obviously, but that is not your fault since I did not give you all the necessary information to have a more complete plan. On our next meeting, I will bring in writing all the products and the demographic profile of the people we want to influence,' he stated. 'I do not want to take any more of your time, but you will hear from me soon. Thank you.'

"Before leaving, he dropped a brown envelope on my desk and exited in a rush. I did not know what the content of the envelope was. But that was not what hovered in my mind at that instant. It was the phrase 'demographic profile we want to influence.' To my extra alert mind, the word 'influence' does not connote material product but ideology. Is he trying to reach people by use of modern technology to export his brand of Islamism? Later, I opened the envelope. It was stacked with about ten thousand pounds, crisp and well layered. I did not know what to do. Is it a setup? Buyout or professional payment? However, we have not so far agreed on fees and the schedule of payment."

The whole time the professor was recalling the process by which she was entangled with Mansour and his group, the officers of the Scotland Yard were listening with great interest and intent. Every word she spoke was transcribed on tape; she was aware of it. For the professor, confessing on her activities was a sort of atonement. The more she spoke, the more she felt relieved of the burden she carried for a long time. Once she met Mansour and she drafted his business plan, it was a slipping slope for her. Ultimately, she fell into an abyss where she could not draw herself out.

"Mansour came with the information he said he will bring the next time we met. It was a scant one-page idea on how to use modern technology in mobilizing and organizing people for action. The action was not specified. When I asked him about what 'action' is he talking about, he brushed it aside by saying, 'What I need from you, Professor, is to set up both the organization and technical infrastructure. I do not think it should matter whether I am selling barbecue sauce or an idea on how to live life. Be aware I have an IT expert in the US, especially recruited to help you on setting up the technical aspect of the infrastructure. I have already provided him your email address. His name is Ishmaelov. I hope you work together to expeditiously set up everything.'

"Ishmaelov emailed me introductory message few days later, the school he graduated from and some of the projects he was involved in after graduation. His special strength is in web design and Internet connectivity. He is fascinated on how the Internet, tweets, and other social media networks could be used to reach millions of people across continents. 'Our task should be to reach people in the most appealing way by social groups. In other words, we should categorize them by age, education, and profession. I hope, Professor, when you draft your plan, you would incorporate these suggestions. How do we reach the youth? The military, police, doctors, and other professionals? I pray we have a good working relationship.' That was the content of his message in summary.

"Ishmaelov was an expert in his field. My cooperative work with him has taught me a great lesson. I have learned how technology could enhance the developmental and managerial aspect of an organization. If it were not used for destructive ideological pursuit, all we have developed could be used as a master plan for any organization to develop. Once the infrastructure was established, the information that were input was a shock to me. It called for the youth for jihad against the West. In many ways, it was not blatant but yet dangerous. Each social group was addressed in different ways. The youth, especially the disaffected individuals, were told their problems were societal, and for them to remedy their problem, they have to reorganize society. Destroy and rebuild an Islamic way to create a just society on earth, it demanded. To make matters worse, it was presented as a war between the West and Islam. The West had waged wars against Islam from the outset of Islamic Umma to present without letup the crusades and the destruction of Islamic civilization in the Iberian Peninsula with Alhambra as its center. And the modern wars in Palestine, Iraq, and Afghanistan are brought up as historic evidence. The Islamic Republic of Iran is put under siege by the infidels to further hamper or destroy Islam, fulfilling its mission of creating Allah's will on earth. The design of the message was to attract Western-born Moslems to attack Western institutions. The targets were military, financial, communications, transport, and power installations. The plan is to paralyze Western societies through coordinated attacks.

"The other aspect of the message was to identify individuals that have worked against Islam. Especially Moslems who had criticized against the aims of the organization. They could be professionals, intellectuals, writers, and business people. These group of people were looked with vehement hatred. They were targeted to be eliminated. Death was the dispensation to be given to these group of people because they are traitors to their faith. The shrill nature of the message scared me. But I thought it was extreme and full of absurdities I convinced myself nobody is to rally behind it. The first few weeks, there were no responses from a reader, even though there were substantial visitors to the websites. It looked my assumption was confirmed that people will be curious, but the call for action will be ignored. The main message was action, vengeance against Western enemy. At this stage, the alarm bell was ringing in my head, but still I considered the whole effort as posturing without any reason to be fearful. But as time went by, I started to notice a different kind of message—vicious, with people volunteering to be an army of Islam to fight America, Britain, and the rest of Western Europe. These are people who have been born in the West, with pluralistic culture and tolerance for religious diversity. I was shocked, to say the least. Mansour and Ishmaelov did not seem to be surprised at all. It was as if they expected it all along.

"They were methodical, using the organizational structure I helped them plan. They organized youth group and groups of other social classes. The youth were the most responsive, and many were recruited. College educated from solid middle-class backgrounds are among the recruits. Ahmed Gillani was among the first recruits. He was born and raised in England. He attended the best schools and graduated among the top in his class. After college, he moved to Canada and slipped through the border into the USA. He did not seek employment. He became a full-time recruiter for the organization. Among his recruits was Kapoor Shah, another brilliant engineering graduate and dedicated member of the organization. The two became the core leaders of the group in the US. Their mission was to recruit youth, preferably American-born Moslems or Americans converted to Islam. Once the young people are sufficiently indoctrinated, they were to be assigned for a 'mission' to accomplish—assassination of 'enemies of Islam' and destruction of installations that will affect the smooth functioning of society. Creating mayhem was seen as tactical way of winning over the 'enemy.'" Thus, the investigation by Scotland Yard toward the professor's involvement was finalized. Scotland Yard transmitted all the gathered information to the FBI.

*****

To prepare themselves for the task, Ahmed Gillani and Kapoor Shah were involved in a rigorous physical training. Every morning before dawn, they ran around a city park before any of the regulars. In a local gym, they did all kinds of physical training. Target shooting was done at a long-abandoned quarry pit. It was outside a city where few people visit. A retired US Army officer was their instructor for target shooting. He was licensed and legal, according to the county and state authorities. Both men took the physical and shooting training very seriously. There was no day when they missed the scheduled training program.

Part of their duty was to know their environment thoroughly. Neighborhood by neighborhood, they explored to gather information where the police station was located. The demographic makeup, ethnic and economic, and major intersections were also studied. The idea was to know as much as possible the city for possible escape routes and hideaways. The density of traffic at different times of the day was also noted for some particular streets. The aim was to train gun-carrying religious ideologues. The selection of targets was left freelance. It could be from a casual conversation among friends and family members. Most of the individuals selected for elimination had been people who, for some reason, were either opposed to radical Islam or people who, by their lifestyle, had been declared apostates and bad example for other Moslems. It was either to preempt or destroy real antagonists for aims which radicals stood for. The dispensation of the punishment was decided by local leaders. To avoid apprehension of the chain of leaders, each cell or local organization was designed to operate autonomously. It raised funds through solicitation or strong arm, which meant part of the funds was sent to a central organization. But in practice since the local groups did not raise sufficient funds, the central groups had to subsidize them. Money had never been an issue. They had enough of it. All the same, they lived frugally.

The gun-toting newly minted radicals were anxious to be in action. Individual targets were selected. All the minutiae of their habits were thoroughly studied. The beautiful and unsuspecting Amina was among the targets. She was an easy prey. Most of the time, she walked to different places alone—shopping, walking in the parks, and coming and going to work. She had no reason to fear of any danger, except for the occasional random danger of living in a big city. Her routes were populated with people at all times. That had given her a sense of safety. There was no reason for her to take extra precaution. There were few times her phone rang with someone ranting some undecipherable language. She dismissed them as nuisance. What else could she think? She was respected and loved by all people who met her, at work or social occasions. She held malice toward none. In the warped mind of the radical Islamists, being a good, decent person was inconsequential. All those who did not follow their religious script were condemnable. Even consorting with people of a different religion could be used to declare fatwa against a person.

The killers did not Come at a time when there was a rush of people in the morning but rather conveniently chose their time during a lull time when security was less alert because people's movement in and out of the building was relatively low. They made themselves blend with the people who lived in the building, wearing casual and yet designer clothing and holding a laptop in a case. Within the bag was the hunter's knife, sharpened and ready for an expeditious kill. They were two, seemingly talking about an issue of gravity when they passed the security checkpoint. The security unsuspiciously buzzed them in. Their stride to the apartment was purposeful. There was no hesitation, no stumbling, and no visible emotion on their faces. There was the confidence bestowed upon them by their religion and God. It was the fulfillment of their scriptural understanding. All blasphemers and apostates and those who brought dishonor to Islam and family and tribe should be punished.

A businessman who vociferously and categorically condemned al-Qaida and its terrorist activities was gunned down in his office. The talented, intellectual writer, Hassen Ali, was found decapitated in his apartment in the city. His crime was for advocating that Islam needed reform, especially for alluding that Quran was outdated and should not be followed literally.

It was Amina's cold-blooded murder that had awakened the usually silently suffering moderate Moslems. It galvanized them to action. The press and law enforcement officers were alerted. The victim's friends acted as catalysts by making sure no resources were spared from apprehending the culprits and bringing them to justice. From the outset, people understood the existence of underground groups of radicals spread within the US and abroad.

It had been a few months since Ahmed Gillani, Kapoor Shah, and Amin had been arrested. Bail had been denied for all three. The prosecutors, under the able leadership of the US attorney, had been building the case against them. A dossier of evidence had been collected. Motive and means had been established. The only thing that they wanted to unravel was the network of the people involved. And that was why it took time.

As all cases ultimately had to be decided in the court of law, so was the case of the three. The court date was set for midsummer. Families were engaged in many activities with children being out of school. Even people who did not have children were busy enjoying the seasonal activities that were not possible in winter. It was presumed that the case would attract less attention than otherwise. In the usual theatrics of court, both attorneys for the defendants and the prosecutors were ready to argue why their case should win. Outside the court, to win the war of public opinion, the attorneys, in particular that of the defendants, had been portraying their clients as pious intellectuals who had done nothing wrong, except being victimized by zealot government agents.

The line had been drawn. Each side was ready to use all means to win. There was so much at stake. For the government to lose a case against the three would mean a real setback on bringing the radical movement to a halt. A win for the radical jihadists would embolden them and accelerate their recruiting and the fight against the "infidel" world. The court case was started with that backdrop. On both sides, first-rate attorneys were aligned with long experience on myriad cases. They had either defended or prosecuted criminals of all ilk and colors.

On midsummer, June 25, the court was in session to hear the opening argument by the attorneys. The jury had been impaneled, and the judge had ensconced in his chair to officiate the drama which had an international implication. Outside the courtroom, several reporters and TV cameras and satellite transmitters were waiting for the actors to voice through them. The security was very tight with plainclothes officers and uniformed officers standing on several corners.

Suddenly, there was a rush by the media people, some stretching their microphones toward a moving group of people. The prisoners with their guards had arrived on special reinforced prison van. They were handcuffed and surrounded by sheriff officers.

In a sort of defiant sound, one of the prisoners chanted, "Allah Akbar!" It was the sound of Ahmed Gillani, defiant to the end.

The two other prisoners did not make any noise as they walked with their heads bent, seemingly oblivious to the hubbub of the crowd surrounding them. The attorneys were not giving interviews to the media. The media had to report only that they had witnessed the passing of the accused in front of them to the courtroom. It was reported, however, by some with great embellishment to make it look as if they had seen and heard some worthwhile event.

Inside the courtroom, the defendants were led to their side of the seating.

As soon as all were seated in their proper places, the judge called the court to order. He then asked the defendants one by one how they would plead their case, guilty or not guilty.

It started with Ahmed Gillani; he chose to ignore the judge's question. In an act of defiance, he avoided to look at the judge's direction by turning his face backward. The judge warned Gillani that he might be held in contempt of court. "Contempt! Haha!" Gillani responded.

The judge, with a stern voice, warned Gillani that he was in a court of law. "You are an intelligent man. I do expect you to behave appropriately. The consequences of your behaving otherwise would result in your imprisonment."

Ahmed Gillani remained defiantly incorrigible. The judge ordered the bailiffs to take him and slapped him with thirty days in jail. That did not seem to faze Gillani from the gestures of defiance he exhibited as he was being taken out of the courtroom.

Both Amin and Shah pleaded not guilty with their attorneys on their side. The judge, after hearing the pleas of the two, decided the next court date would be some three months later. The prisoners were denied bail and were taken back to their cells to brood over their fate in their solitary cells. Amin was the most pitiful looking. His face was sapped of any energy he looked like a living ghost. Kapoor Shah looked like a person with some conviction left in him.

Before inviting the lawyers to give the opening statement, the judge gave a cautionary remark to the jury that what the lawyers said in the opening statement was not evidence but an overview of what evidence they might bring during the course of the trial.

As protocol demanded, the prosecutor was the first to give the opening statement.

"Mr. Harvey, if you are ready, you may proceed," the judge advised.

"Thank you, Your Honor," Mr. Harvey said. Facing the jurors, he started, "Good morning, ladies and gentlemen. As the court has informed you, I am going to address you in what we call the opening statement. It is a bird's-eye view of what the evidence of the case will be. In any trial, since the case may not necessarily be presented in a logical or chronological sequence of events, the opening statement is to give you some kind of overall picture to follow the evidence that may come in bits and pieces.

"Now the case that you are sworn to give judgment to is serious. It is a case of murder and conspiracy to commit murder. The evidence will show that the accused had committed the murder of a young lady, Ms. Amina Mohamed Nur, and the attempt to commit murder against Mr. Abdul. The evidence will also show that Mr. Amin Mohamed Nur had conspired against the individuals and to commit further terrorist acts in the US."

The prosecutor continued with grave seriousness and solemnity of the occasion to build the case against the accused. He intimated about the motive and evidence that brought the conspirators to the court of law. He reminded the jurors of the importance of the duty to which they were entrusted not only for the sake of justice on behalf of the victims but also for the nation against terrorism. "Thank you," he concluded.

The judge asked the defendant's attorney to give his opening statement.

Mr. Witt thanked the judge and started his opening statement. The strategy of Amin's lawyer's opening statement was to paint his client as a young man who came under the influence of well-trained cadres of jihadists, alienating him from his family and friends and coercing him to commit crimes, for which he was deeply remorseful. Here was the highlight of the statement.

"The young man in front of you is a mere twenty-seven years old. In the short twenty-seven years, he had seen so many things in his life which most of us may never experience in our lifetime. He was born in a war-torn country where many young people were forcibly recruited to fight one side or another. It was a bloody war that had affected the whole population. Amin had seen random killings in the streets of his hometown by government agents. Among the dead were neighbors, friends, and kith and kins.

"His father, a respected businessman and devout family man, had been a victim to the regime's repression. He was taken prisoner on suspicion of supporting antigovernment rebels. He was among the fortunate few to come out alive from prison. Because he was afraid the next time he may not be so lucky, he fled from his country with his family in tow. It was a difficult journey. The experience had left a very young Amin very much affected. Abruptly, he left his friends, relatives, and neighbors and came to a country and culture alien to him. The comfort of familiarity had been lost to him. The readjustment was harder to him than any other members of his family.

"Soon, he started to withdraw from the family activities that he enthusiastically participated in his younger age. Unfortunately, at this time, he started to befriend individuals who prey on young people in a state of confusion. They used religion and social atmosphere to create a semblance of spiritual and life's peace. Young Amin immersed into the life of the new friends. Their agenda was to recruit jihadists. For the young impressionable mind, it was seductive. Peace, harmony, and unbelievable bliss in the afterlife was promised with the certainty of messianic message. He bought the whole concept lock, stock, and barrel.

"The drifting away from the family was completed when he migrated to Pakistan without even telling his parents. He just disappeared. Nobody knew where he was, even if he was alive. The next time he surfaced, at least to his family, is when he was apprehended in committing a crime that he regrettably was involved.

"Amin is remorseful for the crime that he committed as part of a fanatical group. He is ready to accept his punishment whatever justice wills. You, the jury, have unenviable position to take a measure of the crime and the accused. In this case, the accused is a victim too. His vulnerability, having fallen into the hands of jihadist terrorists. Once you have fallen into their clutches, there is no way out alive. You will hear from the accused himself how he was coerced to commit heinous crime with a gun pointed at him. If there was any wavering or any suspicion of absconding the group, he was threatened with bodily harm and had witnessed others being executed for opposing the bloody mission of the jihadists.

"So today, Amin is not here to deny facts or minimize the heinous crime committed for which he was a party. He has repeatedly expressed his heartfelt remorse. What I am pleading on his behalf is for you to understand the whole picture of the tragedy. There are many victims here. Tragically, some have lost their lives. No one is here to minimize the loss for the families and friends and the anguish and the sadness that had befallen them. All of us here, including the accused, wish it never happened. Our wishes can never reverse it. We only pray that God would give strength and solace to the families. Thank you for listening." Thus, the defendant's attorney concluded his opening statement.

*****

A month after he cooled his heels in a cool, darkened cell, Ahmed Gillani pleaded not guilty with no show of any of the bravado he showed in his last court appearance.

The court date arrived in August about the end of the month. Ahmed Gillani was the first to appear in front of the judge. He had already rejected any representation by lawyers. He was to represent himself against the strong advice of the judge.

Here was the opening statement of Ahmed Gillani. Facing the jury and the judge, he started by saying, "*Bismillah ir-rahman ir-rahim*. Good morning to you all. I am not here to defend myself or my brothers in Islam. There is nothing to defend. We are here being persecuted by a government and a court that should not have any prosecutorial right over us. I will explain. But I will ask your patience and open-mindedness. For too long, you have been indoctrinated by a system that do not have legal mandate in the eyes of God. It will need your extraordinary willingness to listen to what I say, and then you will reach the conclusion—it is the US government that should be brought to court and not Moslems like us who were doing our duty of Dawa, the teaching of the true religion, Islam.

"Since the time of our prophet—peace be upon him—the forces of evil have tried to destroy Islam. There were unceasing campaigns, mostly from the West, to stop and eliminate the true religion. Its followers had been persecuted mercilessly. History is replete with the struggle between good and evil, and all Moslems are called by God to fight on the side of good by all means necessary. It is a call to rid the evil and the misguided way of life. Each one of us is a *mujahid*, God's soldier. We do what we do to fulfill God's will, to please him, if you will. God alone has sovereignty, and his laws should rule the world as written in the Quran and Hadith. The only government that is mandated by God is the one that applies the sharia laws. Negating the will of God, taking the sovereignty from God to man, is an affront to God. As Moslems, this is unacceptable to all God-fearing people. Jesus Christ was a good Moslem. He defied the unjust laws of Caesar. He had put his life in danger for the sake of truth. All good people have done that throughout history. All good people are followers of Islam. For 'Islam' essentially means to submit to the will of God. Tawhid, as stated in the shahada, teaches us that there is only one God, and he has no partners. Men can't be his partners and replace his laws with their own.

"To Moslems, as Fathi Yakan has written in his treatise so many years ago, Islamic teachings and rules are comprehensive and designed by Allah to govern the affairs of man at all levels of community, from family to the whole of human race. Islam alone can provide the power for Moslems to liberate oppressed people from the control of those who worship the false gods of modernist and postmodernist cultures. The adoption and adaptation of capitalist, socialist, communist, or other man-made systems, either in whole or in part, constitutes a denial of Islam and disbelief in Allah the lord of the worlds. Moslems in an Islamic movement are true servants of Allah, and their obedience is only to Allah, the Almighty in all matters of life. It encompasses not only religious affairs but also worldly affairs. This is because Islam teaches us followers there is no segregation or separation between religion and worldly affairs. The servitude of man means that he must reject all man-made philosophies and systems that, by nature, lead mankind to submit to the false gods of materialism."

As Gillani continued his rambling discourse, the audience in the courtroom, jury, judge, attorneys, and the few observers in the room were visibly confused. They seemed to say and were later confirmed by remarks of some of them, "Is he proselytizing his religious beliefs or defending against the crime he and his partners are accused of?" Since no word was uttered by him on the murder and attempted murder for which they were accused, it was believed that he, in particular, was ready for "martyrdom." Or was it a brilliant tactical decision to get at least some dissenting jury members that the court would have to declare mistrial? Ahmed Gillani and his friends were aware that the government had enough evidence to find them guilty. Maybe Gillani chose not to defend on the case, understanding the futility of the situation, and instead chose to make a bigger case on the underlying reason why they were involved in the crimes for which they were accused.

Even though his rambling discourse seemed disjointed, Gillani, at the end of his opening speech, gave a summary of his thought: "The court has no judicial right to try us as it is not mandated by God's law, the sharia." They were not criminals but "an army of god" jihadists to fulfill the will of God which was to rid evil and bring virtue to humanity. "Since Islam is the only true religion, all other beliefs are idolatry, and followers of falsehood with whatever means should be brought to the right path. *Alhamdulillah*," he concluded.

As Gillani sat by his assigned chair, the judge, with his glasses down closer to the tip of his nose and his head bent to look at the next defendant with his naked eyes, started to order Shah's attorney to give an opening statement.

A loud noise disrupting the quiet that prevailed came from the defendant's side. Both Gillani and Shah started to chant, "Allah Akbar! Allah Akbar!" The judge ordered for order by gaveling several times. However, the defendants continued to chant both in English and Arabic, "God is great! Allah Akbar!"

When it was clear they were not to stop, the judge ordered the bailiffs to take them out of his courtroom and decided to continue the trial without their presence.

Amin was seated quietly with his head bent and his countenance both sad and pensive.

Amin, in a dark prison cell, was haunted by the death of his father. At night, the image of his father in a darkened camouflage would visit him to question him why he had been betrayed by him. It was not the kindly father he had known all his life. The ghost of his father was menacing, with claws on both hands like that of a wildcat, ready to mince him to pieces. Amin was terrified by the new image. He cried for forgiveness, but it was not a forgiving father that visited him in the dark cell in seclusion. The wind that accompanied the father was that of a howling storm with the intensity to match, strong to sweep him into the abyss. Amin pleadingly stretched his arms toward his father. The father wanted none of it. Instead, he scolded his son, "You murderer, do not touch my body." Amin, more scared by the stranger figure, coiled and ran into the corner of the room. The strong wind that followed the ghost picked him up from the ground and swirled him to the ceiling of the room and dropped him to the ground. At the end of the nightmare, Amin found himself on the floor, soaked in his nightmarish sweat. The experience was almost real it tortured him during the day.

Amin tried to pray to the God on whose service he had committed the murderous crime. But even his god had betrayed him. He could not make sense of his prayer. Several times, he repeated, "Allah Illalah Mohamed…" He could not even finish the prayer. His being rejected by all became more devastating to him. Amin feared the darkness that the night would bring.

His days were no better. The ghost of his father had become his constant companion, a torturer. It came in different shapes and creatures, one more menacing than the other. It had come as a bird, a hawk, suspending him in the air and throwing him into a well so deep that he couldn't crawl out. Only, the hawk would pick him up to further torture him. He woke up with body shaking and sweating profusely.

He had dreams of falling toward hell with flame engulfing him and screams of people coming from every direction. He was afraid to close his eyes, lest his torturers would visit him in a form that he couldn't anticipate.

His wakefulness couldn't deliver him any relief. The eyes of his dying sister looked at him like that of an owl with hatred and derision. She taunted him as a coward and crazed sheik. When the image of Amina appeared in his nightmarish memory, he tried to block his mind, but to no avail. Her image was too powerful. Her image couldn't be sated. He tried to beg her for mercy.

Neither the sunshine of the day nor the darkness of the night could protect him from the taunting and torture of his conscience.

He seldom saw the image of his mother, Fowzia. When he did, it was an image of a prematurely aged woman huddled in a corner. She did not curse or threaten. But in her quiet demeanor, she seemed to say, "How could the son who was born from my womb be so cruel and murderous? Was there any ancestral curse on me that had not been soothed with proper sacrifice to have met these tragedies?"

Wailing Voices

The town clung on a side of a mountain. It had two rivers flowing throughout the year. During the summer season, the water level only covered the foot, the washed-up rocks and gravels clearly visible. During rainy season between July and September, all the rain that fell on the surrounding area tumbled down to the rivers, carrying fallen trees and the top-soil of the mountains, evermore denuding it of the vegetation.

Those of us who were born and raised in the area over the years had observed the change of the topography of the mountains. The once-thick forest was a domain to so many predators, like hyenas, wolves, and, some said, lions. None of us dared to climb the mountain. The big trees had been felled by villagers for firewood and the construction of their abodes. The smaller trees were uprooted by the heavy downpours and carried into the rivers. There were no efforts to stem the erosion of the land; the land had become barren with rocks jutted like misaligned teeth.

My name is Matheos Haile. I was born in 1983. Growing up, I had a good life with many friends.

Abiy was my closest friend. Our parents were good friends too. Only on a few occasions, we missed seeing each other. Every day we spent time together. Meals we ate at either of our houses after spying whose mother had prepared our favorite meal.

On weekends, we were inseparable from sunrise to sunset. We would play on the outside, soiling our bodies and clothes. Football was our favorite sport; we played on the grassy field adjacent to St. Gabriel Church. Animals grazed on the field. Every time we wanted to play, we had to drive them out, upsetting the herders. The area to where we pushed the animals was wooded. With eucalyptus trees and pine trees, it was difficult for the herders to watch the cattle from afar.

There were only two schools, both to eighth grade level. One was public ran; the other was ran by missionaries. In the public school, there were about two hundred students on all levels. We attended the public school. It was close to our neighborhood. Every morning, Abiy and I, tucked with our school-bags, would walk to the school. Even at a young age, there was no need for chaperone. The idea of any-one hurting a child never crossed the mind of the community. Adults cared for young children as their own. They would look for their safety, and when a child misbehaved, they would not hesitate to repri-mand the youth. The community was a large family for a child.

The years between 1983 and 1998 of my child-hood, for the most part, were carefree and uneventful. Nothing seemed to premonish what was to come. That would change the course of our family and tens of thousands of others. We were uprooted and deported to Eritrea.

I am recounting of our family's deportation in an unlikely place of Kenya. After fleeing from Eritrea, I ended up as a refugee in Kenya. In Kenya, I met my childhood friend Abiy, who had also fled from Ethiopia and became a refugee. What a coincidence. We were meant to be together. It was the work of the god of love. Serendipitously, we met at a refugee registration camp and jumped to hug each other. Laded with emotions, our faces were covered with tears. We started to look at each other head to foot to make sure we were not dreaming. We had so much to talk, so much catching up to do, yet we were both oddly quiet, mulling in our minds the events of our sudden separation.

Again, Abiy took the first step to thaw our frozen situation. He recalled some old friends and gave an account of their lives. Tedros, or Ted as we lovingly called him, was in Kenya too, he stated. "And he has been here for almost two years."

Ted was our mutual friend. I was excited. Part of my childhood was being recovered, albeit in another country. "Do you know where he lives?" I asked.

"Certainly. We can go there now if you don't have any other plan."

"Plan? Are you kidding?" I responded. "What plan can a refugee have other than the struggle of day-to-day life? Take me now," I implored. We walked sprightly with urgency.

On the way to meet Ted, we started to open up the events that led to our current situation. I started that the last five years were the most trying times in my life.

*****

In July 1999 early morning, a knock that almost broke the door of our house woke us up. My father jumped off his bed, clad on his pajamas and slippers, and opened the door after inquiring who was knocking. He was ordered to open the door immediately by a voice familiar to us all. It was a Tigray People's Liberation Front cadre by the name of Mahdere, who had been to our house on many occasions soliciting funds for this or that charity in Tigray.

As ordered, my father opened the door and found himself surrounded by several uniformed officers. Perplexed by the show of force, he asked meekly, "What is going on? Is anything wrong?"

Mahdere rudely pushed my father and ordered everyone out. My mother by then was dressed in her daily garb and praying to the Virgin Mary and an array of angels. My father tried to talk to Mahdere and elicit his help as an acquaintance for some time. The cadre was in no mood to hear the pleas of anyone. He opened the doors of every room and was taking stock of what or who was in there. Finally, he ordered us to pack our belonging as we were to be deported out of the country.

The news of a group of security officers surrounding our home circulated in our neighborhood. Many people came out to register the event in their minds. Most of the people were baffled by the whole situation. They did not have any clue on what to do.

Mr. Dereje and his wife, Tirunesh, with their son, Abiy, and their daughter, Amsal, came right to the front door of our house, where the security officers stood. Our family was separated from them by the line of officers.

Mr. Dereje asked my father, "What is going on, Haile?"

"Well," said my father, "Mahdere is kicking us off our house and deporting us from the country."

"Incredible!" was the word that came out of Mr. Dereje. "Mahdere, who just came to this part of the country only the last few years, had the temerity to deport a family who had lived here for half a century and who had helped to build the church and school and created jobs in our community. This travesty is not going to happen," he stated.

Soon, Aba Berhanemeskel, the spiritual leader of our family, arrived. He drew out his brass-made cross from the side pocket of his shirt and commanded, in the name of Jesus Christ, Mahdere and the officers to refrain from deporting the God-fearing Christian family.

Mahdere realized he was in a jam. If he used force, important members of the community might revolt, and his relation might sour, making his work untenable. But he was determined to deport the family. He made a tactical withdrawal by ordering the officers to leave the place. However, he emphatically told my father the deportation was inevitable. He left the premise.

Aba and Mr. Dereje were relieved, believing that they forced Mahdere to reconsider and abandon the decision.

My father though understood that the victory was temporary. He thanked everyone, especially our spiritual leader and dearest friend Mr. Dereje with his wife Tirunesh and his children, for their support. "We are going to be deported soon as Mahdere has told me in Tigrinya before he left. I never thought that this day will come. It was always my hope that my wife and I will get old here and our children will grow up to be men and women and start a family from here among you all who had been very kind and accepted us as one of you. You have joined in my happy days, and you have supported me in my bereavement when I lost some dearest members of my family. Times have changed. There is going to be a lot of challenges to all of us. But I tell you, all of us will be okay. Our loving God and the spirits of our ancestors will protect us. I don't know when we will be deported. To some of you, we may not have a chance to say goodbye. I want to tell you now I will never forget you. And I hope, under better circumstances, we may meet again. God be with you."

Mr. Dereje impatiently waited for Haile, my dad, to finish his farewell speech and said, "What a foolish talk, Haile. You are not going to go from here. This community will make sure that nobody touches you. If Mahdere is to deport you, then he should deport us from wherever we came from. My wife and I are from Gojam. Adane is from Wollo. And here, Tumsa is from Arsi. Let them send us to where we came from. He is from Tigray. He had only been here less than five years."

After a while, people started to disperse to do the work they had suspended. Tirunesh and Mr. Dereje sat in the verandah and started talking with Aba Berhanemeskel and my parents. We children all went to the backyard to play. Each of us though was burdened by the event that just happened.

My father knew our deportation was inevitable. When his business license was revoked, it became certain. He was getting ready for the day the last knock at our door would come. He drafted a contract giving Mr. Dereje the power of attorney to be responsible for all the assets to be left—our residence with the furniture, the commercial property where the business was located, and an automobile—without consultation with Mr. Dereje. He made sure that the witnesses had signed the transfer of power of attorney. Among them was the most respected clergy, Aba Berhanemeskel.

Few days later, there was a celebration of St. Gabriel's Day. All the adherents of the Orthodox Tewahedo Christianity in the area congregated to pray and throw a feast. Mr. Dereje and my father were among the elders who organized all the festivities for more than three decades. As usual, they worked very hard to make this year's celebration to be a success. It was very hard on my father, knowing this might be his last participation in the occasion.

In late afternoon when all the celebrants went home and all equipment was moved to their proper places, Mr. Dereje and my father sat to just relax.

"Dereje," my father started, "I am going to ask you one last favor, and I hope you will not protest at all."

"What is that, Haile? If it is within my means, you do not have to worry. I would gladly do it."

At that moment, my father pulled out a paper and handed it to Mr. Dereje.

Mr. Dereje looked at it. He wore his glasses and read it attentively. "What a nonsense, Haile. Mahdere is not going to deport you." He tried to give the paper back to my father.

"In the name of St. Gabriel, please accept my request," my father pleaded. "I have no one to ask, except you. I know it is a heavy responsibility that I am putting on you. But I do not have a choice. I am doing this, if we are deported, to have somebody that I trust and respect to take care of my interest. Only if we are deported."

Mr. Dereje relented by saying, "I will keep the documents, but it is unnecessary as you will not be deported."

Few days later by midmorning, a security offi-cer in a civilian garb came to our home. He ordered my father to the kebele police station. At the station, my father was detained, and he was informed that we were going to be deported on the same day. He was escorted with three officers back to our home where everyone was loaded on a police van with a few luggage that were already packed. It was done surreptitiously with none of our neighbors noticing. The children, three of us, were confused. Only my mother started crying. My sisters, who were nine and ten years old, joined her.

My father reprimanded my mother. "What is the matter with you, woman? Are you not going to the land of your ancestors? Stop crying," he thundered.

Soon, everyone was quiet. The van never stopped until we reached the capital city, Addis Ababa. We were taken to a place where all to be deported were deposited.

The buses to transport us were lined up just outside the camp. The ground was muddy, but our minders never cared about our luggage. Some were dragged, soiling our clothes.

After a chaotic and abusive loading process, the buses started driving northward. We had no idea which route the buses would go, the Gojjam-Gonder Road or Wollo-Tigray route. A few kilometers on our way, it was clear the bus was driving north to the Eritrean border via Tigray. I was trying to observe the houses, trees, and faces of people on the streets. The people seemed oblivious to what was happening on the crowded buses that passed close by them. I was expecting people to show some expression of sadness, anger, and outrage. Instead, people were walking, oblivious to the anxiety of people so precipitously thrown out of their homes. I knew deep in my heart though that my friend Abiy and the beautiful Amsal with the rest of the family were crying over our departure. I should mention I had a crush on Amsal, and I always suspected she liked me too. My dream had been, when I grow up, to get married to her.

The buses were traveling slowly, passing villages and small towns. As it was raining, not too many people were outside. The deportees in the bus were mostly quiet. Few were trying to cheer up the crowd; I am not sure if they were successful. People were overwhelmed by what had befallen them. The young people, sensing their parents' anxiety, were more subdued. The armed military guards escorting the deportees on the bus were also quiet. They did not seem to be proud of what they were doing, at least in our bus.

*****

This was my second long distance trip on a bus. The first time, I remember, was when I was about ten years old when Abiy and I traveled with our fathers to Debre Libanos to partake in the annual celebration of St. Tekle Haymanot at the monastery built bearing his name. Both of our parents adopted St. Tekle Haymanot as their patron saint. Our trip then was full of joy. Abiy and I felt very privileged to go on the trip with our fathers. We felt we were treated as adults. Most of the passengers were religious pilgrims. Halfway along the trip when the sun was at its peak, bright and hot, the half-asleep passengers were fully awakened. Mr. Dereje and my father started to sing spiritual songs, and soon, some of the pilgrims joined them. It was exhilarating to see elderly and middle-aged men to sing with such emotion and energy. The monastery was located in a valley nestled between two mountains. The road that led to the church was steep, and drivers had to negotiate it carefully.

The legend is that St. Tekle Haymanot, a devout monk, stood on the side of the mountain for many years on one leg. To the adherents of the Orthodox Tewahedo Christian church, he is a symbol of piety and perseverance. He is one of the most important patron saints to Ethiopian Tewahedo followers. Throughout the country, there are many churches that bear his name but none as important as the one at Debre Libanos.

As we descended the mountain, the driver was pointing at different sites—the burial ground of notables and also the alleged mountainside where St. Tekle Haymanot stood for many years. When we heard the story, we were in awe that a person so dedicated could stand on a spot on one leg for so long. We were told the miracle happened because the angels were supporting him as crutches. As we reached the church, we disembarked from the bus and headed to the church. A humanity of pilgrims had already assembled—young and old, men and women of all social strata, and from panhandlers to people who gave alms.

The church was full with believers to the brim. There was no way for us to get inside the church. We had to settle outside the church. We dropped our bags that carried food supplies, sparkling water, and some extra clothing. Our fathers spread a garment on the ground and started praying by prostrating, facing the church. We followed their every movement and prayed Our Father In Heaven.

We had not eaten any food as true believers should not eat any food before church services. Abiy and I were very hungry. I prayed to St. Tekle Haymanot to give me strength, as he was supported by the angels.

After almost two hours of praying, I confided to Abiy, "I can't do it anymore. I am hungry and tired." And so was he, he said. "Let us get some biscuits and juice," I suggested.

The problem was the bags were right by the side of our parents. I tried to pull the bag toward us. To our relief, both our parents, almost at the same time, asked us if we were hungry and tired. We said yes.

"Go ahead take what you need and eat under a shade away from people. Make sure you meet us by the bus later on," they advised.

Happily, we took the biscuits, bread, and juices. We covered them under our jackets and sat on a secluded mountainside to eat. We thanked the saint for listening to our prayers. After we ate our food, we decided to explore the area on our own. The huge perimeter of the church was encircled by small houses of the monks, priests, and functionaries at the monastery. The church was relatively new, built by the late emperor Haile Selassie's financial contribution; it supplanted an old church. The area was a topographer's delight. The mountain range, divided by a deep valley and river at the bottom of the gorges, was a stunning view. The escarpment formed by a millennium of erosion had exposed the rocky cliffs that could challenge a mountaineer. Abiy and I decided to sit and enjoy the cathedrals of cliffs that nature had built. It was a view that could inspire the uninspired.

When the pilgrimage concluded, we headed back to our homes. One of the things I noticed was that the two parents had formed a close friendship owing to their similar upbringing. My father grew up in a very religious family, his father and so many of his forbears being priests in their ancestral village. He was trained as a deacon on his way to becoming a priest. Mr. Dereje was also born to a priest father and chief priest grandfather, and he served as a deacon in his youth. Both of them left priesthood by influences that I might explore subsequently.

*****

The subdued deportees' trip had continued nonstop for over five hours. Young children whose mothers were holding them were crying due to exhaustion and long restraint. The driver of the bus, a sturdy young man in his midthirties, was quiet all along, except for a few exchanges with the guard seated close by him. All of a sudden, the bus was stopped in an open space. The guard ordered us to get off the bus to stretch and relieve ourselves. One by one, on both sides of the bus, we got out and looked for bushes and other forms of shades to get privacy as we relieved ourselves.

Twenty minutes later, we were ordered back into the bus. The passengers, for reasons unknown to me, started to talk with each other in a hushed voice, each explaining the circumstances under which they were being deported. Everyone had a different story to tell. Some were taken from their home early morning; others were taken from workplaces without warning and never given time to bid farewell to their loved ones. Many people had no luggage and had only a few change in their pocket.

There was a graceful gentleman; he was a retiree from the Ethiopian army. "I have served in the Ethiopian army for thirty-two years," he said. "I have served Ethiopia, protecting the country along the Somali border. I have led a battalion during the Somali invasion and paid sacrifice for my country. Now the new Ethiopian overlords have declared me as an enemy of Ethiopia, unworthy to live in the country." He was completely confounded by the deportation of him and so many of his friends who were loyal Ethiopians. "What are we going to tell

Eritreans now? Are we going to confess that we were against their independence struggle?"

The bus continued its travel without incident, avoiding stoppage at cities and towns. We had crossed the border of Shoa and entered the Wollo region after driving for almost six hours. The intermittent rain had made driving slow, and the quiet but attentive driver had been very cautious. We passed the market town of Kamisee where people from all the surrounding villages and merchants from as far as fifty kilometers would meet and purchase wares and farm products. On this day, people in the hundreds had crowded the side of the main street, and some nonchalantly stood in the middle of the street. Donkeys, mules, pickup trucks, long-haul trucks, and several minibuses were also on both sides of the street. The bus driver was driving at a snail's pace, constantly blowing the bus's horn. People were busy to notice the passengers of the bus.

On our way, we passed Kombolcha and arrived at Dessie, a historic capital of the Wollo region. Dessie was a sizable city situated on a high plateau. Some of the famed leaders of Ethiopia came from the region, including Empress Menen, the late wife of Emperor Haile Selassie. Upon arrival at Dessie, the driver, after talking to a guard, stopped at a side street and dismounted from the bus and went to a hotel and restaurant clearly visible. We were not allowed to get off the bus, even though we wanted to stretch our legs and relieve ourselves. About twenty minutes later, the driver came back. By then, already a group of people had surrounded the bus. Some were peddlers; others were curious onlookers. The guards made sure no one came close to the bus. We never felt threatened by the crowd. There were no untoward activities that we could observe.

Crossing the Wollo region would take us to Tigray region, the contiguous land before we arrived at the Eritrean border. To go to Tigray, we had to pass towns, such as Haik, Wurgesa, and Woldia. Past Woldia was the border of Tigray as delimited by the new regime in Ethiopia. Tigray was the home of Mahdere, the official that ordered my family's deportation. It was also the home of the ruling power in Ethiopia. Understandably, we were worried as we crossed into the land of our tormentors. The more the bus was driven into the hinterland of Tigray, the more people got frantic. The older officer who was also a senior to the three other officers sensed the uneasiness of the passengers and reminded his colleagues of their duty to take all the passengers safely to the border of Eritrea. Obviously, this he did to calm the nerves of the deportees.

Darkness was enveloping the land. As the sun set, the driver who had been on the wheel for over ten hours was showing exhaustion, yawning repeatedly. After driving a few kilometers, he veered to the right away from the street to a field where he brought the bus to a stop. He declared this was where we were to get some rest for a few hours. Most of us rushed out of the bus to stretch our muscles and relieve ourselves. One of the guards lighted a flashlight to help spot spaces for people to rest. People sat with their backs supported on tree trunks, stretching their legs. Many others, especially mothers with children, chose to stay in the bus to get a nap in any way possible. About three hours later, everybody was ordered back to the bus. Our drive northward commenced.

The trip was uneventful until we reached the city of Mekelle. Mekelle is the capital of the Tigray region. It was the seat of power of Emperor Yohannes IV over a hundred years ago. Since the power shifted southward under Emperor Menelik II, the city had remained at a standstill for lack of sufficient investment. Some thought it was a deliberate policy of the previous regimes. Be as it might, Mekelle now is one of the important metropolises in Ethiopia as the new leaders of the country are from the region.

The time was eight o'clock in the morning when we arrived at Mekelle. The sun was hot at that early hour; many people were on the street. The bus had stopped for refueling. The driver and two of the guards got off from the bus.

People who noticed the guards recognized this was not an ordinary passenger bus but a bus full of Eritreans on deportation. What happened after that was a scary pandemonium. Soon, the bus was surrounded by an angry mob ready to lynch the passengers. There were shouts: "Hand us our enemies! We want to give them justice!"

The senior officer gave an order to the other three officers to protect the bus. He told the crowd, "We have strict orders to take the people to the border, and that is what we are going to do." The bus driver, alarmed by the situation, jumped into the bus before the tank was full. He drove the bus after blowing a warning horn. It was shocking; it was the face of mob hatred.

I always think what would have happened if they had their way. Would they have cut us to pieces? Thank God, we left Mekelle with our skin and body intact.

Few hours later, we arrived at Adigrat. Adigrat is the last town of import close to the contested border between Ethiopia and Eritrea. It had become an important military supply depot and heavily fortified. For reasons unknown to us, we were kept in the bus for several hours. There were few other buses with passengers parked on the side of the road.

After sundown, we were driven close to the border and were ordered to disembark from the buses and travel on foot in the direction pointed to us. With children crying, tired older people, and luggage to carry, we walked the hilly route toward Eritrea. There was talk that the border area was planted with explosives. In the darkness, we might step on one that might maim or kill us. The other danger was that the Eritrean defense forces might shoot us, mistaking us for enemy troops. We prayed for God to protect us. As a possible signal to the Eritrean forces, we were talking in Tigrinya loudly, signifying that we were not clandestine enemy intruders. It worked. The Eritrean forces recognized us as their nationals deported from Ethiopia, as no enemy would alert its adversary by speaking so loudly. As we came close to the border, units of the Eritrean Army were helping the children, the elderly, and the sick cross the border into safe haven.

I arrived in Eritrea two days before my sixteenth birthday. It hit me that, a few months earlier, Abiy and I had planned to celebrate our birthdays together by inviting friends to a party of food and beverages. We had saved some money, and we were going to beg for more money from our parents. We wanted to make it memorable. I was sad that didn't happen.

Here I was in Eritrea with my future so opaque. I should say the Eritrean defense units on the border showed us so much kindness and empathy. For the last few days, sympathy and kindness was what we had missed.

We were directed to a makeshift shelter where we were registered, with all relevant information—names, age, education level, and where from Ethiopia we were deported. The government of Eritrea issued us a card, and admission to Eritrea was made official. The government also provided us with blankets, pans, and plastic plates—the most basic to start life. It was a gesture much appreciated.

From the port of entry, we were transported to destinations of our preference. My family decided to settle in Asmara, the capital city, as we had close relatives there. From Senafe, the town close to the border to Asmara was about three hours' drive. We arrived in Asmara early afternoon. No one waited for us at the bus depot; our relatives were not informed of our arrival. My parents, after a discussion on where to go, agreed we would be at our maternal grandparents' home. The reason was that the house was bigger and only three people resided there.

The humiliation of being dependent on his elderly in-laws was clearly visible on my father. He kept saying, "It is going to be only for a short time. Soon, we are going to be self-supportive and have our own place." Our mother was trying to lighten our father's mood.

My grandfather was a strong septuagenarian with an engaging personality. He would wake up early morning and walk to church and then go to his business. The idea of retiring never crossed his mind, even when my grandmother suggested, "Now that we have Haile and Abeba here, they can run the business," Haile being my father and Abeba my mother. His response was "Are you wishing for my early death? To retire is to beg for early demise."

My grandparents were living by themselves since my uncle and my aunt had been drafted into the Eritrean Army at the start of the border war with Ethiopia. There was no news about their condition, but rumor had it that my uncle had died in combat and my aunt was assigned to a military medical facility around the city of Tessenei close to the border with Sudan. Few times had we spoken about them as my grandmother would close the subject by giving short answers. It seemed to me she was afraid that she might hear bad news about them. It was obvious it was her daily agony. An unspoken internal torture, during the day, she would stand on the corner of the compound, spaced out with her face contorted.

The country was in a state of war. The news was all about the war in cities, and townspeople and supplies were constantly moving to the war front. Young people above the age of eighteen were called to serve in the army after a short training at Sawa military training camp. Those who failed to report to serve and those who had absconded from national duties were rounded up from their homes and streets and forcibly taken to the camp. Avoidance of service resulted in severe punishment, imprisonment, and beatings. Rumor had it that the punishment was bordered to torture with some fatalities.

Few days after my sixteenth birthday, my father asked me to accompany him to the city center. I thought he needed company or to show me the city's main business area. I walked alongside him mainly talking about my school.

He was concerned if I had adapted to the new school environment. He advised me to study hard and be a good role model to my younger sisters. "A man," he said, "should be hopeful about his future. The situation will come to pass. Everything will be okay. Be brave."

"Father," I said, "I will be the best student." That brought a smile to his face.

We kept walking leisurely to our destination. We made a turn to a street, and some army trucks with several young people loaded on them and uniformed army officers around the trucks were visible.

Some young people were running away with officers pursuing them. Suddenly, we heard shots being fired, aiming toward the running youth. The young people made a sharp turn on a corner. We didn't see anyone being hit by the bullets. Soldiers shooting at young citizens in a city center, in broad daylight, was surreal to me.

Sensing danger, my father said, "Let us go back home."

We made a turn and started walking hurriedly. There was an order to stop from behind us.

We saw a soldier a few steps away coming toward us. We stopped. He asked, "What is your name?"

I answered, "My name is Matheos Haile," in my Amharic-accented Tigrinya language.

"How old are you?"

"I just turned sixteen," I replied.

My father said with pleading voice, "He is only sixteen."

The officer rudely said, "I didn't ask you."

I repeated, "I just turned sixteen last week, and we were deported from Ethiopia recently."

Sarcastically, he said, "So you are sixteen and two meters tall and eighty kilograms in weight. You must have eaten too much raw beef."

I didn't see the joke. I kept quiet. He measured me with his eyes from toe to head and ordered me to get on the truck. I cried, "I am only sixteen. I can't go to the army."

My father, in a desperate voice, begged the officer, "This is only a kid, sixteen years of age. Do not look at his physique. We have a document at home to prove it. If you give us time, he can bring it. Until then, keep me under your custody."

The soldier was in no mood to hear our pleas. He shouted, "You liars!" He added, "All of you who came from Ethiopia are liars." He grabbed me by my collars, pulled me to the truck, and forced me onto the truck.

I was crying, and many of the others were crying too. My father, holding his head with his two hands, was shouting and protesting his sixteen-year-old son was forced onto the truck. Passersby were sympathizing, but no one dared to help.

The trucks were driven in the direction toward Keren, a northern city, on our way to Sawa military camp. The soldiers guarding us were cruel. They were constantly throwing epithets at us that were very demeaning to our mothers and always ready to strike us with their batons and rifle butts. I felt like a prisoner of Eritrea, not a citizen.

"God," I prayed, "get me out of this country. Take me to any place, dear Lord, just out of here."

The truck was packed, impossible to sit. On every turn, our body was shifted to a different direction, pushing one another. Nonstop, we traveled for about five hours before we reached Sawa, situated in the Gash-Barka plains of western Eritrea.

Sawa was a sprawling camp with facilities dotted all over the place. Hangar-like structures for dormitories of recruits, officers' residences, offices, storages, bakery, and kitchen facilities were built at different corners of the camp. Within the camp, there were prison cells where young recruits were incarcerated and brutalized. An open field for training and army drills was within the camp. The area was a dry, parched land with dust blowing all over.

On arrival at Sawa, we were ordered to stand in line. One by one, we were registered.

To the registering officer, I gave my name, place of birth, parents' name, and then my age. I told him, "I am only sixteen years old, and I should not be here."

He ignored me and put my age as nineteen after measuring me with his eyes. "Go ahead!" he ordered me.

I stood with the other registered recruits.

After completion of registration, an officer came and gave us a stern instruction on what was expected of us. He reminded us that the country had been invaded by Woyane, the dominant ruling group in the Ethiopian government, to reverse our hard-won independence. "Each of you are obligated to defend the country."

While the officer was talking, I was thinking, "Why is it that the young has to die for a war started by mainly older men? Why don't those who started the war fight it too?" Fleeting through my mind came the image of my friend Abiy and my dear Amsal and the rest of the family. I asked myself, "Is it possible that I may aim my gun against my childhood friend who may be on the other side of the border? If I had to do anything, this will not happen."

On the second day of our arrival at Sawa, several officers came to our dormitories and shouted to wake us up. We were ordered to dress up and follow them to the training ground. It was the beginning of our military training.

The news of the war on the border was grim. An intensified war ensued on all fronts. The unofficial report of the war was that along most of the border from the Assab front to Tserona, Adi-Keshi, and the flash point of Badme, the casualty was heavy. Hundreds of thousands of people were displaced from their villages, abandoning their homes and all their assets, mainly cattle and farms. War creates misery and spreads it to people who may be far from the combat zone. I was miserable, and so were my family and millions of other families in Eritrea and Ethiopia.

The military training was rudimentary. Run, jump, and mount were the exercises meant to strengthen our bodies. We were trained to disassemble and assemble a weapon and do range shooting. With that short training though, it was a body in the frontlines, not an efficient fighting group.

We were sent to the combat zone assigned to different brigades. I was assigned to the Second Brigade on the Tserona front. Only a few months ago, the area had seen the bloodiest combat. The Ethiopian army had made a frontal attack on the fortified trenches of the Eritrean Army. Many young combatants died without any change of territorial control. By the time I arrived at my assigned place, the conflict was in a lull with few sporadic shootings. It was a relief the war had ebbed. As required, we had to report to the commander's office.

The commander of my battalion was a middle-aged man with graying hair and slim but with a sinewy frame of body. He introduced himself as Colonel Hamid. In a slow, deliberate speech, he instructed as to be alert at all times. "Make sure your weapons are always on your side, loaded." He ordered one of the guards to lead us to our assigned spot.

As we started to walk, he called me back. I was perplexed. He asked, "How old are you?"

"I am sixteen years old," I responded.

Momentarily, he turned his face away from me and then said, "You don't speak Tigrinya well. When did you come to Eritrea?"

"About four months ago," I answered.

"Okay!" he exclaimed. After some thought, he said, "You are going to stay with me until I find you an appropriate assignment."

Few days later, a supply truck arrived loaded with carts of ammunition and other supplies. We unloaded the truck and made it ready for another trip. Colonel Hamid ordered me to go onto the truck with a sealed note at hand. The truck driver was informed to whom the note was to be delivered.

After traveling for about thirty kilometers, we stopped at a place where several shipping containers were parked.

The driver announced, "Here is our destination."

The place was buzzing with activities. Some young people were loading while others were unloading boxes and crates from several trucks. It was a depot for all the supplies to the combat zone of the region.

The commander of the depot was Wedi Wush, short and agile with eyes that seemed to penetrate deep into your mind. He was also a fast talker, impatient to those who were slow. He read the note from Colonel Hamid. He asked, "How did he know that you were sixteen years old?"

"I told him," I answered.

"He took your word and accepted it as a fact?"

"Yes, it is a fact," I replied with a tone of frustration.

"As far as I am concerned, you are nineteen years old. That is what the document shows," he asserted.

With that, he called an officer and instructed him to take me to a jobsite. I was ordered to load trucks with other young men. The job itself was not hard as there were enough hands to cooperate. All the people who worked on my side were draftees for national service. Most of them had served more than the mandated time of eighteen months, with no determined date on when they would be relieved from service. It was sad to see so many young people disrupted from their education and future careers. The war never seemed to end. There might be silence of the guns for a short period with each side rearming more. The savagery of this war was more baffling as it was both senseless and unnecessary. Everyone on service agreed on this point. Why war? Was it not possible to resolve border issue peacefully? Were the questions debated among the youth, although surreptitiously?

After a few days on my new assignment, I started to make friends, especially with three young men who seemed to be much closer to one another. I was happy to have people with whom to talk.

It helped me divert my mind from the agony of constant worry about my parents and sisters. The image of my father holding his head in agony was my everyday nightmare. All my life, my father was a pillar of our family—loving and hardworking with an impeccable integrity. He was respected by the community and all who had come to know him. In this situation, he was reduced to a helpless, crying man. I hoped to see my father and hug him with my mother and sisters.

My three friends were Yohaness or Johnny, Isaak, and Habtom. All were drafted to Sawa in the same year from the same school. They had been in service for almost three years. They had known one another at school, even though they weren't friends. Their friendship was established after they were assigned here. I understood why they were so close to one another; they brought memories of their school, teachers, students, and incidents and create a comedy out of them. They had the penchant of looking at people and situations in their funniest way. Despite our grim situation, they were always in jovial mood. They never called me by my name Matheos, or Mati as my friend Abiy used to call me, but by a sobriquet, Amharai, that they gave me. Amharai means one who is of the Amhara ethnic group of Ethiopia, as my Tigrinya speech was accented by my upbringing speaking Amharic. It was not meant as an insult. Actually, they enjoyed listening to my not-so-lustrous Tigrinya. They were curious to know about my upbringing in Ethiopia. I told them how happy my childhood was and my friendship with Abiy and many others. Their appetite was whetted to know more. They were more interested to know how we were treated by the two regimes that ruled Ethiopia, the dictatorial military regime under Colonel Mengistu Haile Mariam and the current ruling regime dominated by the Tigray front. It was through the prism of their experience that their perception on Ethiopia was shaped. For them, the Mengistu regime was a time of terror and of intensified warfare when villages were burned, young people were garroted by piano wires and thrown in city streets, and curfew was from sunset to sunrise. Their encounter with Ethiopians was mainly with the army that treated them as potential enemies.

In May 1991, Eritrea became independent, and the situation changed for the better drastically. It was a time of hope. Peace had come at last.

By 1997, rumors of war were in the air. And in May 1998, war broke out seven years after peace between the two countries. My friends believed the war was triggered by the Tigrean leaders in the government of Ethiopia to reverse the independence of

Eritrea. I was not sure what to say, for the whole situation was new to me. Only now I had started to learn about the prolonged conflict between Eritrea and Ethiopia. Growing up in Ethiopia, the conflict in Eritrea was scantly discussed in my home, at least in my presence. My upbringing in Ethiopia intrigued my friends and broke several of their misconceptions. I told them under the Dergue, the military regime life was not easy for Ethiopians. Young people were press-ganged to go to war, and from what I had heard from my elders, many young people were killed by the regime's "red terror" campaign. During the red terror, the regime didn't discriminate what region and ethnicity one belonged; it eliminated thousands of young people.

Discussion about our lives created confidence and trust among us. Trust was one thing deficient in this place; there was always surveillance and spies amidst the young people. Every activity of individuals was monitored. Any infraction of the myriad of regulations at the camp was severely punished. When it came to punishment, no one was more creative as the regime in Eritrea. All its punishments were adaptation of cruel, inhuman medieval forms at its worst. They gave it fancy names, "otto" and "helicopter." The otto was when they would tie both arms and legs and tie them both together, exposing the bare-foot soles upward where the detainee was beaten. The helicopter was essentially the same restraint, except the detainee was raised over a post, swinging above the ground. It was excruciatingly painful.

Considering the severity of the punishment, having few trusted friends was preferred.

The four of us, though a crowd, were very compatible. Since we were the loudest when we laughed and talked, no one suspected us as conspiratorial. Our commander looked at us as harmless and fun loving with some infantile behavior. That worked for us.

Each of us had worries about our future. Was our fate and future going to be indefinite service to the country as military men with no hope of building a career of our choice? We shared our anxieties among ourselves.

We looked into all possibilities to be released from service. We had been told it would never be granted. To abscond from service during our short leave to visit family was a risky proposal as the army would send officers to apprehend us and bring us back to camp. It would result in imprisonment and punishment in a dingy underground prison. The only option left was to flee the country by crossing the border either to Sudan or Ethiopia.

We thought of this option seriously. "How are we going to flee without being caught on the way? Is it safe? Which way, Ethiopia or Sudan? Will Ethiopia allow us to enter the country after the bloody war? Where in Ethiopia can we go? How are we going to support ourselves? How about Sudan? Will it be safer? Is it possible that we could be deported from there? How about the language? We don't speak Arabic. Is it possible that the Eritrean security forces would kidnap us from Sudan? There is a rumor how Eritrean Army deserters had been kidnapped from Sudan to face execution." These and many other questions were bothering us. We decided to gather information discreetly.

In December 2000, a ceasefire agreement was reached between the government of Ethiopia and the regime in Eritrea. Since the ceasefire, our workload was reduced substantially. Our commander did not want us to stay idle. He organized us into work groups to work on construction, agriculture, and rehabilitation of different facilities. It was a hard labor. Our workday started at 6:30 a.m. through 2:00 p.m. We were given a short break to eat the usual bread and lentil soup. The abysmal treatment made us determined to run away whatever the risk might be.

As we went on leave to visit family, which happened infrequently, we gathered information on what route to take, where the security checkpoints were located, who could be of help—smuggler or guide—and what we needed to carry with us. Each of us had gathered plenty of information. The easiest route from where we were stationed was to cross the border by the Tserona plain into Ethiopia. It was heavily fortified, and yet there were hills and bushes to provide camouflage. The early morning before sunrise was the best time to cross the border as the guards might be tired and would not be alert.

At work, we were assigned to different work squads, but in proximity. It was for the construction of a new feeder road. We used shovel and hoes to clear and move boulders. It was a hard work under unremitting sun. Our lunchtime was at about eleven o'clock in the morning. Each member of a squad was to remain with his team. We disregarded this silly order, and we joined one another at a site median to all.

Isaak's unit leader was the only one who expressed anger at this minor infraction of order. On the third day while at lunch, he came to where we were sitting and started to berate Isaak.

Isaak tried to ignore him, but the guy would not let go. Finally, Isaak stood up and told the guy to stop harassing him at his break time. "You can only order me at work. Right now I am on a break. Break time is my time to use the way I see fit."

The unit leader, fuming with anger at the challenge, hit Isaak with a stick on his left arm. Isaak instinctively punched the guy with his right fist on his face. Since we were standing only a few feet away from the ruckus, we held the unit leader to restrain him from further escalating the situation. While this was happening, more officers came and ordered all of us to stand to attention and follow them to the camp. The unit leader, angry and with bruised ego, was threatening with all kinds of punishments. At the camp, we were placed in detention. The guards were instructed to keep us in a cell until the commander was informed of our assault to a unit leader.

In the cell, we were kept for four days. The first day, neither food nor water was provided to us. Early morning on the second day, bread, sweetened tea, and water were served.

Four days later, the guards took us out of the cell to the commander's office. We were handcuffed as we entered the office.

The commander was seated and writing and didn't raise his head as the guard announced our arrival. Few minutes later, he pushed the pad to the side and ordered the guard to stay outside after closing the door behind him. "So you young guys have assaulted your superior officer," he remarked.

Isaak, the most voluble of us all, said, "Commander, they have nothing to do with it. The problem was between me and my unit leader. He, the unit leader, was picking on me since the day I was assigned under him. He finds fault in everything I do—if I sit, stand, work—for reasons I do not understand. He was obsessed with me. On the day we had the altercation, he came to where I was eating my lunch and shouted that I couldn't be on the spot. I asked why, and I reminded him it is break time and on my own time. He took it as a challenge and hit me on my left arm with a stick he was carrying. Look at the swelling and bruise." He pointed them to the commander.

The commander, after listening calmly, asked, "Were you trying to challenge your leader?"

"That was not my intention, Commander," Isaak answered. "I was only trying to make him leave me alone for a short thirty minutes during my lunch.

The rest of the time I was at his command, I do not respond to all the insults he hurls at me all the time."

Facing the three of us, the commander asked, "When you restrained the unit leader, were you trying to help your friend to kick him? Why didn't you restrain your friend?"

"Commander," I responded, "our friend was not holding a stick. It was the unit leader who was using it as if he was to hit a donkey."

The commander smiled, maybe for my inarticulate use of the language or the expression of hitting like a donkey. "Well," he said, "until further notice, the four of you are going to be working around here, close to my office, and I am going to watch what mischief you are up to. Go to your rooms now and stay there." The dormitory was only about fifty meters away. He was unusually soft in handling our case. Under other circumstances, he would allow the unit leader to decide the punishment over the offender.

With everybody out to work, we were left alone in the dormitory. It gave us a good opportunity to plan our escape from the country. It was already decided to cross the border into Ethiopia. The escape from the camp without our absence noticed was the question that befuddled us. The other problem was the distance to the border; it was almost fifty kilometers, not a walking distance.

Isaak came up with an idea of requesting a transfer to the frontline. Since ceasefire, the area was quiet from gunfire; there was no danger for us.

"But what excuse can we give for transfer?"

"Well," Isaak continued, "I could use my antagonistic relationship with my unit leader. I would argue it would be better for both of us to part. Maybe we can use the same excuse as he considers us as partners in his humiliation. Let us sleep over it."

We all agreed. After much thought, we could not come up with a better idea. The question was "How do we approach the commander, and what if he assigns us to different units far apart?"

On our third day in the camp in proximity to the commander's office, we decided to do some work on our volition—clearing the camp of debris and leveling the gravel on the walkways and straightening some of the fences. We started late in the afternoon, right after everyone—except for some officers, guards, and the commander—left the camp. Clearing the debris, papers, worn-out shoes, rags, and plastic bags was our first target. The four of us worked diligently to clear the section of the camp. In three days, we accomplished what we set out to do. The guards and few of the officers had come to notice our work and complimented us. We were not sure if the commander realized it was our effort. Leveling the walkways would take us to the front of the commander's office and his entry. It was a hard work. But it fitted well with our purpose of impressing the commander. Through three days of hard work, we made a difference. The camp looked well cared for, to the delight of everybody, especially the commander.

The commander invited us to his office by sending one of the guards. At the office, he commended us for the work we had done. "I am impressed by your work ethic and your teamwork." He continued, "You can be good role models to all the young people, and I will keep you as a team."

"God works in mysterious ways. Hallelujah," we said.

This was a dream come true to remain as a team and be on good terms with the commander. All the while, the rest of the recruits and the unit leaders thought the work was part of our punishment. Actually, we encouraged that kind of thinking; it worked to our best advantage in mollifying the frayed ego of the unit leader.

The day after we had a conversation with the commander, we took a day off to talk to the commander to request for transfer to the frontline in the Tserona area. After mustering our courage, we headed to the office to plea for our transfer. The stars seemed to align on our favor, so we took advantage of it.

The friendly guard at the front office greeted us warmly and asked us what brought us to the office.

"We wanted to talk to the commander," we responded.

"Yes. Keep this to yourself. He is very fond of you guys." That boosted our moral. He went inside and came back in a couple of minutes to let us into the office.

The commander was in his spartan office with a few papers spread on his desk. The filing cabinet was placed in the corner. The coat hanger was a nail on the wall. There were no pictures, except for a dated map on the east side of the wall. Two cups and burned-out metallic kettle were on a small cabin behind the commander's chair. The kettle needed a good brush to remove the caked charcoal on the surface. The room portrayed the personality of the man.

He was a veteran of the war of independence and had remained loyal to the goals of the movement. Most other commanders had been corrupted by power and money. He had remained simple, uncorrupted with total loyalty to his people and country. The quality endeared him to the regular army and his people but did not favor him with the leader of the country, and that was why he had remained a colonel. In present-day Eritrea, it was the sycophants, opportunists, and blind loyalists to the president who are holding key government positions. A man of integrity, like our commander, did not have a chance. But that didn't seem to bother him. He did his duties with total dedication.

This time, he invited us to sit on the outdoor-type chairs placed on the side. He moved his chair to face us. "How do you do?" he asked.

"We are fine, Commander. Since we have been assigned here, we looked for things to do, to be useful and contribute in whatever way we can. It was our wish to paint your office and some of the rusting metals, but there were no paints or brushes. It may also look superfluous at a time when our country is at war."

He was listening attentively, impressed by our commitment and zeal for hard work. He was not aware of the snare prepared to control him and get our way.

I continued. I was direct on my appeal. "We came here to request for transfer to the Tserona front, where we can be more useful." The Tserona front had seen some of the major wars. It was devastated with serious damages to infrastructures that would need immediate rehabilitation.

"To the Tserona front?" he asked with animated curiosity. "But that is the frontline of the war. Do you have a death wish?"

"No, sir. We are young. We want to live much longer. But if it was the will of God that we die doing something constructive for our country, so be it."

He sunk into deep thought and then said, "We fought long and hard and sacrificed some of our best brothers and sisters for our children to live in peace. I am weary of wars, my sons. I hope this last war was truly the last. As for your request to be transferred, give me some time to think about it. Come tomorrow afternoon to my office. I will let you know my decision."

We thanked him for giving us the opportunity to present our plea.

The night was cloudy with thunderstorm and lightning as if the heavens were at war. It was a sleepless night for the four of us, both by the sound and the anticipation of what decision of the commander would be. By daybreak, everybody left to different assignments, except us. As people were leaving, some were expressing sympathy for the punishment levied on us to clear the compound, and few were envious, especially those who were under the command of Isaak's unit leader.

We went around the camp to look for something to keep us busy. The camp looked clear of any debris. In the afternoon as appointed, we went to the commander's office. The guard ushered us in immediately.

"Good afternoon, sons," the commander greeted us. He invited us to sit on the chairs that we left the previous day. "I radioed to the commander on the Tserona front," he continued, "of the possibility of you joining his unit. I had recommended that you be kept together as a team. But he said, at this time, they have more hands than they can use, given the insufficient supplies. So that possibility is out."

Before we expressed our disappointment, he continued, "But the commander in the Tessenei-Barentu front is willing to have you under his command. He needs more workers at the Alighider plantation. The work will be hard, cotton picking and harvesting vegetables. So make yourselves ready to move to the western front in Gash-Barka plains. I should warn you it is hot and hard work."

It was kind of a surprise as we all planned to cross into Ethiopian via the Tserona front. But Alighider was far from the Ethiopian border, close to the Sudanese border. We had to redraw our plan as the flight to Ethiopia was out. We thanked the commander for his kindness and promised that we would be ready to leave anytime.

For few days, we hung around the camp doing virtually nothing until, on Wednesday afternoon, we were instructed to travel to Asmara, the capital city of Eritrea, and report to the army headquarter with a sealed envelope.

The driver with whom we were traveling had been a driver for twenty years. Before independence, in the first ten years, he was hauling supplies to the Eritrean Liberation Front from Sudan to the base area in Sahel, northeast of Eritrea. He boasted that he knew Sudan like his own backyard. Casually, we asked him about Sudan. He gave us invaluable information that we thought would be helpful to our plan. Kassala was the first town close to Tessenei once you crossed the border to Sudan. There were many Eritreans who called it home, he informed us. He talked about Khartoum, Port Sudan, and the Sudanese people and how hospitable they were to the thousands of Eritrean refugees.

After almost an hour of driving and talking, the driver turned to me. "Your Tigrinya sounds like Amharic. Were you deported from Ethiopia?" he asked.

I responded, "Yes, with my parents and sisters. We were deported in 1999."

The driver, whose name was Tesfay, continued, "Where are your parents?"

"In Asmara."

"How old are you?"

"Eighteen years old. I was conscripted when I was sixteen years old."

"How did it happen?"

I told Tesfay how I was forced onto a military truck on the street of Asmara while walking with my father.

Tesfay exclaimed, "Oh! Oh! Wait a minute. Are you the son of Haile Wedi Keshi?"

"Yes," I said.

"I am sorry, my son. I am your second uncle on your father's side. I have known about your situation. I was not able to get any information about you from the army due to the fact that the conflict information was scarce. I am glad you guys are alive and safe. I will take you to each of your parents."

An hour later, we arrived in Asmara.

The truck stopped at the Godaif neighborhood where my parents had settled at my grandparents' home. It was evening with a few people walking on the street. We all got off the truck. Tesfay and I walked in front, followed by my three friends. We knocked at the door, which was opened by my sister, Azie. She shouted, which drew everybody to the door. There was a lot of excitement, with my mother crying of joy and relief. We were seated with Tesfay explaining the serendipitous meeting of us. My friends were eager to go to their homes and meet their families. However, my mother insisted they had to eat dinner first. After dinner, Tesfay drove them to their doors.

The next morning, we were supposed to meet at the army headquarter, but Tesfay suggested that we stay at home until we hear from him.

My parents were talking highly of Tesfay as the one who had tried hard to locate me and help me get released from the army. I thought here was a guy that we could trust with our plan.

On Friday morning, my friends came to our home. It was secluded on the periphery of the city; the home was fenced with two-meter high walls on all sides.

While having tea in the compound, I told them that Tesfay was trustworthy, according to my parents, and we should seek his help or advice. All agreed.

By midday, Tesfay came to our home on a bus. After we exchanged greetings, he asked us what our plans were.

After looking at one another, I told him, "Our plan is to go to Alighider and work."

He asked again, "Do you know the work condition at Alighider? What is going to be your future after working as cotton pickers for many years?"

We were quiet for a while, not sure how to bring our true plan without risking divulging our secret.

Tesfay thought we were clueless young men with no idea what we were getting into. He hinted how he had seen many young people immigrating to Europe, US, and Canada through Sudan. "Those young people have opted to improve their lives elsewhere. Maybe those people had someone to help them cross the border into Sudan, and also, they had people who gave them shelter in Sudan. If you guys have the mettle of taking a risk, I know a way to help you. I have lived and worked in Sudan for many years. It is my second home. I have friends who can help you in any way they can. Now tell me. Are you ready to travel across the border?"

We saw one another with smiles on our faces and answered him with a categorical yes.

He advised us not to share the plan with anyone. "I mean anyone, not even your family. We will notify them once you have arrived safely in Sudan. The next few days, stay underground. Do not make yourselves visible. Have some rest. I will contact you when all is ready."

For a week, we had not heard from Tesfay. We were worried. If this mission failed, we might have to go to Alighider and face the punishment for being late. That would complicate our plan to flee across the border. We all spent the night at my grandparents' home with my family.

Early next morning, Tesfay appeared at our door. He loudly said, "Good morning!" And he asked, "Madam, do you have breakfast for an uninvited guest?"

My mother responded in good humor, "You fool. Who said you are a guest? Come inside and sit. The tea is almost ready."

But Tesfay was in a hurry. After my mother went into the kitchen and only the four of us were left in the room, in a low voice, he announced, "Everything is ready. I have a pass for all of you. It allows you to travel to Gash-Barka area without any harassment at checkpoints. We will travel in two days, early morning. I am going to transport supplies to Tessenei and Gulj."

Two days later, we met at an appointed place just outside the city. Early morning, we started our journey toward Tessenei. Tessenei and Barentu were located in the vast expanse of land in western Eritrea. Both were important trading centers, with traders crossing to Sudan to import and export commodities. Since the border with Ethiopia closed and, thus, the closure of cross-border trade and transportation, the two cities had grown both in population and importance. New faces from across Eritrea were seen in the main streets and cafés of the town. Our coming to the city would not create consternation or unusual curiosity. The route was familiar to us. Some two years ago, we had passed through it to go to Sawa as recruits to national service. In both situations, there was a feeling of uneasiness and apprehension. We didn't know what awaited us on either Sawa or on our escape to Sudan.

Tesfay was very encouraging. He told us that the route had been crossed by many Eritrean youth in an attempt to chart the course of their life. Some had crossed borders and sea and ocean to reach Europe and North America. They had built a life of comfort and success. "I advise you, once you reach the nations of democracy, take advantage of the opportunities provided to you. Do not waste your time frivolously, and be good citizens of the host countries."

It sounded like an unrealizable dream to us at the time.

He turned to me and said, "You may not know him, but your father's cousin is in the US. He is a very successful professional. I have got his address and telephone number. Once you reach Khartoum, call him and tell him your situation. He may help you. Your father and I will call him and urge him to help you."

My friends said they did have families in Europe.

After traveling for about fifty-five minutes, we passed through a checkpoint. The guards knew Tesfay and called one another with friendly sobriquets. They did not bother to check our IDs and passes. Tesfay told them that we were going to our assignment in Tessenei. We passed through several checkpoints without incident.

In the afternoon, we arrived at Tessenei. Part of the load had to be unloaded. We helped with the unloading with the other recruits stationed on-site.

Tesfay was happy with our voluntary help in the task. "You deserve a reward," he said and took us to a small café and bought us dinner. It was much appreciated.

The next road of our journey was to take us much closer to the border of Sudan. Tesfay was quiet. Something was in his mind. Maybe there was trouble ahead. We kept quiet, deep in our own thoughts about our future, families that we left behind, and the rest of the trip, which we understood to be most critical of all.

As the sun set, darkness was enveloping the land. On the far mountain range, a light like a weak flame was shooting. As we drove closer and closer, with total darkness, even the mountains disappeared. Few kilometers farther, we saw some flickering lights. As we came closer and closer, we saw a village with huts.

Tesfay stopped the truck and said, "I am going to visit a friend at the village. Stay put inside."

We waited for almost an hour before he came back with another person, obviously a native of the area by the way he was dressed. He introduced the person as Nuru. Nuru spoke Tigrinya well.

"This gentleman is going to be your guide from here until crossing the Sudanese border. He is my friend. We have known each other for twenty-five years. Follow all his instructions. He knows every hill and every nook and crook of the area. Be brave, and God be with you. Here are some contacts in Kassala and Khartoum and of the uncle in the US. Go ahead and follow Nuru. Ciao!"

Nuru took us into a small hut that was empty, except for some tools and a jug made of goatskin full of water. He gave us some water, a precious commodity in the semidesert area. "Our trip will start at four a.m. You will need some rest. Go sleep on the straw-made mattress with the cowhide on top," Nuru advised. "The trip takes about three hours on foot. The aim was to cross the border before seven a.m. We will carry water in a small jug, carried alternately by each of us." Nuru left to spend the night with his family in another hut. He told us he would be back early morning.

There was hay, most likely a feed for their animals, piled on the side of the hut. We spread some of it under the mattress to give us better cushion. We went to deep sleep immediately until he woke us up at three thirty in the morning. We threw some cold water on our faces and started the journey.

It was dark, but Nuru said, "I don't need a light on this route. Just follow me on single file." We followed him quietly.

On the mountain range to our left, there was a military outpost. To avoid it, we went northward before we turned west away from the ranges. We followed a valley until we reached the Sudan-Eritrea border.

Nuru made sure that we crossed far enough into Sudanese territory and instructed us to follow the side road that would lead us to Kassala. He praised us for keeping pace. "You are going to reach Kassala in a short time."

Kassala was a midsized town, with houses with worn-out facades. It was a market town with a booming trade between the neighboring towns of Tessenei and Barentu on the Eritrean side. There was a sizable Eritrean community settled since the fifties.

The morning we arrived in the town, we walked by the main street until a young man approached us. He asked if we were Eritreans in English.

"Yes. Do you know any Eritrean?"

"Come," he said and led us to a group of men sitting and having tea.

We greeted them in Tigrinya and asked them for Mr. Abdulaziz, a name given to us by Tesfay.

"Abdulaziz, *aiwa*," an Arabic expression, said one of them. He pointed us to a store across the street and said, "That is his store. You may find him there."

At the store, a young man was organizing the shelf with goods.

"Good morning," we greeted him.

"Good morning," he responded. "How can I help you?" he added.

"We are looking for Mr. Abdulaziz. Tesfay sent us to see him."

"Oh! Tesfay. I know him. I am Ibrahim Abdulaziz, the son," he introduced himself.

We introduced ourselves one by one.

He invited us to sit by the pile of sacks and said, "My father will come soon." Apparently, Tesfay did a lot of business with them for supplies to the Eritrean military and established friendship.

Mr. Abdulaziz was fair skinned, tall, and with a strong frame of body. On the head, he was turbaned and dressed with jellabiya or thobe, the way Sudanese men dress. As soon as he saw us, he asked, "Are you Tesfay's family? You made it fast. I was expecting you tomorrow. It is all right. I am glad you came safe. Ibrahim will take you home to rest and have a meal. You need your rest before your trip to Khartoum."

Ibrahim, who spoke Tigrinya not so well, had to mix English, Arabic, and Tigrinya all mangled together. We understood each other. He was trying to be helpful, and we were very grateful. We ate a sumptuous lunch at a Sudanese restaurant.

After resting a whole afternoon and night, the next morning, Ibrahim took us to his family store where a van awaited to drive us to Khartoum. The trip to Khartoum took about eight hours.

The driver was Hamid, dressed with grease-stained coverall and a chain-smoker whose evidence could be seen on his decayed, browned teeth and bloodshot eyes.

At the start of the trip, we asked him if it was okay to open the windows to ventilate out the smoke.

"It is fine with me as long as you don't complain of dust and wind."

The dust, rust colored and blown by desert wind, engulfed the cabin of the van with vengeance. We were covered with dust that our eyelashes, hair, and clothing took the color of the dust. The driver said this was khamsin, a sandstorm originating from the Sahara and blown to the coast of Sudan. We had to close the windows, but the dust specks remained suspended, making our breathing difficult.

Khartoum, the capital city of Sudan, was a historic city. It was transected by the Blue Nile and White Nile. Outside the perimeter of the city was a vast expanse of desert. It had seen many heroic battles between the Mahdists and the Anglo-Egyptian forces, most famously led by Charles "Chinese" Gordon, who was killed after Khartoum was put under siege. A movie, *Khartoum*—directed by Basil Dearden and starred by Charlton Heston as Charles Gordon and Laurence Olivier as Muhammad Ahmed, the Mahdi—depicted the fall of the city under the rag-tag army of the Mahdi and the death of Gordon, the British governor.

After the difficult journey in a dusty and smoke-filled cabin, we arrived at Khartoum. Hamid took us to a neighborhood where Eritrean émigrés and refugees resided, as he was instructed by Abdulaziz. He left us at a café where most of the customers were Eritreans of all ages. By our dusty look, we were conspicuously identified as new arrivals. People were eager to hear our story and about the situation back home. We were invited to share tea, a flatbread, and boiled pureed fava beans drizzled with olive oil and lime juice. We ate heartily as we had only a small meal on the way. We asked our hosts if they knew of Habte Wedi Hawe.

They pointed us to a middle-aged man, dubbed as the unofficial mayor of the neighborhood.

"Sure." The gentleman knew him by saying, "Even birds of the area know Wedi Hawe. He should be here anytime unless you are in some urgency." He called a young man and asked him to take us to where Wedi Hawe was.

The young man had been in Khartoum for two years. He explained the challenges of life, the constant harassment by the police, and the fear of either being deported or being kidnapped by the Eritrean security agents. "If you have money," he advised, "pay a smuggler to arrange for going to Europe or North America."

We arrived at Wedi Hawe's home. He was seated with two young Eritreans.

"*Merhaba!*" he greeted us. "Which one of you is the son of Haile Wedi Keshi?"

"I am. Matheos," I said and extended my hand to greet him. Instead, he hugged me and hugged my friends.

He invited us to sit at chairs on the verandah while he wrapped his business with his guests. He was already informed of our arrival by Abdulaziz by phone.

Habte, Wedi Hawe as he was popularly called in the Eritrean community, was affable, with pleasant disposition. It didn't surprise us that he was popular. He made us feel at home. He saw that the dust with sweat had caked on our faces, so he told us to take a wash at the improvised shower at the back of the house shaded by corrugated metal sheets. It was pleasant to take a shower after so many days. He gave each of us a piece of fabric to wrap our body as we washed our clothes and got it dry.

Wedi Hawi came late in the afternoon after making some errands. He was single and living in a sizable home with few furniture. As to what he did for living, we had no clue, but he did seem to live in comfort, from his look and the way he carried himself. He asked each of us what our plans were.

I told him, "I have a number to call my uncle in the US that Tesfay gave me in Eritrea."

"Of course. I know him. He is my kinsman. Good person," he added.

My friends also told him the contacts of their relatives in Europe.

"Good," he intoned. "If they are able and willing to help you financially, the rest leave to me. I will get you all the documents to help you travel to your destinations." Apparently, Wedi Hawe was some kind of wheeler-dealer who arranged for people to cross borders, legally or otherwise.

About midnight Khartoum time, I made a phone call to my uncle in the US. Fortunately, he was at home and responded to my call. I introduced myself as his nephew, the son of Haile Wedi Keshi.

"Oh yes. I have never met you since you were born after I left the country." He inquired about my health and the family.

I said, "I am fine, and I am in Khartoum with Habte Wedi Hawe. I need your help because I fled the Eritrean military service. Wedi Hawe can explain more in details." I handed the phone to Wedi Hawe.

Wedi Hawe and Uncle Solomon exchanged long greetings that included reminiscence of their childhood and some of their youthful escapades. To the issue at hand, my uncle agreed to finance the cost of my trip. I was exhilarated. But my friends were not so fortunate; the families they contacted expressed their inability to help them at this time, except for Yohaness whose cousin in Saudi Arabia promised help.

Wedi Hawe had concluded an agreement with my uncle on the amount to procure documents and cost of air transport. Yohaness and I were set to travel to the US if all the arrangements were made.

To apply for US visa, we had to go to either Cairo or Nairobi as there was no US consular service in Khartoum.

Ten days later, Yohaness's cousin, Kidane, from Saudi Arabia, arrived in Khartoum. He located us by asking for Wedi Hawe's address. It was a surprise to Yohaness and the rest of us. Amazingly, Kidane, except for some graying hair, looked like Yohaness. When asked about it, they said they were their fathers' children. That evening, he invited us to dinner and gave us shirts, pants, and underwear that he brought from Saudi. He came to make arrangements with Wedi Hawe for his cousin's travel. At dinner, he asked us what drove us into exile. We told him all about our experience and the hopelessness of our future under Eritrean military service.

Kidane came for a few days. He met and discussed the whole plan with Wedi Hawe and gave the money for the service. Generously, he volunteered to contribute money for our two friends' expenses for them to travel through Libya to Europe. The travel to Europe was by crossing the Sahara into Libya and the Mediterranean Sea into Italy.

The first to leave Khartoum were our friends, Isaak and Habtom, to Europe. It was arranged expeditiously with a group of Sudanese, Somalis, Ethiopians, and four Eritreans, including our friends. Wedi Hawe negotiated with a Sudanese smuggler, and an agreement was reached. The trip partly was to take with a land cruiser and, as they reached the border to Libya, on foot. Inside Libya, a different smuggler would take them to Tripoli. At the Port of Tripoli, they would board a boat to Italy. We promised to keep in touch with one another. I gave them my uncle's telephone number in the US.

As our friends left, Abraham and I felt sad. We had been so close for the last two years and, in particular, since we left the camp and traveled to Khartoum. Our situation was different; it was necessary for us to get a passport and an entry visa to the USA. Wedi Hawe was working through his contacts to secure us the documents.

According to Wedi Hawe, it took so many pleadings and bribes to get our passports. He had to create a biography of both of us as born in Ethiopia of Eritrean family. We left Ethiopia before we were put in detention on the account of our Eritrean heritage. The passports were secured. Nairobi, Kenya, was preferred to apply for US visa.

The travel took us through South Sudan and northern Kenya. South Sudan was in rebellion against the central government in Khartoum. That made our travel fraught with danger. It took us four days to cross the border into Kenya. From the border, we boarded a public bus to go to Nairobi.

Nairobi was a sprawling metropolis with a cosmopolitan flavor. In the city center, people from all races—Europeans, Asians, Arabs, and natives—mingled in a rush to perform their daily jobs. The traffic was crowded with cars of different models and taxis with blaring music. It was a dizzying experience.

We had information where Eritrean and Ethiopian exiles lived. The refugee community lived in proximity to each other for the comfort of safety in numbers and support in case of mishaps. The Eastleigh neighborhood was a residence for most of the refugees from the Horn of Africa. For any refugee, it was a starting place to make contacts and gather information. In the small cafés in the area, people congregated to relax and share experiences. That was where we made our first contacts. We asked for information about affordable motels or youth hostels.

Kibrom was the person to whom we talked. He was an Eritrean refugee who had lived for four years in Nairobi. "Oh, my friends," he said, "as refugees, you can't afford to live in any sort of hotel. Too expensive. But you can share rooms with other refugees who are in the same predicament as you are, waiting for resettlement in Europe or North America."

Then he took us to another café crowded with people of Ethiopia and Eritrea. He introduced us to the group as new arrivals and looking for a place to stay. "Of course," he added, "they are going to share expenses."

Many of them offered us to share a space. Grateful with the offer, we ate dinner and went with Abel to his place of domicile. The area was a ramshackle neighborhood of refugees and Kenyan underclass. With rubbish strewn all over and houses made of corrugated zinc, plywood, and pieces of wood, it looked as a place neglected by municipal services. We had been advised by Abel and others to be careful of pickpockets, neighborhood hooligans, and the police.

"The police are corrupt. They harass refugees to squeeze some graft money. It is safe to carry a few dollars to bribe the police. Otherwise, you end up in custody."

After the weekend, Abel took us to the café where we met him. Kibrom, our interlocutor, was having breakfast. We sat on the chairs by his table. "I hope that you are starting your refugee life on a right footing," he said.

"Thank you. It is good so far," we responded.

He shared his experience with us and what we should do to gain some legality for our stay in the country. "Register at UNHCR as refugees, number one," he emphasized. "UNHCR may help you resettle in third countries in Europe or North America. It may take a while, but until then, you have legal reason for you to stay in Kenya." He gave us the address to get registered. "Mind you, resettlement takes a long time, sometimes years. There are people who had been waiting for four years," he added. That was a bummer. That deflated our hope of shorter resettlement time.

In the afternoon, we ventured to see parts of the city. Haile Selassie Avenue was the main thoroughfare to the business district. The area was very vibrant with activities. As we walked, the information of spending several years waiting for resettlement worried us. The wasting of our youth in limbo was worrisome. Besides, how were we going to support ourselves for years? Yohaness came up with an idea of moving to Kampala, Uganda, where several of his relatives had settled.

"Hmm," I murmured. "I don't like the idea of separating from my friend, but I understood his concern. I have to stick it in Nairobi for my uncle to send me documents to submit to the US consulate for entry visa."

Next morning, Yohannes decided to go to Uganda, after he made a call to a cousin who had established a retail store business. We shared the decision to both Abel and Kibrom. Kibrom said it was not a bad idea as he could pursue his efforts for resettlement from Uganda. Yohannes left for Uganda by hitching a hike on a long-haul truck with an Eritrean driver Kibrom knew. I stayed in Nairobi with my new friends Abel and Kibrom.

*****

After such a long updating of my story from the day I was deported from Ethiopia along with my family to my friend Abiy, we reached the place where Tedros hung around.

Unfortunately, Ted was not there, and when we asked the other Ethiopians at the café, they said they did not see him today. I was eager to hear about Abiy's family and how Mr. Dereje, Mama Tirunesh, and my dear Amsal were doing. When I thought of

Amsal and the family, I get choked with emotion. There was not a single day I had stopped thinking of Amsal, Abiy, and the rest of the family. Now more than any time in the last three years, I felt I would see them in the near future, God willing. I sensed Abiy was hesitant to talk about his family, and I couldn't figure out why.

As the day was waning, I was thinking of going to Abel's house for the night. Abiy asked me to stay for a little longer. He was making a telephone call on his mobile phone. Apparently, someone answered the phone on the other side. Abiy was animated as he was talking. Without saying anything, he handed the phone.

"Hello?" I called, and I heard a voice unmistakably of my sweet Amsal. For a few seconds, I froze, and some indecipherable words came out.

"Amsal," she said. "Have you forgotten me?" she said in jest.

"How can I forget, dear Amsal?" I responded after I regained my composure.

We asked of each other's health and situations. I told her how I missed her and the rest of the family.

"Maybe you will invite me when you go to America?"

"I will love to," I answered her.

"Tiruye"—as she called her mother—"wants to talk to you."

Mama Tirunesh asked about everybody in my family. When she was about to end her talk, she implored me not to be separated from Abiy. "You both grew up together as brothers. And stay together," she advised.

I promised her we would not be separated. Mr. Dereje was not at home at the time.

Afterward, Abiy said, "Do you know why I didn't tell you about my family? I wanted you to hear their voices and talk to them directly."

"Thank you, Abiy. You are a brother," I told him.

Abiy asked, "Where are you staying?"

I responded, "At Eastleigh neighborhood."

"Oh! We live in the same neighborhood."

I told him how I found the roommates.

"If you want, you can live with us. I share with two roommates. They wouldn't mind," he assured me.

"As of tomorrow, I will move with you. But tonight I have to go to Abel's. I would be ingrate if I left without an expression of gratitude."

At Abiy's place, I encountered an unexpected problem. Abiy had two roommates who had recently emigrated from Addis Ababa. One of them opposed vigorously for a "secessionist" to live among them on account of Eritrea's separation from Ethiopia. Abiy calmly tried to explain to him that I was his friend as close as a brother, that we grew up together, and that he was the one who invited me to live with them.

The guy wouldn't budge. He stood fast and said, "He is not welcome to live with us." To escalate the confrontation, he came close to my face and said, "Why don't you go and live with your own people?"

I saw the guy with such pitiful small stature but a temperament unmatched. I swear I could punch the guy and send him flat to his face on the ground. I remained patient out of respect for Abiy. But Abiy was getting upset and warned the guy to shut up and, if he didn't like it, to get the hell out.

As the situation heated up, the third roommate intervened by saying, "Calm down, guys. What is this? We are all in the same boat, fleeing from our homes. If we were happy at home, we wouldn't be here. So let us live in peace and share a small corner of this place with our guest."

After things got quiet, I felt obliged to make a comment. I told everyone, "I came here as a friend. Outside of my family, nobody is as close to me as Abiy, and I was happy when I met him in Nairobi. I have a promise not to separate from him. I have no intention to cause aggravation to anyone. Thank you."

I was still waiting for documents from my uncle in the US. To get updated about them, I called my uncle collect. He informed me, in two weeks, I should get the documents via DHL, and he asked how I was doing. I told him of my excitement in meeting my childhood friend Abiy and that we were staying together.

"Very good," he said.

I told him I had ran out of money.

"I will send you money through MoneyGram, and pick it up by showing your passport as an ID."

I thanked him very much. Two days later, I went to the MoneyGram office and collected five hundred dollars. That was plenty of money for the modest life we lived. When I offered Abiy to go to dinner, he suggested to buy some rice, vegetables, and beef and cook at home. We could share it with our roommates, he said. I agreed. As always, he was considerate.

Almost two weeks since I talked to my uncle, all the documents he had sent arrived. I picked them up from the DHL office in downtown Nairobi. The documents included an affidavit of support, financial statement, employment letter, and a letter from a senator's office submitted to the consulate in Nairobi. All the documents that he sent me copies of, the originals of which were submitted to the consulate. In a note, he advised me to wait for a notice of an interview from the US consulate. I was so elated I gave all the documents for Abiy to see.

Things seemed to take the right course for me. I was worried for Abiy. His name was not coming up on the resettlement roster. I thought of asking my uncle if he could sponsor him, but I was afraid it might be tasking his generosity.

I had to call my uncle to acknowledge the receipt of the documents. I called him at about midnight Nairobi time, and it would be an early evening in central time US. As I hoped, my uncle answered the telephone.

"Hello! I am Matheos." After exchanging greetings, I told him of the receipt of the documents.

"Good. Now you have to wait for the appointment notice. Make sure you do not change address. Or if you have to, you let me know immediately so I may update the consulate of your new address. Be patient," he advised, "and stay out of trouble." He added, "I will send you money in a couple of weeks."

I thanked him for all the help he was offering me. With a pleading voice, I said, "Uncle, I have one more favor to ask you. I hope it isn't too much. It is about my friend Abiy. He has been here for many months, waiting for some country to call him for resettlement, and it is not happening. Is there any way you can help him?"

He was quiet for a minute or two and then said, "Let me think about it. I can't do it because I am in the process of sponsoring you, but I will ask some friends. I will call you on it."

I thanked him again and ended our telephone call.

Abiy was not aware that I had asked my uncle to sponsor him. I was waiting until there was a positive response. It would be my dream to see us both travel to the US and start a new life.

The highlight of my life since I started living with Abiy was to call Ethiopia to speak to his family. We set time on Sunday late afternoon. Invariably, it was Amsal who answered the phone, to the delight of my heart. She said she eagerly waited for the phone to ring. The first ring was the time when she answered it. I should admit my heart pounded when I heard her voice and every time I talked to her. Amsal was different. Her voice, bright eyes, well-aligned milky white teeth, shoulder-long silky hair, proportioned frame, and good mores made her more attractive. I loved her all the time.

On this particular Sunday call, I told her all my documents had been submitted to the US consulate and I was just waiting for the interview date. "If everything goes right, I might migrate to the US, but I will always call you from there."

Lovingly, she said, "I hope you will."

I also mentioned that I had asked my uncle to sponsor Abiy and that he said he would see what he could do. "Maybe Abiy and I will travel to the US together."

"That will be great. I envy you both. I wish I could join," she said.

Driven by my emotion, I said, "I wish you were too, Amsal. I love you so much."

Maybe because of the suddenness of my expression of love, she paused and said, "I love you too."

Her four-word response had a magical effect on me. That moment, I wanted to hug, kiss, and caress her. We spoke for a longer time than usual, expressing our hopes and goals. I was encouraged enough to tell her my hope at the moment and forever to be with her.

"I will wait for that day," she said tenderly.

Abiy was sitting in the café, seated among young people. I joined him and handed him the telephone. "It has been a long talk," he remarked without a hint of sarcasm.

I simply said, "I guess it was."

On the fourth day after I talked to him, my uncle called me on the telephone to give the good news about Abiy's sponsorship. He said his brother-in-law, a famous attorney with great political connections, was willing to sponsor him. What he needed now was a short biography of Abiy that should include his full name, date of birth, education, parents' name and address, and siblings' name and address. "To expedite it, either email it or fax it to me at the number provided."

I promised we would fax it that day and thanked him before we ended the call. I rushed to Abiy to give him the information and work on the biography.

Abiy saw me with a big smile on my face. "What is with you? Did you win a lottery?"

"Come! Sit down! I have something to tell you." I told him the news.

He remained silent with mouth open and no words coming out. After he caught his breath, he said, "I cannot believe you did this for me. You don't know how grateful I am."

"Let us sit down and work on the biography," I urged him. In the late afternoon, we faxed it to the USA.

There is something about hope that brightens the spirit of a person. Hope allows one to dream of a better tomorrow and the future. Abiy and I had every reason to look at our future with much hope. Deep in my heart, I started to believe that we would depart from Kenya in a few months.

While waiting for date of an interview, our life had become routine. We walked the streets, rendez-vous at the same café, trade jokes, and sometimes discuss current events and sports, especially the British football teams. But my mind always diverted to my obsession, Amsal. Wherever I went, she was always in my mind and now more than ever. I was not sure if Abiy knew what made me change my disposition in the middle of our talk, among others.

Abiy's documents arrived five days later. We checked if everything was in order, and it was. Mr. Donald Boone, the sponsor, was very meticulous. He filled all the forms and included his financial statement prepared by a certified accountant and his three years' tax documents. He included his business card with a note attached advising us to call him as soon as we received it. As advised, we called Mr. Boone at his office. Unfortunately, his assistant informed us he was in court. We left a message and hung up the telephone.

We celebrated by going out to dinner at an Ethiopian restaurant. As always, we talked about our childhood. We remembered the time we went to Debre Libanos monastery and about some of the eccentricities of the people that crossed our lives.

Then Abiy said, "Wouldn't it be nice to call your parents and talk to them?"

I was hesitant to call, for fear that I might put them at risk if the telephone was being monitored by the Eritrean government.

"But," he insisted, "I am the one who is going to call them. And I will hand over the telephone to you and talk to them without mentioning your name."

Since I left Asmara, Eritrea, it would be my first time to talk to my family. In Sudan, Wedi Hawe connected me with Tesfay who informed them of our safe arrival. My uncle Solomon from the US, every time he called, informed me that everybody was fine.

The telephone was ringing a few times. Abiy was about to hang up when it was picked up.

Father answered it. "Hello! Who are you?"

"Abiy. I am Abiy Dereje. How are you, Baba Haile?"

Father said, "Abiy!" My father repeated, "What a miracle! Where are you calling from? How are you doing? And how are Dereje and Tirunesh and Amsal?"

Abiy said, "I am in Nairobi. Everybody is fine."

Father said, "Did you know your friend is in Nairobi?"

Abiy said, "Yes. He is here with me, and we live together."

"Blessed be the Lord! Blessed be the Lord!" Father intoned. His excitement was infectious. Father added, "How is Aba Berhanemeskel, our priest?"

Abiy said, "He is fine, except getting old and fragile. He always remembers you in his prayers and our family too."

Father said, "I know! I know! Dereje and Tirunesh are more than friends. They are brother and sister to me and my family."

Abiy said, "Matheos wants to talk to you."

I said, "Hello, Abaye. How are you?"

Father said, "Oh! My poor son, how are you? We are all fine, except for missing you dearly. Your mother and sisters are fine. They are out to visit some family now. They will be disappointed for not being here when I tell them you and Abiy called."

I said, "We will call back in a few days. Give them my love. Abiy and I are fine. Do not worry about us. Uncle Solomon is helping me generously."

Father said, "He is a blessed brother. Let me talk to Abiy."

I handed over the phone to Abiy.

Abiy said, "I am here, Baba Haile."

Father said, "Next time you call Dereje and Tirunesh, tell them we are fine. I am anxiously waiting for the day to see them all face-to-face. And to Amsal, pass our love to her and tell her the girls remember her all the time."

Abiy said, "I will do so, Baba. And please pass my regards to all."

The telephone call ended.

I turned to Abiy and thanked him for his thoughtfulness. The call was for me to talk to them. I was happy to hear Baba Haile was fine.

We both said how sad it was to divide people on account of a piece of land inhabited by the same people and how stupid it was to go to war and cause the death and destruction far beyond the number of people in the contested area. To claim victory after this disaster was immoral. If there was victory by either side, it was pyrrhic.

Lately, I had been thinking of my friends who fled from Eritrea with me. Yohannes was in Uganda, but we lost communication. The two others, Daniel and Habtom, left from Khartoum to go to Libya, crossing through the Sahara Desert with a final destination to cross the Mediterranean Sea to reach Europe. There was no means for me to reach Europe.

In the evening, I made a call to Yohannes, but there was no response. I left him a message with my phone number.

About midnight, the phone started ringing. Abiy said it must be my call and handed me the phone.

"Hello!" I responded. "Is this Yohannes? How are you doing?"

Yohannes said, "I am doing really well, working for my uncle in his store and import-export business. He is paying me well, and he has promised me to help me start my own business. I have decided to settle in Uganda. It is a good country. There are many people from countries of the Horn of Africa. The government is tolerant of refugees as long as you respect the laws of the country, and Ugandans are very hospitable. And how are you doing? And your friend?"

I said, "Abiy and I are fine. We are sharing a place together with two other roommates. Our case is in course with the help of my uncle and his brother-in-law in the US. All documents along with the application had been submitted. We just are waiting to be invited for interview."

Yohannes said, "I wish you all the best. And don't forget to get in touch with me before you leave to the US. Have you heard from our friends in Libya? I am always worried about them."

I answered, "No, I haven't heard about them. I pray to God to protect them."

Yohannes said, "Listen, it is getting late. I have to wake up by early morning. I will call you soon. Good night."

I said, "Bye! Yohannes, let us keep in touch."

I told Abiy, "Yohannes has decided to settle in Uganda and start business with the help of his uncle."

"I wish him luck," Abiy expressed.

It was getting late, so we went to sleep. The neighborhood we lived was one of the seediest parts of the city. Refugees who most were bereft of resources lived in the neighborhood. But life could be challenging with drunks shouting in the middle of the night, music blaring from the underground bars and bordellos, and night thieves prying into houses, stealing, and sometimes physically attacking residents.

On this night, about twenty minutes after we turned off the light to sleep, someone tried to pry open the door. All of us heard the noise, and Abiy shouted, "What do you want, son of a bitch? You open the door, you are as good as dead. *Wo Allahi!*"

The thief or thieves ran hastily before the threat was materialized. After things calmed down, I asked, "Since when did you convert to Islam, Abiy?"

Without losing a beat, he responded, "Thieves around here are scared of the Somalis. I was just sending them a message. It worked, didn't it? I am not sure if it is the pretentious Somali threat or the voice of awakened people that scared them."

The next morning, our two roommates had conspired to do little theatrics on Abiy's bluff the night before. One of them went outside and pretended as a thief trying to break into the house while the other, in fright, shouted, "Allah, help us!"

It was a hilarious drama, but Abiy bested them by saying, "Last night, you were not laughing. You were quiet, scared like a rat. I saved you, cowards." He laughed. It became a morning talk at the café among friends.

Tedros, our friend whom we were supposed to meet over two months ago, never showed up. Some said he had moved to Eldoret in southern Kenya. Others said he left to South Africa. I was sorry to have missed him.

In December, rumor was rife that the Kenyan government had ordered all refugees to be rounded up and moved to remote refugee camps. The camps were so remote and without adequate supply of water and food, and communication was difficult. It would be difficult to follow up on appointments for interview with consulates or refugee agencies. For urbanized youth, it would be almost impossible to survive in the camps. Disease and death were rampant for lack of adequate medical facility. Those who had lived in Kenya for a while had found ways to avoid the roundup by making themselves invisible until the situation subsided. If one was caught, the immediate thing to do was to bribe the arresting officer. We made sure to store enough supplies of rice, canned foods, biscuits, tea, sugar, and powdered milk at home. That was enough to keep us during the time of roundup. Usually, it would last a few days. It was halted on the fourth day. We escaped the onslaught of roundup.

The life of a refugee was filled with a mixture of fear and hope. Away from home and nurturing community, it was a constant struggle to stay afloat.

Both my uncle and Mr. Boone had received the acknowledgment of receipt of the documents for our visa application. We were also advised to appear in person with official identifications on February 7. Coincidentally, our interview dates were set on the same day at different hours. We had about forty-five days before the interview. While waiting for our interview, Abiy and I received notices from the MoneyGram office to appear with IDs. I knew it was money sent by my uncle, but Abiy's was a surprise. In the morning, we rushed to the MoneyGram office, and to our joy, both my uncle and Mr. Boone sent five hundred dollars apiece.

"Gee!" Abiy intoned. "This is godsend. I never expected it. How am I to repay this generosity? I can't wait to meet these gentlemen."

We were happy with our good fortune, and we took it as a good omen for our future. The same day, we sent faxes to both of them, thanking them of their generosity, and we promised them we would not disappoint them.

In the evening, we decided to call Ethiopia and Eritrea. Abiy told his family of the generosity of Mr. Boone and that our interview was set for February 7. "Pray for us," he pleaded with them.

I spoke to them. After greeting Ababa Dereje and Tirunesh, I talked with Amsal. I told her of our impending appointment at the Embassy of US. I even intimated with hubris that we might be in the US in three months' time. "Once I am settled in the US, I will do all my best for you to join us. That is a promise," I told her.

"I will be excited," she responded.

"I love you so much, but it is getting late. Until next time. Sweet dreams, my dear. Of course, about me."

"Certainly, I will, my dear. I will," she added.

Yohannes called early Tuesday morning. The call was so early we were alarmed it could be some kind of warning. Abiy answered and handed the telephone to me.

"Hello!" I called. Yohannes was on the other side.

Yohannes said, "I am sorry I called you so early, but I was awakened from Italy by our friends. They are safe in Sicily. Once they are registered, they will be allowed to go to the mainland. Their plan is to travel farther to England. But it will be a few months before that happens. I am happy they crossed the Mediterranean safe. From what they told me, it was a rough journey." Yohannes continued, "The sea was turbulent. Food was inadequate, and the boat was overcrowded. It was a miracle that they arrived at Lampedusa without any casualty but a lot hungry and exhausted. You may get a call from them. I have provided them with your number. I hope Abiy wouldn't mind."

I said, "No, don't worry. It will be okay with Abiy."

Yohannes said, "Talk to you next time." And he ended the call.

"Is Yohannes all right? He calls at this early hour," Abiy asked with concern.

"Everything is good. He called to let me know our friends had crossed the Mediterranean safe into Sicily."

"Glad to hear that," Abiy expressed.

With our interview set and some money in our pocket, our appetite for touristic adventure was whetted. Kenya was famous for its wildlife. People came from all over to have a rendezvous with lions, zebras, elephants, leopards, and so many other beasts. There were many ways of traveling to see the animals in their natural habitat. The price for arranging the travel could cost from several thousand dollars to a reasonably less expense. We chose the cheapest way where a driver in an all-terrain automobile was to take us and have photoshoot in the Masai-Bora area.

We arranged a tour with a tour guide with a Land Rover to take us with four other local tourists and stay in the wilderness for the whole day. He advised us to wear comfortable attire and shoes, have a camera ready, and carry something to eat and drink. Early morning, we met our guide at the appointed place. The other four people were already seated in the automobile, and we took our seats. The driver had driven many times through the wild game park that he was familiar where the different species of animals would congregate. Of course, we wanted to see them in the safe enclosure of the Land Rover. The Land Rover had a retractable roof, so people could stand with heads out to observe and take pictures.

The first animals we saw were zebras and giraffes grazing with total abandon. We took several pictures. As we drove farther into the park, we saw animals of different species. We saw a pride of lions with cubs under the shade and the lioness standing with tongue hanging out and breathing with audible sound. We were only about ten meters distance. It was awesome. We took pictures as the driver had stopped the car for us to look closely. The animals didn't seem to begrudge us at our ogling and intrusion into their domain. With total disinterest in our presence, they seemed to say tolerable nuisances. Yet none of us ventured to step outside the automobile fortress. The driver kept driving farther on the dusty road until we saw a herd of elephants crossing the path. The gigantic animals were moving to the more thickly forested part of the park. There were about eight of them with three youngsters. The head of the family, a humongous elephant, was looking at our direction, maybe observing if we were a danger to the members of his family.

"How do they protect themselves?"

The guide driver told us that elephants were very protective of their families.

"But where are the Masai people?" we asked.

The driver said, "We will go to a Masai village soon. You can talk and socialize with them, albeit with respect." He changed direction toward the city but in a different route.

After driving for about twenty kilometers, he stopped at a cluster of huts. He stepped out of the car and started calling out people. Several people from different huts came out to greet us. He spoke in what I thought was Swahili. There were women, men, and children.

A man spoke in English. After welcoming us, he asked if we had seen different kinds of animals. To which we responded positively.

The men were tall, sinewy, and graceful. The women were dressed in their traditional garbs, bare breasted, with no inhibition. If it were not for their dress and ornaments, they looked like so many of our people. We took pictures with them and gave a few dollars as a token of our appreciation.

From there, the driver took us under a big acacia tree where we sat and ate food that we carried with us. He warned us to stay alert as animals might ambush us. The car was parked only a meter away with doors left ajar. Our driver was a gifted tourist guide. On our way back, he entertained us by mimicking the different voices of animals and birds.

In Nairobi, we developed the pictures and showed them to friends at the café. We thought we had earned a bragging right for coming so close to wild beasts in the African savanna. But among the refugee community where activities of such nature were considered vanity, people looked at us with sarcasm. It didn't take long before a moniker was attached to our names. Abiy became Tourist Abiy, and I became Tourist Matheos. The next few weeks, the joke was "Is your next trip to scale Mount Kilimanjaro on a hot air balloon?" Yes, it was infantile, but for people who scrimped to feed themselves on a daily basis, maybe we were insensitive to brag about our touristic adventure.

It was the first week of January, close to the celebration of Christmas of Orthodox Tewahedo Church. It was a time of joy and gift exchanges. I thought of Amsal. *How about sending her a surprise gift?* I shared my opinion with Abiy, and sure, he agreed that would make her thrilled. I bought a sweater, blouse, shirt, a pair of shoes, and a handbag. I packed them into a box with a letter of expression of my love for her tucked inside and sent it on DHL to Addis Ababa. Five days later when we called to wish the family a merry Christmas, Amsal was so excited for the first time in her life. She was out of words, except to say "I love you." Those three words were a poem to my ears and made my life enjoyable.

On Christmas Eve, we went to the Ethiopian Orthodox church to pray and celebrate Christmas among our people. After the ritual of celebration ended, we decided to hang around to socialize with the congregants. There was plenty of food and beverages organized by volunteers. There were many—by my estimate, about six hundred—people. The women were in their beautiful dress and the men in an all-white traditional clothing. The whole atmosphere was festive. Amharic speakers and Tigrigna speakers were in a communal celebration. Politics, region, nationality, or citizenship mattered little. I was happy. It was a long time since I had been among so many of my people in a religious celebration.

Actually, it was at Debre Libanos monastery, when Abiy and I traveled with our parents to celebrate the St. Tekle Haymanot annual celebration. The gathering of people in the church had another function—social function, where old friends would meet and renew their friendship and relatives would meet and catch up on their situations.

Tedros had traveled to celebrate Christmas at the church. He was a member of the church from the time he came to Nairobi. He saw us from a corner and walked toward us and touched the back of Abiy. He stood behind us.

When Abiy saw him, he turned his face to me and said, "Look who is here."

I made a turn and saw Tedros and blurted, "Hi, Ted!" with excitement.

He responded, "Hi, Matheos!" with a coolness of a person stranger to another.

It did not stop me from giving him a hug, which I believed was reciprocated involuntarily because he didn't expect it. Abiy sensed the uneasiness of both of us and suggested that we go outside the church, to which we all agreed. As we came out of the church, the day was breaking. It was still very early morning to see much activity in the street. Few automobiles and fewer people were moving on the streets.

As we walked, I was asking myself, "Is there something I did to my friend Tedros for him to be so cold towards me?"

Tedros told us that really he was talking to Abiy because he avoided eye contact with me, that he came the day before from Eldoret, and that he was going back in two days. He was admitted to an Adventist-run college.

"Wow! Exciting! Congratulations!" Abiy exclaimed. "Matheos and I are also hoping to go to the US. Our interview date is on February 7. Matheos's uncle is the one who is helping us by sponsoring him, and his brother-in-law is sponsoring me."

"Good luck," he said.

As we walked, we saw an open café, and Abiy suggested to have coffee. All agreed, and we sat on the outside seating. It was warm for that hour. We ordered beverages.

And Abiy, true to his nature, asked Tedros, "What is wrong? Why are so you cold to our friend

Matheos? He has been asking about you since he came to Nairobi, eager to meet you."

Tedros disingenuously said, "Didn't I say hi to him?"

He was still avoiding my face. I started to get annoyed. Who cared if he didn't want my friendship? But I was curious why he turned to be unfriendly.

"What is the matter with you, Ted? This is unlike you. Is there something that he did to annoy you?"

Ted said, "I have stopped to talk to Eritreans because they are our enemies."

Abiy looked at him sternly for some time, surprised by the answer. I was about to respond, but Abiy stopped me by gesturing with his hand. Abiy said, "Are you serious, Teddy? You know our friend and his family. He is a friend born among us, grew up with us, and played together with us. We ate at each other's homes. We are more like brothers than friends. How can you label him enemy? You know the circumstances under which they were expelled from Ethiopia in spite of the protestation from our families. Did they try to hurt anyone? Didn't they cry for being separated from us? They didn't start the war. They were victims of it, like thousands of others. I still consider him as my dearest friend and brother, no matter what the politicians say or do. That is all I want to say, and Matheos has nothing to be ashamed of or apologize for." Abiy stood and said, "Let us go," without bidding bye.

We walked quietly to our home to get some sleep. We rested for a few hours and woke up as the midday sun got hotter.

As we were eating lunch, I brought up Teddy. "I couldn't believe. It is not the same Teddy I grew up with—"

"Let us forget him," Abiy interrupted. "I am not interested in talking about him."

In the afternoon, the telephone rang, and it was Teddy.

Abiy answered it. "Hello," he said. And then he was quiet. Teddy told him he was leaving in the morning. He wanted to talk to us before he would leave. "It is all right. We can meet anytime." The time and place were set for four thirty in the afternoon.

Teddy was a bit awkward when he approached the table. He extended his arm to greet us. He gestured for the server to take orders. He ordered juice and invited us to order anything we wanted. We were already drinking sodas and politely declined by saying, "Thank you."

Teddy, in a soft voice, said, "I am sorry guys for what happened yesterday." He continued, "After you left, I thought about the whole thing, including our childhood. All the good times we spent together, the mischiefs we did, and the tight bond we had, which was an envy to many of our classmates. All came back to me. It helped me think what matters most is the character and friendship of the individual rather than race, ethnicity, and national origin. I am sorry to act the way I did. I value your friendship. I hope we put this episode in the past."

Abiy looked at me to observe my reaction. I gave a nod of acceptance. We stretched our arms in friendship, but Teddy stood and gave me a hug. The gesture reignited our old friendship. He was eager to hear about my story since the expulsion. I told him the long story until my arrival to Kenya. He heard me with full attention and sympathy. He asked about my family. He was back, the old Teddy. Teddy postponed his travel back to Eldoret by two more days. The three of us stayed together the whole time, reliving old experiences, laughing, and reminiscing old memories. It turned out to be the three most memorable days of three friends for a long time.

Two weeks were left before our interview date. Every day we were waiting anxiously for our fate—of going to the US and starting our life with hope of the future or being stuck here as refugees bereft of any hope and security.

In the meantime, the routine of our life of going to the city where fellow refugees would congregate in cafés continued. Abiy called a group of refugees huddled together "the table of rumor factory." He even segregated the different groups by the creative rumor they peddled. It was the few individuals that made the difference. Some were so inventive in their rumors they could either terrify you or entertain you by their stories. We loved to join the most creative group of all. Every day they had stories to tell on the foibles or successes of individuals. All the stories must be taken with a grain of salt as most of them turned out to be fantasies or imaginations of the individual storyteller. But what was a refugee to do, with plenty of time at hand and few things to do? All the rumors started with "Have you heard of such and such person or such and such incident?" Then everyone opened their ears to imbibe in the funniest or saddest creation of the imagination. Of course, there would always be someone to confirm the story with embellishment, and at times, there were others who tried to debunk the story with their own take on the incidents.

One of the distinctive qualities among the young refugees was the habit of sharing. We shared food, money, housing, and sometimes clothing. It was the temporariness of their life that made them avoid hoarding. There was a deeper feeling: "I left my home, my family, and all my possessions. What is the point of being selfish when I don't know what is going to happen tomorrow?" Actually, Abiy had a better term for it. He called it "communal happiness" or "communal misery," whichever spectrum of feeling one shared at a certain time.

On February 7, we got off our sleep early, took a shower, and dressed in clean, well-pressed shirts and jackets. Our fading shoes were polished. All the copies of the documents were organized in a manila folder, and we got our passports in our pockets and two extra passport-sized photographs ready. We walked out of the house to meet with the consular officer. I had the earlier appointment, with Abiy almost three hours later, but we went together, encouraging each other. When it was thirty minutes into the appointment, I showed my invitation letter to the person at the gate and to the clerk at the front door. I was guided to sit at the waiting area to hear for my name to be called. I tried to distract myself by reading the assorted magazines on the desk. I ended up looking at the pictures, beautiful pictures, of the different places in the US.

"Mr. Haile," someone called.

I got confused. Nobody had called me by my father's name.

I didn't respond until the clerk told me, "It is for you. Get into the room to your right."

"Thank you," I said and walked into the room where a young consular officer was seated behind a big desk. There were two chairs on the side of the desk to which I was invited to sit on one.

The officer said, "Good morning," to which I responded likewise. He seemed to be a nice guy, I reassured myself. He asked me for my passport and the extra pictures and the several documents on file pertaining to my application.

The interview started with checking my biographical information.

The officer asked, "How are you related to your sponsor?"

I answered, "He is my uncle on my father's side."

The officer asked, "Do you know Abiy Dereje?"

I answered, "Yes, he is my childhood friend."

The officer said, "But he is from Ethiopia."

I said, "Yes, from the town where we were born and grew up."

The officer asked, "Do you know his sponsor?"

I said, "I know he is my uncle's brother-in-law. It was my uncle who arranged the sponsorship."

The officer said, "I grew up in the town where your uncle and Mr. Boone live. My parents still live there. Mr. Boone is a very famous lawyer with powerful connections."

I replied, "Oh! Interesting. What a coincidence."

The officer said, "What is your plan in the US?"

I said, "I want to further my education and start a career."

The officer stamped the visa on my passport and signed it. "Good luck. Maybe when I visit my hometown, I might meet you."

I said, "Thank you very much, sir." I felt like being reborn at that moment. He guided me through the door. I said, "Thank you again," to him and to the clerk. She approvingly smiled at me.

I rushed to see Abiy. Even the air smelled different. The shining sun looked brighter, and the blue sky was majestic. I felt God was celebrating with me. Abiy was in a corner seat, hunkered like an exhausted traveler. When he saw me smiling, his mood changed. Instinctively, he knew the news was good and smiled before I even told him the approval of my visa. I just handed him my open passport for him to look for himself. We jumped like little kids, catching the curious look of passersby.

Some three hours later, Abiy went through the same gate and doors to see the same consular officer. It took slightly longer for his interview as the officer asked him about the escape from Ethiopia and school documents. Fortunately, Abiy had included the school papers and some letters from his family and friends corroborating the reasons of his flight. With the documents and a strong and credible sponsorship from Mr. Boone, the officer granted him an entry visa. In our personal history, February 7 was etched as the most important day.

Immediately, after securing our visas, we faxed the news to my uncle and Mr. Boone. As for calling our parents in Ethiopia and Eritrea, we decided to wait until the date of our departure was determined. I was tempted to call Amsal and break the good news, but I deferred, to Abiy's suggestion, to wait for our departure date. Of late, I had been using every reason to call Amsal at least once a week. This would have been the best news to tell.

In the evening as we were celebrating the occasion with friends, the telephone started ringing. Abiy handed it to me; it was my uncle and Mr. Boone. They expressed their happiness for us being granted visas and asked when did we plan to travel.

"We are ready anytime, as soon as it could be arranged."

"Okay, then we will contact the travel agent. We will update you the soonest. Good night."

With visas secured and tickets to be arranged by our sponsors, we called Ethiopia and Eritrea.

My dear Amsal answered the telephone with her sweet melodic voice, "Hello!" to my delight.

And I said, "How are you, lovely lady?" And without waiting for her response, I said, "I have good news to tell you. Abiy and I are going to America."

In excitement, she shouted, "Tiruye! Abaye! Come here! They are going to America! America!" she repeated.

We talked to the parents and told them, with the help of their love and prayers, we had been granted visas, and we might leave Kenya in two weeks.

"Oh! Bless you, sons! Be good and pray and praise the Lord," they advised.

Amsal took the telephone back and said, "You are not going to forget me once you are in America?"

"Not in a million years, my dear. I love you and want to spend the rest of my life with you. And that is my solemn pledge," I confirmed.

Abiy called my parents in Eritrea and told them the good news—that our life as refugees was to end and our new life in America was to start.

They were so happy, and they advised us to never separate and to support each other. "God be with you, my sons," my father prayed.

We were informed that our flight was scheduled for February 28 on a KLM flight through Amsterdam and Atlanta, Georgia, and on a local flight to Chicago.

My uncle called and informed us to pick up the tickets at the KLM office and the money at MoneyGram. "February is the middle of winter," he said. "Bundle up, it is going to be cold. Have a scarf, sweater, and heavy coat. Donald and I will be at the airport in Chicago to pick you up. Have a safe trip. If you have any concerns, call either one of us. See you soon."

The flight was at ten o'clock in the morning to Amsterdam, Netherlands. It was a jet plane with a comfortable seating. It was a smooth flight, and we arrived at the Schiphol Airport safely. The connecting flight to the US on Delta Airlines was in the evening. We had a few hours in between. We sat at a café in the airport terminal while waiting for our flight, admiring the elegance of the airport. The terminal was crowded with people rushing with their luggage in tow in every direction. "Where are all these people going?" A sign of commerce and progress.

As the time came close for boarding, we went to the gate where our flight was to take off. We boarded the plane crossing the Atlantic Ocean mostly in darkness. The sky was brightened by a full moon and bright twinkling stars adorning it. The flight was interesting. It took us to Scotland and crossed the ocean to reach the Canadian sky and then southward to Atlanta. It was tiring but nonetheless exciting. At the Atlanta Airport, we changed to a local flight to go to Chicago.

At the Chicago airport terminal, my uncle and Mr. Boone were standing and looking for two young men that they had never met before. It would be very easy to identify us among the overwhelming Caucasian passengers. Out of caution, however, my uncle Solomon was holding a cutout cardboard with our names inscribed in big letters. We joined them. After exchanging salutations and telling them how the trip was, we collected our luggage and exited the airport to go where the car was parked. Oh! Was it cold! Never had we imagined such bone-chilling cold. Remember we came from tropical Africa. Once we get into the car, the heat was blasted full, to our relief.

To relieve our anxiety of a life in such a frigid clime, our hosts comforted us by saying, "Don't worry, it is only for a few months. Spring will come with its bright sunshine and ambient weather."

It was very difficult for us to imagine that, in a short few months, the weather could change drastically.

Donald was the driver. He had already told us to call him by his first name. "No more formality. We are family and on first-name basis," he added.

It was a bit awkward for us because we came from a culture that frowned calling a person older or with a degree of achievement by just first name.

But Uncle Solomon said, smiling, "It is okay. He is Don."

The car was luxurious, big, and with leather seats—the type only dignitaries would drive in our country. We were already in dreamland.

After driving for about forty-five minutes, the car was stopped in front of what looked like a restaurant.

"Time for something to munch," Don announced.

In the restaurant, we were handed a book-like menu with food items whose names were strange to us. In the restaurants we catered in Africa, menus were not written. The choices were only three items, and we ordered among them. Befuddled by what to choose, Abiy and I looked at each other. And then he pointed at one familiar item, hamburger, and so we ordered. It was juicy and delicious, and crispy fries were on the side.

On the way, Uncle Solomon was pointing us the different towns and cities that we were passing. Snow was falling, piled on the street sides like a pile of cotton. The trees had shed their leaves, looking like dead trees. We were in awe with everything we saw.

We arrived in Milwaukee by late afternoon. Uncle Solomon and Don lived about half an hour outside the perimeter of the city. Uncle Solomon and his wife, Erin, lived in a big house with their dog. At the house, Sarah, Don's wife, and his two children— Rebecca or Becky and Albert or Al—with Erin waited for our arrival. As the door opened, we saw a big sign in bold letters, festooned with balloons, "Welcome, Matheos and Abiy." Everyone shouted welcome and started to hug us and took over our luggage and took the several clothes bundled over us to fend off the cold.

After we settled on comfortable chairs, Don gave a welcoming speech slowly and in simple English. He said, "We are all happy that you have arrived safe. Now you are part of this family. We are here to make your transition to life in America smooth. Do not hesitate to ask for help when needed. Al has volunteered to take you on a tour to the city." He faced Al and said, "Thank you, Al. If you want to make a call to Ethiopia and Eritrea, Sol will help you." Pointing toward the dining table, he added, "Now is the time to feast. Erin, Sarah, and Becky had worked hard to prepare the food."

We thanked them all.

Before the dinner, we were led to our rooms. Wow! Two separate bedrooms with big beds. This luxury was to spoil us. When we were left alone, we looked at each other and said, "Is this real, or are we dead and in heaven?"

We refreshed ourselves and joined the rest of the family in the dining room. The dining table was big and could sit eight people. A variety of food was ready on serving dishes. It was a very enjoyable dinner, and the easy and loving relationship among the people was evident. Everyone made us feel at home.

After dinner, we were so tired it was a struggle to keep our eyes open. It must have been the time difference and jet lag. They urged us to go to sleep, and we had the most comfortable sleep we had in a long time. In Nairobi, we stayed in a dingy little room on mattresses on the floor. Our bedsheets were cleaned maybe once a week. Our body was washed from an improvised shower with pails of hanging water from the sidewall. Water was scarce. There were times when we couldn't take a complete body wash, actually more often than not. Already, in a single day in the US, our life had changed immeasurably for the better.

Al came early for a tour to the city and its surroundings. We had breakfast at home—scrambled eggs with bacon, pancakes, and freshly squeezed orange juice.

Erin offered us coffee, but we were not coffee drinkers. "Aha! You came from a country that gave coffee to the world, and you don't drink it," she observed.

When we were about to leave the house, Erin offered cash to buy us some clothing. Al said he would rather use a card instead of carrying cash. Erin agreed. We left the house not understanding what they meant by card. Al took us to the city, neighborhood by neighborhood, and some of the iconic sights, university campuses, and lakeshore area. Our last stop was at a mall.

The mall was so big with multitude of shops, big and small. At the men's clothing store, Al told us to choose shirts, pants, and jackets and check for sizes in the fitting rooms behind the counter. We chose different pieces of clothing. On the jacket, the price was 120 dollars. I immediately converted it to Ethiopian currency, and I was shocked. It was over 1,000 birr, a two-month salary for the average worker. This was outrageous. I couldn't make them spend that kind of money, I protested. Abiy agreed. Al was confused on what we were doing, constantly checking on the price tags. We told him it was too expensive and to take us to a cheaper place.

He said, "This is an average price."

"Average price!" we expressed our surprise. It was only at the insistence of Al that we took the clothes. They were very nice, we admitted.

"How was the tour of the city?" Erin asked.

"It was beautiful. Al was a great guide," I answered.

"Yes, he is great." Erin had a special love for her nephew and niece.

We had to make a call to our parents and, of course, to my dear Amsal. About midday, we called Ethiopia.

Amsal answered it on the first ring. "Hi, Americans!" was her first remark.

Abiy told her kindly, "You can say that," and updated her of our situation and how it had turned out—far better than we ever dreamed. "It is marvelous. Our hosts and their families are wonderful. They are spoiling us, sister. Yesterday they bought us expensive clothing. With our new attire, you may not identify us. If I may say so, we look elegant. Can I talk to Tiruye and Abaye? I know Matheos is salivating to talk to you. Before he bites me, let me finish my talk."

He told his parents of our safe arrival in the US and how our hosts, Uncle Solomon and Donald, picked us up from the airport. "We are being treated so wonderful. You don't have to worry a thing about us. These are very kind people."

"God bless them," Abaye prayed. And he added, "Don't disappoint them."

After talking to me and advising us to be respectful to our hosts, the telephone was handed back to Amsal.

I was lost for words. I kept saying, "I wish you were here. Everything is marvelous."

She said, "I am happy for you. And with you there, I know I would have loved it."

"That is my dream," I promised before we hung up the call.

As we were getting ready to go to Don's place at the invitation of Sarah, we saw Erin donned a hat, scarf, heavy jacket, and boots that we saw in movies featuring American farmers. We were curious why she was dressed like that. And then we heard a scratching sound coming from the sidewalk in front of the house. We peeked through the window, and Erin was shoveling the snow.

We said, "We are here, two young men sitting, and she is doing the hard work. It is not right."

We changed our clothes and wore sweaters, winter jackets, head covers, and gloves. We went out. Erin insisted that she was all right and that she had done it all the time, but we were equally insistent that we had to do it. She finally relented. We cleared the entryway and all the sides and sprayed deicer; all was clear when we placed the shovel in the garage. She was so happy for our being considerate. In the evening, she told everyone of our shoveling experience. Everybody complimented us for being helpful.

The removal of snow from the sidewalk became our chore. We never expected it to be a business that would make us money during our school years.

Erin took us to the Boones' house around six o'clock in the evening. Everybody was there, except for Sol. He was stranded on traffic owing to the heavy snow. He called and informed Don that he would be late and that it was all right, without him, to start the dinner.

Don said, "Let us give him about forty minutes unless someone is famished."

"We can wait," all assented.

Al took us to the basement where so many gadgets were available—computers, video players, and all kinds of sport equipment. It must be a well-used room as we observed from the muscular body of Al. With the direction of Al, we tried some of the games. We were novices, but he said with a few practices, we would be good at them. He demonstrated a few of the games when Becky shouted, "Sol is here! Come upstairs!"

Sol greeted us in Amharic and asked how our day was, and we responded, saying, "Wonderful."

The dinner table was covered with an array of foods and beverages. We each dished from all and ate to our fill. At dinner, Erin repeated our clearing of the snow to Sol. He was very happy and appreciative of our help to his wife and our good manners.

Al picked up where Sol left and, with obvious humor, said, "There is no free labor in America. I work for my father at his law firm, and he pays me.

If he fails to pay, I will sue the shirt of his back."
Everyone laughed.

But an idea came tangentially from the humor.
Erin said, "Al, you gave me an idea. If Sol and our
young men agree, why don't they clear snow in the
neighborhood for a fee during winter and take care
of lawns in the summer. What do you think, Sol?"

Sol agreed, "It is a great idea as long as it doesn't
interfere with their education."

Hence, a business was created. Erin was
respected and had many friends in the neighborhood. She amazed us. The next morning, she drafted
a flyer of the type of service we would provide for a
reasonable fee.

The neighbors had been made aware of our
arrival, and after Erin called for service, almost all
of them offered us the job. Erin secured us a map
of the area and marked all the houses. The first day,
she went with us door to door to introduce us to
the people. We met Mrs. Walter, Steven, Franklin,
McGrath, Rossati, Mitchell, and Marquez. All of
them were very nice and welcomed us to the US and
their neighborhood.

Fortuitously, a heavy snow fell that night, so the
next day became our first day at work. At five thirty
in the morning, we were ready to clear the snow. We
dressed properly for the weather. We started with
the closest house, that of Mr. and Mrs. Walter. We
cleared the steps, entryway, and sidewalks and spread
deicing salt.

As we were clearing the next house which was contiguous to the Walters', we heard Mr. Walter, standing on the front door, called his wife, "Honey! Come and see what the young men did. Good job."

We did clear all the houses and finished in less than four hours.

Back at home, we were eating breakfast when Erin saw us and asked, "Are you already done clearing the snow?"

"Yes," we told her.

To make sure everything was done right, she went and checked every house. She was happy, so were all the people. She collected the fees and compliments.

In the meantime, Mrs. Walter asked if it was possible for us to walk her dog twice a day.

"I will ask them," Erin promised.

As soon as she stepped into the house, Erin said, "Hey, rich guys! You have earned two hundred dollars, and all are happy. You did a wonderful job." The walk-a-dog part we didn't understand, and we looked at Erin, baffled. She explained, "You take the dog to the park and walk it around."

"What? Like a shepherd behind his livestock?"

"Not like that. The dog is on a leash around the neck. You just hold it and walk in the park."

"All right, we will do it," we accepted. I was thinking, "I couldn't wait to tell Amsal about our new career as shepherds of dog. She will laugh her heart out."

So many things were involved with dog walking. It was not idly walking, whistling your favorite tune. You had to clean after the dog. You either had to carry a small scoop and broom or a plastic bag and some other bag to collect the poop and dump it into a garbage bucket. We preferred the plastic bags. Mrs. Walter demonstrated for us how to pick up the droppings by placing the plastic bag to cover our hands and pick up the poop and then fold the bag tight and place in another plastic bag that we would carry over. The name of the dog was Kuba.

Mrs. Walter said, "It is Kuba with K."

Behind her back, we said, "Does the dog know the spelling of its name?"

As Erin instructed us, we took the dog to the park a few blocks away. Actually, it was more fun than we thought. There were several people walking dogs, young ladies and elderly people. When they saw us, they commented Kuba had a new walker. Apparently, in this small community, people knew one another's dogs. Kuba was a well-trained dog. We walked a good distance in the park. Mrs. Walter had instructed us to bring back the dog in an hour for its meal. Interesting, even dogs had designated time for their meals.

About three thirty in the afternoon, we went to Mrs. Walter's place to take Kuba for the second walk. The dog was already leashed and waiting for us. We followed the same as the morning. There were many more dog walkers. What we noticed was that dog walkers seemed to have some camaraderie.

Every time one passed, they would have a short chat, mainly about their dogs and the weather. They tried to communicate with us, but our limited English was an impediment. So we just smiled. And when they said, "Kuba looks good," we would say, "Thank you," even though we thought it was the silliest thing talking about a dog's look. People don't say, "You look like a dog" to compliment you. On the contrary, it is when you are at your worst when people say, "You look like a dog."

The day was deceptively bright with sunshine, but it was cold. Something was out of sorts in the situation. Where did the heat that bright sunshine emitted get dissipated? In Africa, if the sun is bright, surely it would be a hot day. Nonetheless, the frigid weather didn't stop people from jogging, walking, and playing with their dogs. And we were enjoying the frantic activities.

Erin and Mrs. Walter made sure everybody in the neighborhood knew about us and the service we provided. People were told how polite, conscientious, and trustworthy we were. Several people approached Erin for us to walk their dogs and clear the snow. By the end of the second week, we had eight dogs to walk, four for each of us. We had planned strategically which dog to pick up first. Having more dogs on a leash was a bit more of a challenge as the dogs had different temperament. We walked the dogs five days a week. On weekends, the owners wanted to spend time with their dogs.

On Saturday, Al introduced us to his girlfriend, Alexandra. She was out of town since our arrival. He brought her to Erin and Sol's home where we met her. She already had information about us. As she saw us, she asked, "Which one of you is Matheos?" I just raised my arm. "And, of course, you are Abiy." She stretched her arm to greet us and wished us to have good life in America.

Erin, from across the room, commented, "They are already Americanized. They work as dog walkers and snow removers of the neighborhood."

"I am impressed," Alexandra said. "In such a short time, you are doing what most young American did. I was a newspaper distributor. I used to wake up very early morning and drop papers in every door in the neighborhood."

On Sunday, we were up early morning at six thirty, ready to start the day. We were determined to go to church.

Erin, who was a devout Catholic, attended mass every Sunday. As she was up and ready a few minutes later, she saw us dressed up. "What is up, guys? Where are you heading this early morning?"

"We want to go to an Orthodox church."

"Oh, gee! There are no Orthodox churches in this area. In Milwaukee, I know there are Greek Orthodox churches and Eastern Orthodox churches. But they are far from here, and there is no public transportation. Sorry, I would not be able to give you a ride. I have to be at church. I tell you what. Why don't you go to my church today, and next week, we will get up earlier, and I will drop you at one of the Orthodox churches."

We agreed. We went into an impressive Catholic church. People were getting into the church at the time of our arrival. The inside of the church was stupendously elegant—stained glasses, religious icons, and stuccos that looked like medieval art. The service started at eight o'clock in the morning with a regular Catholic doxology, followed by the priest's homily, and it ended at about ten thirty in the morning. We liked it and decided to come to the church regularly. As we were about to leave, we were introduced to the priest and deacons and several of the parishioners. All wished us well. On our way back home, we told Erin how much we liked the service and that we had decided to attend regularly.

"Are you sure? Is it because you didn't want to inconvenience me of driving you to Milwaukee?"

We assured her that was not the reason, but we felt at home in the church.

Sol had prepared breakfast—what he called brunch—with a variety of choices of food and beverages. It was much appreciated by all of us, especially by Erin who gave him a kiss.

In the afternoon, we decided to explore some of the interesting places of the town on our own. We had a map marked with different spots with the help of Erin.

She gave us fifty dollars and some advice of not staying exposed to the cold for long. The weather wasn't severe today. However, long exposure could cause hypothermia. "If you are cold, get into a café or shopping area. It is always heated."

The first place we went to was the village center, where the municipal office and many boutique stores, cafés, and restaurants were located. In a café, we sat and observed the movement of people, most carrying shopping bags. We ordered tea.

To our surprise, the fast-talking young server asked us, "What kind of tea do you choose?"

We were not aware that there were many choices of teas. Randomly, we chose Earl Grey. We thought Mr. Grey must know about tea. It wasn't a bad choice. Sipping our tea, we started talking about our life, the amazing turn it had taken, and the good people we had met. We were blessed. It must be the prayers of our parents, we agreed.

In the evening, we had an appointment with Sarah to talk about our education. She had volunteered to follow up with our admission to schools. Sarah was already at home when we were back. She asked if we had enjoyed our tour of the center of town. We replied yes, it was enjoyable.

Then she delved into the school situation. "You will start school first week of April, but before that, you will have to sit for test on English proficiency, to determine the level of your English and to be assigned classes accordingly. The classes are called ESL, English as Second Language. They are not credited for college. The idea is to make you ready to attend college and to be able to communicate in the society." Sarah continued, "I know Abiy has completed high school and carries documents to prove. Matheos, you do have one more year left to complete high school. You may have to take GED. It is a high school equivalency program. If you successfully complete the program, you could be admitted to college. The school you will be attending is a community college, not too far from here."

We told her we saw it as we walked to town.

"Good," she said. "The test, you will take it next week, after you had walked the dogs."

Early morning on Monday, we lined up our leashed dogs and went to the park to "shepherd" them, as Amsal put it. It was becoming fun; we had started to identify the personalities and eccentricities of each dog.

We liked Kuba, our first dog. It was the laziest of all, but everything it did was predictable—where it would poop and when it would scratch its back.

The names of the dogs were interesting and creative. The Mathewses' family dog was April; it was a female dog and joined the family in the month of April.

Lucky was the dog of the McGrath family, brought from shelter a day before it was to be made to rest.

Amigo was owned by the Stevens. Mrs. Steven told us the dog was littered by their friend's dog. She explained, "*Amigo* is 'friend' in Spanish."

The Franklins' dog was Buddy, a husky dog, and Mr. Franklin said, "That is a real buddy." He trusted him more than anybody. Abiy commented what a sad situation it was to trust a dog than a person.

The gregarious Mr. Rossati called his dog Butana. He explained it was derogatory in Italian while laughing hilariously. "This bitch is like a prostitute." He laughed again. We had a hard time understanding him. We liked him all the same. He was always good and generous to us.

The Marquezes' family dog was Hunter. "What does he hunt?" we asked.

"Nothing, maybe his food at home. But our daughter who was five years at the time we bought him called him Hunter, and it stuck."

Curiously, we asked, "What do you mean 'we bought him'? Where do you buy a dog? Is there a dog market?" likening to the livestock market in our country.

Mr. Marquez explained, "There are pet stores that specialize in dogs."

"What a country!" we exclaimed.

Sarah came at eleven o'clock in the morning to take us to the college for the proficiency test in English. We walked there. Sarah led us through the maze of the building to the admissions office, where we were registered by showing our passports and social security numbers. The personnel at the office were very efficient. Sarah was familiar to them. Even the people in the back office came to greet her and us. One of the people led us to the testing room. He handed us the test and bid us to sit anywhere. The time allotted for the test was one hour. And we both finished on the time prescribed.

The tester took our finished work and instructed us to wait for A few minutes before he told us the result of the test and what level of English class we should attend. When he came back with the results, he said, "Not bad, level 4." He gave us a handout with instructions on what books we would need to buy and the date and timetable of the classes. We bought the books at the school bookstore and went home.

In the afternoon, we walked the dogs on our regular route. On returning the dogs, the Walters' family dog Kuba was our last. Mrs. Walter waited for us at the door. After taking the leash of the dog, she asked us if it was possible for us to go with her to the hardware store to buy some paints.

"Sure. We could do that any time you are ready."

"Good. I would call Erin to tell her that I have detained you here for a short time. I don't want her to be worried."

We bought two different colors of paints, a gallon of each, and a few paintbrushes and paint rollers. With the purchase, we went to the Walters' home and deposited them into the garage. To our surprise, Mrs. Walter wanted us to help her paint the garage floor and sidings the next day. Abiy and I looked at each other. We had never held a brush, and we didn't know what to say.

"Let us talk to Erin. She may explain to Mrs. Walter our predicament."

Erin, with her can-do attitude, said, "To paint a surface is easy. In the morning, I will go with you and show you how you could do it. In no time, you will catch up and do it."

The painting was done, thanks to the help of Erin. Mrs. Walter was very happy and paid us handsomely.

There was a very interesting tradition between Erin and Sol. At the end of the day at the dinner table, they would tell each other what happened in their life during the day.

On this occasion, Erin had a story to tell about our new experience of painting a garage floor and siding. She declared, "It is a new business for these young men."

Sol, after attentively listening to his wife, turned his face toward us and said, "Wonderful. How was it?"

We gave credit to Erin as she showed us how to handle the brushes and the stick of the paint rollers and to lay the drip cloth and the technique of painting, and we did the work. Mrs. Walter was satisfied.

"With ethos of hard work and attitude, you will be successful. Keep it up," he advised.

The weather was getting balmy by the day, and the park where we would walk the dogs was getting crowded. People were taking advantage of the comfortable days. Some leisurely walked with their children in tow. Others were playing Frisbee, throwing the disklike material to another person or to their dogs. It was alive and enjoyable. People had started to become familiar with us. And some, out of curiosity, asked us where we were from. And some exchanged names with us.

On Monday, Erin went back to work after a few weeks of hiatus, and we were ready to start classes in the afternoon.

Our English teacher was an aging hippie with a long ponytail, bespectacled, and dressed in floral shirt and baggy pants. He introduced himself as Bill Makredis. "You can call me Bill," he said. He had traveled and worked as an English instructor in Africa and Greece. He welcomed us to his class and advised that we made use of the language frequently to get used to the pronunciation of American English. "Class attendance is mandatory. Absence of three classes will force you to repeat the course," he warned. He demonstrated the use of the language lab, the earphones, selection of course, and different switches on the equipment. He released us early on the first day of class.

At five o'clock in the afternoon, we were already at home. We checked the refrigerator for food. There were plenty of cold cuts to make sandwich, which were not appetizing to us. We decided to prepare food that we had learned in Kenya—rice with chicken and sautéed vegetables. All the ingredients needed were available, including herbs and spices. We boiled the rice with herbs and spice and browned the chicken and added it to the rice to further cook. The broccoli florets and carrots were grilled and smeared lightly with garlic-infused olive oil. Food was ready a few minutes before Erin opened the door.

Erin said, "What is this aroma? Something cooking." Before she unloaded herself of her bag and file she was carrying, she came to the kitchen to observe and saw the rice with chicken and vegetables colorfully ready on serving dishes. She couldn't hide her joy and amazement. "I don't know what to say," she said. "Thank you. I can't wait to tell Sarah and Don." She picked up a fork and tasted the rice. "Wow! It is tasty! Wonderful!" she exclaimed. "I didn't know you guys were great cooks."

Sol came a few minutes later.

Erin was still in the kitchen. "Come here, honey," she invited her husband. "A feast is ready for your dinner."

He hugged and kissed her and observed the meals on the serving dishes. He looked at us appreciatively and said, "Good job again." We had prepared food that was enough to feed ten people. "Tomorrow I am going to take some to lunch and brag among my coworkers the talent of my nephews. It is positive proof that all the things that I have been telling them were not fiction."

Just before we sat for dinner, Erin called Sarah and told her. Sarah invited herself. She was always welcome at the house. Don was out of town. She brought a bottle of red wine from her collection. It became a real feast.

Erin was checking for messages at the home phone. There were two messages from Mrs. Peterson and Mrs. Katz to inquire availability of us for spring cleaning over the weekend. She asked us if we wanted to take the work.

"Yes, we are available on Saturday and after church on Sunday."

The schedule was set with the two families. As we were taking more work, Erin thought it was necessary to put all the schedules written and placed on a cork frame in the kitchen area.

On Tuesday, we went to the public library and secured library cards by showing our IDs. We borrowed some books on English language instruction. We studiously read the books by constantly referring to the dictionary for words that were unfamiliar to us. With our diligent study and the help of a tutor, we were ready for GED and college.

"Dog shepherds" had become our sobriquet given to us by Amsal. Every time we called, she answered by calling us, "Hello, dog shepherds!"

This time, since our business had expanded to painting and moving stuff, we told her that moniker was not appropriate. We bragged we were businessmen. Our business was "Abiy and Mati General Services."

She responded, with good humor, "It is not as cute as 'dog shepherds.' I will stick with it." In a serious note, she said, "Only six months are left before completion of high school, and I have not decided what to do after that. I would love to come to the US and be with you and go to college. Otherwise, I hope I would be accepted at Addis Ababa University."

"Dear Amsal, my dream is for you to join us here. I have been thinking about it. So far, I didn't discuss it with Abiy or my uncle. I may do that soon. I pray that I see you soon."

My last conversation with Amsal lingered in my mind. If I shared it with Abiy, would he say, "Great, let us find a way to help her come here"? Or would he quip the refrain used by our ancestors, "A river does not have a place to sleep, and it carries logs with it"? Notwithstanding how he would respond, I was determined to share it with him. Besides, it was going to be about a year later. Hopefully by then, we might have our own place. Another advantage would be that she would be helping us in our business, earning her expenses. I pondered over the idea for a long time, and I liked it.

In the morning as we were walking our dogs, I asked Abiy to sit on a vacant bench.

"You want to take a break so soon?" he asked.

"No. I have some thoughts that I want to share with you."

"What?" he asked.

I divulged what was itching in my mind.

Abiy listened attentively and then said, "You want her to come so eagerly."

I said, "Don't you?"

"Yes, I do, Mati. But isn't it too early for us to take a responsibility of this kind?"

"Abiy," I responded, "it is going to be a year later. I only want to start the process now."

"How?" he inquired.

"I am going to ask Erin and Sol to help."

"I can't do that, Mati. They are doing a lot for us and again to add some more responsibility on them. No, I can't do that," he repeated.

"My dear friend, do not worry. I will," I responded. "Besides, in a year's time, we will be on our own. Amsal is not going to be a burden. She will work with us and live with us. The only thing Erin and Sol will do is sign some documents to get her a visa."

"You want her to come so desperately," Abiy added.

"You know I do," I said frankly.

"All right, it is your game. Let us see how you are going to play it," he ended.

Before I shared my idea with Erin and Sol, I decided to find out what was involved in applying for a visa. At the college, there were foreign students that I befriended who must know the process to secure a student visa. To make sure if there was a variation of applications from different countries, I asked Nigerian, Lebanese, and Indian students. Each told me the same process—an acceptance from an accredited college and financial statement showing the ability to finance the education and living expenses. With that information, the next step was to ask Erin and Sol if they could sign the document. Abiy and I were willing to pay her travel expenses and living expenses upon arrival in the US. The questions were "Who should I ask first, Erin or Sol? And should I talk to them at the dinner table?" After cogitating the idea in my mind, I decided to talk to Erin first. Erin, as a woman, might sympathize better. I postponed telling her to Saturday when she was relaxed at home.

On Saturday at ten thirty in the morning, we went to help the Peterson family with their spring cleaning. We cleared all leaves, paper scrubs, and plastic materials that the winter snow had kept buried. Inside the house, we boxed all winter clothing and sealed them to move to the basement storage. We washed windows by spraying them washing detergents and water. We helped rearrange furniture. The older furniture, we dropped at the back of the house to be picked up. Five hours later, we were done.

As soon as we entered the house, Erin said, "Just in time. We are going out for dinner with my brother's family. Go get ready," she advised us.

We would have preferred to stay at home, but we couldn't say no to Erin. We took showers, changed clothes, and joined them in the living room. We joined the Boones and Alexandra at a restaurant in Milwaukee. A live band was playing, and we were seated alfresco. All nine of us sat there. "Less noisy," Sarah suggested.

The menu was very expensive with enticing names, mostly in French. It was our first time to eat shrimp with the encouragement of Sol. We enjoyed it.

After dinner, we moved to the area where live music was played and people were dancing. Dan and Sarah moved to dance, followed by Alexandra and Al and Erin and Sol. Becky was trying to make us dance, but we were too self-conscious. Becky joined her brother and Alexandra. Abiy and I were admiring onlookers. After an enjoyable evening, we went home a little after midnight, and the next day, we had to go to church.

As we set to go to church on Sunday morning, Erin suggested that we take some of the flyers for Abiy and Mati General Services to distribute among the congregants. We took several copies. The church service was attended by a large group of believers who seemed to know one another. This was our second attendance at the church, and at the end of the service, as people were walking out, we were greeted by many of them. Erin, who was standing next to us, was telling about our new service business and handing them the flyers. Some already indicated their need for our service.

Sol attended church rarely; on this day, he was working on the yard as we were parking the car. We changed our clothes and joined him in the yard and helped to straighten the edges and clean the muddy entryway. As we were working, Sol asked us about the church, given our background as members of the Orthodox church. We said that the difference was mainly in language. Otherwise, we didn't see much difference.

He said, "I am glad you guys are open-minded and see the commonality rather than dwell on the differences. It is important to have that attitude in everything you do in life," he advised us.

In the afternoon at the Katz house, we did yard cleaning and preparation of the vegetable garden with the direction of Mrs. Katz. We adjusted some parts of the fences that were bent by heavy snow and wind. Mrs. Katz said she might need service on planting tomato and other vegetables.

From the Katz family, we went home to catch up with our studies. After finishing our work, I saw Erin talking over the phone in the living room. I thought it was an opportune moment to talk to her about my plan in regard to Amsal's move to the US.

As soon as she finished her telephone call, I moved toward her. She sensed that I wanted to talk to her and asked, "What is it, Mati?"

I answered, "I have something to ask you, Erin."

"What is that?" she asked. "Come sit here."

I shared my plan and showed her the pictures that Amsal sent two weeks ago.

"Oh my god! She is gorgeous," she stated.

And I told her she was the younger sister of Abiy.

"That is icing on the cake," she quipped, a term I never heard before. "We are going to share this news with Sol as soon as he wakes up from his nap."

Sol was holding a book, walking to the study room, when Erin asked him join her in the living room. He complied and sat by her side.

"I have got a story to tell you, beautiful story," she added.

"What is that? You are so animated, Erin."

"Well," she breathed, "our Mati is lovestruck."

"What are you talking about? With whom?" he asked.

Erin pulled out the pictures and said, "With this beautiful young lady."

It was his first time to see the pictures. "Where is this pretty young woman?" he asked.

"That is the dilemma. She is in Ethiopia. And do you know she is Abiy's younger sister?"

"All right, that makes it very interesting." He was quiet for a while and then said, "Is it not too early to get into such commitment? You just started school. That demands a lot of time."

Erin interjected, "It is not going to be right now. It will take about a year. What Mati wants now is for us to help him in securing her visa to come to the US. Well, listen, you may have to talk to Don. He is the attorney."

"Okay! I will call Don later at home."

Don had several questions before he gave his suggestion. The questions came to me through Erin. "How serious is the relationship between the two of them? Are they planning to get married? If so, why don't they get married and bring her as a spouse? If she comes as a student, she may not be eligible to work. And how is he going to support her? How about his education? Could it be a distraction?"

To all the questions, I gave the answers, and Erin was satisfied with my thoughtful answers. But she thought the best way to bring her was as a spouse. For that to happen, I might have to travel to Ethiopia.

This might require a whole new planning, and I had to share my idea with Amsal.

I updated Abiy on what Don and Erin said in regard to Amsal's visa.

His response was one of caution. "I am with them. You are rushing this thing. But it is your thing, as I said before."

"Abiy, it is going to happen," I reassured him.

I took a few days to think about the whole situation before I called Amsal.

Few days later, I called Amsal and shared the different options of securing her a visa and told her I was advised the easiest and best way was through marriage. "It might be presumptuous on my part to consider the marriage option before I ask you if you want to be my wife. Now I ask you. Will you marry me, Amsal?"

"Yes, I already am your spouse spiritually," she responded, to my delight.

"Here is the proposal then. Next summer, I will come to Ethiopia, and we get married. No ceremony needed. We get a civil marriage at the municipal office. With the marriage certificate at hand, you will be eligible to apply for immigrant visa at the US consulate."

"I love the idea, Mati. Should I share it with my parents?"

"Maybe we should wait until closer to the time," I replied. That settled, I went to my studies.

The number of clients for our business was expanding. For the next month, we had reservations to do all kinds of odd jobs, including the dog walking. Some of the neighbors gave us work to help us financially. People had come to recognize our high standard of performance, punctuality, politeness, and honesty. Throughout the village, we had come to be known as Abiy and Mati. People were willing to rearrange work schedules with our time for school time. We were always working or doing our studies with an occasional time for recreation. But we were happy.

May came with its pleasant weather. I was ready to take the GED exam, and Abiy had applied at the local community college where we had been taking ESL courses. By midmonth, I took the exam; it was much easier than I thought it would be. It was the help of the tutor and ESL courses that prepared me for it. I became confident to start college at the same time as Abiy.

On the weekend, Kathleen and Edward Boone came for a visit from St. Paul, Minnesota. They are parents of Erin and Don. They had welcomed us over the telephone, and they promised to visit us at a convenient time. As soon as we met them, we knew it was from the parents the gregariousness and kindness inherited by Erin and Don. They were transparently kind people. They brought us some gifts well packaged with welcome cards stuck in them. We thanked them for their generosity and kindness. The usual reserved Sol was very affable with the parents. They talked about work, politics, and some of the projects that Sol was involved as project manager for a major company. Kathleen and Erin were quietly talking, sitting by the dining table when Sol called Erin and asked if she had made a reservation at a restaurant, Edward's favorite dining place.

Erin had told her parents what was going on in our lives—the business, school, and Amsal. This happened at the time when we went to work.

When we came home in the evening, Edward saw me with a wink on his eye and invited us to sit by him in the living room. He said, "Things are going forward for you guys. I am so happy. And Erin told me you have a young woman in Ethiopia."

Shyly, I said, "Yes, Amsal. She is Abiy's sister."

"So I heard. That is great. If there is anything to help, don't hesitate to tell us. Both of you," he added.

Abiy and I said, "Thank you very much."

Kathleen said, "We have told Erin and Sol to bring you to St. Paul to visit us when school is out. It is only a few hours' drive."

We said, "We will be happy to come and visit you. Thank you again."

The next morning, which was Sunday, everybody agreed to come to church. Except for Alexandra and Al, everyone came to church. Sol and Don who were not regular attendees showed up in honor of Kathleen and Edward. We were a few minutes ahead. We waited for them at the entryway. They beamed when they saw us, and we followed them into the church.

From the church, we went to a local restaurant for brunch.

As we were eating, Sarah said, "If Mom and Dad"—that was how she called them—"come to town every weekend, I may convert to Catholic." Sarah was a Methodist.

"Sarah, we love you all the same" was their response.

And she said, "You know I love you too," with authenticity, no hint of pretention.

The afternoon job we had at the Reeves family was physically hard. It was moving out heavy furniture to be stored in a carriage house at the back and replace them with newer ones. We had to place the older furniture on the second floor of the carriage house. The steps were steep and narrow, which made it more difficult. As it was challenging, more than two people had to work at the same time. After much struggle and sweating, we finished the job. We should mention though that the cash reward was very generous. We went home to rest our aching muscles. Erin left us a note saying that they were at the park close to the fountain if we chose to join them. We stayed at home to rest and to do some studies.

Five weeks later, Abiy's admission arrived, followed by my passing the GED with excellent results. It was confirmed both of us would be in college at the same time. Compliments to our tutor who continued to challenge us with advanced math and science lessons in addition to English.

Amsal's coming to the US was going through spousal unification. Of course, I would have to travel to Ethiopia to get married to her. That would happen only during summer when school was in recess. Optimistically, she would be here in about a year and half. It would be agonizingly long, only aggravated by our regular contact over the telephone and not being able to see and touch each other.

Time management was very important, as Erin explained to us many times. For we were going to be busy between school and work, we had to schedule everything so that we used time optimally—time to work, study, eat, and sleep. Every minute had to be used productively. We were good so far. We allocated four to five hours a day for our studies. Work was twenty-five hours, weekend included.

Our living arrangement would remain the same. Erin and Sol had extended our stay until we complete first year of college or the arrival of Amsal. We had small expenses for the occasional purchase of groceries and sundries. We had been saving most of our income. That was at the insistence of Erin and Sol. We would have been happy to contribute part of our income to the family.

In summer, a lot of activities happened. People would go picnicking, traveling, and enjoying the many activities in the city. On Tuesday evening, Al dropped to visit with Erin on his way home, and he told her he and Alexandra were going to Milwaukee for the summer food and music festival. "We can take Mati and Abiy with us if they are not busy."

Erin said, "Good idea. They certainly will enjoy it. I'll tell them as soon as they come from dog walking. Hold on! I will call them."

"Hello!" I answered the phone.

Erin told me, "Al and Alexandra want to take you to a festival in the city."

"It would have been nice, but we have a commitment to do work at the Robertsons' home."

"No! I forgot," Erin answered. "Wait, I will call Sheila if she can postpone the work for another day, if it is not urgent."

And she did. "Sheila said no problem, it could be done next week."

With the commitment vacated, we traveled to Milwaukee and partake in the festivities with Alexandra and Al.

The festival was a yearly event attracting thousands of people from all over Wisconsin and from other states. Music was played by world-class artists of so many genre, and food vendors of all ethnicities and American staples were sold on-site.

Alexandra and Al were guiding us to the different food vendors.

"What is that you want to eat?" Al asked.

To which Alexandra suggested, "How about barbecue? That is typical American." She added, "I think."

Al agreed. We bought food from a vendor that specialized in barbecue food, chicken and ribs. We carried our food close to the music site. It was a good summer day with wind blowing from the lake, cooling the hot summer heat to pleasant temperature. While listening to the blues music, we enjoyed the ribs and the Dr Pepper drinks. The barbecue was delicious—sweet and spicy smothered with sauce—and there were roasted corn and biscuits on the side. We sat and listened to music played by several bands for almost four hours. We went for a second round of meals. Abiy and I wanted to have more of the ribs and ordered them with trimmings. We sat for more music.

About ten o'clock in the evening, we drove back to our homes. We thanked Al and Alexandra for a great day as we parted. Erin and Sol had already gone to sleep. We also went to our respective rooms.

The next day while we were having lunch, I was telling Erin and Sol about the music festival in Milwaukee—how enjoyable it was and the food, barbecue ribs, was "finger-licking good," a phrase that I had picked up from the Kentucky Fried Chicken slogan.

Erin and Sol looked at each other. And Sol said, "So you ate ribs. What kind of ribs was that?"

Perplexed by the question, I answered by pointing toward my ribs, except bigger.

"Did you know what those come from?"

I was getting a little suspicious, but I answered they must be from cattle.

"I am glad you enjoyed it." And he ended his query abruptly. Which made me think what was all about it. This was not a fasting period for Orthodox adherents. It left me curious why Sol was so interested about the ribs.

At the time, I did not pursue the issue, except to ask Abiy if we had violated the fasting period. Abiy assured me it was not a fasting period. But then I said, "Why were Erin and Sol eyeing each other and Sol was asking about the ribs as if it was the first ever that we ate meat?"

It was the next day that I knew the puzzled questions from Sol about the ribs. The ribs were of pig, pork ribs. In our religion, the Orthodox Tewahedo Church background, we are not allowed to eat pork meat. The one time we had bacon was a turkey bacon that Sol made sure to state it was not from pork. Since then, Erin had made sure no pork product was brought into the house. Abiy and I assessed our feeling about it. The thing that surprised us was how our upbringing had tenaciously clung to our psyche. The ribs we enjoyed, but when we were made aware they were from pork, we felt a modest disgust. Immediately though, we questioned our feeling. "What is wrong with eating pork?" Some traditions were so archaic and did not have any relevance to life today. This was one of them, and we shed it off our thinking.

The Robertsons' work that we had postponed, we did it on Tuesday right after walking the dogs. Sheila was planting new flowering plants, like hosta. We picked up the plants from a nursery a few blocks away on the main street. We prepared six flower beds on the side of the house visible from the sidewalk. When the flowers bloomed, they would give joy to the eyes of every person that walked close to the house. They were a variety of colors carefully selected by Sheila to be aesthetically pleasant. Partly, it would show our handiwork. The whole time we worked on the yard, Sheila was giving us direction for every step in leveling, planting, and watering.

Mr. Robertson was seated in the living room close to the window, looking at what we had been doing. His wife said he had been sick for a few months and was recuperating at home. Both of them looked as old as Erin and Sol, maybe in their forties.

In the few months that we had been in the US, our English proficiency had improved to the extent that we could conduct conversation unabashedly on any subject with anyone. At the dinner table, we were most voluble, telling our experiences in exile and the way to exile.

Erin listened to us with much fascination. "How is it that as young as you guys are, you can experience so much of life's challenges that many people here will never experience in a lifetime?" She found some of them hilarious, like the time we went to the game park and became a laughingstock to our friends who somehow begrudged us for being vain to be tourists while so many were desperately hustling for a meal to eat. The moniker attached to our name was what tickled Erin.

I received my acceptance letter at the local community college as Abiy had received it previously. We had planned to register for the same courses for obvious reasons, to study together and help each other. A catalog of the courses was included with the acceptance letter. We chose four courses for the fall semester in consultation with our tutor and Sarah.

We were registered early. Fortunately, all classes were open. Sarah bought us all the school supplies and textbooks required, and Don mailed a check for tuition payment. The courses that we chose did not conflict with the twenty-five hours each of us worked in a week.

The weekend before classes started, Erin and Sol took us to Lake Geneva, Wisconsin, to see the colorful fall foliage. The golden and purplish colors of the leaves adorned the surrounding hill of the lake. It was breathtaking with the weather at a pleasant midsixties. We took a boat tour around the lake. The captain of the boat was telling us who owned the different mansions by the lakefront. Lake Geneva, the town, was small with several hotels and restaurants that catered to visitors who came from Chicago and other places. Sol drove us around the perimeter of the lake to see some of the neighborhoods. Grand houses owned by the rich and famous were built by the hills close to the lake. Another great day and great experience.

On our way back home, Erin said our next trip would be in November when we would travel to Minnesota to celebrate Thanksgiving holiday with her parents. She explained the meaning of Thanksgiving celebration. She briefly said it was a day when families would get together and give thanks for a year past. It was a neat idea, we thought. Who, more than us, should give thanks and celebrate to our God and to all the families that welcomed us and helped us to be part of their families? It was appropriate to have such a day where everyone in the nation would give praise to their creator. It should be adopted the world over.

School started in earnest in the third week of September. On the first day in class, we were given a syllabus by each professor. The syllabus contained not only the chapter-by-chapter lessons, what was expected of us to cover, but also how grading was to be done and other requirements to pass the class. Our last class ends at 1:45 p.m., giving us enough time to walk our dogs. The evening was reserved for studying with a break for dinner and a short chat with Erin and Sol.

I heard a profoundly disturbing news from Asmara, Eritrea, over the phone. My father told me my two younger sisters were ordered to report for the national military service at Sawa training camp in western Eritrea. I had gone through the process while I was in Eritrea. Two months had already passed since the time the order had arrived. They were hiding by moving to an address of a relative. If caught, they would be punished severely. It was only a matter of time before the military would send officers to fetch them and, if they could not find them, to arrest our father. The Eritrean "national service" is an ambush to an indefinite servitude. Young women were turned into maids of officers and forced into concubinage. If they dared to reject the unwanted advances of an officer, they might end up in a jail made of metal cargo containers or in a dingy underground cell. The inhumanity of some officers in the Eritrean military had been documented by escapees fortunate enough to be resettled in Europe or North America. No one was held accountable, for there was no rule of law.

Would I let my sisters fall into the hands of rapacious officers? It was not going to happen if I had anything to do with it. I knew my father would do everything in his power to protect them. The only option he had was to help them cross the border into Ethiopia, a dangerous attempt but less dangerous than to let them be abused by military officers. I promised him I would to talk to Tirunesh and Ababa Dereje to help them once they crossed the border.

I discussed with Abiy the plan, and he was eager to help. He suggested we send money to Eritrea to defray the expense for the payment to smugglers. The estimated cost was about two thousand dollars. Which we immediately sent it through a third party that would advance the money in Asmara within two or three days.

In the evening, we made a call to Ethiopia. Amsal answered. She was alarmed because we never called midweek.

I told her, "Why are you anxious? Can't I call my love any time I want? My reason for calling on a Thursday is that Azie and Aida are planning to come to Ethiopia."

"Wow! Are you serious? If you are joking, I will never forgive you," she said.

"I am serious, dear."

"I can't wait to see them. You don't know how much I miss them." In her excited voice, she called her mom and dad to come to the phone.

Ababa Dereje was on the phone. After exchanging greetings, I shared the danger my sisters were facing and the plan of crossing the border into Ethiopia.

He said in anguish, "What is this world coming to when little girls can't live under the shield of their parents? Mati, my son," he continued, "the day they crossed the border, I will personally go and pick them up and bring them here. Do not worry. Tell them to call me the moment they crossed the border. I will not let them spend a night in a refugee camp."

I thanked him, and after talking to Tirunesh, I handed the phone to Abiy to greet them.

On the same day, I called Asmara and informed my parents what Ababa Dereje said.

"I never had doubt that Dereje will come to the rescue of my girls. The only worry I have now is how safely they cross the border."

In the next few days, we worried day and night. Four days later, we received the good news that they had crossed the border safely, and the smuggler had taken them all the way to the town of Shire. From Shire, they contacted the Dereje family. Amsal informed us that her dad had already flown to the city of Axum and traveled to Shire to pick them up. Without consulting Abiy, I withdrew two thousand dollars and sent it to Ababa Dereje to cover his expenses. Only later did I tell Abiy, and he mildly protested by saying it was unnecessary.

Azie and Aida, accompanied by Ababa Dereje, arrived at their home. Amsal and Tirunesh were eagerly waiting for their arrival. As soon as they approached the door, Tirunesh welcomed them with joyful ululation while Amsal jumped to hug them. They checked one another for the changes they had shown since they were separated with so much delight and amazement.

Ababa Dereje intervened by saying, "Give them time to refresh themselves. They are tired after a long trip."

After a bath and a change of clothes, they joined the family. A feast was prepared in their honor. Azie and Aida were very happy to be in the home of the family who was part of their upbringing.

Amsal sat in between them, asking all kinds of questions. She was visibly happy to have them both. She had always considered them as sisters. Their sleeping area was arranged in the same room. At night, they were talking until the wee hours, laughing and murmuring. Their laugh could be heard in the other room where the parents were sleeping.

Ababa Dereje reprimanded Tirunesh when she got out of bed to order them to go to sleep. He said, "Let them talk and laugh. They had missed each other for many years."

In the morning, even an explosion could not have woken them up. They slept to almost noontime.

The next day, many well-wishers, old friends, came to visit, including Aba Berhanemeskel, the spiritual leader of our family. The priest led them in a prayer, thanking God for bringing them safe to their birthplace, and he prayed that our parents would come soon to join the community from which they were separated suddenly and forcibly.

After the friends left, Amsal took them out to visit the neighborhood to view some of the changes. A few things had changed, except many of the people were newcomers. The house, our birthplace, was occupied by a new family. Amsal and her parents had avoided any contact with them. Mahdere, the cadre who forcibly evicted us and expelled us from the country, had been murdered by an unknown assailant. His position had been replaced by a local man, Mr. Abebe, who was much gentler in dealing with people. Amsal knew him well, but Azie and Aida barely remembered him. There were a few buildings erected on the field where our brothers used to play football during break time. Some of the neighborhood streets had been resurfaced. They used to be so muddy during the rainy season we avoided them and took a longer route to go to school. They met several people that we knew during our childhood. They stopped and greet them and asked them how our parents were doing, and a few had invited them to come to their home. In a few days, they were settled and started thinking about their future.

The next time I called Asmara, I informed my parents that all was well with Azie and Aida and that Ababa Dereje had traveled all the way to Shire to take them home.

"Blessed be the Lord! God bless Dereje and his family," my mother prayed.

Few days later, we informed Erin and Sol the travails that Azie and Aida had gone through and safely and that they had arrived in Ethiopia.

After listening to the whole story, Sol said, "The next time, if any situation arises, share the information with us. And now what is the plan with the young ladies?"

I answered, "For now, we are relieved that they are safe and comfortable. As for the future, we will see what could be done. Obviously, we will be in contact with them. I would want them to go to school, and that is what Amsal suggested too."

The semester was about halfway, and several tests were ahead of us in the coming week. We had been doing good in all the quizzes we had taken so far. Our tutor was giving us instruction in advance of our classes. In spite of our busy schedule with our work and classes, we were involved in different campus activities, international students club being one of them. There were students from seventeen countries represented in the club. It had been very educational through the interaction with such diverse cultures. The club had planned to hold an event, "International Day." Each member was to bring something unique to his or her culture. It could be food, craft, music, or dance performance.

Abiy and I did not have any idea what to do. We brought it up at dinner while seated with Erin and Sol.

Sol said, "Yes. I remember the experience in college. I did not have a clue what to do. A Nigerian friend suggested to just show up in our folkloric costume. The problem was we didn't have the costume. A simpler idea is what we needed. We just put a sign 'Get Your Name in Ethiopian Script.' People responded, and several names were written. We remember one young man by the name of John. When we wrote his name with two Ethiopian alphabets, he was excited that two English alphabets could be combined to make one Ethiopian alphabet. The event went well, and we contributed our modest share."

The results of our midterm tests were out. We did very well with straight As for both of us. Don was always involved with our education. Erin faxed him the report card. He called to congratulate us and invited everyone for dinner on Saturday at their home.

Our business was going strong. For lack of time, we had to politely decline some jobs. Since our savings had grown and we continued to earn money, we decided to send some money regularly to our parents, about two hundred dollars every month to each family. Converted to local currency, that was a good sum. Our families were very appreciative.

Amsal, Azie, and Aida were very happy that their brothers had grown up to be very responsible. The three of them were inseparable when they went to the market and church and to visit friends. The first time they went to church, they accompanied Tirunesh and Ababa Dereje.

The elderly priest Aba Berhanemeskel gave a blessing to the family and reminded the congregation that Haile and Mr. Dereje were the prime movers to build this blessed church. And he said, "We hope Haile and his wife will come back and pray among us. Let us pray to God." And he led the congregation to prayer. It was heartwarming to the family and us when we heard about it.

On Saturday, we had dinner at Sarah and Don's place. Becky was at home, helping her mother in arranging the table as we arrived. They congratulated us for our good grades and declared the dinner was in recognition for our achievement. At dinner, we talked, among other things, about our future transfer to a four-year college and the visit to Minnesota on Thanksgiving holiday to celebrate with Kathleen and Edward. Fortuitously, Kathleen and Edward called while we were relaxing after dinner. Don first talked to them and told that the dinner was in celebration of our achievement at school and handed the telephone to us. And they congratulated us and expressed they were eagerly waiting for our visit to their place. We thanked them both.

About the transfer to another college, Becky was telling us how important it was to apply early once we identified which college we preferably wanted to attend. "If you maintain your grades, any college will be more than happy to accept you. Your choice will depend on what you want to study—engineering, business, liberal arts, etc. Now is the time to do some research on the universities in our area, like

Milwaukee. There are several great universities without going far."

We listened and agreed with everything Becky said.

The next day, we skipped going to church to catch up on our work that was postponed for the weekend. In the morning, we saw flurries of snow, auguring the coming of winter. But during the middle of the day, the temperature was well above freezing point. No trace was left on the ground. We were done with our work before Erin came home from church.

Sol was at home doing some work he brought home. When he heard the door open, he came out of his office and met us as we were to change our uniform. "How was work?" he asked.

"Not bad," we answered.

"I did not see you eating breakfast this morning."

"Yes. We ate cereal and juice before we left," we told him. But it was more of an invitation to talk, so we sat by the living room.

He asked, "How are the families doing?"

"Everybody is fine. The girls are settled and happy. They are reacquainting themselves with their birthplace, meeting old friends, and making new friends."

"How about Amsal? What is she doing? Is she at school or working?" He had talked to Amsal on two occasions.

"She has passed the college admission test, but she has delayed registration by a semester. The university is about a hundred kilometers farther, and she did not make a living arrangement in time. And besides, with the arrival of Azie and Aida, she decided to stay with them for a few months."

"Very nice," he said. "Maybe it is time for her to send her transcript and apply for college here."

It was unexpected. Abiy and I looked at each other and didn't give any comment.

"I know it was agreed," he continued, "that you will go and marry her and apply for spousal visa."

"Yes, that is what I was planning," I reminded him.

"I know, but applying for college does not change the plan. It is only going to help her start right after she arrives here."

"Oh! That is good idea," we agreed.

"All right, we will send her application forms and ask her to send it back with her transcript included."

Soon, Erin walked in. "Hey, my men! What conspiracy are you hatching up?" she joked. Sol shot back to overthrow the queen of this little empire. "Don't even think about it," she shot back. After taking off her jacket and hat, she came and joined us. "I can't believe it. All the women at the church were asking about Abiy and Mati. I think they are falling for you, at least a few of them."

Erin was checking the refrigerator, when we volunteered to make lunch of our famous chicken and rice. "Oh! You guys are a doll. Thank you," she said.

Right away, we started to work in the kitchen. In forty minutes, a lunch of chicken and rice and variety of grilled vegetables were ready. We announced lunch was ready. It was already set on the dining table. Sol opened a bottle of wine. We all enjoyed the lunch. After lunch, we moved to the study room to finish homework and study.

On Monday morning right after we walked the dogs, we went to school about half an hour earlier before classes would start. I used the time to go to the office of admissions and registration to get the application form and catalog of the school. I told the clerk at the office I needed it for my fiancée who lived in Ethiopia. She gave me the documents and advised me to follow all the requirements described in the form, including test for TOEFL (Test of English as a Foreign Language). In the afternoon, I mailed the documents and my note to Amsal.

My aging grandfather's health in Asmara was getting worse. He was exhibiting symptoms of dementia. My father was running the business that Grandpa managed for almost six decades. At home, my mother and the help were taking care of him. My grandmother was seventy-eight years old; she was in good health for her age, but she lacked the physical strength to take care of her husband.

It was sad to hear that the man who was the epitome of strength and stubbornness of character was now reduced into such helplessness. According to my mother, sometimes he didn't even remember us, but then there were times when his faculties were sharp and he would ready himself to go to work.

In the evenings, my father would walk him and take him to the workplace. It was about three kilometers round trip. If he got tired, they would sit at a café among people who had known him for years. My father thought it was therapeutic. He even deluded himself into thinking that he might regain his faculties. "I know," he said, "my father-in-law is as obstinate as mule. He is going to snap out of it. Mark my word."

My mother was more realistic. She said, "Sadly, I only pray that he goes peacefully."

Both my mother and grandmother had accepted that there was no turning point; he had reached the sunset of life. And that was what doctors had told them, "Just make him comfortable. Medically, there is nothing to be done."

Few days after I sent the document to Amsal, she received it. She was not expecting anything like that and didn't know what to make of it. She called us to get information and know what our plan was. I explained to her to fill the forms and attach all required documents and send them expeditiously.

"I have to tell you something, Mati," she said pleadingly. "I hope you wouldn't be angry at me."

"What is that?" I asked.

"After the mail arrived, I told my mother what the package contained. You know what she said? 'So Mati wants you to be with him soon?' I looked at her with disbelief. And she continued, 'I am not born yesterday, Amsal. You don't think I had no suspicion what you two are up to with those long phone talks?

327

A mother has extra sense, my dear daughter.' I can't lie to my mother, so I spilled all the beans. But I asked her not to tell my father. 'Why? He will be happy. You know how he feels about Haile and his family, and I concur Mati is the suitor to my daughter, and your brother must have agreed with the proposal.' With much relief and joy, I said, 'Yes, Mother.' But I still begged her not to tell my father because I want to surprise him when we are ready to exchange vows. 'All right, my lips are sealed.' She gestured with her mouth closed, but her eyes were exuding joy. 'Oh! I love you, Tiruye,' I said."

"Amsal, make sure you send all the documents." I was even more anxious now that Tirunesh had given her approval.

The much-feared-yet-anticipated visit by the Eritrean security agents looking for Azie and Aida came. At the time they came, my father was at work. It was Grandfather, Grandmother, Mother, and the help who were at home. My grandfather was seated outside, and the gate was secure to make sure that my grandfather would not stray out of the compound. The two security agents on civilian clothes knocked at the gate loudly, which startled my ailing grandfather. The young help ran to see who was knocking so loud. She saw two men. Before she asked them to identify themselves, they pushed her to the side and entered the compound, heading toward the house. At the door of the house, they ordered her to open the door after announcing they were security officers. Her mouth dropped, and she pushed the door inside.

Rudely and with no concern for the privacy of people living, they headed to the living room. My mother and elderly grandmother, who had heard the commotion by the gate, were already standing in the living room.

My strong-willed grandmother was the first to ask who they were. And after they identified themselves as members of the security, unimpressed she told them, "Don't they teach you to respect people's privacy? You just broke into the living room of elderly citizens. You are not our invited guests. You don't have to force your way into the middle of someone's house."

One of the officers, quite taken by my grandmother's defiant tone, said, "Mother elderly, we are ordered to fetch Azie and Aida because they failed to report for national service duty. Where are they?"

My grandmother, as defiant as ever, said, "We are parents. We feed them. We give them shelter. We love them, but we don't follow them as guards wherever they go. We don't know where they are going. Find them and have a good day. We are done with you."

The officer, flabbergasted by the audacity of the old lady, backed toward the door. But at the same time, he said, "They should report within twenty-four hours to national service at Sawa military camp."

Azie and Aida were not to be found obviously, but that didn't end the case. In Eritrea, the sin of the child would fall on the parents, guilt by association, and the penalty could be imprisonment or financial. There was no place to challenge the penalty, no place to plead, and no court to appeal to.

The health of my grandfather was getting worse appreciably. He had lost his memory. Like a toddler, even his words came out jumbled. His muscles were atrophied. He had to be carried for his daily sun. He had to be fed and cleaned. The end was nearer, and it came after his eighty-ninth birthday. People came from all over to mourn his death. Families, friends, and business associates all came to pay their last respect to a man who had faced so much grief when he lost three of his sons in the war of independence. He had carried his grief stoically, giving solace to his wife. He started a business by sheer fortitude and ability to make friends. The business had become a distraction from the deep grief locked deep inside him that brought dementia upon him.

After the death of a family member, some close friends and family members would remain with the bereaved for a few days to give them solace and take care of them. On the third day of the internment of my grandfather, two young security agents came to the house and asked for my father Haile. Some who were seated close to the door told the agents that he was grieving the death of his father-in-law.

The agents said, "We are aware of the situation. However, we want to speak to him."

My father heard the conversation and stood from the corner where he was seated close to my mother and grandmother.

As he walked to talk to the officers, my grandmother followed him. And before he spoke, she said, "What brings you boys?" she asked.

"We are from the internal security and want to take Haile for a few questions at the office."

"Can't you see we are grieving? Don't you have some respect for the dead? Aren't you created by the same God?"

"We are sorry, madam. We have orders, and we have to take Haile with us," the officer retorted.

My grandmother, whose anger was building up, exploded. "You ape!" she scolded the officer. "This is the house of my three sons who died in your war. I didn't even see their remains. You abandoned them in the wild without giving them proper Christian burial. You cowards, you must have been hiding when the likes of my sons were fighting. That is why you are here to harass the mothers who lost so much. You don't even show any scratch. Yes, you coward. To harass an old mother is not courage. I will be dead before you take my son-in-law. Go tell your boss and your government, if you can call it that. I am ready for them. Get out of my house before I take out your eyes!" she fumed.

Some of the mourners stood to restrain my grandmother. They begged the officers to come some other time. The officers, humiliated by the words of my grandmother, walked out. The danger with the security agents was that they wouldn't flinch. They might back out at a time, but sure they would be back with full force. And they would take their revenge more brutally on anyone who had shamed them—be it old, young, or invalid.

It happened only a week later. The Eritrean regime, unpredictable on many important issues when it came to brutal security enforcement, was always predictable. It came in force. There was a litany of evidence over the years. On Monday morning, it was two people who had come to arrest an old lady and an unarmed middle-aged man, my father Haile. The crime of these elder citizens was for two young women who had avoided the notorious national service. The national service had gained its notoriety by the abuse the young recruits faced at the hands of the officers. Some had dubbed it as "modern-day slavery." They herded the two out of their house to a waiting van with two more officers inside. My father appealed to the officers to leave my grandmother alone and take him.

My grandmother was defiant. "I am going. I want to tell to the face of their boss what I think of him. These cowards who show their manhood against unarmed elderly people. In the battlefield, they were hiding underneath a cave. And you tell me you brought freedom. What freedom have you brought us? Is this freedom? Take it with you to your Sahel, to your Nakfa."

The whole time, they were telling her to shut up. After fifteen minutes of a drive full of contention, they arrived at the station. All the officers got off the van and ordered my grandmother and father to get off the van. My grandmother was shouting with all her energy, attracting the attention of many people in the compound.

The colonel who headed the station came out. He recognized my grandmother. He came closer to her and said, "Calm down, Mama Abrehet. What is the problem?"

She looked at him and recognized him and unleashed her disdain for him. "You ask what the problem is. You dog, you ordered your bullies to bring me here, and now you have the temerity to ask me what the problem is. You and your government are the problem. Let God bring the wrath upon you, you scoundrels, scum of the world!" she cursed.

My father had been taken inside, and they started interrogating him of the whereabouts of Azie and Aida. "I don't know. They have disappeared, and we are worried."

"Have you reported to the police of their disappearance?"

"No. Families are looking for them all over."

"I think you are hiding them or helped them to cross the border. If you don't bring them in forty-eight hours, we will hold you responsible. Now go and take your mother-in-law with you. Report to this station on Thursday."

My mother, who was left behind with the help, was a total wreck. She didn't believe her eyes when she saw them being dropped off a taxi. She jumped off her seat and hugged them as if they had been away for years.

As ordered, my father went to the station on Thursday—of course, without Azie and Aida.

The officer said insultingly, "Did the old woman regain her sanity?"

My father looked at the officer sternly and told him, "I have never met a saner person than my mother-in-law."

The officer changed his tone and asked, "Where are the two girls, your daughters?"

"I don't know. Go search your prisoners-packed prisons," my father responded. "Maybe they are in one of them."

Uncharacteristically, the officer showed patience. "Mr. Haile, since you have failed to bring your children, the penalty could be imprisonment or monetary or both. It would be my decision for you to pay a penalty of thirty thousand nakfa for each girl. Until the sixty thousand nakfa is paid, you will be held in detention."

My father was ready for the penalty, except that he was not carrying the cash at the time. He asked the officer if he could go to the bank and withdraw the money.

The officer assented, "You will be escorted by an officer to the bank and come back with the money."

Forty-five minutes later, my father was on his way home after paying the penalty. It was the better outcome, all family members agreed. All these incidents I was informed by my father months later. I was glad none was sent to prison, even though I believed it was a gangster's blackmail to charge money for children's avoidance of national service servitude.

*****

Thanksgiving was fast approaching. We were to travel to Minnesota on two vehicles. The SUVs were wide enough to accommodate everybody comfortably, and besides, it was only a few hours' drive. We would be leaving on Wednesday and would be back on Saturday. We notified all our clients to make arrangements to walk the dogs for the three days we would be out of town. Most of them were traveling out of town, taking their dogs along.

Only one of our clients was staying at home with her children and grandchildren coming to visit, but she was agreeable. "Don't worry. Go have a good Thanksgiving. My grandchildren will walk the dogs for the three days."

The drive to Minnesota took us about four hours. By the time we arrived, it was dinnertime. Kathleen and Ed greeted us with smile and hugs. After we unloaded and placed our luggage into our assigned sleeping area, we were led to the dining area. Kathleen had prepared enough food to feed the whole group. It was a great dinner and an amiable companionship.

Becky was talking to Abiy with animation. I did have a suspicion she liked him. Every time we visited her home or any place, they would meet, and she would choose to sit close by him. Abiy was a man of few words but carried himself with grace. I might be prejudiced, but he was an elegant person. I would not be surprised if Becky fell for him.

On Thanksgiving Day, with Becky included, all the men went sightseeing, mainly for the benefit of Abiy and me. The city looked abandoned. There were a few people walking, and there were fewer cars on the street. Most businesses were closed, except for a few food stores and restaurants. After roaming the streets, we went back to the house.

Kathleen and Edward owned a ranch house with a vast land on the back. There was a small lake just outside the perimeter of the property. According to Edward, it was a relaxing fishing spot.

In the afternoon, we were ready for an early dinner. The center of the dinner was a big roasted turkey with trimmings and a variety of dishes to be savored. As we sat for dinner, Alexandra and Al called to wish us happy Thanksgiving. They went on a vacation to Hawaii. They bragged how they were basking in beaches with temperature in the nineties. In Minnesota, the temperature was freezing. But inside, not only was the temperature warm, we were also abounded by the love all around us.

After dinner, we moved to the basement entertainment area, where a big-screen TV was the center attraction, and watched football. Abiy and I were watching with a kind of detached amusement of the bigness of the players, their agility, and the jumping of players on top of the opposing players to grab the ball. We thought it was violent. How was it that these big guys could take so much punishment and walk with seemingly no pain? Becky was explaining the rules of the game. All the rest were enjoying, totally engrossed by the movement of the ball. They had a little friendly bet; they called it sweepstake. They had a column of names vertically and scores for each on the different quarters of the game and which team would be the winner.

Friday, the day after Thanksgiving, was a big shopping day. We went to the Great America Mall, a giant indoor shopping area where hundreds of stores of every size and type were located. In the middle of the mall, there was a big area for the entertainment of children and adults. The mall was crowded. It looked like the whole city had merged into the same place. Don said people came from other states and abroad to shop there. It was one of the attractions of the Twin Cities; the two cities of St. Paul and Minneapolis are called Twin Cities.

The ladies wanted to do some shopping while the men lounged at a bar within the mall. The bar was crowded with people watching football and drinking. Americans were crazy for sports, we observed. It might be true what a Nigerian classmate had told me, "Americans buy newspaper just to read the sports section."

The ladies, loaded with bags of shopping exploits, stood at the bottom of the escalator, waiting for us to join them. We drove to the house. Kathleen pulled out two sweaters, hats, gloves, scarves, and earmuffs as a gift to both Abiy and me. We were very appreciative of her kindness.

The Saturday before our trip back to Wisconsin, we had lunch at a Scandinavian restaurant, a buffet style. At lunch, Edward asked me how things were going with Amsal's situation.

And I updated him with the process of applying for college for her and then the application for visa as a student. "Hopefully soon, she will mail the application and relevant documents."

"Good," he said. "Let us know if there is anything we can help," he reassured me. I thanked him for his generosity.

On our way back to Wisconsin, the weather was crisp and clear, and the ground was covered with a smattering of snow, auguring the arrival of winter. The frenetic activities in the parks and streets had slowed down. But there were those who enjoyed winter sports who prayed for a pile of snow to fall.

On Sunday, we went to church. The sermon was on thanksgiving, not the holiday but the expression of gratitude to the Lord for the marvel of life. Father Branagh was at his best—jovial, informative, and energetic. He asked each of us to take stock why we should be thankful to our Lord and to think of the sick, hungry, and those snared by wars and conflict. "Make your life remarkable. Make the meaning of your life important to humanity," he exhorted. He brought up that Mark Twain had Tom Sawyer attend his own funeral and listen to how people had eulogized him. It was the need to know how people remember us after our demise. He concluded his sermon by saying, "Let us make our lives worthwhile and life enhancing." And he quoted Ralph Waldo Emerson, "To leave the world a bit better whether by a healthy child, a garden patch, or redeemed social condition, to know that even one life has breathed easier because you lived—that is to have succeeded."

For the week after the holiday, we had planned to spend every spare time to study in preparation for the final examinations. Our tutor had essentially become our cheerleader as we were doing very well at school, particularly in mathematics and sciences. As we had planned, we had a very busy week between our work, classes, and studies. By the week of the tests, we were well prepared, and that helped us maintain our excellent grades.

Amsal called to inform me that she had sent the application for admission and the documents. I told her about our Thanksgiving trip and enjoyable time with Kathleen and Edward. She was intrigued by the turkey as part of the holiday dinner. "Turkey, what is that?" was her first question.

I had to explain to her that a turkey looked like a very, very big chicken. Her next question was "Does it taste like chicken?"

"No," I said. "To me, without the trimmings and the side dishes, it is bland. I wouldn't even have eaten it. But it was a very enjoyable dinner with wonderful people."

With her curiosity intact, she handed the telephone to Azie and Aida. They had meshed with the family. Except for missing our parents, they were happy.

By the time Amsal's documents arrived, a full-blown winter covered the land with inches of snow. The northerly wind was blowing hard, dipping the temperature to bone-chilling cold. We covered every part of our body with piles of clothing, except for the eyes and nose. As we walked our dogs, cursing at the cold, we were amazed to see some people walking nonchalantly, covering their bodies lightly. Children were building a snowman and throwing snowball at each other with glee.

Since the school had been on break for winter and the holidays, we were working extra—snow removal and some odd jobs besides our regular dog walking. We were always busy, and within the community, people had come to know us well. We worked hard and honestly to maintain our reputation. It had served us well.

The dog walking gave us joy. The dogs had become an extension of our family. There were six breeds, and over the months, we had come to know the different behavior they possessed and their likes and dislikes. They seemed to know us too. Whenever we arrived at the doors, they would wag their tails, knowing full well that we were there to take them out of the confines of their home.

Abiy joked, "I wouldn't be surprised if one of them call over the phone and say, 'Come soon and take me to walk.'"

Before we started working with the dogs, we never had any idea of the various breeds of dogs. Dogs were dogs, like humans with different looks. Now we were reasonably versatile on some of the dog breeds.

Lately, Becky was coming to our place more frequently. She had all kinds of excuses—to tell us about different universities and their programs, to take us to a play in Milwaukee, or to take us to the shopping mall where her favorite café was located. We never said no to Becky because she was such a good-hearted person. She was very attractive but slightly overweight. She always talked how she planned to go on a diet and regimen of exercise. But she would postpone them for lack of time, her excuse.

Erin was curious about the frequency of Becky's visit, but she never said anything until a Sunday after church. I was seated in the living room, watching TV, while Becky and Abiy were playing computer games in the study room.

Erin came to the living room and sat next to me. "Is it okay if I sit here, Mati?" she asked.

I looked at her, questioning because she always sat by me. "Why ask?" I was thinking. "Sure, Erin, if you want to watch the news."

"Yes, news," she remarked.

I suspected news was not what brought her to the living room. She looked twice toward the study room, and then she brought up what was in her mind. Half in jest, she asked what was going on between Becky and Abiy.

I was caught by surprise, and I acted suspiciously, for I had suspected that Becky had an eye for Abiy. I said, "I don't know." And I continued, "I know Abiy like the back of my hands. There is nothing going on."

"I know, Mati. I understand, and I believe you. Abiy does not keep secrets from you." In a low voice, she said, "Between you and I, Becky likes Abiy," she confided.

"Did she tell you?" I asked.

"No, not yet," she answered. "I know my Becky will soon come and confide in me if my suspicion is correct. She always does," she said matter-of-factly. "But keep it to yourself, Mati, until Becky says something."

"My lips are zipped," I assured her. With that, she left me to watch the news.

I never kept secrets from Abiy. Between the two of us, we were always open since childhood. But since I gave my word to Erin to keep locked about them and my suspicion about Becky's feeling for Abiy, I didn't tell him anything. It was not easy. I was anxious for Becky to confide on her aunt so everything would be out in the open. Abiy and I were very fond of Becky. I hoped this situation wouldn't complicate our friendship. She had become a surrogate sister since we arrived in the USA.

Since the arrival of the month of December, people talked about the Christmas season. The newspapers and TV were filled with advertisements enticing people to buy this or that gift. The town streets were adorned with Christmas decorations, and most of the houses' Christmas trees with colorful lights and decorations were set up. The town in the main commercial district had placed a big tree beautifully adorned with lights and Christmas-specific items. In the shopping mall, a plump bearded man in red-and-white uniform was seated—Santa Claus. Young children would sit on his lap and take pictures. Sometimes even mothers would stand by his side and take pictures. Music was played at the mall, auguring the Christmas season. And the malls were crowded with shoppers of Christmas gifts. We were told Christmas was the busiest time for most of the stores. From what we observed in the US, Christmas was more secular. People of other religions also celebrated it, especially parents with children. It was inevitable as the barrage of advertisements would force parents to buy something for their children. Otherwise, the children might feel deprived as their friends and schoolmates would talk about the gifts they had received.

Abiy and I were swayed by the culture, and we bought several items for Erin and Sol and the Boones. There was also a special gift for Becky. We wrapped them with the help of the store clerk and hid them in our room, unbeknown to Erin and Sol. We bought a Christmas card and mailed it to Kathleen and Edward. The mood on the streets was joyous. Invariably, people would greet us, "Merry Christmas." The spirits of the people seemed to be uplifted during the season. There was something magical about it. Except for the bitter cold, even the atmosphere seemed to exude joy. The trees, loaded with melted snow and then frozen, looked to be adorned with diamond crystals replacing the shredded leaves.

On Sunday after church, we picked up Sol at home to buy a Christmas tree at Menards. On the parking lot, they had set up an area where pine trees of different sizes were sold. There were many families buying trees. We joined the people and started to choose a tree; Erin chose a tree about six feet tall. We stood it in the corner of the living room. We helped Erin adorn it with decorations from the past year. After lighting the tree, we ceremoniously sat at the dining table close to the tree and sipped on hot cider garnished with cinnamon stick.

Abiy and I had planned to invite them for dinner. We told Erin. Sol had already been informed.

"Thank you. How did you know I was tired to cook dinner?"

We suggested a Japanese restaurant that we had heard serve a special steak.

Erin said, "That is too expensive. Let us go to a Thai place."

We insisted we could afford for one night. She relented. Since we arrived at the restaurant earlier for dinner, there were several tables unseated. They sat us right away. It was an elegant restaurant with an open kitchen with all the activities of the chef and his staff visible from our table. It was theatrical—the chopping, flipping, and decorating the dishes. Erin and Sol ordered tempura and sushi. We ordered steak, miso soup, and green tea, which was served first. They gave us chopsticks to feed ourselves with for the side dishes. The only time we saw them was in movies.

Erin saw us looking at the chopsticks with awe in our faces. "Is this the first time?" she asked. Meekly, we answered yes. She demonstrated how to hold them. "But if you would rather use forks and spoons, they can provide you."

We were relieved. Food was good. And Erin and Sol were happy, and so we were.

*****

Amsal's acceptance letter to the college came earlier than expected. They sent a copy to Erin and Sol and mail to Amsal. Since we received the letter sooner, I called Amsal to inform her of the good news. She was excited and cried loudly. She called everybody, and I talked to them. The only question they had was when she was to travel to the US. I explained the process briefly that she would need to get a visa from the US consulate in Addis Ababa. And after that, we would purchase the ticket for her flight. Her school would start in spring, so she had to be in the US sometime in March.

"With Amsal coming, we have to make changes in our living arrangement," Abiy suggested.

I concurred, "We should explore a place where the three of us can live, maybe a three-bedroom apartment. But it should be done with the confirmation of her visa."

As frequently as we saw Becky, it was rare that Al came to visit his aunt. He was very busy with a new job at a prestigious law firm in Milwaukee. His father was hoping for him to join him at his firm, but Al decided to experience practice outside his father's tutelage. Don agreed with condition that he should be back to work with him. On Saturday, Al called Erin and asked if it was okay that he would stop at home on Sunday after church.

Erin said, "Anytime, Al. I miss you."

As promised, Al came about three o'clock in the afternoon, about the same time we came back after clearing snow for our clients. He asked us how our Thanksgiving holiday was and about our school. We told him it was the most enjoyable holiday, and at school, we were doing fine. We were exploring different universities to transfer.

"Wonderful," he said and went into what brought him home. Al declared that he had proposed to Alexandra, which she accepted. Erin was ecstatic, and we congratulated him, wishing him well.

Two weeks after we received Amsal's acceptance letter to the college with a catalog included, she received the letter. The next process was to apply for visa at the US consulate. It could be done in person or online. Abiy suggested better to apply in person. That way, if there were issues, she could respond right away. I concurred and advised her to do the same.

"I will ask Azie and Aida to accompany me," Amsal remarked. "They will be my crutches if the consular officer denied me visa. I can see myself collapsing to the ground."

I said, "Don't be a fool, dear. There can't be any reason why you will be denied. All documents are legal and in order. The college is accredited. You can take Azie and Aida to accompany you since the wait could be long."

In Asmara, the militarization of the country continued unabated. The rounding up of young people and sending them to Sawa boot camp was intensified. A young man who was helping my father at the store was taken while walking to work. My father was saddened because the young man was reliable and hardworking, and he was also the breadwinner to his elderly parents. Recalling my forced conscription from the street while walking with him brought up bitter memory. He considered the young man as his son. The family had lost one of their sons at war; a daughter was under the national service, and the only son left was gone. They were left alone without any means to support themselves. The father was long unemployed from a shuttered bottle manufacturing factory. At seventy years of age, the prospect of employment was almost nonexistent. The mother was bedridden of sickness, most likely the result of deep grief. My father, aware of their situation, offered a part-time job to the gentleman, mainly restocking and as a guard. I was proud of my father for being so considerate and empathetic to the situation of the family.

We kept ourselves very busy during winter among school, work, and getting ready for Amsal to join us. On her first appearance at the US consulate, her visa application was not granted. She was required to get a security clearance from her local administration. The clearance had to show if she had been a good citizen with no criminal or security-related blemishes on record. She was a bit confounded. The insinuation that she needed a security clearance felt an affront to her upright family with unimpeachable character in their community. Notwithstanding her feeling, it was a requirement to get the document.

After she told her father, he said, "So what is the problem? Let me take you to Abebe, the new administrator of the area, and he will write you the document without hesitation."

The next morning, they were in front of the office when Abebe noticed the father. "What brings you this early, Mr. Dereje?" he asked. He greeted them politely. After the father told him the situation, he said, "No problem. Have a seat. As soon as the secretary arrives, she will write you the clearance. She will be here in a few minutes."

Fifteen minutes later, the document was ready. It was read to them before it was sealed. The envelope was stamped, to prove it was not tampered. The next appointment at the consulate was in three weeks.

*****

Becky registered at a yoga training program close to our home. She had to attend the classes three times a week. After the classes, she would drop by our home. Playing video games with Abiy was her favorite pastime. She said it relaxed her nerves. On Friday within the week she started the yoga training, she dropped by at home. But instead of her usual video game, she sat with her aunt in the living room. Erin had arrived from work early, and Sol was on a trip for a conference. Becky was talking in earnest with her aunt. I had my suspicion of what they were talking about as I was watching the gaze and the easy smile. Abiy never indicated on how he felt about the attention he was getting from Becky. I hadn't said anything since I promised Erin to keep it to myself. They talked for almost an hour when Becky asked me if I was interested to go to a movie. I excused myself by claiming of having to catch up with some work.

Abiy, who was a distance away from us, accepted the invitation, unaware of my decision. He readied himself by putting his winter attire. When he noticed I wasn't ready, he asked, "Mati, when are you going to get ready?"

"I am tired. You go ahead, Abiy," I responded. My intention was to give them some privacy.

As they were getting out, I noticed Erin giving a wink to Becky. Clearly, Becky had confided to her aunt. Soon, after they left, Erin asked me what my thoughts were with love between them.

"I have no idea, Erin. We never brought the idea of romance with Abiy. Well," I continued, "Abiy is unattached. He is fond of Becky. He may even love her. It may trouble him because he considers her like a sister."

She challenged me, "How about your relationship with Amsal? You grew up together like brother and sister, from what I gather."

I saw the hypocrisy in my response. To get out of it, I said, "Let us see what brings this evening. It may develop into romance before the end of the night."

The clock ticked late. About midnight, Becky dropped Abiy in front of the house. Erin had gone to sleep. I stayed up reading and talking to Amsal over the phone.

Abiy saw me and asked, "You are still up."

I pretended I was busy, and I wasn't aware of the time. Truth be told, I was waiting for him.

He saw in all directions to make sure Erin was not on any side of the room.

"Erin went to sleep about an hour ago," I assured him. "How was the movie?" I asked.

As if he was awakened from sleep, he retorted, "The movie…uh…uh…was not bad."

"What was is it about?" I asked him.

Again, he kept saying, "Uh…" He absentmindedly said, "Uh…kissing, shooting, driving fast—the usual kind."

"Are you okay, Abiy?" I asked, as if concerned for his well-being. Abiy was fine. He was processing the event that occurred a few hours back, and he didn't know how to tell me.

I was about to walk into my bedroom when he said, "I don't know how you will think about me after this evening, Mati." Uninterrupted, he told me the details of the evening's event. "As soon as we walked out of the house, before we got in the car, she hugged me passionately and tightly, expressing how happy she was that we were spending the evening together. I said I was happy too, not knowing how to answer otherwise. As we walked into the car, she extended her arm and held my hand. In the car, she started the engine to warm it up. She complained how cold it was and started to rub my shoulders and neck. Before I reacted, she pulled me and kissed me. Smack on the lips. I kissed her back. I would be lying if I said I didn't enjoy it. Mati, since she started to give me special attention, I have liked Becky. I would have discouraged her a long time ago if I didn't feel flattered and enjoy it. She is a beautiful and genuinely good person. But I am so filled with guilt of betrayal to Sarah, Don, and Erin. They treat me like a member of the family, and I do this. At this point, I am filled with self-loath. But at the same, I am in love with Becky."

I listened to him with sympathy. "I know, Abiy." I totally understood his feelings.

He continued, "How am I going to look at Erin's eyes and Sarah's and Don's?"

I felt it was time to share my opinion. "Abiy, don't worry about a thing. Erin knows everything. She had noticed the attraction between the two of you. Becky had already confided with her about her feelings towards you. You know why I didn't go out with you earlier? I wanted to give you privacy. Only the two of you have to confront and deal with your feelings."

"Are you serious, Mati? Erin knows? And she is okay with it?"

"Absolutely. She is very approving," I said with a smile.

He was not sure what to make of it and remained quiet. With that, we parted to our respective rooms to sleep.

On Sunday morning, we were ready to go to church when Becky drove her car to the front of the house. "I came to go to church with you," she declared.

"I hope you do it every Sunday," Erin answered.

She hopped into Erin's SUV. Abiy was all blushed. The whole time, he was looking down. I found it so hilarious to see my dear friend in a situation strange to him. I was seated on the front passenger seat with Erin driving. Becky and Abiy sat on the back seats side by side. The whole trip, Becky held tight Abiy's hand. At the church, Erin led us to four open seats and made Becky and Abiy sit next to each other. I thought I saw Abiy sweat. Poor guy, he was all nervous. I thought Erin was having a little fun to see him sweat a bit. After church, Erin invited us to a brunch at our favorite restaurant. We sat in a booth with Becky and Abiy sitting on the same side, Erin's suggestion.

She later told me she wanted to observe their body language if they were in love. "Small gestures, glances, and touches are telltale signs of a person's feeling."

In the evening, Erin had to pick up Sol at the airport in Milwaukee. She invited me to drive with her, and I readily accepted. Becky and Abiy were on their computer games. As we were driving, the case of Becky and Abiy came up obviously.

"I think they are in love with each other," she quipped. "It is early to conclusively say, but from my observation today, they are in love. What do you think?" she asked me.

I said, "You are right. In fact, Abiy is very fond of Becky, except he feels guilty of betrayal to the family."

"Why?" she asked.

"Well, he feels that he had been treated as part of the family, like a son. And to have a romantic relationship with Becky looks sort of incestuous."

"If they really love each other, we will make it official, and that may make him feel at ease," Erin hoped.

Sol's flight was delayed by an hour. Waiting in a café, I surmised how our life was to change in a few months, when Amsal would arrive and if the relationship between Becky and Abiy would flourish. I brought up the need for us to find a place to live.

Erin agreed. "Maybe not far from us."

Almost two hours late, the flight arrived. Sol was exhausted. I helped him carry his luggage to the house. Becky's car was parked on the spot we left it. As Erin and Sol entered the house, I left to my previously appointed work; it was to make some errands for Mrs. Katz.

By the time I came back home, except for Sol, all three of them were in the living room, watching a movie.

Abiy was relaxed. He said, "You shouldn't have gone alone. I was waiting for you."

"The job was easy. No need for both of us to go. Besides, Becky was here. I didn't think it was fair to leave her alone."

I didn't know what to make of it. Abiy was sitting so close to Becky, almost hugging her on a love seat, and Erin was seating spread out on the sofa. "Did Erin force them to sit that way?" I asked myself. But they didn't look like two people forced to sit close. They seemed to enjoy the closeness of their bodies. No one was forthcoming with an explanation of the change in the last few hours. And I didn't ask for explanation. I joined them in watching the movie. Appropriately, the movie was about two young people in a romantic relationship in an island.

As soon as the movie ended, Becky stood to go home. She exclaimed, "I was comfortable here, but I got to get ready for tomorrow!"

As she walked to the door, Abiy followed her to her car. They gave each other an intimate hug and kiss.

I was eager to hear from Abiy what happened while I was gone to pick up Sol at the airport and work at Mrs. Katz.

The only comment I heard from Erin was "Did you see the lovebirds?" And she was broadly smiling. I suspected she had something to do with it.

Abiy came back triumphantly, and we moved to our study room. While we were organizing books and materials for school in the morning, he started the story of the day by saying, "You can't believe what happened today. After Erin and you left to Milwaukee, we were playing computer games. Soon, we started touching and kissing each other passionately. I told her how much I love her, except that I feel guilty on what the rest of the family may feel, I sensed.

"She said, 'But we are not committing a crime. We are just in love. There is no guilt in love. Erin knows, and she had nothing but great things to say about you.'

"'How about Sarah and Don? What are they going to say?'

"'Right now, they don't know,' she said. 'We will deal with it in time. But believe me, they are not going to disapprove of a person that I love, particularly one who is as good as you.'

"After that, I was more relaxed and enjoyed the rest of the time. When Erin and Sol came into the room, I didn't hear them. Becky was sitting on my lap, and we were kissing each other. I almost dropped her to the floor.

"Erin turned back away to give us privacy. After brewing herbal tea, she invited us to the living room. And forthrightly, she said, 'Abiy, there is nothing to be embarrassed about. I understand you two are attracted to each other. Ain't nothing to be embarrassed.' She encouraged me. She directed us to sit at the love seat. And that is how you found us," he concluded.

"How do you feel now?" I asked.

"Honestly, Mati, I am happy and in love."

"Great," I said.

After three weeks, the appointment for Amsal to appear at the US consulate arrived. With the security clearance in a sealed envelope and other documents, she came to the consulate. She handed the documents to the consular officer; it was a different person.

He looked at all the documents carefully and said, "Everything is in order, except the sponsors do not fully describe how they are going to support you. Are they going to pay for living experiences, medical insurance? They have committed themselves to pay for your education. Now we need a statement of committal to support you with living expense. Once you bring that statement, you will be granted a visa."

Amsal was very disappointed, and she called right after the interview. I was disappointed too. I called Erin and shared the news.

"There is no problem. It could be done tonight," she calmed me. She discussed the situation with Don. And Don said he would make his secretary draft the statement, and it would be signed and be ready soon. The statement, signed and notarized, was sent via DHL for express delivery.

In the town that we lived, there was a small newspaper that was published weekly and distributed free at different vendors. It reported mainly on events and personalities in the town. Newborn children, weddings, new arrivals, and the deceased were reported. But sometimes events as mundane as breakup of relationship and the start of a new relationship were included. One morning after Becky and Abiy were seeing each other, Sarah saw a picture in the front page headlined "The Lovebirds." It was Becky and Abiy holding hands. Sarah picked up the paper and drove home. On arrival at home, she called Erin at work and read her the short note on the paper with pictures.

Erin feigned ignorance and said, "Can we talk about it later, Sarah? I am quite busy right now."

Sarah agreed and hung up the telephone. She felt like calling her husband but changed her mind, reminding herself this was not a calamity. But she was ready to confront her daughter as she arrived at home. The whole afternoon, she was pondering all the emotional feelings this relationship would trigger, based on race, class, and culture. She paused. "With Erin and Sol, I have been around interracial marriage. I know how loving the relationship they have built, and the family had been happy about their marriage."

At school, Ashley, a schoolmate of Becky's, had brought a copy of the newspaper and shoved it at Becky.

Becky gazed at the paper for a few minutes before she jokingly said, "The cameraman is no good. We look better than the picture. Next time we have a college party, you will see him." And then she walked away.

Ashley was ready to talk, but Becky's reaction shut her off. Ashley was a gossiper in the college. She had showed the newspaper to anyone who had given her time. The gossip went like this: "Rebecca Boone had imported a lover from Africa." In the cafeteria, there were sneers whenever Becky would pass a group of women. Becky was not a person easily intimidated, and if anyone dared her, she was ready to return the dare in kind or more. She had two strong-minded friends at school, Gwen and Jane. They went to the same elite Catholic high school, and when one was attacked, they would gang up to make life a hell to the attacker. Ashley became their target.

It started with the look, the look of hate and disdain. It was a look of foot to head with no words exchanged. After a few times, it started to work in the mind of the person. Ashley was terrified to see the three friends. She tried to talk to Becky on two occasions, but she was ignored. Soon, the gossip died.

After finishing our afternoon work, Abiy was planning to go to a show with Becky. Becky had bought two tickets. But Erin called Becky and asked her to come to the house before the show.

"Can I come tomorrow, Auntie?" Becky suggested.

"I need to talk to you tonight, dear."

"All right, I will be there around five p.m."

"Fine," Erin agreed.

Becky came at the appointed time. She was not sure why Erin insisted for her to come tonight.

"Sorry to mess up your evening schedule, but I have something to talk to you. Sarah had seen the picture in the newspaper, and she is not happy a secret of such importance had been kept from her. She asked me if I knew about it, and I pretended that I was busy to talk. I think you have to come clean with her."

"Was she angry?" Becky asked.

"I sensed disappointment rather than anger. Disappointed that her daughter didn't confide in her, considering the close relationship that you both have."

"I love my mother," Becky remarked. "And my dad," she added. "I will talk to her honestly tonight."

"Good girl." Erin hugged her. Erin told her to call after she talked to Sarah.

*****

"Dinner!" Sarah said, looking at her daughter.

"Thank you. I just had dinner at Auntie's place."

"Oh! I should have thought," Sarah snapped.

Becky looked at her mother's face to read her feelings. But it was not possible because Sarah avoided looking at her. Becky knew that when her mother was unhappy with a person or persons, she would avoid looking at them.

Don, the lawyer, understood the dynamics of emotions, and he intervened at this point. "Becky," he started calmly and slowly, "what is going on between you and Abiy?"

"That was what I was going to tell you," Becky responded.

"After the whole world knew and talked about it," Sarah angrily snapped.

"I am sorry, Mom and Dad. That is not how I wanted it to be. Abiy begged me to wait for some time until he deciphers the emotion between loving me and what it may make you feel about it. I know I love him, and he loves me. But he felt that he betrayed the family that accepted him as one of them. Mom, Dad, I love you. I do not want to disappoint you in any way. And it is what Abiy said too. Of all the men I have dated, he is the most mature, decent, considerate, intelligent, and goal oriented. I love him dearly. I know he loves me."

Don looked at his daughter intently and then at his wife whose face had relaxed and said, "The most important thing for us is your happiness. We do not have any doubt Abiy and Mati have the qualities you described. But we do not want to be left in dark about the future of our children."

Becky called Erin as promised and informed her all was fine in the home front.

After the call, Erin thought it was time to talk to Sarah, and she dialed the phone. They talked for a good forty-five minutes while Becky was busy with schoolwork and Don was immersed in reading.

After finishing her work, Becky called Abiy to update what had transpired between her and her parents. Abiy was eager to hear how they reacted. She simply said, "Fine."

For Abiy, "fine" was such a nondescript; he wanted to know what they said and how they reacted. "Was it acceptance because they believed in our love or acceptance because they could not change the situation—"

"Abiy, you are becoming hysterical," Becky interrupted. My parents are not cynical unless truly they believe they would not agree just to be agreeable. Believe me, I know them. Just relax. I will see you tomorrow. I love you," she said and hung up the phone.

*****

Amsal, escorted by Azie and Aida, went to the consular office with the new affidavit of support clinched on her hand. The line at the gate was long. They had to wait for almost two hours. It was bearable because the three of them together were talking and, at times, giggling. Once in the office, the officer remembered her and asked for the documents. She laid everything in front of him, including her passport. After checking the documents, he stamped an

F-1 visa on a page of her passport. He wished her good luck and to study hard and be good citizen while in the US. "Thank you," she responded.

Outside, Azie and Aida were waiting anxiously. When they saw her face with a broad smile, they knew it was good news.

She hugged them with her passport open to show them the visa seal. "Let us go home and call Mati and Abiy and tell them the good news," she stated.

Azie suggested, "Let us call them right now from our cell phone." After hesitating, considering the time in Wisconsin, Amsal agreed.

I answered the call on the fourth ring.

Excitedly, she told me, "A visa had been granted, and I am outside of the consulate with Azie and Aida."

I said, "Wonderful! I am so happy. Abiy is sleeping in his room. I will tell him in the morning. I will call you in the morning. And give my love to Azie and Aida."

Abiy was awakened by the ringing of the phone at this late hour. He splashed cold water on his face and went to my bedroom. He was concerned by this untimely call. "Is everything okay?" he asked as he entered the room.

"Can't you read my face? Amsal just called with visa on her hand."

The idea of finding an apartment became more urgent. With Amsal's coming soon assured, a convenient living arrangement was important. In the town, we had developed many acquaintances, mostly through our work. Among them was Mr. Rossati, the loquacious and perennially happy person who owned several commercial and residential properties in town. He had hired us to do odd jobs at different times. He had always been appreciative of our work and generous in his payment. He first came to mind to ask for apartment in one of his buildings. Erin might also be of help as she was very resourceful. We needed a three-bedroom apartment, preferably with two bathrooms.

In the evening, we brought up the issue of housing with Erin and Sol. They both supported the idea, and Erin promised to contact some landlords.

Becky and Abiy had been going out steady for the last five months. Their relationship was getting tighter, and the love toward each other was palpable. Every minute outside school and job, they were always together. When we transferred to the university in Milwaukee, Becky joined the same university. With Becky's great sense of humor, she brought out Abiy's on-the-spot one-liners. We made friends. Our table at the cafeteria was always crowded with young people of many nationalities. Everyone thought of Becky and Abiy as a great couple. I was hatching a plot to arrange an engagement party for them on the same day that I would propose to Amsal, of course, after her arrival in the US. And I would discreetly assess the wishes of both with the help of Erin.

As several people had been told of our search for a three-bedroom apartment, we had several offers.

Mr. Rossati was our choice to be our landlord. He showed us a three-bedroom apartment with one-and-a-half bathrooms about a mile from our residence. He gave us a good deal. If we agreed to take care of the common areas—like the stairs, the sidewalk, and the corridors—and clear the snow during winter, we only have to pay 150 dollars per month to cover utilities. It was a great offer that we signed on happily. Erin and Sol were happy and reminded us, "Mr. Rossati is trying to help you." We were very grateful and promised not to disappoint him.

The flight ticket for Amsal was purchased to fly her on Ethiopian Airlines from Addis Ababa to Frankfurt and then on United Airlines to Chicago, Illinois. Her flight would be on mid-May, with winter giving way to early spring. Erin had suggested the three of us—Becky, Abiy, and I—should pick her up from the O'Hare International Airport in Chicago. Becky owned a fairly new Honda Accord, and we all had driver's licenses that we could relieve one another if need be. Becky was excited to meet Amsal. They had talked over the phone a few times, although Amsal was not aware of Becky's relationship with her brother.

Our busy life had become busier, preparing a new life in a new residence. The apartment looked amazing when the furniture was arranged with the guidance of Erin and Becky.

Mr. Rossati was the first nonfamily to come and visit our apartment. He said, "Wow! It looks great." And he even made a joke, "Maybe I should move here, and you move to my place." He gave us some keys for the building to have access to the areas that we agreed to service.

Amsal arrived at the O'Hare International Airport in Chicago, Illinois. It was early morning when the airplane landed. We had arrived at the airport earlier. The day was a bright spring day. The days before were rainy and cloudy. On the day Amsal arrived, the sun had come out shining to welcome her. The process of going through customs and immigration took about forty-five minutes. It was the longest forty-five minutes for me. I was so eager to see her the wait was torture. Then she emerged pulling her luggage, so beautiful and elegant, and walking confidently toward us. She saw us on the other side of the glass door and waved at us. I waved with both my hands up. I couldn't believe how much she had changed in the few years we had been separated. The many pictures she had sent me did not do justice to the real beauty of Amsal. With a height of about five feet and eight inches, she was elegantly beautiful. It was an emotional meeting. We hugged each other warmly for a good time before we even spoke a word of greeting. After a long trip, understandably she was tired, but the excitement had energized her. Becky and she hugged each other like they were friends for a long time.

She was surprised to see me as a six-feet-tall and bearded man. She joked, "I guess America has a booster for growth. Both you and Abiy had changed but, I am glad, for the better. My men are handsome."

We walked to the parking lot side by side. I was in awe by the grace and beauty that enveloped her being. In the car, we sat side by side with Becky driving and Abiy seated on the front passenger seat.

She told how everybody had come to Addis Ababa Bole International Airport to see her depart. "Dad, Mom, Azie, and Aida. We cried over each other's shoulders, with Dad stoically watching. But I could see his eyes were filled with tears. They sent their love hundreds of times."

We drove outside the perimeter of the airport to merge onto I-94 west highway. Becky suggested that we stop for a snack on the way, but Amsal insisted she was not hungry. About halfway, she was so tired and couldn't open her eyes and laid her head on my shoulder to take a nap. We kept quiet for the rest of the trip so as not to disturb her.

About ninety minutes' drive took us to the front of our apartment. As the car came to a halt, Amsal woke up from her slumber.

"Good morning," we told her. "We are home."

"God, I was so tired," she responded.

We unloaded the luggage and led Amsal to the apartment. We had already set up the extra bedroom for her. With the help of Erin, I bought pajamas, robe, slippers, towels, and a few other items specific to a woman. We placed the luggage in her room.

She was impressed by the apartment and her bedroom. "Is this bedroom for me?" she asked suspiciously.

I said, "Yes, dear."

"It looks comfortable," she remarked.

"You deserve it," I responded.

I led her to visit the rest of the apartment. She was amazed how organized it was. Becky and Abiy were patiently waiting in the living room while I was acting as a tour guide. Before she sat in the living room, I asked if she wanted to take a bath.

She said, "Yes, it will relax me."

I filled the bathtub and prepared everything she needed. After the bath and a change of clothes, she joined us in the living room. She looked more stunning with the dress I sent her a few weeks ago.

We were invited for dinner by Erin and Sol. We arrived at six o'clock in the evening. They were ready to welcome Amsal. As we parked the car, they came outside to greet her, and they greeted her like a princess.

Erin came close to my ears and said, "Mati, you didn't tell me she is such a gorgeous young woman."

After sitting for a few minutes to get acquainted, we drove to Bruno's Italian restaurant. Erin had already made a reservation, and we were seated upon arrival. Bruno's was an elegant high-end restaurant. It was spacious but always crowded by people who came from Milwaukee, Madison, and other small towns.

Becky had been on a diet for the last three months. She ordered salad and grapefruit juice. Since she started dieting, she had become a svelte beauty by dropping pounds.

Everybody else ordered foods from the expansive menu. Amsal ordered the ravioli with spinach salad. She liked it and ate a piece of chocolate cake for dessert. The conversation was lively about life and future. I was surprised by Amsal's English language skill. She had no problem conversing with the group.

After dinner, we went to Erin and Sol's place for coffee and tea. Becky and Abiy sat on the love seat close to each other. We sat on the larger sofa with Sol and I bracketing Erin and Amsal. Becky was speaking to Abiy close to his ears, which made him smile, and she planted a kiss on his face. Amsal's eyes opened wide, caught by surprise at such a clear demonstration of love. She kept quiet.

After the coffee and tea drinking was over, before our departure, I stood to clear the cups and wash them.

Amsal volunteered to help. She followed me to the kitchen. While I was washing the cups, she told me what was in her mind. "Mati," she started, "what is between Becky and Abiy?"

I said, "What do you mean?"

"Mati, you know what I am asking about. You saw the kiss."

I cut it short by saying, "They are in love, Amsal." She was quiet.

As Becky drove back to our place, Amsal and I sat at the back seat holding hands, our initial show of affection in a physical way.

As Becky and Abiy went into the bedroom, I lingered with Amsal to gauge her feeling about Abiy's relationship with Becky.

She said, "It doesn't bother me as long as they have mutual love and respect. My only grudge is why it was kept secret from me all the time. We were calling each other."

I assured her that they loved each other and that Becky was a wonderful young lady.

Wistfully but in jest, she asked, "When are you going to introduce me to your secret love?"

At that instant, I grabbed her by her waist and planted a warm kiss on her lips and said, "Now you know who my love is."

We sat amorously in the warmth of our bodies until we started to fall asleep. I helped her to go to sleep in her room. It took me a while to sleep, rethinking of the event of the night.

Next morning, I was the first to get up from bed. I checked if Amsal was awake by peering through a crack of the door. She was still asleep like an angel. I came close to her bed and gave her a soft kiss on her brow. She woke up and saw, I suspected, my longing eyes. She asked me to sit and gave a hug and a kiss. How lovely, I thought. I couldn't resist kissing her.

After almost half an hour of tender hugging and kissing, Amsal had to get ready for us to go to church. I knocked at Abiy's bedroom to wake them up to get ready. We arrived at church a few minutes late. Erin was already seated. We joined her.

It was the first time for Amsal to attend a Catholic mass. At the end of the service, Erin asked her to stand up to introduce her as a new member of her family who just arrived from Ethiopia. As people were leaving the church, they welcomed her. Most expressed admiration of her beauty and elegance.

Erin and Becky took Amsal with them as we had to go to do some work. The work took us three hours. By the time we came back at Erin and Sol's place, it was about four o'clock in the afternoon. Only Sol was at home. The three ladies had gone to visit a mall. On their way back, they stopped at the Boones' for Amsal to meet Sarah and Don.

For dinner, we decided to surprise Amsal by cooking at home. We had stacked supplies before her arrival—fried chicken, flavored rice, sautéed spinach, and salad.

When she tasted the food, she said, "I am glad you guys are good cooks. I was afraid I will be the cook of the house. With two cooks, I don't have to worry. And I would enjoy what you concoct in the kitchen."

Becky had left to go home for the night and get ready for school tomorrow.

We had agreed that Amsal would go with us to the university. As we had staggered classes, one of us would be with her until classes ended. After dinner, Abiy and I had to work on our studies while Amsal was flipping the remote control, watching different shows on TV.

As we finished our work, we joined her, but Abiy said he was tired and went to sleep. My suspicion was he wanted to give us privacy. I sat with Amsal, and she reclined by putting her head on my lap, looking up at me. I kissed her and massaged her scalp, neck, and back. Looking at her beautiful face, well-chiseled teeth, sexy eyes, and delightful curves was so arousing. I had to fight to restrain myself. It was my decision not to consummate our love before we had a formal engagement in a few months. As time was getting late, I led her to the bedroom, kissed her, and left her to sleep.

Early morning, we walked the dogs, and on time, Becky came to give us a ride to school.

On the first hour, Becky didn't have class. She stayed with Amsal, visiting the library and the campus ground. We had agreed to meet at the cafeteria as we finished our class, and Becky was to rush to her class. Several of our friends came and met Amsal.

We asked her if she was willing to go dog walking with us after classes.

She laughed heartily and said, "I can't miss it for the world."

After dropping our backpacks at our apartment, we went to do our dog walking. As we went around to pick up the dogs, all were asking who this beautiful young lady was. Some were ready to offer a job. But we said, "Not yet as her work permit was not in order."

Expecting Becky to give a ride all the time was becoming difficult; it was time to buy a car. We bought a Toyota Camry with a low mileage. It was a good car; the fair price was negotiated by Erin. Practically, the car became Amsal's and mine as Becky and Abiy were inseparable. To school, we alternated cars.

Two months after her arrival, I asked Amsal her feelings about life in the US. I needed to get a clue if she was ready for engagement.

Her answer took my breath away. She said, "I am so happy with my life. I live with the person I love, a brother that I adore, and his beautiful girl-friend. Mati, my life is a dream."

I kissed her and told her how much I loved her and I wanted to spend the rest of my life with her.

"That is my dream too," she added.

On a Sunday evening when the four of us were sitting at home, I pulled a stunt. The previous day, I had bought a ring, and so I knelt on my knees and asked her if she would marry me. She was excited and said yes without hesitation. We opened a cham-pagne and celebrated the occasion. Becky called Erin and announced the engagement. Everybody called to express their congratulations. Amsal loved her ring, took a picture with it, and sent the picture to her parents.

Becky and Abiy discreetly planned to organize a small party to celebrate our engagement a week later. Erin suggested to do it at their place. A few people were invited, family members except for Mr. Rossati and his wife. Food was to be catered by Bruno's Italian restaurant. Amsal and I were the last people to know. Till the day of the party, it was kept secret from us.

On the day of the party, when I was getting ready to go to work, Abiy said, "The work had been rescheduled for the week after." He observed my suspicious look and added, "Call Erin. She is the one who took the message." Erin corroborated it.

With an evening free, I thought I would work on my studies in the corner of my bedroom. Amsal followed me and lay on the bed. As we were cozying up with each other, Abiy declared Erin was expecting us.

As we approached the house, we saw several cars parked—Sarah's, Rossati's, and another car beside Erin and Sol's cars. We looked at each other to read faces if there was something going on. Becky and Abiy pretended knowing nothing. We paced toward the door, looking for some clue indicating what was happening. The lights were dimmed inside. No heads were visible through the shaded windows. We rang the bell, and as we entered the house, a collective voice of congratulations was heard. A big sign with "Amsal and Mati, congratulations" was hung on the wall to the right of the kitchen where the dining table was set. Each person, with Erin being the first, gave us a hug and wished us the best. We were both overwhelmed and left speechless. Erin led us to the love seat reserved for us. They took pictures and videos for posterity.

We enjoyed the dinner, cleared the table, and started enjoying cocktails when Erin stood to speak on congratulating us and how elated she was by all things about us since the day we arrived to live in her house. It was a well-received speech. As she was about to finish her speech, she was looking at Abiy, maybe inviting him to express a few words.

Abiy stood up and welcomed everybody. "Before I express my feelings on this wonderful occasion, I have something to do," he said. And he started searching his pocket as if to take a note that he had written. Instead, he pulled out a little black box and faced Becky and knelt and pulled the biggest surprise of the night by asking her if she would marry him. He said, "The last few months, you made my life the happiest. I can't imagine living without you. Would you marry me?"

Becky was caught by surprise. She stood and knelt right to his face, kissed him, and said yes, to the applause of everybody. There were a few tears shed—that of Sarah, Erin, Becky, and Amsal. I was so happy. I knew how much they loved each other.

Don stood to speak. He said, "This is a total surprise to us. Over the months, we had seen how dedicated they are to each other and how our Becky was happy. It is every parents' dream to see their children happy. We are indeed blessed with our son Al and his beautiful fiancée Alexandra and with our little Becky and the young man who had come to our life and become part of us, now more than before. Abiy and Mati are young men of enormous quality, integrity, hard work, and generosity that we have witnessed since the day of their arrival to the US. Now with Mati betrothed to the lovely Amsal and Abiy to Becky, we wish them all the best."

Sol gave us his blessing and expressed how proud he was of us. Erin admitted that Abiy had given her information of his intent to propose. It was his idea to do it after dinner, and I conceded he was right. A champagne was popped, and that augured our life as couples. We couldn't be any happier. The only regret we had was the absence of our parents. Alternatively, we sent them video and pictures of the occasion.

My friends in Kenya who now lived in Uganda and England came to mind. I had promised to invite them on my wedding day. The wedding day was in the planning. It was to happen after graduation, but I wanted to touch base with them.

Yohannes in Uganda was more accessible. I called him and introduced him to Amsal over the telephone and informed him of Abiy's engagement. He congratulated us and expressed his best wishes. Yohannes had a very successful business in Uganda that expanded to the neighboring countries of South Sudan, Kenya, and Rwanda. Mombasa, the port city in Kenya, had become the hub for his ever-expanding business.

The video and pictures sent to Ethiopia and Eritrea were received. Both parents rejoiced and had their own celebrations among relatives and friends.

Ababa Dereje said the celebration was officiated by Aba Berhanemeskel, who was the pastor for both families since long before our birth. He baptized us at his church as toddlers. He was our spiritual father and treated us with love.

Amsal said, "I pray he stays alive to officiate our wedding."

"I hope so too, my dear," I added.

Our plan was to get married at the church where we were baptized in the town of our birthplace.

Becky had moved with Abiy to live as a couple. The four of us were now living in the same apartment. It became crowded for four. Each of us needed a study area and a place to relax. We discussed the situation, and we all agreed to find separate apartments.

We shared our idea with Mr. Rossati. He offered a bi-level three-bedroom apartment in another of his building. We thanked him, but we wanted to start a family independent of each other. The more frequent contacts would create probable conflict. He came up with an alternative that we lived in two different buildings two miles apart. We said that was fine. We checked the apartments, and we found them acceptable. Since we agreed to continue servicing his building, he agreed that one of the apartments was gratis. We agreed among us that each was to pay half of the rent for the second apartment.

The other apartment was closer to the home of the Boones, so Becky suggested for Abiy and her to move there. On the weekend, we moved to our respective apartments. Erin and Sarah came to help Amsal and Becky arrange the rooms while Abiy and I moved the furniture by renting a truck. Once the apartments were set, our life as a couple started. For the most part, however, we were together.

Life as a couple had befitted Amsal and me. My love and appreciation for her had increased by day. One more thing about Amsal—she always had a joke on hand; time was never boring with her. When she called Ethiopia and talked to Azie and Aida, they would talk for hours, most of it laughing. I tried to listen to what made them laugh so much, but Amsal kept her voice so low I could hardly hear them. When I asked what they talked about, she kidded, "It is girls' talk. You don't need to hear."

When we were young, growing up in Ethiopia— maybe I was about six years old, and Amsal was about four—in family gatherings, they used to make us sing duo. I was the shy one. Amsal was always ready in the front to croon. She dared me to come and join her. Partly by embarrassment and partly by my desire to be around her, I always ended up singing with her. We belted out tunes of our favorite artists—Mahmud, Tilahun, Aster, and many others. Everybody praised us for our talents, and we became the stars of so many evenings. Over the years, I had stopped singing until she reminded me of our joyful past. She always enjoyed humming a tune, especially when she was in the shower or cooking. I would cock my ears to hear the melodious tunes that came out of her throat.

One evening while we were sitting, holding each other, she asked me to sing with her.

"Oh, my dear, you don't want to hear my hoarse voice! I had not sung in many years, and I will sound like a donkey braying." She insisted that I sounded fine and that I should just follow my tune. I was reminded of the happy days of my childhood and the love I had for her at that age. I started to sing. I could see her eyes wide open and overjoyed.

She said, "Mati, you are an incredible singer. Don't ever tell me you can't sing."

From that day on, we would sing in the kitchen, in the bed, and while driving to go places. After she exposed me as a hidden talent to the family, I was asked many times to join her and sing. She had a knack of changing every family or friends gathering into a celebratory occasion. I loved her dearly.

Amsal was not only fun but she was also serious about life. As we lay on our bed in the warmth of the embrace of our bodies, she would lay her hope of life of having children and a happy family. "School has to be a priority at the time," she quipped.

I added, "I can't wait to see a brood of little Amsals and Matis."

"How many children do think we should have?" she asked.

I simply answered, "With you, the more, the merrier."

"Four children are what we should have, God willing," she stated.

"Amen," I said. Nothing in life is finer than living with a person you love and respect.

*****

Azie and Aida, as they crossed to Ethiopia, had been registered by the Red Cross and the United Nations High Commissioner for Refugees (UNHCR) as refugees. The organization helped refugees resettle in a third country. Canada, US, Australia, and several European countries were the main resettlement destinations. The process might take many years. A list was drawn from the thousands of refugees to be interviewed. The purpose of the interview was to establish how credible the story was. The names of those found credible were passed to the sponsoring countries for consideration of resettlement. We were for hoping Azie and Aida to be resettled in the US. On their behalf, Abiy and I had filed appeals and presented necessary forms and documents to different sponsoring organizations. Until their turn, they continued to live with my parents-in-law. It was only on technical and legal terms that they were considered refugees.

Amsal and I had promised our family in Ethiopia that our wedding would take place among them in our hometown. We had to plan ahead to make the necessary arrangements. Tentatively, the date of our wedding was set for mid-December, right after graduation. There were about seven months for preparation. In the meantime, we were making arrangements for my parents to travel to Ethiopia to partake in our wedding.

We had shared our plan with Erin and Sol and the Boones. Erin and Sol had confirmed their plan to attend. Since Abiy and Becky were planning to wed in early spring in Wisconsin, the Boones decided to stay home. But Becky and Abiy planned to travel with us. Becky, Azie, and Aida were to be the bridesmaids.

In the seven months before the wedding, many preparations had to be done—venue to be secured, musicians to choose, and guests to be invited. All things in Ethiopia were being organized by Ababa Dereje and Tirunesh with the help of Azie and Aida. Amsal was in constant contact with them on her choice of musicians, venue, and guests to be invited.

Our business of dog walking and general services had expanded. Many new clients had been added, and Amsal had joined us as a partner. The three of us had several dogs to walk, segregated by species and temperament.

For landscaping, we had befriended a gentleman by the name of Jose. Jose was a very skillful, hardworking man. He immigrated to the US some five years ago from Mexico. His family resided in Mexico, hoping he would legalize his status and bring them to join him. He was introduced to us by Mr. Rossati; he had worked as repairman on his buildings. We bonded with Jose quiet well, maybe because of our refugee experiences. We became refugees to escape from repressive regimes, and Jose escaped from an oppressive economic situation. We all left our families behind. Jose had left his young children and wife. Every evening at the same appointed time, he would sit on the stairs to our apartment building and call and talk to each member of his family. He was such a dedicated father and husband. If there was an event happening in his family, he would share it with us—child's birthday, school achievement, all reasons for celebration. He felt so much empathy for his wife's dedication. "She is a dedicated mother and blessed wife," he prided. He was genuinely proud of her. His parents, who lived in the same area, supported her despite their ages. Jose was the only son to his parents. His two sisters were married and lived in Mexico City. Only on occasion would they visit the family in Morelo, where his ancestral home was. Isn't it sad to see a family separated in desperation to make a living—children left without embrace and guidance of a father and a wife deprived of the love and companionship of husband? If it were not such a topsy-turvy world, people like Jose—law-abiding, God-fearing, family loving, and hardworking— should have a home anywhere in the world.

As we were getting busier with school and preparation for our travel to wed, we were using the services of Jose more frequently. Jose was happy getting regular work, and we were happy because our business was done timely and to the high quality we expected. Abiy and I had plans to delegate our job to him when we would travel to Ethiopia.

The news of my parents traveling through Kenya to Ethiopia was more problematic. At the

Ministry of Foreign Affairs, they were asking them all kinds of questions about their travel—why, where, and when. My father had decided to stay home to take care of the business and my aging grandmother. My mother was to travel alone.

Amsal had a pile of stuff for our wedding. Our extra bedroom looked more like a small storage for a store outlet. Decorations and gifts were systematically separated and boxed with clear labels. When I asked her how she was going to transport them, she had already planned that each of us would carry only one luggage for all we needed. The extra luggage permitted would be stuffed with her hoard. She had already discussed it with Becky. Amsal was doing all the preparations while taking a full load of courses at school. Her grades were excellent. Her skill of time management always amazed me. Time was allocated for all activities, and she was disciplined to live by them.

Erin had started a tradition, what she called "a night out of the ladies." One night a week, they would spend an evening together. Sometimes they would go out to dine. At other times, they would go to a show. There was no particular day; they planned depending on circumstances. Infrequently, Sarah would join them. Most of their conversation revolved around the two weddings coming a few months apart.

Amsal and Becky were planning fabulous big weddings with families and friends gathered to celebrate.

Our wedding in Ethiopia was a forgone conclusion; it would be big with all the family members and friends gathering. And I was delighted with it as it would give me the opportunity to celebrate with people who meant so much to both of us.

Abiy was a bit apprehensive. Not many of his families could be part of the celebration because the wedding was going to take place in the US. The cost of the wedding would be exorbitant, even though the Boones had promised to cover most of the expenses.

We were graduating at the end of the year. We had already submitted the necessary forms declaring our intent to graduate. All the required courses had been achieved with high grade point averages. We had been exploring possible employment opportunities with companies around Milwaukee. There were promising responses. There was no rush for us to start a job right away. We had many plans, like travel and wedding. The option of graduate education was also being considered.

Azie's and Aida's schedules for interview for resettlement to either Canada or the US had been set. They had to travel to the Tigray Federal Region at Shemelba for the interview. Shemelba was a desolate area where a mass of desperate Eritreans escaping repressive regime had camped. The decision of the resettlement of Azie and Aida, having been registered there upon crossing the border into Ethiopia, would be decided in the area. Their choice was to come to the US.

Their prayer was answered as they were to be resettled in the US. We were all happy that they would join us, expanding our family. Amsal was the most excited of us all. It would take a few more months after the wedding before they would travel to the US. Until then, they would be busy organizing what needed to be done for the wedding.

Goatherd in Exile

There were no schools in our village, neither in the adjacent villages. Nonetheless, education was never in my agenda nor my parents'. My lot in life was to be a small farmer and goatherd like my fore-bears. I never resented it because I never knew any better. Life was never easy. There were times when drought hit our area and rainfall became meager. The harvest we collected was severely affected, making the coming months difficult, and hunger set for the family and livestock. Livestock died for lack of grass. Truly, it became a survival of the fittest.

Our social gatherings were during weddings, baptisms, and celebrations of a particular angel that a family adopted to worship and make devotional sacrifice for. My family celebrated St. Michael's Day, which would fall in the month of November every year. People would gather at our house, some from neighboring villages, to pray and partake in the fes-tivity. A couple of goats would get slaughtered for the occasion. And my mother, with the help of some women kinsfolk, would prepare the food and home brew to be imbibed by guests. The priest and deacons had to open the celebration by praying and giving blessing to the family and attendants.

People were devout to Orthodox Christian Tewahedo church. They would pray without fail every day and attend church regularly, particularly on Sundays. The priest was important in the social life of the community outside the ecclesiastic duties. He acted as a mediator in conflicts, whether it was domestic or among members of the village. He officiated engagements and weddings, prayed for the sick for speedy healing, led at burial for the dead, and gave solace to the bereaved. No planned financial compensation was allocated for his services. Farmers might provide a portion of their harvest, which most did, but it was not obligatory. The priest, for the most part, was of farmer class and did his own farming for sustenance. He was as impoverished as the rest of the farmers and truly lived the life of the community he served.

When sick, the villagers would resort to traditional medicine. There were individuals who concocted different remedies by using roots, leaves, and shrubs. Sometimes, perchance, it worked, and the community would heap honors as a miracle worker to the traditional medicine person. Oftentimes though, the villagers would die of maladies that should have been treated and cured with proper prescriptive medicines. The life expectancy of the villagers was very low.

I emerged from this background. A village with primal innocence. A dusty, rusty life unexposed to modern technology but with strong traditional values and respect of parents, elders, and the community—the core values that guided the later part of my life.

By the seventies, a new situation appeared to emerge in my area. New faces who spoke my language albeit with distinction in accent came. They were young and armed with rifles and handguns. They were dressed differently from the local people, covering themselves to the ankle and wearing shoes unlike the villagers. The villagers were wary about the newcomers, who didn't attend church services and never observed praying. Their religion, as repeatedly proselytized by them, was revolution—to bring education to enlighten us and health care system to cure our sick. They brought new ideas that started to create havoc to the foundation of our life. New ideas started to creep in our minds. We were made aware slowly that there was a better way of living than we thought our lot in life. I certainly was captivated by the young people.

War Came to Our Village

The villagers who had tolerated them with circumspect had started to be vexed by the transgression of the cultural norms of the community, criticizing the church as anachronistic and regressive, keeping the people in chains by having so many sacred days in which believers were not to work. If one defied them, sanction was ordered by the priest, and one was made to prostrate for a certain number of days. The ideas of the young rebels were sacrilegious and affront to their faith and God. The rebels, seduced by their ideology and fanatically holding on to the promise of creating paradise on earth and creating an egalitarian society sans exploitation, were not cognizant of the sensitivities of the villagers.

The once-peaceful village that had lived in blissful doldrum was disturbed by having active adversaries within the area. The government forces were in pursuit of the rebels. The relation with the rebels soured further as the village children were enticed by young crusaders. They started to neglect their daily routine of herding the livestock and helping in the farms. The rebels, by starting a literacy program, taught the young people how to read and write. Soon, books and talk with the rebels expanded their vista; they felt suffocated by the primitive life in the village. They heard of cities, electricity that turned dark nights into a bright daylight situation, and of cars made of metals that could travel faster than horses. A dream was born. Dream of one day, maybe sooner than later, joining the humanity that enjoyed those miracles. The rebels encouraged them on their dream. A dream was something to have; to realize it was another. Fortune, however, had a strange way of happening.

In late seventies, the Ethiopian political situation was chaotic and brutal. War was in many fronts in the country. The military regime had unleashed a bloody campaign against the youth. They called it "red terror." Young people in the thousands were joining the different opposition fighting movements, and more were fleeing the country to neighboring countries as refugees seeking safe haven. Ethiopia became a focus of cold war rivalry with the Soviet Union and Cuba on the side of the military regime, supplying it with personnel and military hardware, whereas the West had tacit support, if less active, to some opposing forces of the regime.

Emboldened by the massive support, the regime intensified its brutal persecution of the war and suppression of the youth in cities and towns. That helped to swell the young fighting against the regime. Unfortunately, most of the young people were not ready for the rigor of life in the backwoods. Their political skills were deficient. Soon, they were fractured on ideology and strategy of how to conduct the struggle. At times, the differences led to skirmishes. In desperation and disappointment, many chose to cross borders and join the growing refugee population.

Life in Exile

The trek that led us to cross the border was in the western part of the country, with a rugged landscape and sparsely populated area. It was infested with malaria-causing mosquitoes, venomous snakes, and wild animals. Many young people had lost their lives in crossing the area. The presence of a few people carrying arms gave us some sense of safety, especially from nocturnal animals. To protect our body from mosquitoes, we covered ourselves with few clothes we had carried, except our eyes. We traveled early morning before the sun reached its height to avoid the heat.

The Sudanese and Ethiopian border did not have a mark to signify the beginning of one country's territory and the end of the other. We crossed into Sudan uneventful. We continued our travel north-west until we reached a small town. It was amazing to me. I saw houses made of stone with the roof made of zinc corrugated metal. But that was not what attracted my curiosity immensely; it was the automobile. The automobile with four circular footings was a machine beyond my imagination. How it moved with no horse to draw it was beyond me, and it was not in a downward slope. The city youth started to explain to me about a substance called gasoline mixed with air and spark to ignite it that helped the car to move. It was still a miracle to me. It was only years later that I understood the compression and expansion that caused the movement of the machine parts that caused the motion of the car.

From this day on, my life became a continuous adventure of discovery.

The small town's name was Gedaref, the first town upon our entry into Sudan. Compared to my dusty village with thatched houses, it looked like a metropolis with better-built houses. The people spoke Arabic, a language unfamiliar to me. The distance and disconnection with family and the familiar was heavy on me. By going farther from my home and country, I was hurtling into the unknown. Many questions were worrying my mind: "How am I to survive? Will there be anyone who would hire a goatherd or farmer, the only skills I have?"

My cotravelers' optimism was infectious. "Don't worry, you will adapt," they kept encouraging me. "Language, you will pick up in a short time, and you will find a job to support yourself" was their word.

In Gedaref, there was a hastily organized refugee camp. Several hundred people of all ages from my country were encamped. I was told some were officials of the imperial regime who had escaped from persecution by the military regime, Dergue. They dreamed of going back and regaining their old position once the new regime faltered, but my new friends thought it was a pipe dream, unrealizable under any circumstance.

After a few days' stay at the Gedaref camp, we moved north to Giref on our continuing journey toward Khartoum. Before we left Gedaref however, we were registered by the UNHCR as arriving refugees, and we were provided with identification cards.

We traveled to Giref on the bed of a truck. I noticed the difference in landscape between my village and the area around Gerba. Coming from the verdant hills in my part of the country to the sandy plains with bushy vegetation was a huge contrast. Along the way, there were a few goats and a herd of camels. It seemed to me the life of the people was harder than mine. The reason of our travel through

Gerba was that the destination of the truck driver, who was of Ethiopian descent, was Gerba. He assured as we wouldn't have any problem to hitch a ride to Kassala since many trucks passed through the area.

Indeed, two truck drivers were willing to give us a ride to Kassala. We arrived at Kassala in the afternoon. It was a hot and dusty day. Kassala was a much larger city. I never thought as many people could live in one area. The little glass bulbs that brightened the dark night were everywhere. I was becoming more acclimated to the city living as days went by. In Kassala, there was a large émigré population from our country. Some had been living in the city for a long time. They owned stores, long-haul trucks, and taxis.

My First Job in Exile

One day with one of my friends, we went to a truck stop where drivers would take break and refill with petrol and inflate the tires.

As I was looking at the truck and the size of the tires curiously, the owner of the truck arrived. And he asked me, "What is your name, son?"

I responded, "Belay."

"How old are you?" he asked again.

I said, "I don't know, but my mother used to say I was born two days before St. George's Day" (Kudus Giorgis Day).

He laughed. "You look strong. Do you want to travel with me? To help me along the way, I will pay you for your services," he said.

My friend was more excited than me. He said, "This is good opportunity to learn about truck and how to drive it."

I accepted the offer. It was a challenge for a person with no mechanical concept.

But the driver was very patient, and he helped me with how things work, all the time encouraging me. "I was a novice like you when I started few years ago," he said.

Soon, I learned how to use a jack to unbolt a deflated tire and change with another tire, how to gauge the oil level, and how to check how tight and balanced the loads were on the truck bed. The driver, Tedros, at times let me sit in the cabin of the truck and showed me the handling of the steering wheel, the clutches, and the braking system. Working on the truck was very exciting to me. Not only was I exposed to an experience that I wouldn't have dreamed in my little village but I also was exposed to the experience of traveling to different places.

We traveled to Khartoum, Port Sudan, and Juba in South Sudan, a troubled area with a war against the central government in Khartoum. We never faced any danger. There were a few times that we saw some trucks burned by explosive mines along the way.

A few times, we had crossed to Uganda and its bustling capital, Kampala. Uganda, with its impressive greenery, was a contrast to the landscape of Sudan.

Kenya was one of my unforgettable experiences, as the most developed and peaceful country. The roads were well paved and appreciated by Tedros. The farms impressed me most. The plants were lined straight like a phalanx of soldiers standing orderly. The irrigation system with metal tubing was ready to hydrate the plants when needed almost instantaneously.

Nairobi, with so many of its towering buildings and streets crowded with so many cars, was awe-inspiring. I wondered how many people lived in one of the buildings.

When I asked Tedros, he said, "All the people in your village and many more spaces to spare."

"Oh my god, I am glad I didn't die before I saw this" was my reaction. I started to bless my rebel friends who opened my eyes of a world unknown to me in my primitive village.

When we traveled to Kenya, our destination was Mombasa, a port city impressive in itself, hotter, and on the bank of a vast ocean. Many ships were perched on the port, traveling to countries whose existence I didn't know. Tedros told me countries in Asia, Europe, America, and Australia. I started to dream big. Maybe one day I would visit those distant lands and see for myself.

A Dream Was Born

Every place I had traveled so far had differences in language, dresses, and way of life. In the area of Khartoum, the natives dressed in a free-flowing garb that was proper to the arid, hot clime. In South

Sudan, the nomadic people dressed in a piece of colorful fabric that covered the torso and carried a stick.

I came to observe that every hour or two we drove, we reached a place where different ethnic group lived. Usually, they saw one another with suspicion and, at times, with hostility in competition for water and grazing land. While I was in my country, I never had any concept of a country. My village and the contiguous villages were the extent of my knowledge of geography, and there was only one language, Amharic. I was astounded that so many kinds of people and languages existed in the world.

Every day, my life was full of excitement. Every new discovery of culture, language, and geography excited me. Sometimes I wished my parents, siblings, and the people in my little village saw me. They would not have believed the goatherd of the village had changed so much.

Last night, I had a dream of going back to my village. As I arrived in my village, all the people were dressed in white. My father uniquely was dressed in low flowing thobe as most Sudanese men wore. As I came to the group of villagers, they were singing as the women were ululating and the young people, including my siblings, were clapping. Birds in the thousands were flying high over the crowd. I was happy, only to wake up from the dream.

The next morning, I shared the dream with Tedros.

He said in his usual gentle and soothing voice, "Oh, Belay, one day you will be back to your village in a glorious way. You are going to do great things to your family and the village."

I heard him with earnest, and I prayed that would come to be true. From that day onward, it became my life's watchword. I dreamed of helping my village build a school, a medical clinic, and roads to make ease of accessibility. It was only a dream now, but I would work hard to bring it to fruition. Dreams are not illusion. As Al Barca had said, they are guideposts to life. We dream of future achievements and ambitions and strive to accomplish them.

During the day under the visible sun, I started to look at things that could be done in my village. Irrigation system that could water the land without waiting the scourge of unpredictable seasonal rain could benefit the community. I thought this might be doable. It could benefit the community immensely to cultivate a variety of vegetables and stable grains throughout the year.

Months after working as an assistant to Tedros and having learned how to drive a truck, I shared my wish to secure a driver's license and be a driver. Yes, indeed, Tedros agreed.

Goatherd Became a Truck Driver

After working for almost a year as an assistant on a long-haul truck, I graduated to become a driver. With the encouragement of Tedros, I tested and secured a truck driver's license from the Sudanese government in Khartoum. The pivot of my life changed within a short time. I continued to work with Tedros as a second driver. As two drivers, we were able to traverse more distances, driving alternately. We were continuously on the road, except for inspection and service of the truck. My income had increased, and so was my savings. This went on for a few months, until we split by me going to be a driver for another owner of a truck. Tedros and I split amicably.

As a solo truck driver, I barreled past many villages and towns. I made a decision where to stop. I came up with the idea of stopping at towns and exploring the business environment in the area. After several stops, I started to establish relationships with vendors and gathered information of the products they sold, where they got them, and how much they charged for them. An idea was created, the possibility of me being the wholesaler to the vendors.

The idea Incubated in my mind until fatefully I met a Kenyan of Indian descent, and I shared my dream of the business idea. The name of the gentleman was Mukhtar, a man of vast business experience and network of connections. He was impressed with my idea and set a date for us to meet and draft a business plan. Our business plan was rudimentary, with a few products to distribute. Clothing, loose fabrics, and a few packaged food products were the initial items we considered. The capital investment was minimal. It was deemed foolhardy to put substantial investment at the start.

The distribution and sale of products was easier than I thought. The vendors were happy to get the products at their doors and at reasonable prices, saving them time and expense. Each vendor gave me a list of products that they needed on every trip. My customers' number increased as many people came to know about my services, and my line of products increased according to demands. My profits skyrocketed, and I saved a substantial amount of money. After two years, I was able to buy a Mercedes long-haul truck.

On quiet nights, I prayed to God for the blessings bestowed upon me. I wished my family was close by to share my good fortune, particularly my brother that I left behind, who most likely was herding goats. I wanted him to come and join me in the venture of life.

A Message to My Village

I never rested from looking for ways to connect with my family. There were people who cross-border traded who might be of help to create the connection. As my village was remote with no telephone or road connections, whoever was willing to help me might seek to be compensated handsomely. I was ready to pay for it. I contacted a middleman who had contacts with the cross-border traders and shared my desire to hire a person who would be willing to travel to my village and take a message. I told him I was willing to pay a fee for the service. He agreed to find me a reliable person and agreed how much it would cost me. We exchanged telephone numbers and parted to go our ways. I was filled with hope of connecting with my family.

Few weeks later, Gebre called me over the telephone with the good news of identifying a gentleman willing to take my message. The man was leaving in a week. I had to be at Gebre's place soon. At the time, I was in Port Sudan in line to load my truck. I pulled out of the line and took a bus to Khartoum. I arrived early morning, tired and dusty. I rested in a hotel room for couple of hours. I refreshed, changed dress, and headed to my appointment.

Gebre, or Gebremariam as his proper name was, had been living in Khartoum for decades. Arabic was his choice of language, but he spoke both Amharic and Tigrinya. He was well attuned with the Sudanese culture and had a widespread network of contacts with the people. Among his friends were high government officials and successful entrepreneurs. He was married with two children and resided in the most desirable neighborhood of the city. The frenetic situation in his office showed the man was of multifaceted activities.

At the time I went to his office to make a deal with potential messengers, a few people were waiting for attention from Gebre. I had to sit and wait for about an hour before he turned his attention toward me and the messengers.

I had identified the Ethiopian man in wait as the messenger. I greeted him in Amharic, "*Tenastlign.*"

And he responded, "*Tenastiign indemen arefedk.*"

"Do you live in Khartoum?" I continued.

"No. I am here for business. My residence is in Gondar," he responded.

I knew then he was my messenger-to-be. I introduced myself as a native of Gondar in a small village called Ader.

The man said, "I am here to meet you. Gebre mentioned you want to contact your family left at home."

"Oh yes! Wonderful," I said. I introduced myself again as Belay.

And he responded, "Good to meet you, Belay. I am Tilahun." Tilahun was aware of the reason of our being at Gebre's office. After pausing for a moment, he said, "Sadly, the situation in our country is bad. The conflict in the north is getting worse. And the government, instead of seeking peaceful means of finding a solution, had escalated the conflict. The fratricide had continued unabated. So much death and destruction, so many people displaced and fleeing the country to seek refuge in other countries."

I found Tilahun as a likeable person, and I was happy that he was willing to take my message to my village. We avoided to talk about the business that brought us to the place in fairness to our interlocutor, Gebre. Gebre was busy with so many people who had come ahead of us. There were people of different nationalities in queue to make their deals. He was of many talents as a tour guide and expediter through government bureaucracy.

Interestingly, among the people seeking attention were young scholars from a university in Europe who came to do exploration and study in the Nubian Desert. It was only after I asked what the *ferenjis*, as we call Caucasians in my country, that I was told to dig and study the history of the Nubians long gone. I had no idea that one could study history by digging sites. Amazing. In some ways, it was sacrilegious to me to dig the remains of people long gone. Wouldn't it anger the spirits of the ancestors? Could it bring doom to the descendants who collaborated on the act? There was an alarm in my earnest concern.

Later, Gebre calmed my serious presentiment of disaster. He said, "No doom is going to happen. The digging is done with utmost care and respect for the remains of the ancestors. It is done to study how they lived so that we learn more about their life."

Tilahun, with better education than me, agreed with Gebre.

Gebre segued to the business at hand. "I guess you have introduced yourselves to each other," he observed. "It is not necessary from me to explain why you are here."

"Yes," I said. "Tilahun is the kind of person I was dreaming to meet and help me connect with my family. He knows my village, and I hope he will be willing to take my message."

"Good," said Gebre. And he asked Tilahun if he was willing to take the challenge.

Tilahun's response was affirmative. "I will be happy to be a carrier of good news to parents who may be worried about a lost son." But he said, "It is a very remote and difficult terrain. The only means of travel was on a mule."

I agreed to pay Tilahun six hundred dollars and Gebre two hundred dollars for his service. It was worth the expense. Tilahun promised he might be back in three months. After that, I gave the names of my parents and my brother, Tafere, and wished him well. We parted ways. I had to go back to Port Sudan where my truck was parked. It was an eager wait for Tilahun to bring me any news.

The season had started to get hot. The land had dried, and the khamsin sandstorm was blowing vigorously, blinding the eyes with visibility almost nil. There were times when I parked my truck until the situation calmed down and the dust settled on the ground. The heat evaporated the moisture from the ground, leaving the soil caked with dendritic lines. When the rainy season started, the caked soil wouldn't absorb it, causing floods and erosion to the already-depleted organic matter of the topsoil. The flood made driving hazardous, and vehicles were detained at different safe spots.

My business, both on hauling goods from different places and the distribution of goods to vendors, was going strong. The opportunity to expand further was there, except that it couldn't be a one-person operation. My brother's arrival could be of great help.

Civil Strife in South Sudan

My main distribution business was in Juba, South Sudan, and small towns along the highway to Khartoum. In South Sudan, a war was raging between the South Sudan rebel groups fighting to secede and Khartoum, Sudan, tenaciously trying to hold it by deploying an army and following scorched earth policy with the use of ground and air force. For many years, the war was waged in remote areas with little effect on the highways and towns that I crisscrossed. However, lately, the war was closer to towns. There were times the convoys of trucks were escorted by the army. In spite of the rumors of war, I had never faced any violence by either side, and business continued unimpeded.

Message from Tilahun

Six weeks after Tilahun took my message, he sent via telephone a message from the city of Gondar that he succeeded in meeting my family. The message was passed to me by Gebre, and he added that Tilahun would be coming to Khartoum in about a month. I was ecstatic by the news and hoped for the details when Tilahun would arrive in Khartoum. For now, I had to continue with my work routine. My financial situation was soaring as my business expanded. I continued to work feverishly with little respite. Money became the demon that drove me. But I had a purpose.

Lately, an opinion started gripping my thought. "How could I improve the life of my family and my village? Many things are lacking in my village. Priority was school. How could it be done? I have the means of building the structure, but how about teachers?" I needed somebody who could advise and guide me on what I should do. Gebre was the person that came to my mind.

Along the way of doing my business, I started looking at how schools were built in small communities. Most of the schools were built of cement blocks with corrugated zinc roofs. In some places, school walls were built of stones, which gave me the idea of its feasibility in my village as stones were ubiquitous.

Before I knew, the month was gone, and I received a call from Gebre inviting me to come to Khartoum the soonest. Tilahun was back and was ready to give me all the news from home. I went in three days.

Message from Home

Three days later, I was in Khartoum at the door of Gebre's office. My eyes couldn't believe what I saw as soon I stepped into the room. "Is it a dream or reality?" I asked myself. I saw my brother standing with arms stretched to hug me. "Tafere!" was the word that popped out of my mouth.

My younger brother, dressed in the clothing that I sent with Tilahun, came rushing and hugged me. It was a joyous hug, warm and tight. He had grown up since I left him. He cried, and I cried for happiness. I had to look at him from foot to head to recheck for reality. Except for his ponderous walk as he was not used to wearing shoes, he looked like a town boy. Gebre and Tilahun were looking at the drama unfolding, standing and smiling on the side. They didn't want to interrupt the excitement of the two siblings. How did this happen? It was Tilahun's work for which I was immensely grateful. I hugged and thanked Tilahun, and I said, "How can I repay you for this?" It was beyond the call of duty.

Gebre invited us to a small room with a few chairs and a table.

Tilahun started telling me about his travel to my village. "I hired mules and a guide to escort me all the way. It took us about ten hours to reach the village. We arrived there just before sunset. It was easy to locate, your parents' home.

"A villager returning home from work at his farm greeted us and curiously asked, 'You are strangers to the village. Are you passing through? Darkness is catching up. It is not advisable to travel in the dark.'

"I responded, 'Actually, we are visiting the village.'

"The farmer curiously asked, 'Who may it be you are to pay a visit?'

"I replied, 'The family of Aleka Demeke.'

"'God bless you. Aleka is my friend and my neighbor. But what brings you to Aleka's home at this late hour?'

"To assuage his obvious concern, I said, 'We are here with welcomed news.' Before he further inquired about the message, we arrived at Aleka Demeke's house.

"The farmer shouted, '*Enante betoch!* This house! Aleka, how are you? I have brought you two guests. They look like they came from a far place.'

"The family came out from the little hut, surprised on who could be visiting at this late hour. After exchanging greetings, they invited us to sit at two boulders that made part of a fence that corralled the livestock. I could tell from their faces they couldn't figure out what these strangers dressed unlike the villagers were up to.

"To relieve them of their suspense, I pulled a picture from my pocket and handed it to Aleka Demeke. It was the first time that he had ever seen a picture. The only human figures that he had seen were the icons of angels painted on sheepskin in the church. He looked at it intently. He touched the surface with his fingers. The more he saw, the more confused he became. And he passed it to his wife. She was befuddled by the picture. The son, standing between the parents, recognized his older brother and shouted excitedly. The mother and father in tandem repeated, 'What a miracle! Oh! Holy Trinity, my son's image on a piece of paper.'

"I calmly told them, 'Indeed, it is your son, and he sent me to visit you. He lives in a country called Sudan. He is doing very well.'

"Your mother started to cry and ululate loudly. The neighbors were alerted by the wailing, and ululation came rushing. Soon, the whole village assembled in the field close to the hut. They made me repeat the story, and I obliged. Each villager wanted to know the details out of curiosity, especially that the village son had become the proprietor of a truck. I had to explain what a truck is and that you managed to make it move and cross long distance. 'Oh! What a miracle!' each gasped.

"The younger son was fascinated with the story of his brother. With eyes wide open and ears close to me, he attentively took in every word. It wasn't difficult to imagine what was going on in his mind. To see with his own eyes his brother and his achievements, maybe the whole village youth was thinking the same. It was a cultural shift. The opening of a new vista far beyond the limitation the little village could offer.

"The village people were mesmerized by what they heard and the way we were dressed. We had shoes, the sneaker type, appropriate to the season and the travel. Our pants and jackets were alien to them. Most of the villagers were barefooted and covered themselves above the knee, narrow at the bottom and wide on the side, and with heavy cotton sheet on top. The women wore clothing that covered their ankles and lighter cotton sheet on top. The men invariably carried a stick about a meter long for both protection and as a crutch when they stood and talked. In the group, mainly the men talked, with the exception of elderly women. There was deference for the aged people. When an elderly person spoke, everybody would listen quietly. If the person was of the ecclesiastical class, special respect was bestowed.

"As the time was getting late, people started to disperse and went to their home until only the family and us were left. The package brought from Sudan, a gift from Belay, was distributed to the family. It was mostly clothing and sundries. The mother was resistant to change her style of clothing. She even called the clothing unchristian and unbecoming to a religious person.

"As our mission was accomplished, it was time for us to find a place to spend the night and start our journey back to our homes early morning. The family hut was very small, and there was no motel in the village. We decided to spend the night in the church premise. The family insisted to slaughter a goat on our behalf, but we declined as we had brought some packaged foods for our journey. The son, in his new attire plodding ponderously, guided us the route to the church. It was a small church surrounded by trees. It is taboo to cut trees in church premise. There were few monks who lived in shades close to the church. We joined the monks and, in jest, said to ourselves as overnight monks. We tied the mules in a grassy area surrounded by boulders as fence from hyenas.

"We woke up early morning, drowsy with aching backs from the discomfort of sleeping on solid ground. The mules were readied to start our journey as early as possible.

"Unexpectedly, the young son came rushing toward us. He must have run as he was breathing heavily. This lanky young man of seventeen years looks more of fifteen-year-old.

"'Anything wrong, son?' I asked.

"He nervously responded, 'I want to go with you to be with my brother.'

"'Oh! Son, your brother didn't tell us to bring you to Sudan. Besides, your parents wouldn't allow you to leave, and my travel to Sudan will be a few weeks later.'

"I could see the disappointment on the face of the child. He seemed determined to go on the trip. The mind had been awakened by the exciting life on the other side. I imagined there will be a migration of so many of the young people of the village.

"Leaving the young disappointed man behind, we started our journey back in earnest.

"Our trip back was uneventful. We followed the same route, except in the opposite direction. The village never came out of my mind, its remoteness from any urban area and civilization. No school, no medical services, and yet people seem to live happy, unaware of the world outside. Now they have been exposed to the world—the existence of a world more complex yet exciting—away from their small hamlet. A young son, through sheer serendipity, discovered that world and brought it back to his village through a message and few products of his new world.

"After traveling about two hours, we decided to get some rest as our back and sleepless night was wearing us. We unsaddled the mules and sat in a shade close to a clean spring water.

"I was about to doze off. I heard of footsteps getting closer and louder by the minute. It was the young man who followed us, determined to join his brother. We were put in a dilemma—take him back to his village or let him join us on our trip. I decided to let him travel with us piggybacking alternately on two mules."

About the Author

T. W. Gabriel currently resides in Chicago, Illinois, and is a father of two sons. The stories in this book are extraction from the experiences of hundreds of refugees from the Horn of Africa.

Daniel

CPSIA information can be obtained
at www.ICGtesting.com
Printed in the USA
JSHW030932310722
28655JS00001B/1

9 781638 813262